CITY OF MARGINS

CITY

OF MARGINS

A NOVEL

WILLIAM BOYLE

PEGASUS CRIME
NEW YORK LONDON

CITY OF MARGINS

Pegasus Crime is an imprint of
Pegasus Books, Ltd.
148 West 37th Street, 13th Floor
New York, NY 10018

First Pegasus Books paperback edition March 2021
First Pegasus Books hardcover edition March 2020

Interior design by Sabrina Plomitallo-González, Pegasus Books

ISBN: 978-1-64313-692-9

10 9 8 7 6 5 4 3 2 1

Printed in the United States of America
Distributed by Simon & Schuster
www.pegasusbooks.com

Dedicated to the memory of David Berman.
Thank you for the songs and poems.

From a distance,
The city looks like broken glass.
—Joe Bolton, "Little Testament"

I'm the fire, I'm the fire's reflection
I'm just a constant warning to take the other direction.
—Jim Carroll, "City Drops into the Night"

She believed that all life from the womb to the grave was a coincidence. She knew that in the womb it was indubitably coincidence; in fact, everything about the womb was coincidence, from what went in it to what came out of it. She believed in coincidence as a pilot believes in air. He doesn't see it, but he's flying many tons of steel on it, so it must be there.

Her whole life was a series of coincidences, one stumbling after another.
—Chester Himes, *Pinktoes*

PROLOGUE

JULY 1991 | SOUTHERN BROOKLYN

"I was with Suzy when it happened," Donnie Parascandolo says, stepping away from the kitchen counter, his beer getting warm in his hand. "I'm telling you. I don't know what it is about this broad. She loves the fights. She loves grilled cheeses. She loves Rudolph the Red-Nosed Reindeer. She's around when weird things happen."

"No shit she loves Rudolph," Sottile says from the couch, thumping his chest. "I love Rudolph."

"You love Rudolph?" Pags says, moving over to the fridge for another Bud.

"Look at him," Donnie says. "Of course he loves Rudolph. He probably jerks off to Rudolph. You jerk off to Rudolph, Sottile?"

"I tried once," Sottile says without hesitation. "Didn't do nothing for me."

They all laugh.

They're in Donnie's living room. It's a big house for a guy by himself. He had a family once, a wife and a kid. Donna was his wife. Donnie and Donna. Perfect. They had a wall plaque with their names on it, a match made in guinea heaven. And Gabe was their kid. Donna came up with the name Gabe. Always sounded to Donnie like the name of a first baseman who batted .232, hit about six homers, drove in forty-something runs, but kept his job because he was good with a glove. Gabe was a troubled kid. Moody. His second year of high school, a little over a year before, he offed himself.

Nothing too bad happened that Donnie knew of to prompt it. It was in Gabe's blood, the depression or whatever. Hanged himself in the cellar from a water pipe. Donna found him. They lasted about two months after the funeral and then got a divorce.

Donna still lives in the neighborhood, over on Eighty-Fourth Street. She said she didn't want anything from him, money-wise. She just wanted to try to start over. She took her records—she loved her records—and a few boxes of Gabe's stuff and moved into a small apartment she rented from some lady who used to play pinochle with her mother. He let it go. What else could he do? Other than the stuff Donna claimed—some of Gabe's books, baseball cards, toys from when he was a little kid, and even some of his clothes—Gabe's room is just as he left it. Donnie keeps the door shut and never goes in there.

He's been on-again off-again with Suzy for about six months now. Nothing serious. No way he'll ever let her move in. At forty-four and with a dead kid in his rearview, he doesn't mind the feeling of being free. He likes being a cop okay. He likes drinking with Sottile and Pags. He likes eating Chinese food and pizza and buttered rolls every meal. Truth is, he likes not having to worry about a kid anymore. Having a kid meant stress. School, doctors, a million expenses. Never mind the fact that you've got the pain of another existence on your hands. He learned that the hard way with Gabe.

Sottile and Pags don't have kids, thank Christ. They never fell down that hole. Well, Sottile did briefly. Back before Donnie knew him. His baby was born dead. The wife died not long after. Donnie doesn't know what her name was. Sottile didn't feel like he had anything in common with Donnie, being that his kid never lived. Pags was allergic to getting too close to women. That makes it easier for Donnie to be around these guys. They were married with kids, he'd have to choke on his emotions over Gabe. He doesn't talk about that stuff, but it's there in his memory. Gabe as a baby in his arms, sleeping on his chest, playing around on the living room floor, dressed like an elf for Christmas. Can't just wipe it all away.

Now he's got his routine with Sottile and Pags. There's the job, number one. There's going to Blue Sticks Bar or the Wrong Number after they get off or coming over here to drink and watch the Yanks. And then there's the side work they do for Big Time Tommy Ficalora. Donnie's been into this from the start, but it's amped up since Gabe's death. Tommy is the head of one of the neighborhood crews. He likes having cops and ex-cops on his payroll. They mostly do strong-arm stuff for him, collections and whatnot. Sometimes they transport shit. Sometimes they get rid of things that need to get gotten rid of. Sometimes they do real dirty work. Donnie's good at that, breaking an arm, choking a guy out, going further when it's mandated. He has no trouble reconciling being crooked and being police. Pretty much every cop he knows is crooked in some way. They all take bribes or steal outright. Most take payoffs for protection. Some are into insurance fraud, burning bars down for the mob, that kind of shit. The ones who have wives cheat on them or beat them, though Donnie was never one of those. At least one he knows is into raping hookers, and nobody will pinch the crazy fuck over it. Many work for the opposition in their spare time, and many work for the opposition while they're on the clock. They're bad a million ways. They betray any ethics they once had. It's the culture.

Anyhow, comes down to it, Donnie doesn't mind having this big house to himself these days. After Donna split, he thought he might sell it and get a small apartment like she did, but he likes wandering around, opening and closing doors, sleeping in different rooms, looking out windows for different angles on the sidewalk and the P.S. 101 schoolyard across the street. He just doesn't go in the cellar or Gabe's room.

"You were saying?" Sottile says.

"I was saying what?" Donnie says.

"You were telling us about something that happened that Suzy was there for."

"Shit, that's right." Donnie pounds the rest of his beer and rips a loud belch.

Pags claps, his can thunking against his palm. He's back on the couch next to Sottile. The TV's on behind them, the sound low, the game coming back from commercial. It's the bottom of the tenth. The Yanks are trying to finish up a close one against the Angels.

"Let's watch this and then I'll tell you," Donnie says. He goes over to the fridge for another beer. He opens the door. It's a sad scene in the fridge. Six Buds left. A thing of olives from Pastosa. Some Parmesan cheese. A quarter of a roast beef sandwich. Yesterday's container of lo mein leaking, leaving brown smudges on the shelf. He pops the beer and slams the door shut. He joins Sottile and Pags on the couch.

The Yanks are taking Howe out and putting Farr in.

"Now?" Sottile says.

"Okay," Donnie says. "We're just sitting at Lombardo's. I've got the veal. Suzy's got the fish. We're having a little wine."

"That's when he comes in?"

"Fucking Dunbar. Just struts into the joint. He's got a nice-looking broad on his arm."

"So, what's he say?" Pags says.

"He says, 'Parascandolo, you clean up nice.' Then he turns to Suzy, and he says, 'How much is he paying you? It's not enough.' He laughs his ass off."

"You ignore him?"

"I say, 'Good evening, Captain.' Something real polite like that."

"Tuck your dick between your legs."

"Fuck am I supposed to do?"

The game's back on. Donnie pounds the arm of the couch. Yanks need one. *Come on.*

"So, that's it?" Sottile says.

"That's just the start," Donnie says.

"What's the rest?"

"Wait, wait. He's got it. Two down here."

"Jesus Christ, you're really dragging this out."

Farr gets the outs. Donnie stands up, puts the beer on his TV table next to the videotapes he has out from Wolfman's. *Pacific Heights* and *Cobra* and *Young Guns II* again. He rents the same movies a lot.

"Okay," Pags says.

"The rest is I go into the can after dessert, Dunbar's in there pissing. He tells me he knows how I feel about him, how youse two feel about him, how all the white cops in the department feel about him. That's what he says. 'All the white cops.' We're all white cops."

"So, you grew some balls and told him to go shave Sharpton's bush, or what?"

"I said, 'I'm a fair guy. I give everyone a fair shake.' He says to me, 'You think you're hot shit. You think you're Stallone.'"

"You do resemble Sly. But a more washed-up version. Sly would have to let himself go for years to play you in a movie."

"Fuck you," Donnie says, but he's laughing about it. Sottile and Pags kid him about his looks a lot. He's a little washed-up, sure, but he's a handsome bastard. Sottile and Pags are Dennis Franz type motherfuckers, donut-bellies, the kind of guys who have pit stains and bristly mustaches decorated with crumbs and wear boxers that smell like they've been washed in a corned beef bath.

"Back to Captain Dunbar, come on," Sottile says.

"So Dunbar jabs his finger against my chest. His eyes are all bloodshot. He looks like Yaphet Kotto. I can tell he's a few drinks in."

"Sly and Yaphet Kotto," Sottile says. "Showdown in the can. Tension's high."

"Who's Yaphet Kotto?" Pags asks.

"You don't know Yaphet Kotto? He's from *Alien* and *Midnight Run*."

Pags nodding now.

Donnie continues: "He says to me, 'I know you've had it tough the last year, but you better get your shit together or you'll be washing windshields on a street corner somewhere.' Then he does this—if I may say so—*offensive* Italian voice: 'Capisce?'"

"No shit," Pags says.

"Hand to God," Donnie says.

"This guy's got stones. What'd you say?"

"I grab his forearm as he's about to jab my chest again. I say, 'Have a good night, Captain Dunbar,' and I give him this big shit-eating grin."

"Cool and collected," Pags says. "I bet that drove him wild."

"You're something, I'll give you that," Sottile says.

Donnie gets up and goes over by the TV. He leans down to shut it off just as the news comes screaming on. He pauses because the woman behind the desk is the one he likes and she's wearing a red dress tonight and has on murder-red lipstick. But then she's gone and some reporter in a trench coat is at a crime scene somewhere, standing in front of a blinking traffic light. Donnie twists the knob to off.

He roams over to the window behind the TV and pushes back the curtains. It was up to him, he wouldn't have curtains like this. He'd have blinds or nothing at all. These curtains, his mother made. They're papery and frail. He won't take them down because they're hers but also because he doesn't give enough of a shit to put in the effort.

He's looking at the schoolyard across the street now. A light hangs next to the basketball hoop and casts out a cone of brightness. He sees chalk graffiti on the blacktop. He's thinking it looks like a sad painting. The darkness all around, the half-busted hoop, the circle of light, the stillness.

Just then he sees little Antonina Divino emerge from the darkness. Well, she used to be little. She lives around the corner with her father, Sonny, and her mother, Josephine. Donnie used to watch her do laps around the block on her bike. See her with her Hula-Hoop in the schoolyard or playing hopscotch with her friends. Cute kid. Always full of energy. Gotta be fourteen, fifteen now, wearing nothing but a white bra and pink shorts. Laughing. Her brown hair draped over her neck. He can't imagine what he's seeing is real. He's thinking maybe she's on drugs. He's about to call Sottile and Pags over.

That's when Mikey Baldini steps out of the darkness and wraps his arms around Antonina. Mikey's old man is Giuseppe, who's in the hole to Big Time Tommy for twenty-five large. On the docket for tomorrow, by pure chance, is a visit to Giuseppe, Big Time Tommy saying it's time to kneecap the guy if need be. A kneecapping's the beginning. Then both arms get busted. Then, it comes to it, the guy goes for a swim. Donnie would just as soon skip steps one and two. Giuseppe's a pathetic piece of shit. And look at his kid out there. A fucking freak. Donnie only knows him from a distance. Back from his first semester of college upstate with those things, those plugs, in his ears, and a plain black line tattooed on his chin—fuck's that all about? Good-looking once maybe, in his Our Lady of the Narrows uniform, but now he looks like a real scumbag. His hair all knotted up. Wearing a dirty hoodie. A kid like this, he's scoring with little Antonina? To mention nothing of the fact that she isn't of age.

"What's going on?" Sottile says, as Donnie charges into the empty bedroom at the back of the house. Donnie ignores him and grabs the Louisville Slugger he keeps behind the dresser.

"What'd you see?" Pags asks.

"Jesus Christ." Sottile gets up reluctantly. "I'm trying to tie one on here."

"Antonina from around the block," Donnie explains. "She's fifteen, tops. Giuseppe Baldini's son's there. He's looking like he's about ready to fuck her on the concrete under the basketball hoop."

"No shit," Sottile says.

"Let's go," Pags says.

They're out the front door now, Donnie leading the way, the bat held at his side, Sottile and Pags fanned out behind him. As they cross the street and pass behind a parked van, they head for the main entrance to the schoolyard on the corner.

Donnie can see through the chain link. Mikey's kissing Antonina's neck. His hands are on her hips. He looks up at the sound of their feet. Antonina does, too.

The three men enter through the gate. They're in a dark stretch of the schoolyard now.

"Who's there?" Antonina says.

"Don't move," Donnie says.

"What the fuck?" Mikey says.

Donnie comes out in the light, Sottile and Pags at his side. "Step away from the girl. Put your hands up."

Mikey looks like he's about to shit himself, probably over the presence of the bat.

Antonina recognizes Donnie. "Mr. Parascandolo," she says, her arms across her chest now. "It's okay. He's my friend."

"This is your friend?" Donnie says to her. "How old's your friend? You're what, fifteen? He's eighteen, nineteen, right? That ain't kosher."

"Who are these guys?" Mikey says.

"You don't know me?" Donnie says.

"They're cops," Antonina says to Mikey. And then to Donnie: "Leave him alone, please. We were just having fun."

"He give you something?" Donnie asks.

"What do you mean?"

"You on drugs?"

"Mr. P, I don't do drugs."

"You're in school at Kearney, right?"

"Right."

"This is what they teach you there? Go ball the first freak who comes along? Look at this prick."

Donnie sees Mikey's face in full now. That black vertical line tattoo from the bottom of his lip to the bottom of his chin is surrounded by little black dots.

"What's that tattoo all about?" he asks the kid.

Mikey jumps in, his voice wavering: "I got to be friends with some crust punks up in New Paltz. They did it for me. Looks badass." He's loosening up, thinking maybe the bat's just for show.

"Hell's a crust punk?" Donnie says. "Kid's lost his goddamn marbles. I'm gonna call you Chin from now on. And what's that junkyard shit in your ears all about?"

Mikey shrugs, thumbs the black plugs that have stretched his earlobes to the size of nickels.

"He likes it," Donnie says, miming the voice of the kid from the Life cereal commercials. Pags and Sottile laugh.

This Mikey, this piece-of-shit freak right in front of him who'd never be mistaken for a happy-go-lucky kid in a cereal commercial, takes a bottle of MD 20/20 from the pocket of his hoodie, unscrews the cap, and slugs from it. A healthy three-, four-second slug. This bum, drinking his bum wine, he's alive and well and Gabe's gone forever—that's what Donnie's thinking a few beers in.

Donnie, keeping the bat at his side, goes over and grabs the MD 20/20 from Mikey.

"You want some?" Mikey asks. "Have some. I'm in a sharing mood."

"A smart guy," Donnie says over his shoulder to Pags and Sottile.

"Real smart, seems like," Pags says.

Donnie looks down at the bottle. Red Grape Wine flavor. He's had MD 20/20 a handful of times, sure, but only the Orange Jubilee and Peaches & Cream. Thunderbird used to be his poison when he was coming up. He flicks off the cap and takes a long swig. Then he brings it over and passes it to Pags, who takes a quick hit and passes it to Sottile, who hesitates, wiping the mouth of the bottle with his sleeve before nipping at it like it's Dom Perignon.

"You been drinking this?" Donnie asks Antonina. "He's been giving this to you?"

"No," Antonina says.

Donnie raises the bat across his chest. "You been feeding bum wine to a fifteen-year-old girl?" he asks Mikey.

"Fifteen?" Mikey says. "I thought she was sixteen, I swear."

Donnie gets the bottle back from Sottile. He guzzles it, drinking what's left. He belches and chucks the bottle over his shoulder. The glass shatters against the concrete over by the chain link fence behind the basketball hoop.

Mikey gulps. He's sweating.

"Just let us go," Antonina says.

"Where's your shirt?" Donnie asks.

"Right over there," she says, pointing into the dark.

"Go get it. You want the whole neighborhood to think you're a little puttana?"

Antonina keeps her arms crossed over her chest and rushes toward the building. Donnie can make out her movements. Only barely. She's by a dark doorway, reaching down, picking up a shirt. She slips it on. She comes back. Her shirt's pink, and it says ASTROLAND in white script.

"Your folks know where you are?" Donnie says to Antonina.

She shakes her head.

"Maybe I should go over and talk to your dad. I bet he'd like to know what you're doing out here."

"Please don't. Please put the bat down. Mikey's nice."

"I'm scaring you, huh? Maybe you need some scaring."

"Donnie," Sottile says, "let her go. She's a kid."

"And what about *him*?" Donnie says, stepping closer to Mikey with the bat out. "He's in college. Mr. Fucking Chin. He's got coward blood running in his veins, let me tell you."

He's talking about Mikey's old man, the degenerate, but he doesn't say it outright. Mikey doesn't know Donnie, doesn't know he does side work for Big Time Tommy, maybe doesn't even know how deep in shit Giuseppe is.

"Look, Mr. Parascandolo," Antonina says, level-headed. "It was my idea for Mikey to come here. I thought the schoolyard would be dark and quiet. I snuck out to meet him. I was stupid. It was stupid."

"It *was* stupid," Donnie says. "Very stupid."

"We're being respectful. We're not giving you any trouble. Just let us go."

"Let's just go, yeah," Sottile says. "This is over."

Donnie looks at Pags. "What do you think?"

"It's not right, that's for sure," Pags says. "The wine. The shit in his ears. He's too old for her, I agree about that."

Donnie steps closer to Antonina. "A girl like you just don't know how to use your head, and that's a shame. You're young. You got a lot of years ahead of you for mistakes. You should *think*. Next time you might not encounter cops nice like us."

"I'll think," she says.

Donnie turns his focus back to Mikey. "You shouldn't have come here, you know that, right?"

Mikey nods, staggers a bit. He's maybe a little drunk off that bum wine.

"You heard me?" Donnie continues. "You shouldn't be with a girl like this. You know that, right? She's too young. She's got decent parents."

Another nod.

"Next time you don't have the luck to bump into cops like us, I can assure you of that. You'll be handcuffed and locked up. You fuck a fifteen-year-old, you're a sex offender." Donnie pauses. "But maybe you don't give a shit. And maybe you don't give a shit for cops. Maybe you and your 'crust punk' friends spit on cops? Huh? That's what you do?" He mimes spitting on the ground. "'Fucking pigs,' I can see you saying it now."

Donnie likes seeing the fear in Mikey's eyes. He likes the idea that the kid started out one place, thinking he was gonna just score a piece of pussy, and that he's ending up here, practically shitting his pants, tuned down totally by a tough guy with a shield behind him. Donnie feels as good as he's felt in a long fucking time. Pags is riding the vibe, too. Throwing a fright into a freak like this. Good old-fashioned fun. Sottile, not so much. But that's okay. Sottile's maybe a little bit too nice, a little bit too soft, but that's one of the things Donnie likes about him. Sometimes it's good to have a fat, soft angel on one shoulder to keep you out of too much trouble.

"Come on," Sottile says, reaching out and prodding Donnie in the ribs. "We're all finished here."

Antonina gives a look of relief, like with Sottile there it's possible they'll get out of this soon.

Maybe, Donnie's thinking, he should give the girl more shit. "You were gonna let this punk screw you, weren't you?" Donnie says to her.

Antonina knows better than to respond at this point.

When Mikey opens his mouth and starts to talk, Donnie instinctively lifts the bat one-handed and cracks Mikey in the side of the head with it.

Mikey drops to his knees, one hand pressed over his ear, the fingers extended out over his temple and forehead, the other hand on the concrete, keeping him up. There's some blood showing in his hair. Donnie clocked him good.

"Jesus Christ," Sottile says.

Antonina goes over and puts her hand on Mikey's back. Donnie looks at her. Her face is saying a million things, but she can't make words. She's got fear and regret in her eyes.

"You okay?" she finally asks Mikey.

"You learned something tonight," Donnie says to Mikey. "What not to do. How not to be. Straighten up before it's too late."

"That was fucked, Donnie," Sottile says.

Donnie snaps back at Sottile: "You got a bad streak of limp-wrist in you, you know that?"

"Mikey, you okay?" Antonina asks again.

Mikey's still on his knees, wincing, his eyes squeezed shut.

"He'll survive," Donnie says. He turns and leads the way out of the schoolyard, Pags and Sottile fast on his heels, leaving Antonina huddled over Mikey. "Let's go to the Wrong Number," he says to Pags and Sottile.

"Sure thing," Pags says, laughing. "That was fucking funny, Donnie, you playing Whac-A-Mole with that kid's melon. Maybe you knocked some smarts into him."

"Fucking idiots," Donnie says, thinking about Mikey's face tattoo, his stretched earlobes, his dirty hoodie, his crust punk pals or whatever, and thinking about his arms around little Antonina Divino. They got doom ahead of them, he knows that much. "I could use about ten million beers."

Blue Sticks, their other main haunt, is a cop bar, but the Wrong Number is just a plain old neighborhood dive. It's where Donnie met Suzy. He took to spending more and more time hiding out there after Gabe died and Donna left. It's only a few blocks from his house.

When they show up at the Wrong Number now, he, Pags, and Sottile stroll in, triumphant-seeming, as if they've just won a softball game in clutch fashion. Donnie sets his bat in the corner like it's an umbrella.

Maddie, the bartender, is crumpled on a stool near the register, smoking up a storm. She's wiry and grizzled, wearing a wool hat even though it's not cold, drinking her gin out of an empty black olive can, a pack of unfiltered Pall Malls in the breast pocket of her bowling shirt. Three other old bastards sit at the bar with Buds. It's dark except for the neon beer lights and the dull bulbs dangling from loose sockets in the ceiling. The TV's showing the news, a white line zipping up and down the screen. The sound of the reporters babbling on is the only noise in the joint.

"What'd you fucks do, rescue a cat from a tree?" Maddie says, grinning behind her cigarette.

"That's firemen," Pags says.

"We just did some off-the-books etiquette training," Donnie says, bellying up to the bar. "Give us three shots of Jack and three Buds."

Pags and Sottile settle on stools on either side of him.

Maddie moves slowly but gathers their beers and then pours their shots in glasses that Donnie can only assume the best about.

Donnie raises his shot glass and waits for Pags and Sottile to lift theirs. "Chin-chin," he says, tapping their glasses and then putting back the shot. He follows it with a quick pull from his beer.

Pags and Sottile take their sweet time with the shots.

"You see what I did there?" Donnie says. "'Chin-chin' in honor of our good friend Chin out there."

"You think that's like a sex thing, that tattoo?" Pags asks.

"Fuck you talking about?" Donnie says. "A sex thing how?"

"I don't know. Like witch shit. He's upstate with those hippies doing god-knows-what. They're maybe fucking goats in the woods, you know?"

Donnie laughs, finally plopping down on his own stool. "That's just drunk assholes, getting their kicks, waking up to realize they look like monsters. Where you gonna get a job with that shit on your face?"

"And what's with the ears? Must fuck up your ears pretty good to jam those things in there."

"Maybe he gets fucked through his big earholes," Donnie says.

They laugh.

"You didn't have to whack him like that," Sottile says.

"I'm getting sick of your negativity," Donnie says, flashing a smile. "Besides, it's only a matter of time before that kid winds up in the same spot his old man's in. Speaking of which, consider what we did a warm-up for tomorrow with Giuseppe."

Donnie motions for Maddie to refill their shot glasses. She comes back with the bottle of Jack. Donnie tosses a couple of twenties on the bar. Maddie pours the shots and takes money for the two rounds, leaving the change piled there in front of him. Donnie loves to see money sitting on a bar. His uncle Pencil Pat—skinny as a rail, the smooth-dressing fuck—used to do that at his hangout, the Cockroach Inn. Throw down a few bills and just let the bartender pull from it as he needed to pay for drinks. Something about it makes Donnie feel on top of things.

"Chin-chin," he says again, downing the second shot. Pags and Sottile follow suit.

On the TV, the news winds down. The WPIX station identification bumper comes on the screen. Donnie zones out looking at it, the two 1s looking like the Twin Towers wrapped in a circle. It's hypnotic as fuck. Designed that way, probably. Maybe that's all TV is. Hypnotism.

Pags and Sottile are watching the tube now too, nursing their beers.

A commercial plays for Lucille Roberts. Broads in spandex working out. Next is an old-timer in stupid glasses pouring cereal into a bowl, saying something Donnie can't make out. This one's for Total cereal.

Donnie's not even sure what time it is. Maybe eleven. There's no clock on the wall in the Wrong Number, which is a good thing. Maddie locks up at some point, but there are nights she just doesn't close. Some guys, they sleep right there at the bar or in a booth or they just keep drinking all night. Maybe tonight will be one of those nights for him, Pags, and Sottile. They're not on the job tomorrow. Their only obligation is the Giuseppe thing for Big Time Tommy.

Cheers comes on now. There it is, confirmed. Eleven o'clock. Still early. Donnie angles his head and watches for a couple of minutes. He likes that Kirstie Alley.

"I wish they showed nothing but the Lucille Roberts commercial on a loop," Sottile says. "I could watch it my whole life. Especially that one chick on the exercise machine."

"One day soon they'll be showing pornos on regular TV," Pags says. "Mark my words."

"I'll take Rebecca," Donnie says.

"Who?" Sottile says.

Donnie points up at the screen. Kirstie Alley in a blue dress, her hair over her shoulders, standing at the bottom of the front steps in Cheers and laying into Sam Malone about something.

"I'm a Diane guy," Sottile says.

"Course you are."

More shots, backed by another round of beers. They're settling into something good here. Donnie's feeling loose-limbed, relaxed.

But that third shot sparks an idea.

"We should go get him now," Donnie says.

"Go get who?" Pags says.

"I got my load on," Sottile says. "Let's sit still for a sec, huh?"

Donnie whispers to them, not that Maddie can hear him or even gives a shit what they're talking about: "We should go get Giuseppe now. Two-to-one odds he's playing cards with Pete Wang in the back room at Augie's."

"You think?" Pags asks.

"He's not home with his wife, no way. It's not that late. He's in the hole to Big Time Tommy, he's not laying bets over at the club. Where else is he gonna go? You were with me last week when we were on his tail. Trust me. He's playing cards with Pete Wang."

"He's got no dough, how's he get in a game with Wang?" Sottile asks.

"Always with the fucking questions." Donnie sucks down his third beer and the rest of Pags's. He pushes what remains of the money to the edge of the bar. A good tip for grizzled old Maddie with her gin in an olive can and her unfiltered Pall Malls. He stands and leads the charge out of the Wrong Number, grabbing his bat as they exit.

Sottile protests the whole way, insisting he was just starting to feel good, that maybe they should put their energy into going to pick up some street-walkers in Coney.

Augie's is a couple of avenues over, a corner deli with a back room where owner Pete Wang holds card games a few nights a week. Donnie doesn't know shit about cards. Maybe it's poker or blackjack or fucking Go Fish they play.

But Sottile's question was legit: If Giuseppe's scratched out, how's he pay into the game?

Still, Donnie's banking on Giuseppe's presence at Augie's. These degenerate fucks always find a way. Donnie's seen enough of them to know. He's seen them on the job, and he's seen them in his work for Big Time Tommy. If there's a ticket on a train that'll take them lower, they'll hop the turnstile to board. As his old man used to say, "A chi vuole, non mancano modi." *Where there's a will, there's a way.* Giuseppe's wife—Rosemarie's her name— she's probably sitting at home, crouched at the kitchen table, praying her rosary. Her no-good husband's out gambling away whatever they've got, and her fuck-up of a son's trying to throw a lay on a girl probably just got out of her training bra.

Augie's is dark when they get there, but that doesn't mean anything. They stand on the opposite corner, leaning against the brick wall of a hair salon.

"So, we do what?" Sottile asks. "Stand here and wait? Or storm in?"

Donnie clanks his bat against the sidewalk. "Let me think."

What they wind up doing is waiting there, Sottile getting impatient, saying it'd be nice if they'd at least had the presence of mind to bring along a fifth of Jack. Donnie's plan is to pounce on Giuseppe as soon as he comes out of Augie's, bring him back to the house, throw him in the trunk of his Ford Tempo, and take him out to the Marine Parkway Bridge. Forget about kneecapping the pathetic shit. Toss him straight in the drink, that's what Donnie's thinking. Get this headache off his hands. Give that punk kid Mikey a dead dad to deal with and a debt to inherit. He wants to take something from somebody the way Gabe was taken from him.

"This is ridiculous," Sottile says.

"Go home," Donnie says. "Take your tampon out and get your beauty sleep."

Pags cracks up.

"Funny," Sottile says.

It's another half hour before Giuseppe comes staggering out the side door of Augie's, his flat cap in his hand, his shoulders slouched. It's the pos- ture of a perpetual loser. Probably lights candles at the shrine of Our Lady of the Perpetual Loser, the mook. He's got a three-day beard and dark circles under his eyes. Guy's a math teacher in real life—he goes to work like this?

"See?" Donnie says. "I got a sixth sense."

"Now what?" Pags says. "You swinging for the fences again?"

"Follow me."

Donnie rushes Giuseppe, leading with the bat. Pags and Sottile scramble behind him. Donnie can hear the whiskey in the way they're walking.

Giuseppe sees him coming and drops to his knees, clasping his hat against his chest, his face full of panic. He knows who they are, of course. They've been around plenty before.

"Tell Big Time Tommy I'll pay in two weeks," he calls out. "Two weeks is all I need!"

Donnie arrives in front of him and reaches out with the bat, gently pressing it against the tip of Giuseppe's nose. Some beak this bum's got. Donnie's noticed it before, but up close it's more pronounced, more cock-eyed, more everything. Giuseppe closes his eyes, drops his hat to the ground.

"You're gonna get twenty-five large in two weeks?" Donnie asks.

Sottile's looking all around, up and down the avenue, at the closed riot gates of other storefronts, peeling back the shadows for faces. He doesn't like being out in the open with the guy like this, and maybe he's right.

"Get up," Donnie says to Giuseppe.

They walk the few blocks to Donnie's house, Donnie prodding Giuseppe in the back with the bat the whole way. They encounter two people, a guy in his twenties wearing headphones and another guy, in his forties or fifties, who seems half-loaded. Neither gives them or the bat a second look. Giuseppe tries to talk, tries to finagle his way out of the trouble he's in, tries to make promises, but every time he opens his mouth Donnie jabs him harder.

The schoolyard across the street is empty now. Antonina's home in her bed, no doubt. Donnie wonders about Mikey—did he have to go to the hospital, or is he back home with his mother, worried about old Giuseppe here?

Donnie's Ford Tempo is parked at the end of his dark driveway. They get in, Donnie in the back with the bat across his lap and Giuseppe huddled next to him, Pags behind the wheel, Sottile in the passenger seat, scooting it in reverse until it bumps Giuseppe's knees. The car reeks of booze.

"So, where we going?" Pags says, turning down the visor and finding the key next to a prayer card from Gabe's funeral Donnie keeps taped there. Pags knows the score. He got right in the driver's seat without questioning anything.

"Drive like you're going to Riis Park," Donnie says.

Pags nods and starts the car. He knows.

Donnie sets the bat down between his legs. He keeps a few things in the car for times like this. One is a roll of duct tape. He's thinking he should wrap up Giuseppe's legs and hands, slap a piece across his mouth. But then he thinks better of it. The guy's taped up like that, no way it looks like he jumped, which is the preferable outcome here.

Pags backs out of the driveway slowly, nearly scraping the car against the side of the house.

"What're you gonna do with me?" Giuseppe asks.

"You'll see," Donnie says.

"I'll get the dough, I swear."

Pags has them in the street now, closer than he should be to a parked car. Donnie knows the car. A Citation. It's Mr. Papia's from up the block. The lights on the Tempo aren't even on. Donnie scolds Pags, tells him to get his shit together. Pags snaps the lights on. Sottile has fallen asleep, and he's sawing wood big time.

They make a right off the block, another right at Twenty-Fourth Avenue, a left at the light on Cropsey, and then hop on the Belt Parkway, eastbound. No traffic at all, just the regular assholes going ninety.

They get off at the Flatbush Avenue South exit, headed for the Rockaways. The drive isn't long, fifteen minutes or less under normal circumstances, but it takes them closer to twenty-five because Pags is going slower than usual, drifting onto the shoulder the whole time. They're not afraid of getting stopped.

"The bridge?" Giuseppe asks. "I'm not a good swimmer. Please."

"Chi ha fatto il male, faccia la penitenza," Donnie says, slurring his words, again summoning his old man, who had a proverb for everything. "'You make your bed, you gotta lie in it.'"

"I'm a good man," Giuseppe says. "I got a family. I'm a teacher. I got summer school. You can't do this."

"You're a good man? My balls are good men." Donnie laughs. "You raised a son ain't worth shit, let me tell you that much."

Giuseppe looks confused. "What do you know from my son?" he asks, even more desperate now. He's reading this as a threat against his family. "You leave my son out of it. And my wife. I owe the money, that's all. You do what you need to do to me, but you leave my family alone."

Real noble all of a sudden, the stronzo.

They stop in the middle of the bridge on the eastern edge. No other cars at this hour. Donnie was thinking the bridge was higher, to be honest. Been a little while since he's been out here, and the last time he wasn't sober either. It's a vertical-lift bridge. In the raised position, it is higher. Regular like this, it's probably only fifty feet down to the water. Giuseppe survives, he survives. He doesn't, he doesn't. No loss either way. Donnie shrugs it off. Though the guy said he can't swim, so odds are good he sinks like a stone.

Donnie looks up at the towers of the bridge, bright in the moonlight. He looks out at the Verrazano in the distance. It would've been a better option as far as height, that's for sure, but there's too much action there.

"Think about this," Giuseppe says. "You're cops, right? You're supposed to protect people like me."

"You don't know us," Donnie says.

Sottile's snoring fills the car.

Donnie acts fast. He orders Giuseppe out and follows him, the bat pressed against his back. He realizes the bat isn't his piece just about then. He wishes he had his piece. This few-second stretch, the guy makes a run for it, what's Donnie going to do? Get in the car and have Pags chase him down, which would be a pain at best and a mess at worst. But Giuseppe doesn't run. Donnie's guess is that Giuseppe's decided this is nothing but a threat. He thinks they're going to show him how close he came to dying, dangle him over the edge even, and then let him off with a final warning. The classic delusion that he'll get a stay of execution. Donnie would bet a million bucks he's thinking he'll straighten up starting tomorrow. No more gambling, family first. He's praying to God in his head, making all kinds of promises.

As Giuseppe gets close to the railing, he's about to say something else to Donnie, but Donnie uses the bat again to shove him forward as hard as he can. Giuseppe wavers and then goes over the railing, the top half of his body flopping forward, his hands looking for something to grab hold of. His legs are up in the air. It takes one more good push on Donnie's part to shake him fully loose, his hand bristling against the cheap fabric of Giuseppe's right pant leg, before the leg is over and the body is over and Giuseppe falls head-first into Rockaway Inlet, screaming the whole way down. Donnie doesn't wait to see how he fairs. He gets back in the car and tells Pags to take him home, he's tired.

JULY 1993

Ava Bifulco knows there's trouble when her Nova starts making that clicking noise again. She's on the Belt Parkway, heading back from a quick detour to Kings Plaza, a bag from Macy's riding shotgun. Last time the car broke down was two weeks ago. She was coming back from her cousin Janet's in Staten Island and the car started making this noise and just stalled out on her right on the Verrazano. Luckily, since she was on the bridge, help came fast. They towed her to Flash Auto, where Sal and his brother Frankie charged her six hundred bucks for this or that. She doesn't even remember what exactly. The receipt's at home. She was hoping to have a few months without any trouble. She's sick of having things that break down. The car. The water heater and washing machine and refrigerator and toilets in the big old house that she shares with her son, Nick. She wants things that don't break down. At fifty-one, she feels like she deserves some easy living. She's got friends her age, they're down in Florida now, and all they do is sit on beaches, read paperbacks, play bingo, go to buffets, rub oil into their skin. But she knows the easy life is a long-shot dream. She's got work—Sea Crest, the nursing home and rehab facility she manages, would fall apart without her—and her mortgage is a few years from being paid off in full, and Nick, twenty-nine but not married yet, relies on her more than he should.

She passes the Knapp Street exit. The noise gets louder. Smoke ribbons up from under the hood. What Ava wants to do is beat the wheel and scream, *Fuck this bullshit!* Instead, she tries to stay calm. She inhales and exhales. She keeps her fingers loose on the wheel. She says a couple of Hail Marys. She takes it in stride as she feels the car die and gets over to the narrow shoulder on the left. More smoke. She's as close to the barrier as she can get. Cars are zooming by her at seventy on the right. Another deep breath. She's got to figure out a plan. Get out and walk and find a payphone off the exit? There's that rest stop coming up, isn't there? But that's on the other side. Still, maybe she can make it there and find a payphone. Yeah, just her. Hopping the barrier and dodging traffic in her black pantsuit and matching mules.

She reaches over to the glove compartment and pulls it open and finds her Viceroys. She pushes the cigarette lighter in and waits for it to pop. Could be worse. Could be dark. The lighter thumps out, spooks her. She yanks it from the receptacle, its glowing orange coils hot against her palm. She's a little unsteady, the thrum of traffic shaking her car. She puts a cigarette between her lips and lights it. She takes a heavy drag. *Okay. What now? Finish your smoke, that's what.*

A car pulls up behind her. She can see in her rearview that it's a gritty gray Ford Tempo with a dirty windshield. The driver is just a dark shape to her. She's nerved up. You never know. This fucking city. Guy could be stopping just to strangle her to death.

He gets out of his car. White. Italian, by the looks of it. A few years younger than her, mid-forties probably. Hook nose, dark hair. He's wearing a white T-shirt and blue jeans and work boots. She watches in the side mirror as he approaches, coming up on the driver's side, away from the traffic. She rolls down her window.

"Can I help you out at all?" he asks.

She smooshes her cigarette out in a heap of filters in the ashtray under the lighter. "Thanks so much," she says. "Piece of junk just quit on me. I've been having a lot of trouble with it lately."

He nods.

She waits for him to make a suggestion.

He doesn't say anything.

"I'm not sure what to do," she says. "My son's probably worried about me. I'm already late getting home."

"I can give you a ride," he says. "To a payphone. You live near here? I can just take you to your place. You can call a tow truck and get the guy to bring it to your garage." He looks out at the passing cars. "You got Triple A?"

"I do. And I don't live far."

"Where's your garage?"

"Flash Auto on Bath."

"Sal and Frankie."

"Right."

"Stand-up guys."

"Wish they did a better job fixing my car a couple of weeks ago."

"Way things go. How about that ride?"

"Sure," she says. "Let me just get my stuff." She grabs her Macy's bag and her purse and gets out of the car, following him back to his Tempo, staying close to the barrier.

"Why don't you just get in back?" he says. "Too hard to get in on the passenger side."

"Good idea." He opens the back door for her. She squeezes past him and climbs in. He closes the door behind her. The back seat is a mess of newspapers and torn-up scratch-offs. She puts the Macy's bag between her legs and clutches her purse in her lap. She's still nervous. He's a stranger, and you can't get in a stranger's car without being worried it could be the beginning of the end. She's heard the stories. Abductions. Rapes. Murders. *But he seemed like such a nice guy.*

He gets in under the wheel and pulls his door shut. It makes a grinding noise that sounds something like the door on her washing machine. "I'm no bad guy," he says. "You can stop worrying. I'm just here to help."

"Wouldn't a bad guy say that?" she asks.

"I guess. Good point." He turns the car on, and soon enough they're back in the flow of things on the Belt.

She turns around to look at her Nova. It's weird to leave it there like that. She wonders if someone will ram it from behind or bust a window and steal the radio or whatever else they can get. Not that there's much in there. Did she lock the doors? Jesus Christ. She can't remember.

"I don't know if I locked the doors," she says.

"It'll be fine," he says. "It won't be there that long. You were abandoning it overnight, I'd say you had something to worry about."

Another thought. She digs through her purse. "Shit. And I forgot my cigarettes."

"You can have one of mine," he says. He reaches across to the passenger seat and comes up holding a silver cigarette case. He passes it back to her.

"Thanks," she says. The case is pretty similar to the one her mother used to carry. She hasn't seen a cigarette case like this in a long time. She opens it and takes out a cigarette. Unfiltered Pall Malls. "These are old-man cigarettes."

He laughs. "Are they? I just started smoking about a year ago. I used to buy Marlboros and rip the filters off, but then I got started on these by my bartender."

"Got a light?"

"Right. Sure." He digs around in his pants and hands her a yellow Bic. "Sorry. The car lighter doesn't work."

She lights the cigarette and rolls down the window and blows smoke out at the other cars. She can really feel this one in her lungs.

"Tell me where to go," he says.

"You can get off at Bay Parkway," she says.

"That's my exit, too. Where do you live?"

"You know the Marboro Theatre?"

"Yeah, of course. I go to the movies a lot."

"Right near there."

"Okay. My name's Don, by the way, just so you know who you're riding with."

"I'm Ava," she says, blowing more smoke.

The exit's looming. He looks back in his rearview mirror. A scuffed green pine air freshener dangles there. Coiled around the string is a twist of palm from Palm Sunday. She wonders if he goes to St. Mary's or Most Precious Blood or St. Finbar or maybe Saints Simon and Jude. Either way, there's that palm and it's a good sign. She relaxes with her smoke, tenses down, tries not to think the worst about the Nova. She's thankful for this Don. A Good Samaritan.

Nick's worried about his mother. She's late getting home from work. Could be she just stopped off at Pathmark or Meats Supreme, but the car's been in rocky shape, and he can't help but think of her broken down somewhere. The nursing home where she works is in Coney Island, and he hates to think of her standing out on Mermaid Avenue with the hood up, waiting for help. He looks at the yellow rotary phone on the wall, expecting a call any second.

He's sitting at their kitchen table with the window open. He's got a plate of cold squash flowers in front of him. Golden, crispy edges. Perfect batter. Ava made them last night with blossoms that Larry from up the street brought over from his garden. The radio's on. WCBS. Traffic, news, sports. He can't focus on any of it. He's got the little fan going. He should change. Put on shorts and a T-shirt. He's still in his work clothes. Button-up yellow linen shirt, blue tie loosened around his neck, blue blazer, blue Dockers. He teaches at Our Lady of the Narrows in Bay Ridge. Journalism and Honors English. Now he's doing summer school. He takes the bus every day, the B1 with a transfer to the B64, leaving as early as he can to avoid seeing students on the route. They only have the one car, he and his mother, and he's not ashamed to live at home with her even though he'll be thirty at the end of August. His girlfriend, Alice, teaches Biology at OLN and wants him to move into her place over Pipin's Pub right there in Bay Ridge, but he likes living at home with his mom. He likes feeling like a kid.

Nick left home for college. SUNY Geneseo. He lived up there for four years. They were okay years. He missed Brooklyn. He took the bus home often. When his dad died his last semester, he started coming down every weekend. And then it just seemed like a foregone conclusion that he'd move back in with Ava, and she seemed thankful to have him. She never grew tired of him, at least not outwardly. She liked to see him fed and entertained and happy. Nick had wanted to pursue a career in journalism, to be the next Jimmy Breslin or Pete Hamill or Mike Lupica, but that stalled out on the tracks. He couldn't get in the door anywhere. Instead, he took the job at Our Lady of the Narrows, his alma mater, and he's been there seven years. Time just rattling by. His twenties over. Just like that. He's one of those teachers students don't love or hate. They find him boring. Maybe a couple here and there latch on to him as a potential mentor and then realize he's got nothing to offer them.

What he really wants is to write a script. He loves movies. Their neighbors, Paulie and Nina Puzzo, have a son, Phil, who lives downtown in a Boerum Hill brownstone and put out a big book on the Diamond Den murders and has another one coming about the Brancaccio crime family. Phil does all these interviews, and he's got piles of material. His Diamond Den book was a bestseller, and De Niro even bought the movie rights, with Phil tapped to write the script. Least that's what Paulie reports. Nick wants to write a script about gangsters, something Scorsese would direct, but he can't settle on a topic. He makes notes, tries to figure out an approach, but everything falls flat.

The phone rings. He rushes over, expecting a harried Ava. But it's Alice. "I could use a drink," she says.

"I can't come all the way back to Bay Ridge right now," Nick says.

"Everything okay?"

"Ava's not home yet. I'm getting worried."

"You always do this. She's fine."

"The car, you know?"

"She's fine, I swear. I wish you'd just come over. Hell, I wish you'd just move in. Think how nice it'd be. We could walk to work every day. We could go down to Pipin's for drinks whenever. Movies at the Alpine. Dinner at Colucci's. Nonstop screwing."

He laughs. "Nonstop screwing sounds pretty good."

"You wouldn't have to jerk off with your mother's Jergens anymore. You know what I'm wearing right now? Nothing. And I'm smoking a cigarette. I bet you're still in your school clothes."

"You're really wearing nothing?"

"I'm telling the truth."

Our Lady of the Narrows is a boys' school, and all the students have crushes on Alice. The other teachers, too. Mr. Maroney and Mr. Miller putting their eyes all over her whenever she passes. Principal Sechiano getting flushed when she talks to him. She's *that* teacher. A little older than him. Thirty-two. Pencil skirts. Librarian glasses. Science-smart. A rack that makes even the closeted Christian Brothers among them howl at the moon. Once Nick confiscated a notebook from Gianluca Spara, a pimply junior, and it was filled with drawings of Alice in various stages of undress. Gianluca was a real-deal artist, and the drawings were good. Some of them were even tasteful. And the ones where Alice was totally naked, well, Nick had to admit they were pretty close to the real thing.

"Tomorrow night," Nick says. "I'm yours tomorrow night."

"My hand's between my legs," Alice says in a hushed voice.

"Alice."

"Just listen. Okay? Can you listen at least?"

He doesn't say anything, and he listens as she moans like a porno and talks him through what exactly she's doing, how she's slowly butting out her cigarette in a clean, clear ashtray she stole from the diner on Fourth Avenue, where she's putting her hands, what her skin feels like, saying how wet she is for him. He can't take it. If he had a car, he'd drive there now. Maybe he should just call a car service. But the thought of Ava trying to get through is keeping him from fully enjoying Alice's show. *She's fine.*

"This phone belonged to my grandparents," Nick says, interrupting Alice. "I can see my grandmother wiping it down with rubbing alcohol when my grandfather had a cold."

Silence on the other end. "Is that you talking dirty?" Alice finally says, laughing a little. "Should I continue?"

Nick gulps. What happens if Ava comes marching in with bags of groceries or something and he's got his hand down his pants, stroking away like a champ? Twenty-nine years and she's never once caught him whacking off. He doesn't want to start now, even if phone sex with his girlfriend is a way less devastating scene than a lonely bathroom tug or living room pillow hump.

"Okay," he says.

"I'm on my bed. I'm really not wearing anything. I'm not lying. I'm so hot. You know I get hot easy when the AC's not on."

"Put on the AC."

"You're really fucking bad at this."

In the front of the house, the door bursts open. "Nick?" Ava calls out.

He hears the sound of a bag being put down in the hall. "I've gotta go," Nick says to Alice.

"Really?" Alice says. "I'm really naked. Like *really*. This is real, what I'm doing. This isn't just talk."

"Ava's home." Nick hangs up the phone and nudges his boner under his waistband, hoping it'll deflate before he sees Ava. Nothing's worse than standing in front of your mother with wood.

"Nick?" Ava says again.

He goes out to the foyer, his hands crossed over his midsection. Ava's standing there in her pantsuit with a Macy's bag at her feet. A man is behind her. Nick doesn't know him, but he looks familiar.

"What happened?" Nick asks. "I was worried."

"The car broke down on the Belt," Ava says.

"Goddamn. Again?"

"This is Don. He was nice enough to stop and give me a ride home."

Nick's wood has shriveled up, but he can't shake thinking about Alice on that bed. He goes over to Don with his hand out. "Thanks so much for helping my mother."

Don smiles. They shake. "It was nothing. It was a tough spot. I've been there myself."

"I know you from somewhere?" Nick says, letting go of Don's hand.

"I don't think so," Don says.

"We've got to call Triple A," Ava says. "The car's just sitting out there."

"It'll be okay," Don says.

"Come in, Don," Ava says. "I've just gotta make this call and then I'll fix you something to eat. I can defrost gravy. It's dinnertime. You must be hungry."

"I should go."

"You got a wife?"

Don shakes his head.

"So you've got nothing to eat at home. Let me make you a nice home-cooked meal. After that, coffee and cookies. It's the least I can do."

Don hesitates and then says, "That sounds great."

Ava leads Don into the kitchen. Nick follows behind. He studies the guy. Work boots and jeans and a T-shirt. A certain kind of guinea swagger specific to the generation ahead of him. His face is familiar, but Nick can't quite place it.

Ava calls AAA. She seems relieved that the truck's on its way to tow the Nova. They'll bring the car straight to Flash Auto, they say, and Sal and Frankie will deal with it first thing in the morning. She manages to catch Frankie in the office before he leaves for the day, and Nick can tell from their conversation that Frankie's being highly apologetic and saying that they'll figure out what's going on with the car.

Nick sits across from Don at the kitchen table. When she's done on the phone, Ava sets plates and napkins and forks in front of them.

Don studies the summery tablecloth first and then the picture of the Virgin Mary up on the wall.

Ava moves to the stove. She goes to work, defrosting an icy block of gravy in a saucepan with a burnt black bottom and a dangling handle. She puts water on to boil for spaghetti. "You divorced, Don?" Ava asks over her shoulder.

"Oh, leave the poor guy alone," Nick says. And to Don: "You give the lady a lift, I bet you weren't expecting Twenty Questions."

"It's okay," Don says. "Yeah, I'm divorced."

Ava pauses, stabs at the gravy as the ice begins to melt away. "My husband died. Pancreatic cancer. Nick was in college. I don't like being a widow. The men at church, they want to go for a walk or take me for coffee. Doesn't sound appealing to me. I get hit on a lot at the place where I work, too. All these old farts."

"I've had an on-again off-again girlfriend for a couple years now," Don says.

"She must want to get married. Second marriages are tough. I mean, that's what I hear."

"We're off-again."

"Ava," Nick says. "Drop the third degree."

"My son doesn't want to get married," Ava says. "He's got a nice girlfriend. Gorgeous. She's got the guys lining up. He still doesn't want to get married. I tell him, 'You better be careful. She's not going to be young forever. You're not going to be young forever.'"

"What can I say?" Nick says. "I like living at home with my mother. I like the home-cooking." He thumps his belly with his hands.

"He can eat, God bless him," Ava says, "but he stays so skinny. How about you, Don? You like to eat?"

"I could take or leave it," Don says.

"Take or leave eating?" Nick says.

"You know, I do it. I grab a roll here, a slice of pizza there. I don't really think about it."

"To each his own," Ava says.

"You want a drink?" Nick asks Don. "I think we've got some leftover scotch from my old man. I like bourbon. I went to Kentucky once, and I came back a bourbon fiend."

"Now you're talking my language," Don says. "Scotch sounds great."

Nick winks at him. "I've got you covered, my man." He goes over to the liquor cabinet and grabs a half-full bottle of Johnnie Walker Red and a brand-new bottle of Maker's Mark he picked up at Liquor One a few days ago. He puts the bottles on the table. "Ice? Soda?"

"Little ice maybe," Don says.

The tumblers are in the cabinet over by the stove. Nick gently elbows Ava out of the way and grabs a couple, rinsing them in the sink. He gets ice from the freezer and drops a few cubes into each glass. He puts one in front of Don. Don pours the scotch for himself. Nick sits back down, peels open the wax on the Maker's Mark, and fixes himself a hefty glassful.

The boiling water hums on the stove. Ava takes out a box of spaghetti and empties it into the water, stirring it with a wooden spoon so it doesn't clump up or stick to the pot. She spoons a little gravy into the water.

"You said you went to Kentucky once?" Don says to Nick. "What for?"

"What do you think?" Nick says.

"A woman?"

"Right. Mallory. I met her in college. We hooked back up a few years later when she was living in Park Slope. Then she split for grad school in Lexington. I chased her down there. It only lasted a week. But I got turned onto bourbon for good. Kentucky's pretty nice. Bluegrass, that's a real thing. Like, the grass is really blue."

"I've never been out of the city," Don says.

"Me neither," Ava says. "Except Jersey. But that doesn't count." She stirs the gravy dramatically, tastes it off the spoon. "I always wanted to go to Italy."

"My grandparents on both sides were off the boat," Don says.

"Same here. We've got a lot of family over there. Calabria. Naples. Sicily."

Don downs his drink and pours more. "My old man's side is from Potenza. He was a bricklayer. He came from a family of bricklayers. My mother's side is from Bari."

"Did you bring your cigarettes in?" Ava asks Don.

"I sure did," Don says. He takes the case out of his pocket and sets it on the table, opening it to a neat line of Pall Malls.

"I forgot my Viceroys in the car," Ava says to Nick. "Don's been nice enough to share his cigarettes with me."

Nick takes notice of the case. It's silver and old-looking. Engraved on the outside with a floral motif. "That's a nice case you've got there," Nick says.

"I like it," Don says, holding it up.

"Where'd you get it?"

"Picked the pocket of some stiff," Donnie says, and he smiles.

Nick laughs. This guy's got character. "'Some stiff.' That's good."

Ava comes over to the table. Don passes her a cigarette and she leans over and he lights it for her with the yellow Bic. She thanks him and goes back to the stove, blowing her smoke away from the gravy and the spaghetti.

"I think I smoke because I like carrying around the case," Don says, taking one out for himself and lighting it. "You don't want one?"

"I don't smoke," Nick says.

"It's a new habit for Don," Ava says. "That's the way to do it. Go your youth without smoking and then take it up in your forties. Nothing to lose."

Something about Don itches at Nick. "I don't know you from some-where?" Nick asks.

Don blows smoke at the ceiling. "I don't think so," he says.

Ava takes the strainer down from over the stove. She wraps a piece of spaghetti around the wooden spoon and blows on it and then slurps up the strand to test it for doneness. "Good," she says. She puts out her cigarette in an empty Cento can on the counter and strains the spaghetti over the sink. She puts it back in the pot and mixes in the gravy. And then she serves them a bowl each with more gravy on top and some fresh grated Parmesan from Pastosa. Nick's in his glory. He's sorry to say this might trump sweet Alice. Don puts out his cigarette and digs in.

The teller at Williamsburgh Savings Bank is Russian, beautiful in a weary way. Mikey noticed her last time he was in to get something from the safe deposit box for his mother. He swore he'd come back and ask her out. He's standing right in front of her now, looking at her through the glass panel between them. She's wearing a light red shirt. The two top buttons are open. Her skin is pale. She's got freckles on her nose. Blue eyes and blond hair. Her name tag reads LUDMILLA. She's waiting for him to say something. He's got a deposit envelope on the counter in front of him. He writes on it with the pen chained to the counter: *Would you go out with me?* He passes her the envelope.

She laughs. "You don't talk?"

He shrugs.

"What's your name?" she asks.

He takes the envelope back and writes his name.

There's an old lady with a shopping cart behind him in line, getting impatient. Another old lady has strutted through the revolving front door with a bag of groceries. The guard is yawning, sitting on a folding chair by the stairs down to the safe deposit boxes. Other official bank people are doing official bank shit.

Ludmilla shakes her head. "Sorry, man."

He sighs.

The old lady behind him says something in Italian. He's throwing her whole day off, he can tell. She's got people to feed, other stops to make. He's an inconvenience.

He turns. "I'm sorry, miss," he says, holding up his hand. "Just give me a minute here."

"So, you do talk," Ludmilla says.

"You get a smoke break?" Mikey asks. "Come outside with me. Give me five minutes. I don't convince you to go out with me, forget we ever met. I'll leave you alone."

Ludmilla takes him in. He's wearing a wispy thrift store T-shirt and has holes in the knees of his wrinkled jeans. He hasn't shaved in about two months, and he's got a beard now. He mostly wanted to cover up the chin tattoo he got from some crust punks his freshman year of college at SUNY New Paltz. His earlobes are ruined from the gauges he wore for two years. He can stick his fingers in the holes the gauges left. It feels weird. But, he knows, he's not an ugly dude. He's got a shot. He bets Ludmilla is thinking he's cute.

Ludmilla calls out to another guy roaming around behind the counter. "Jimmy, take over for me! I'm going out for a smoke!"

Jimmy nods and trudges over.

Ludmilla comes out from behind the counter and guides Mikey through the lobby. They go through the revolving door together, standing close.

Outside, Eighty-Sixth Street is alive with shoppers. It's midafternoon, and people are going from store to store with their bags and carts, hauling fruit and bread and vegetables. It's nice out, not that hot, low eighties maybe. Cars honk under the El, fighting to double-park.

Ludmilla leans against the wall of the bank and fishes a pack of cigarettes out of the pocket of her slacks. She offers him one, and he shakes her off. "You invited me out for a smoke but you don't smoke?" she says.

"Right," he says.

"And your name's Mikey? You don't look like a Mikey."

"What's a Mikey look like?"

"I don't know. Silly." She blows smoke at him. "You're a mess, but you're handsome. How old are you?"

"Twenty?"

"You're not sure?"

"I'll be twenty-one tomorrow."

"Happy birthday."

"So, would you go out with me?"

"I thought you had a plan to convince me."

Mikey shrugs.

"Where will you take me?" Ludmilla asks.

"I don't know. There's a Chinese place I like on Bath Avenue. It's called Sixth Happiness. Or we could go to Spumoni Gardens?"

"Chinese or pizza?"

Mikey hadn't thought this through. Truth is he never thought he'd get this far. Ludmilla's classy. She probably dates rich guys who take her to steakhouses.

"You're not in college?" Ludmilla asks.

"I dropped out."

"You should get your degree."

Mikey can't tell how old Ludmilla is. She's probably only twenty-five or thirty, but she's got this mature thing going on, like she's crossed an ocean and seen some hard shit and lived to tell the tale.

Ludmilla continues: "You flunked out? Someone broke your heart?"

"Little of both," Mikey says, trying not to think about Ginny, who'd busted his heart pretty good and then hightailed it to Maine on a whim with a hippie she met at a fucking Phish show. People really like that Phish shit. It makes them happy, and they're probably fine in the head, rarely as down as him, doing their goddamn hippie dances and making fucking flower crowns. Ginny was okay. He misses things about her but not the way she says certain words because she's from upstate or the way she refuses to call him Mikey, only Michael.

"Do you even have any money to take me out?" Ludmilla asks.

"I'm between jobs right now."

She digs around in her cigarette pocket and takes out a couple of crinkled twenties. She presses them into his palm. "It's not much, but consider it a gift."

He looks at the money. "You don't have to do that."

"Ask another girl out, someone your age. Take her somewhere decent."

"Really, no. I don't need pity." Mikey tries to give her the money back.

She refuses. "Do you have a family?"

"I'm not an orphan!"

"You have such sad eyes," Ludmilla says and then she drops the cigarette to the sidewalk, crushes it under her heel, and heads back into the bank.

Mikey holds the bills up to his face. They smell like they've been in a beautiful woman's pocket all day. He wonders what they'd smell like if they'd been in his pocket. Probably sour sweat.

He walks away from the bank and crosses Eighty-Sixth Street, dodging a bus. He couldn't have anticipated a therapy session with Ludmilla. He also couldn't have anticipated a handout from her. Usually his handouts only come from his mother or Uncle Alberto, not strangers. He must really look like a bum today.

He goes straight to Spanky's Lounge on Cropsey Avenue for a drink. Spanky's isn't his favorite dive bar in the neighborhood, but it's the only one he'll go to since he discovered that the cop who thwacked him with the bat that night in the schoolyard a couple of years back hangs out at the Wrong Number. He found that out the hard way. He was drinking there one night with his friend Matteo—they were about six or seven beers in—when the cop and his two other pals showed. Donnie Parascandolo, the guy's name is. He read about him in the papers last year when he got kicked off the force for punching his captain. Nothing happened that night at the bar. Mikey saw him and left out the back door. Spanky's is closer to his house anyway.

Antonina was out of his life forever after that night in the schoolyard. He figured Donnie had a thing for her and that was at the root of his going apeshit. She *was* too young, anyway. That was also the night his father went missing. His mother freaked out for about thirty-six hours before they got a call from the police. He'd washed up in Dead Horse Bay. He'd jumped from the Marine Parkway Bridge, which Mikey had never even heard of. Initially, they didn't know why he'd jumped. They knew he liked to gamble and there'd been trouble with him draining the savings, but they had no idea he was in the hole to Big Time Tommy Ficalora for twenty-five thousand bucks. That debt fell to them. Mikey went to the funeral with the fat purple shiner he got from the cop's bat. He stayed with his mother for the rest of the summer before heading back up to New Paltz for college. He skipped classes, drank and smoked weed a lot, tried any other drug he could get his hands on, including heroin, opium, shrooms, and cocaine. He lasted into his junior year, when he dropped out altogether, and then he couch-surfed for a while before coming back to Brooklyn in May.

Spanky's is pretty quiet midafternoon like this, Bennie Gibson the bartender sitting there with a racing form, two skeezy alkie ladies drinking at the far end of the bar. Gibson could be thirty-five or fifty-five; he's one of those guys. Pennants hang over a wall of bottles. The *Knight Rider* pinball machine is bunched up in the corner next to an unplugged jukebox.

Mikey orders a beer. Gibson brings it without any talk. It is his birthday the next day—that wasn't a lie. He'll be twenty-one, which means he can sit here and do this legally. His mom is inviting her brother, Alberto, over for "dinner," which isn't really dinner but a big feast in the afternoon. She'll make everything Mikey loves. Ravioli and chicken parm and garlic bread. Uncle Alberto will probably bring a new girlfriend and want to talk about Atlantic City. The conversation will come around to his father, and his mother will start crying, saying she wishes he could be with them.

He misses his father, sure, but he's mad as hell at him, too. Jumping like that. Pussy move. Leaving the debt for him and his mother. He hasn't done anything to help, of course. How could he? His mother's stuck paying it off a little at a time. She's got a decent job, working as an aide at that nursing home in Coney Island, but everything's on her shoulders—taxes, repairs on the house, the car, groceries, bills, and the gambling debt—and he's just mooching off her.

"Hey, Gibson," Mikey says.

Gibson looks over his racing form. "What, kid?"

"It's my birthday tomorrow. Do a shot with me. I'm buying."

Gibson nods. "What're you having?"

"Jäger."

"Christ."

Gibson pours two shots.

Mikey lifts his glass, and Gibson lifts his.

"Happy birthday to me," Mikey says.

Rosemarie drains macaroni in the strainer over the sink. Mikey should be home by now. She's worried, but she always worries. That's her way. She looks at the clock. Quarter to seven. She got home from her shift at Sea Crest an hour ago. The bus was running behind schedule. It had been a long day there. Mrs. Rindone was off the deep end, swatting at her, calling her a bitch. Her boss, Ava Bifulco, was nowhere to be found when she needed her help. The creepy janitor stared at her while she ate lunch, his eyebrows wild, something bronze and pasty gooped under his nose. When Rosemarie started working as a nurse's aide almost twenty years ago, she thought she was doing good, but it's hard and sad, and it's worn her down, and she floats through her hours at Sea Crest on autopilot, trying to avoid looking too closely into the lost eyes of some old forgotten woman whose daughter only visits her on holidays.

It's too early for dinner. Even if Mikey comes in the door now, he won't be hungry. He's almost never hungry anymore. He's getting too skinny. He doesn't think she knows he drinks so much, but she does. It's hard to be a mother. No one tells you that. Or they do when you're a teenager, and you don't listen.

She mixes the macaroni in the pot on the stove with some of her gravy. She puts the lid on to keep it warm. She'll heat it up if she has to. Why does she even cook like this anymore? All she ever eats is toast and fruit. Force of habit. As if cooking like this will summon back Mikey's father, her Giuseppe.

She walks down the hallway and looks out the curtained window in the front door, expecting to see her son unlatch the gate and come bounding up the steps. But there's no sign of him yet.

Raising Mikey alone the last two years hasn't been easy. She didn't bargain for all the other sorts of trouble that Giuseppe's death would bring. You'd think just grieving your husband would be enough. Of course, Mikey's an adult now. Twenty-one tomorrow. How'd that happen? She should be letting him go instead of trying to pull him closer, but he dropped out of college and moved back in with her, and her belief is that no mother should turn away from her child.

College. She should've pushed harder for Brooklyn College or St. Francis instead of letting him go to New Paltz. She had a feeling about that place. Her brother, Alberto, he'd spent some time up there, and he'd said it was a place city kids go to college, they take some LSD, they wind up getting tattoos and living in tents in the woods with rabid dogs. She wonders if Mikey has ever taken LSD. She's not even sure what LSD really is. And he did get a tattoo, right on his chin like an idiot, and now he's got a scraggly beard to hide it. And what he did to his ears with those plugs. His earlobes droop like he's ninety. There are these holes there you can stick your finger in. When he wants to upset her, he plays with the holes.

Back in the kitchen, she sits down at the table and doodles on a notepad. She wishes, as she does so often, that Giuseppe hadn't been a coward and taken his own life. That's how she views him now. A coward. Pure selfishness, doing that. Sure, he'd fallen down a hole with the gambling, but there had to have been some other solution. If he'd just come to church with her more, put his faith in God, instead of being scared into believing that there was no way out.

Twenty-five grand was a lot of money, but it wasn't the end of the world.

She knew that for a fact now. Big Time Tommy Ficalora, who Giuseppe owed, he came around a week or so after the funeral and told her she could pay off the debt little by little. "It's not going away," he said, "but I'll give you some space because I'm a reasonable guy and I have sympathy for your situation."

And here she is, a couple of years later, she's paid off a fifth of what he owed, and Big Time Tommy's not charging her the vig. You ask her, that was a respectful move.

Maybe she should hate Giuseppe, spit on his memory, but she can't bring herself to do that. He was so funny. He wanted to be a comedian, *was* a comedian. He taught math at P.S. 231. Two nights a week, before the gambling was at its worst, he'd go to comedy clubs in the city and perform. He never wanted her to come. He said he wanted her to wait to see him until he got his act down to a science. Fifteen years, he said that. He wasn't much of a drinker, but he got in trouble in the bars betting on baseball and basketball and football. The trouble peaked when he bet the Bills over the Giants in the Super Bowl. When that placekicker missed the field goal at the last second, Giuseppe was done for. Then he managed to get deeper in those final few months before he saw no other option and took the coward's way out.

Rosemarie doesn't feel forty-six. She remembers being a girl and thinking about numbers like forty-six like she was looking up at them. Her mother was seventeen when she had her, so Rosemarie was almost thirty when her mother was the age she is now. Her mother died of heart failure at fifty-five. Her father died of a brain aneurysm at fifty-two. At forty-six, she's both an orphan and a widow, and that's just not a very good family track record. She stays up nights, worrying that she has only six years left, or maybe nine years. She prays and prays about it. She wants a long life. She wants to see Mikey get past whatever this phase is and find a nice Italian girl and settle down. She wants a good job for him, two or three kids, and she wants his family in this house. She'll move into the back bedroom off the kitchen, and he and his wife can have the master bedroom. She imagines herself holding her grandbabies on the recliner in the living room. She imagines singing them to sleep, "Ninna Ninna" or "That's Amore."

The front door clangs open now, and Mikey comes stumbling into the house. He's had a few beers, she can tell. Not even seven o'clock on a Wednesday, and he's drunk. He pauses to find his balance on the radiator by the stairs down to the basement.

Rosemarie stands, traces the cap of the pen she's been holding against the palm of her hand, digging it into her skin, and then falls back into her chair. "Where've you been?" she asks.

"Robbing a bank," he says.

"Very funny. You hungry? I made macaroni."

"I'm not hungry." Mikey sits down across from her at the table. His eyes are bloodshot. The stink of cheap beer emanates from him.

"I can't give you some macaroni? You need to eat. You're wasting away to nothing."

"Ma, please."

"Your birthday is tomorrow."

"I know."

"Uncle Alberto's coming over. He's bringing sfogliatelle, rainbows, and cannoli. I'm making ravioli with chicken parm and garlic bread. Your favorites."

Mikey nods. "Who're you feeding here?"

"Uncle Alberto likes to eat."

"You should bring all this food to a homeless shelter."

"Homeless shelter? What're you saying? It's your birthday. These are your favorites. You can at least eat on your birthday, can't you?"

"Feed people who need to be fed, that's what I'm saying."

"You need to be fed. Have a bowl of macaroni."

Mikey exhales dramatically. "Okay," he says. "I'll eat. You want me to eat? I'll eat."

"There you go," Rosemarie says.

Mikey gets up and goes over to the stove, plucking the lid from the pot. He rummages around in the overhead cabinet and comes out with her favorite red mixing bowl. He empties macaroni into the bowl with the big wooden spoon she's left behind on a dish on the other front burner. He goes to the fridge and gets the small jar of grated locatelli. He pours half the jar over his macaroni.

"What're you doing?" Rosemarie asks. "That's my mixing bowl. Get a normal bowl. And that's too much cheese. Locatelli's not cheap. We need some for tomorrow."

Mikey smiles. "What am I doing? You wanted to feed me. Well, I'm eating." He uses the wooden spoon to shovel macaroni into his mouth. Grated cheese dusts his jacket like cigarette ash. A couple of pieces of half-chewed pasta fall to the worn linoleum.

"Sit down. Take off your jacket. Eat normal." Rosemarie motions for him to sit back down.

He does sit, pulling the bowl close to him and continuing to pig out on the macaroni. He's not enjoying it. He's doing it for show.

"What good is this?" Rosemarie asks. "Why are you even eating? You eat for sustenance, not to make your mother look like a jerk."

"A jerk?" Mikey says, his mouth overflowing.

"That's what you think of me, right? I'm just some jerk who feeds you and gives you money and makes your bed."

Mikey swallows hard, almost choking. "You give Big Time Tommy all your money. Because of what a fuck-up Dad was."

"Don't badmouth Daddy."

"I wish you were smarter."

"That's such a cruel thing to say."

Mikey pushes his bowl away and goes into the bathroom at the opposite end of the kitchen, slamming the door behind him. She needs a new door there or new hinges. She's afraid one good shove will bring it tumbling down. She hears the sink running at full blast, and then she hears Mikey retching. Maybe he's a bulimic. She's seen shows. You eat and you puke, and it's a whole thing. Or maybe he ate too much too fast. Or maybe he drank too much, and the food just didn't sit right.

"You okay in there?" Rosemarie calls out.

The sounds stop. "I'm fine," Mikey says.

"You want some ginger ale and pretzels?"

"Jesus, no." He swings the door open, and he's standing there, wiping his mouth.

"Aren't you cold, walking around in that little T-shirt?" Rosemarie asks. "Go down to the basement and get one of Daddy's old jackets."

"It's summer."

"He's got this nice brown corduroy jacket, you remember? It'll look good on you. I used to love to see him in it. The way he dug his hands into his pockets. I bet some of his toothpicks are still there."

"You sure he wasn't wearing it when he jumped?"

"What is wrong with you right now? What kind of thing is that to say? Angry at the world's no way to be."

Mikey walks past her and goes to the fridge and gets a can of Coke. He pops the tab and takes a long swig.

"You're gonna puke again," Rosemarie says. "You want to puke again? You want to wind up in the hospital?"

"For puking?"

"You think you're a hotshot. One day you'll learn, you're not so big of a hotshot."

"Believe me, I know I'm no fucking hotshot."

"That mouth! Disgraziato."

"Maybe I will go down and get one of Dad's old jackets. Maybe I'll put it on and go jump off the bridge just like him."

Rosemarie crosses herself. "God forbid. Take it back."

"What is this, the schoolyard?"

"Take it back." Her legs feel wobbly. She sits at the table and puts her head in her hands. She rocks back and forth. "Why would you say that? You think it's a joke? You think I'm not afraid of losing you, too?"

Mikey puts his Coke can on the counter, and it's a terrible, lonely sound that fills the room, the can clanking against the wood, the soda sloshing around.

"I'm not gonna actually do it," he says.

She's crying before she can stop herself from crying. She's thinking about how she felt all those long hours that Giuseppe was missing, how she feared he was dead in a ditch, shot by one of Big Time Tommy's henchmen. She's thinking how it was even worse when the police told her that he'd washed up on the beach in Dead Horse Bay with all the broken bottles and old shoes. She'd heard about Dead Horse Bay. It was where the boiled bones of horses had been dumped back when there were rendering plants in the area. This was in the early part of the century. Then it was a landfill. Then it was the place where Giuseppe Baldini was deposited. Whatever he was thinking in those final moments, however trapped he felt, she was sure he must've at least thought of her, of their first happy years together in the house. She wonders if he had doubts after landing in the water. Knowing he wasn't a good swimmer wrecked her. She's sure the impact didn't kill him and that he struggled to stay afloat before drowning. Her poor Giuseppe.

Mikey leans down next to her, and she feels his hand on her back, not quite patting her, not quite comforting her in any meaningful way, just *there*, a hot slab on her shoulder blade. "Oh, Ma," he says. "I'm sorry I said that."

"Do you hate me?" Rosemarie asks, and she turns to him, imagining the boy he was, happy in the driveway, pitching a Spaldeen against the garage, listening to ballgames on the radio with Giuseppe. One day he was a boy and loved nothing better than to come in after playing outside and eat whatever food she'd prepared—squash flowers, spedini, meatballs—and then one day he was no longer a boy and he'd go quietly to his room and shut the door and blast his music.

"I don't hate you," Mikey says.

"The way you talk to me, you must." She wipes tears from her eyes and can taste a stray tear on her lip. She thinks of crying at Giuseppe's closed-casket wake. She thinks of Mikey on a chair, sitting with Father Borzumato, who was there but was disgusted with Giuseppe. Which was understand-able. Her husband threw away God's greatest gift, life.

Mikey's hand moves on her back, scrunches up so she can feel his knuckles pressing down and then releases back into a flat, stiff position. "I don't," he says, and then he stands and his hand is off her, away from her, headed back for the Coke on the counter.

"How's your stomach?" she asks.

"It's fine. I'm fine. It was just from eating like that."

"I don't think you hate me."

"I don't."

"Can you talk nicer to me? Please. Just try."

He finishes the Coke and drops the can in the garbage under the sink. He lets a loud belch rip. "I'll try," he says.

She dabs at her cheeks with a crumpled paper napkin she finds on the table. "Thank you," she says.

He heads back for the front door. "I'm gonna go out," he says.

"Where?" The concern in her voice is obvious, even as she tries to mask it. He must mean the bar.

"The library. And then maybe Wolfman's. I want to get some books and videos."

"You need money?"

"I'm okay."

And then he's gone, out the front door, and she's alone at the table, tearing pieces off the napkin she just used to soak up whatever was left of her tears.

After Don leaves, Ava's washing the dishes while Nick sits at the table with a stack of student papers, sighing his way through, slashing at the stapled pages with a red pen. AAA has called to let her know that the Nova was safely delivered to Flash Auto. The bourbon and scotch are still out. Don's left a couple of cigarettes for Ava so she doesn't have to go to the corner store. "Such a nice man," Ava says, snapping off her yellow rubber gloves after finishing the last bowl and dangling them over the edge of the sink and then lighting a Pall Mall with a book of matches from La Palina. She grabs the Cento can and sits across from Nick while she smokes.

"It was nice of him to help you," Nick says. "He about drained Dad's scotch. And for someone who doesn't like to eat, he really plowed through that spaghetti."

"Shush up," Ava says. "You're so critical."

"You got a little crush?"

"He's nice."

"I'll tell you this: I don't want him for a stepdad."

"I would've been stranded out there without him. This day and age, in this city, not a lot people are kind enough to stop and help. I could've died."

"Everyone breaks down. I was worried, but you're stretching it a bit. I don't think you would've died."

"That Belt's a roller coaster. Who knows?"

"You get his number? He live around here?"

"He said he lives over by the school."

"P.S. 101 or St. Mary's?"

Ava taps ash into the can. "P.S. 101."

"It's bugging me where I remember him from."

"Probably just from around the neighborhood. You see people walking on Eighty-Sixth Street forever, their faces register as familiar."

"Could be, yeah."

"Leaving me these cigarettes was such a nice gesture."

"Okay, Ava, I get it. You're in L-O-V-E."

"Stop." She exhales in his direction.

He swats the smoke away. "I'm trying to work here."

"How's Alice?"

"Probably mad at me. She wanted me to come over."

"You should get a car. Sal and Frankie have a few new used ones in."

"Maybe," Nick says, rubbing the bridge of his nose, straining to make sense of what he's seeing on the page.

Ava never would've guessed that he'd become a teacher. He always enjoyed reading, but she didn't think he had the personality to stand in front of a group of kids. It takes a certain kind of person. Nick's loose around her and Alice, but he otherwise keeps to himself. She's never seen him teaching. She wishes she could. She'd be proud to see him standing up in front of a chalkboard, shaping young minds. Her husband, Anthony, never would've guessed Nick would become a teacher either. He wanted Nick to work for the city like him. Nick couldn't do that. Teaching gave him days that ended by three.

"Well," Ava says, rising, cigarette still clutched between her fingers, "I'm going to take a shower."

"Slip out of that power suit," Nick says.

"Work's nothing but a headache. That Rosemarie's always on my heels. I avoid her. She needs to be able to do something without my say-so."

"That's Mikey Baldini's mother, right?"

"Yeah, you had him in school, remember?"

"I did. Wasn't much in the brains department."

"And then the stupid car. I swear."

"At least you met good old Don."

Ava lurches across the table, slapping playfully at Nick with her cigarette hand. Ashes fall on the paper he's reading. "You're such a screwball," Ava says.

"Watch it!" Nick says, laughing. "I don't want to set these papers on fire. I mean, I do, but I better not."

Ava's bedroom is off the kitchen. After Anthony died, she bought a new bed, a full mattress and a different frame. She couldn't stand the idea of sleeping in their bed alone. She had Nick wrap the mattress in plastic and put it in the basement and then disassemble the old frame and put the pieces in boxes. Nick thought she was crazy. It was a perfectly good bed. He didn't understand. This new bed isn't even terribly comfortable. She bought it at the cheapo mattress place on Eighty-Sixth Street.

She goes into the bedroom now and sits down on the bed and takes a long drag off the cigarette. She unbuttons her shirt but doesn't take it off and kicks out of her shoes. When she's done with the cigarette, she's going to rub her tired feet and then she's going to take a cold shower. She likes cold showers on summer days. But she wants the cigarette to last a little longer. Unfiltered.

Thinking about Don, how she likes his voice and his face and his hair and the cigarettes he smokes, has her feeling guilty. She tries thinking about Anthony instead. She looks around the room for traces of him. A coiled gold chain on the bureau. His rubbed-raw rosary in an envelope next to that. Their wedding picture up on the wall. Taken in the parking lot of St. Mary's. She was twenty. It was the summer of 1962. A wedding picture in a parking lot then looked better than a wedding picture in a parking lot could ever look now. The cars were long, shiny, clean. It was the old church, the one that burned down six years later. Anthony was in a classic tux. He had a Sinatra thing going. She was so young-looking, so unbelievably young-looking, with the veil comb clamped in her dark hair, her gentle face, her pretty dress. She was lucky to get married when she did. Before the fashions changed and everyone looked psycho. The '70s and '80s, those are wedding pictures no one wants to see. Mustaches and velvet. Big shoulder pads. Hair and glasses you couldn't believe.

She goes into the small carpeted bathroom at the far end of the bedroom, an addition that Anthony built a few years after they bought the house and had Nick. They needed their own bathroom. In the winter, it gets cold in there and she has to leave the tap dripping when it drops below freezing. The grout in the shower is moldy, the tiles scummy, but she never feels like scrubbing it clean. She puts what's left of her cigarette in the toilet and flushes. She closes the door and takes off her jacket and pants, hanging them from a hook on the wall. She slips out of her shirt, letting it fall to the floor, standing there in her bra and underwear, looking down at her hips where the pants have cut red lines into her skin. She forgot to rub her feet. She sits on the toilet and crosses her left leg over her right leg and rubs the ball of her foot hard. She was stupid not to wear socks again. The toilet lid is cold against her thighs. She switches to the other foot and reminds herself that she needs to take a Tylenol later. The Tylenol is in the medicine chest over the sink next to her bottles of Alyssa Ashley Musk perfume. All these aches and pains. Getting old is for the birds. What will it be like in twenty years? She won't even recognize her body.

When she's done with her feet, she gets up and brushes back the shower curtain and turns on the water. She barely twists the hot knob, letting the cold run heavy. She unsnaps her bra in the back and takes it off over one arm at a time, throwing it on the toilet lid, cupping an arm under her breasts. She removes her wedding ring and sets it on the windowsill. The girls at work have told her to stop wearing it, but she can't, she won't. She steps out of her underwear and gets in under the water.

She takes her bottle of shampoo from the caddy and pours some into her hand, massaging it into her hair with the tips of her fingers. She closes her eyes and lets the water thrum against her. She falls into thinking about Don again.

She imagines his hands on her.

She imagines pushing down his pants and boxers—he must wear boxers—so they're crumpled at his feet and touching him, taking him in her hand the way she used to take Anthony in her hand.

She imagines him kissing her arms and her thighs and her tired feet.

Anthony would fall to his knees and hug her body to him, kiss her belly, kiss everywhere, and it was the best she'd ever felt. Times like that made her forget about hard work and failure and death and feeling like the world was grinding her down. She imagines Don hugging her the same way.

The cold water feels good. She opens her mouth and lets it stream against her tongue, pound her teeth.

A thundering knock on the bathroom door.

"What?" she says, opening her eyes and groaning. Nick, like a little kid, can't wait.

He says something on the other side of the door.

"I can't hear you," Ava says through the water.

She hears the door creak and feels a draft from it being open. Nick is standing on the other side of the curtain, over by the toilet. She peeks out, only her head, making sure the curtain totally obscures her from him.

"Why are you in here?" she says to him. "Can I have a minute of peace after a long day?"

"I figured it out," Nick says, biting the cap of his red pen. "I was sitting there, grading essays, and I just couldn't shake it."

"Shake what?"

"Figuring out where I know him from."

"Who?"

"Don. Who do you think?"

"Please, just give me a minute to finish up and then I'll be out."

Nick nods. "Sure, sure. Sorry. I was just excited." He leaves and pulls the door shut behind him.

She tries to get lost in the dream again, tries to let the cold water carry her away, but it's over. She can't get back. Nick's made her lose it. She shuts off the water and stands there in the tub, dripping. A rack next to the shower is full of fresh, dry towels. She wraps her hair in one and then uses another to dry her body. Her terry cloth robe is stashed among the towels. She keeps it folded away there because she's caught Nick wearing it a couple of times when she's come home from work. "What?" he said to her the first time. "It's so goddamn comfortable." The next time he just shrugged. "You don't mess with a woman's robe," she told him. She puts it on and then slips her ring back on too, an important after-shower habit. Once, when Anthony was still alive, she left her ring on the windowsill and it somehow dropped behind the toilet and got lodged in a deep gap between an upthrust of carpet and the wall and it took her a while to find it though she knew it couldn't have gone far and she was frenzied and Anthony said he'd just get her a new one if she didn't find it and she said she didn't want a new one, she wanted the one he'd given her on their wedding day.

Out in the kitchen, Nick's moved aside the student essays and replaced them with a couple of folded open copies of the *Daily News*. He keeps stacks of old issues under the bed in his room. He's always looking for stories. Real New York stories he can turn into a movie script. He says he's going to write a script and sell it for a million bucks. She's never seen him sit down and write a word, though.

Ava's still got the towel in her hair, and her robe is cinched tight. "Okay," she says. "What is it?"

"Have some bourbon," Nick says, proceeding to suck down the rest of what's in his glass and then chomping on some ice.

"I'll pass. And you better take it easy. You have work tomorrow."

Work. Nick takes the bus, but she hasn't thought about how she's going to get to Coney Island. She guesses the train will be easiest. At least she can get off and walk on the boardwalk to Sea Crest.

Nick taps one of the papers on the table. "This isn't today's *Daily News*."

"So?" Ava says.

"This is from last summer. A cop went on a bender and clocked his captain."

"I don't remember that."

"It wasn't big news. I just read carefully. Your man Don, he was the cop."

Ava scrunches her forehead and sits at the table.

Nick turns the paper around and pushes it toward her. He taps Don's official police picture. No smile. Hair shorter. But it's him. It's definitely him. "Donnie Parascandolo," Nick says. "Now he's 'Don.' Your boyfriend's a disgraced ex-cop."

"He's not my boyfriend, number one," Ava says, taking a closer look at Don on the page.

"The thing that made me remember was you mentioning Mikey Baldini. This is the same guy, your Don, who hit him with a bat when he was trying to get with Antonina Divino."

"Where'd you hear that?"

"Word gets around in school. Gossip in the halls."

"When was this? Rosemarie never mentioned it."

"Couple years back. She didn't know, I'm sure."

"Must've been right around the time her husband killed himself. I know the Divinos from St. Mary's. Antonina must've been fourteen, fifteen. Sounds like Mikey deserved a whack."

"That's why no one who knew pushed too hard to get Don in trouble, I guess."

She motions at the papers with her hands out. "This doesn't diminish Don in my eyes, if that's what you were thinking it would do."

"There's more."

"What?"

"The name Gabe Parascandolo ring a bell?"

"No."

"That was his kid. Hung himself in the cellar of their house. That's why he and his wife got divorced. Couple of months after the kid did it, they were done. She still lives around here, too. Donna Rotante now—that's her maiden name. Donnie and Donna, pretty cute. You know her?"

Ava reaches for the last cigarette Don left behind. She feels shaky. This is a lot to take in. And Nick looks so pleased with himself. "I don't know her, no," she says. "Let's change the subject."

"This guy's something else," Nick says. "A treasure trove. He's my script. It'll write itself. No more school, no more books, you know how it goes."

"You're drunk," Ava says, still holding the unlit cigarette between her fingers.

"I sure am," Nick says, a twinkle in his eye. "This fucker's my meal ticket. Who better to write about this guy, this neighborhood, than me?"

"Don't be stupid."

"Your Good Samaritan has a checkered past. He ate your spaghetti. Raved about your gravy."

"Don't pretend to know someone you don't know."

A big self-satisfied smile from Nick. He pours himself more bourbon. "I should be thanking you, that's what I should be doing."

"Think twice before you do something stupid," Ava says, and she gets up and disappears back into her bedroom to put lotion on her legs and to watch the news.

Donnie started introducing himself as Don after getting axed from the force but still thinks of himself as Donnie. In his head, when he talks to himself, it's Donnie this and Donnie that, just as it's always been. Being Don to folks he's meeting for the first time is just a small way of distancing himself from the version of him that was in all the papers for going on a months-long bender culminating in sucker-punching Captain Dunbar at Blue Sticks Bar and getting shit-canned so majestically after refusing desk duty and blowing off therapy. Sottile and Pags still call him Donnie. They're the only people left from his old life other than Suzy, and he and Suzy are barely anything anymore. All the cops he would've considered friends thought he'd disgraced himself and the department with the Dunbar thing. Oh well.

He's thinking this because it was still kind of strange to be Don with the woman he picked up on the Belt and her son. It was strange to be in their house. He's not even sure why he picked her up in the first place. The old him might've done that, sure. Before Gabe. The old him was good like that, had, at least now and then, the tendencies of a gentleman. The new him, not so much.

The woman, Ava, there was something about her he really liked. The way she wore that suit and smoked his cigarettes. She was a few years older than him, probably fifty or so, but she actually looked his age or even younger. She stirred something in him. That Italian thing. She was hot like the mothers of some of his friends were hot growing up. He wanted her hands in his hair. He wanted his head on her chest. She was the kind of woman to nurse you back to health. He didn't know that when he stopped, but he wonders if something was guiding him. These few years since Donna left him, he's only had Suzy, and he's sick of Suzy with her broken front tooth and that mascara dripping down her cheeks. He's no prize, he knows that. Booze-riddled. A disgraced ex-cop. But he can still get it up when he wants to, and Suzy's a dead-eyed lump. Ava's got him daydreaming about balling for the first time in a while.

He's on his couch in his boxers, cigarette case and a pint of scotch on the coffee table in front of him next to the phone, the home screen of *Super Mario World* on the TV. He took the cigarette case off some weasel in Bay Ridge whose arm he had to snap. The weasel said it was a family heirloom. "Fuck your family and its heirlooms," Donnie told him. He likes the case a lot. It brings him comfort. It's the thing that really got him started smoking.

The scotch at Ava's went down smooth, and now he's stuck with his usual cheap shit. He takes out a cigarette and lights it with his Bic. He blows smoke at the ceiling.

The phone rings. He picks it up, hoping it might be Sottile or Pags about the new job they've hopefully lined up. Post-force, he's been doing more and more work for Big Time Tommy, with and without Pags and Sottile. Mostly it's strong-arm stuff. Occasionally, it's a drop. One time, he trailed this drug kingpin's mistress to keep tabs on who else she was screwing. Big Time Tommy was pissed at him over Giuseppe. He'd only wanted the bum kneecapped. He'd killed a couple of other guys for Tommy in the time he'd been working for him, before Giuseppe, but it was always sanctioned, and the guys were always bigger, more obvious scumbags. Donnie had earned back Big Time Tommy's trust over the last couple of years with loyalty and silence and quality work. He'd knocked off a few guys since, and shit always went down by the book. Only Big Time Tommy could hand down a death sentence. Having a purpose other than being police felt good. But he was sure Big Time Tommy wouldn't be happy if he knew about Donnie clipping dough off the top from his collections. Donnie's racket: Make the chump pay a little extra, and what's extra becomes his. Dough adds up like that. And it's not stealing from the Ficalora crew, per se.

It's Suzy on the phone now. "Where are you?" she says.

"You know where I am," Donnie says. "I picked up the phone where I am."

"What are you doing home?"

"I live here."

"I thought you were coming over here. I rented a movie."

"I'm too drunk to get back in the car."

Silence from Suzy. "You fucking piece-of-shit fuck," she finally says. "I've thrown away a lot of time on you. I've stuck with you. I want company, you can at least give me company."

"Where's your vibrator? You out of batteries?"

"Jesus Christ. Don't you get exhausted with yourself?"

"I *am* tired, Suzy."

She slams down the phone on her end with a huff. He can picture it. She's probably sitting there on the sofa in her HILL VS. HEARNS T-shirt and a pair of his boxers he left behind one night, her legs unshaven, no deodorant on, bowl of potato chips next to her, cradling that stupid little stuffed Rudolph the Red-Nosed Reindeer she's got. And she expects him to come over and throw a lay on her.

Now, Ava in that suit, that's something he could get excited about. She's probably all clean curves under there. Soft, well-maintained.

It's getting dark out. The kind of sad late-summer dark that pushes in through the curtains and takes over a room. The only light is from the TV. He drops the butt of his cigarette into an empty Bud can on the coffee table. It sizzles in a forgotten last sip of beer. Smoke gushes up from the mouth. He reaches for his scotch, unscrews the cap, and slugs some more.

A knock on the front door. He wonders who the hell it could be. He imagines for a second that it's Ava and that she's got nothing but a mink coat on, her body all goose-pimply.

"Who's there?" he says from the couch.

From the other side of the door: "It's Nick."

He can't make sense of why Ava's son would come to his house. And not that long after he left there. How's he even know where he lives? Donnie doesn't say anything. He stands up and shuffles down the hall to the door. He opens it with the chain on. Nick's there. He looks lit up from the bourbon.

"What do you want?" Donnie asks.

"Can I talk to you a sec?" Nick says.

"About what?"

"Can I just come in and talk to you?"

"How'd you know where I live? Why you knocking on my door?"

Nick lets out a breath. "Okay, let's do this right here. Took me a few minutes after you left, but I realized who you are. The cop who punched out his captain."

"So, you want a fucking medal?" Donnie says.

"You don't understand, man," Nick says. "You're *interesting*."

"I am?"

"You've got a fan in Ava, my friend. Let me tell you."

"I do?"

"Sure, man."

Donnie beefs up his chest. "What do you want from me?" he asks.

"You're it, Donnie," Nick says, his speech slurred. "You're just what I've been waiting for. You should come around again. Ava really likes you."

"Don't call me Donnie."

"Don. Okay? There you go. Ava really likes you, Don. She's been lonely."

"You're drunk." Donnie pauses. "You're fucking with me about this, why?"

"Maybe I've had too much to drink," Nick says, stumbling back toward the gate. Under the streetlights he looks sick and pale. "I'm from *here*. I'm the guy. This is it. Thanks for helping Ava out, Donnie. Don."

"What are you saying? I don't get it."

Nick opens the gate and walks backward on the sidewalk.

Donnie shakes his head and watches Nick disappear up the block and then around the corner.

He decides he'll go to the Wrong Number. He needs a stiff drink after this encounter with Nick. He goes back in for his cigarettes and wallet and then walks straight to the bar.

When he gets there, Maddie's in her usual spot. The place is pretty crowded. Some faces he recognizes from the neighborhood. Others he doesn't. One he does recognize is Dice, Big Time Tommy's fuckmook side-kick. Little guy. Five-three if he's an inch. He's wearing sweatpants and an oversize Patrick Ewing jersey. He's there with a couple of nobodies, guys who look like they cruise up and down Eighty-Sixth Street in shiny cars, windows down, bass thumping, hollering at girls like the animals they are.

Donnie orders a beer and a shot of whiskey from Maddie, and Dice is hovering over his shoulder in no time flat. The guy's a natural-born ball-buster. His nobody buddies are still over at the table. They're smarter than he is.

"What's the what?" Dice asks.

Donnie does the shot, sips the head off the beer. "I ain't in the mood for you, that's for sure," he says.

"That's not nice. I'm gonna see you tomorrow, right? You're on the clock?"

"Fuck off. Let me drink."

Next thing he knows Dice's hand is on his shoulder. Donnie doesn't want to tangle with this shitbird, but he will. The guy rides Big Time Tommy's dick, but Donnie knows Big Time Tommy thinks he's nothing but a joke. He's like a dumb dog that just needs to be fed and kept around. Donnie's not sure what his story is exactly. Must be somebody's son or nephew. Donnie knocks him out, he won't get shit for it.

"Get your hand off my shoulder *now*," Donnie says to him.

The hand's still there. Dice rattles on: "Tell me something funny. I want to laugh tonight. I've had a few. I know you're good for a laugh. I've heard things. This guy's got stories, they say. From the force and whatnot. Shit you saw. What's the craziest thing? You ever seen a guy stuck down a sewer? Or a broad shoving a dead rat up her snatch?"

Donnie turns and pops him in the face.

Dice falls back and lands on his ass, his hands over his mouth. "What the fuck?" he says. "Who you think you are? I'm gonna tell Tommy on you."

Donnie downs his beer, calls for another shot from Maddie. He turns on his stool, the shot outstretched in his hand. He knows Dice won't get up and fight back. That's the thing with bums like Dice—they never do.

"This one's for you, you dumb bucket of fuck," Donnie says as Dice works himself up into a sad squat, defeated. Donnie throws back the shot and laughs.

The Ulmer Park Library is one of Mikey's usual stops. He heads there now, walking up Bath Avenue with his head down, trying not to trip on cracked concrete. He's a pretty slow reader, but he likes sci-fi. When he was nine, his mother took him to the library to get his own card, and *The Time Machine* was the first book he got out.

His mother. He should've just stayed away from home longer. Fighting with her like that was a waste of time and just made him feel rotten. When he said he wished she was smarter, what he really meant was he wished she was interested in things other than him. He wishes she had friends, that those friends would take her out to movies or for drinks. He wishes she liked anything as much as she likes worrying about him. All she has is church and work. And when your job is taking care of old people, dressing them, wiping their asses, watching them shake with confusion and terror, that's not much to hang your hat on. Mikey went to work with her once or twice when he was younger, and it made him upset.

To stop himself from thinking about his mother, he starts thinking about the pretty bank teller, Ludmilla. He's still bummed that she took pity on him like that. Maybe he'd become one of these young guys walking around who already looks washed-up without knowing it. He should try again with her.

His old man. Had he brought him up, or had his mother? That was stupid. Now she'll be crying all night, and he'll have the feeling he gets when he pictures his old man dead on Bottle Beach.

When Mikey gets to the library, it's closed. Just outside the front gate, there's a small box of books. People are always dropping off books for donation. The library has more than they can deal with. Some, they sell up front for a quarter or fifty cents. Others wind up in the trash. People feel like they're doing good giving their old books to the library, but mostly they're just afraid of throwing things out.

He doesn't feel bad digging through this box now. If he finds something good, he'll give them some money next time he's in.

Eight paperbacks are stacked in two piles in the plain box. Pennies are scattered at the bottom. A lot of times, a box of donated books like this would be pure junk, but there's good stuff here, classics, even a sci-fi novel or two. He plucks *The Lathe of Heaven* from the middle of one pile and then decides he should just take the whole box.

He sits down on a bench up the block and looks through the books. Nestled between a copy of *Invisible Man* and *The Heart Is a Lonely Hunter* is a folded piece of paper with perforated edges. He unfolds it and sets it on his thigh. It's a letter that looks like it was typed on a word processor. The single-spaced print is faint, faded. He reads it:

Dear Mom,

I just don't feel right. It's like a burning wire in my gut, this feeling. I guess I'll never be okay. That's just the way things are. It's not your fault. I'm sorry for letting you down. I'm sorry I couldn't be a better son, the son you deserved. Love you.

Gabe

Mikey turns the letter over in his hand to see if anything else is on the back. He reads it again. It sounds like a suicide note. Or maybe it's just an apology. Maybe this Gabe did something that pissed his mother off and he had to write this to try to explain himself. But Mikey can't shake the feeling that it's more than that, a goodbye, a definitive last statement, the kind of thing both he and his mother wished his father had left behind before disappearing.

He wonders how this note even got there. Is it possible that Gabe's mother never even saw it? That it got sandwiched between these two books and forgotten?

He leafs through the pages of all the books, hoping for some clue. Some scrap of paper to drop out. Something, anything else. Inside the front cover of *Frankenstein*, he sees *Gabe 9-F* in big, blocky letters. He looks in every other book, thinking he must've missed Gabe's name elsewhere. But all he finds is a yellow Post-it note sticking to the back cover of *Salem's Lot*. On it, in girlish curlicue script, is written: *New phone # 372-4276*. It's something.

The numbers play over and over in Mikey's mind. He wonders what will happen if he dials. There's a payphone at the deli up the block. He's used it before. One time, when he was fourteen, he used that very payphone to try to call a phone sex line off a card he found on the street on a dare from his friend Mig. They didn't get anywhere with the phone sex line. No way a quarter or even a few quarters would've gotten them past *hello*.

Carrying the box under his arm, he heads for the deli. The payphone is on the brick wall on the side of the store. Tags are spray-painted all around the phone. The things people usually write above phones, too. He digs around in his pocket for a quarter. He has change from the bar he went to after Ludmilla gave him that forty bucks.

He drops the quarter into the slot and punches the number in from memory. He's always been good at memorizing phone numbers quickly, not that he's had many to memorize. A few guys who were good friends for a little while and then faded away. Ginny. Before that, his senior year, Kristy. He never memorized Antonina's number. They were just getting started when what happened in the schoolyard happened.

The phone rings four times and then a woman picks up. Her voice is soft. She's got the sound of the neighborhood in her. Mikey's lost his accent. He made an effort to lose it up at college. He wanted a nowhere accent.

"Yes?" the woman says.

"Hi, is Gabe there?" Mikey asks.

"Who is this?"

"I'm looking for Gabe."

A long pause. Tears in her voice. "I'm his mother. Who are you? Gabe's dead. What the fuck is this?" The sadness turning suddenly to anger.

Mikey is about to hang up, but he doesn't. He keeps the phone pressed against his ear. He listens to her breathing, hears the sound of her licking her lips, swears he can even hear the sound her teeth make biting down on her lower lip.

"I'm really sorry," he says.

"You're sorry?"

"I just found a box of books at the library. I found this number on a Post-it stuck to one of the books. There was a note in the box. I didn't know if it was what I thought it was."

"What note?" she asks.

"A note saying goodbye. From Gabe. I didn't know. I hoped it wasn't . . . I just didn't think it was something that was meant to be in the box."

"Oh, Jesus."

Silence hangs between them for twenty seconds. It feels like ten minutes.

"Do you want me to do something with it?" Mikey asks. "Do you want me to bring it to you?"

"Please," she says, in a hush.

"Just tell me where. I'll bring it now."

She gives him her address. She lives on Eighty-Fourth Street right off the corner of Twenty-Third Avenue. It's not far. He memorizes the house number.

"Who are you?" she asks him.

"I'm just a guy," he says. "I'm home from college. I live around here. My name's Mikey Baldini."

"Thanks, Mikey. I'm Donna. Donna Rotante."

"Okay, Donna. I'll be over in fifteen, twenty minutes."

He hangs up the receiver and backs away from the payphone. He crosses the street and heads up Bay Forty-First Street toward Benson Avenue. It feels good to be doing something with purpose.

Donna hangs up the phone. The call was a sledgehammer to her chest.

Her son, Gabe, killed himself three years ago, and she'd finally worked up the courage to bring some of his books to the library as a donation, thinking she'd send a little of him out into the world. But it was closed when she got there, so she left the box of books out front and somehow—*somehow*—Gabe's last note just to her, his suicide note, was in the box and here was this stranger who'd picked it up and read it and called her because her new phone number was somehow also in that box, scribbled on a Post-it. How did it even get there? How does anything get anywhere? It fell in, or she stuck it on one of the books for some reason or another, most likely. These things happen.

She puts her head in her hands and listens to the emptiness of her apartment. Once, she lived in a house not far from here. She had a husband, Donnie, and they had their baby, Gabe, and he learned to crawl and walk on the wood floors in that house, and she sat in the kitchen and fed Gabe mashed carrots and little bits of pasta and mozzarella, and she wiped his mouth and gave him sippy cups full of apple juice. He grew up, and he went to grammar school at St. Mary's, and he wore his little clip tie and his blue button-up shirt and his dark slacks and his Thom McAn shoes. Donnie was a cop. He drank too much and was gone even when he wasn't on the job. As

Gabe got older, he grew more and more withdrawn. He cried a lot. Donnie gave him hell for that. Gabe was always wearing his headphones, listening to heavy metal. He started cutting his arms with razors. Donnie didn't know that, but she did. She tried to talk to Gabe about it, but he wouldn't open up. She wanted him to go to a shrink. He refused. She should've forced him. When he was fifteen, he hanged himself in the cellar with a belt. Finding him was hell. She can't revisit that scene in her mind's eye. She can't think about his body against her as she held him and tried to get him down from the pipe. Afterward, he was gone, really gone. Nothing prepares you for that.

She left Donnie and rented this apartment from Suzette Bonsignore, an old friend of her mother's. Suzette lives upstairs with her three cats. Both of Donna's parents are gone. Her mother died ten years ago from a stroke. Her father died the year before Gabe from a heart attack. As far as Donnie, she signed off on everything. She didn't want the house, didn't want his pension, nothing, zilch. He went down an even darker path, losing his job and his pension in the process. She'd decided to try to survive her own way. That's all she could do.

This apartment was where Suzette's daughter lived before she moved to Long Island. Suzette isn't in good health. Her daughter doesn't come around much anymore. Donna took it as it was and didn't do anything to improve it. She moved in with just a couple of suitcases of clothes, her records and turntable, and several boxes of Gabe's stuff. Everything else she left with Donnie at the house. The apartment is on the ground floor. There are bars on the windows. The mailbox is missing a screw and dangles next to the door. The couch is torn. She got a nice area rug for cheap on Eighty-Sixth Street, and that covers the scuffed, wooden living room floor. Her bed frame is on the verge of collapsing. Water damage has stained the ceilings in the living room and bedroom. Lights dim on their own. Pipes clank. There's no washing machine, so she has to use the Laundromat around the corner.

Gabe loved to read, but she doesn't, which is why she was getting rid of his books. It hurt her too much to look at them, to imagine him reading them, curled up in bed, a tall glass of water on his nightstand. She'd taken them with her for the connection to him they provided, but that connection was lost.

What she loves is music. She has about a hundred records split between two milk crates in her living room. She has the same turntable she's had for twenty-plus years. It still sounds great. She doesn't even like to watch TV. When she comes home from work—she's a receptionist at Bishop Kearney High School on Bay Parkway—she just likes to pour some wine and listen to her records. Bruce Springsteen, Linda Ronstadt, Jackson Browne, Joni Mitchell, Otis Redding, Carly Simon, and Garland Jeffreys are some of her main go-tos. Music is her only solace. The silence right now is terrible.

When the doorbell rings, she jolts back into the present moment and looks around at her messy kitchen, her sink crowded with mugs and plates, detritus from three or four meals in a row of nothing but coffee and crumb cake.

She's still dressed for work, her black slacks and black blazer and white shirt that she should've washed days ago, but her shoes are off.

She pads through the living room to the front door, barefoot. She hasn't had anyone in her apartment in months, and even then it was just Roberta from work. Does she need to invite this Mikey in? She looks around. A mirror frosted with dust. Blankets swirled on the couch. Crates of records, and a stack that she's recently been playing. Turntable and dusty speakers. A Casio keyboard that once belonged to Gabe, that she's been tinkering with. She took piano lessons as a girl, and she can play a few songs from *Les Misérables* on the piano at Bishop Kearney.

The stranger is there with the box of books when she opens up. He's little more than a boy. College, he said? He's in a ratty T-shirt and wrinkled jeans with holes in the knees. He has dark hair and dark eyes and a beard. He has a unibrow and a big Italian nose. Something tells her he's been drinking— he just has that *look*—but he also seems harmless, tender even.

"Hi," he says. "I'm Mikey. I called."

"Do you want to come in?" Donna asks.

"I shouldn't." He holds the box of books out to her.

She takes it and sets it on the floor just inside the door. "That note," she says.

"I'm sorry. I shouldn't have read it."

"You couldn't have known what it was."

"Still, I'm sorry."

"I don't know how it got in the box."

She says it and realizes it's absolutely true, and her mind plays back the scene from earlier that day, taking the stack of books from the shelf in her bedroom, thinking it was time to let go of some of Gabe's stuff. The note must have somehow been between the books already. When was the last time she'd seen it? She'd read it frequently in the months following his suicide, holding it in her shaking hands just to put her hands where his hands had been. He'd left it for her in the cellar, in a sealed envelope propped on top of the washing machine. She's always wished he'd written more, had taken the time to let her know more about himself. He had become a mystery to her at fifteen. She wishes she could've told him—though she did tell him, in various ways—that everyone goes through hard times and that being a teenager is especially hard. She wishes he would've written more because writing more sometimes helped people get through the worst of it, the writing itself a form of therapy, a way of healing. But Gabe had descended into a darker place than that, and he couldn't get away from it and he didn't write more, barely wrote anything. But he'd written something, and she'd looked at it and looked at it until she lost track of it, and there it is now in this box of books she dumped at the library.

"If you don't want the books anymore," Mikey says, "I'll take them."

She leans over the box and takes out the note, flattening it against her thigh and tracing her finger over the letters. "Sure, I'm glad someone who wants them will get them. Gabe loved to read."

"I like it, too."

"Gabe liked to write. He wanted to write plays, at one point anyway. Do you like to write?"

"No, I can't write. I always got Cs and Ds in my writing classes."

She stands up. "Will you come in? I can make coffee. It'd be nice to have a little company."

"Okay," he says.

She folds the letter, inserting it in the pocket of her blazer. "Just leave the box," she says. "You can get it on your way out."

Mikey comes in and wipes his feet on the mat inside the door.

She guides him through the living room. She notices that he looks at her records first.

In the kitchen, she pulls out a chair for him. He sits, scooching the chair in, trying to figure out what to do with his arms. He settles on putting his elbows on the table.

Donna fills the percolator, the outside dewy with condensation. She scoops Folgers into the basket and then fits the lid on, placing the percolator on a medium flame.

She thinks about what's in her fridge. Some vanilla yogurt that's pretty old, a box of raisins, a last hunk of Entenmann's crumb cake. "You want a piece of crumb cake?" she asks.

"I'm good," he says. "I just ate dinner. I'm pretty full."

Donna sits across from him at the table. "Do you have an apartment?"

"I live with my mom."

"You're in college?"

"Not anymore. I dropped out. I went upstate."

"Upstate where? I have distant cousins in Coxsackie."

"New Paltz."

She nods. "About the note," she says.

"We don't have to talk about it," he says, his voice gentle.

"Thank you. I know." She looks over her shoulder at the stove. The coffee isn't perking yet. She continues: "I want to. Gabe, he was fifteen." The tear's there on her cheek before she even realizes she's crying again.

"I'm sorry."

"It's okay. I'm okay. You're young. Gabe was young. He was having a hard go of it. He was just sad. I tried to get him help." She feels, suddenly, so open with this strange kid. She hasn't been able to talk to anyone about Gabe. Not at work. Not the therapist she tried those first three months. Maybe it's because he's close to Gabe's age. Gabe would be in college now. Mikey could've been a friend of Gabe's. Maybe it's meant to be, her leaving the note, Mikey finding it and bringing it back.

"My father killed himself," Mikey says, and she's struck by his lack of hesitation.

"That's awful," Donna says, pushing forward in her chair. But she's even more intrigued. It's another thing that makes this feel meant to be. "I'm so sorry."

"I was eighteen when he did it. He was in trouble."

The coffee starts perking rapidly. Donna goes over and lowers the gas, the blue flame sputtering under the percolator. Two mornings ago, she'd left the burner on and had woken up to the smell of gas and thought how easy it would be if the apartment just blew up with her in it. But she'd probably take poor Suzette and her cats out, too.

She gets two clean mugs out of the dish drain and sets them on a cutting board next to the stovetop. "Do you take anything?" she asks Mikey.

"Just black," he says.

She waits there at the stove, hunched over the percolator, rubbing her neck. "I lost hope," she says.

Mikey doesn't say anything.

She elaborates: "After Gabe died, I lost hope. It's hard to have hope. I used to go to church. How can I go to church? You know what Father Borzumato said to me? He said we couldn't bury Gabe in my family plot. He said Gabe was going to hell. I don't believe that. I don't know what I believe, but I don't believe that."

"He said the same thing to my mother," Mikey says. "But my mother accepts it. She thinks that's what happens."

"You go to church?"

"Not anymore. I did, growing up."

"You lost hope, too?"

"I guess. I'm not sure I ever really had hope. I don't even know if I know what hope is."

The coffee has perked for a few minutes. Donna takes the percolator off the stove and sets it on a burnt brown oven mitt. She pours the mugs full of coffee, bringing one over to Mikey and then getting the other one for herself.

She sits back down. "That's a good question," she says. "About what hope is, I mean."

"I don't know," Mikey says, holding the mug up to his lips and taking a sip of coffee. "I'm not good at thinking about stuff like that. I'm not really very smart."

"You seem smart." Donna leans back in her chair, the steam from the coffee rising in front of her. "You have a job since you dropped out?"

"Not right this sec."

"You want mine? I can't stand it anymore."

"Where do you work?"

"Bishop Kearney. I'm off for a couple of weeks now."

"Really? I went to Our Lady of the Narrows."

"I should've figured. Gabe went to Lafayette for high school. I don't know why. It's not like it was when I went there. Maybe I do know. He said he didn't want to go to an all-boys school."

"It sucked."

Donna's thoughts stray back to Mikey's father. "Can I ask you a question? You said your father was in trouble. What kind of trouble?"

"Gambling," Mikey says.

"He wasn't the man who jumped from the Marine Parkway Bridge, was he?"

"That's my old man."

She remembers hearing about it. Word was that Mikey's dad—she can't remember his name, though she remembered people saying it—was in the hole to Big Time Tommy Ficalora. Donnie used to work some for Big Time Tommy. He didn't think she knew, but she did. He probably still does. Maybe that's his only work since he stopped being a cop. She thinks of Mikey's dad, painted into a corner by bad decisions, so desperate he had to jump. She didn't read the story in a paper, but it was the kind of thing where you run into someone on the street and they ask if you heard the news and they tell you about this stranger killing himself. It'd happened that way with Gabe, too. He became gossip for all the people who had nothing better to do than talk.

"I'm so sorry," she says.

"It's okay," Mikey says. "He did what he did."

"Can I ask you something else?"

"Okay."

"I heard about your father—what was his name?"

"Giuseppe."

"I heard about Giuseppe just from people shooting their big mouths off. Did you ever hear about Gabe like that?"

"I didn't, no."

"You sure? The neighborhood talks."

"The neighborhood talks, but I don't listen." He pauses, sips some coffee. "You know, there's a lot of . . ." He searches the air for what he's trying to say. "I don't know what word I'm looking for. There's a lot of *something* in our stories."

"Synchronicity?" she asks.

"Maybe. That sounds good. What's it mean?"

"I took psychology in college. It means that coincidences can be meaningful, basically. Things just line up, you know? I think that's what it means. I think it fits."

"You talked about Gabe, but you didn't mention being married. What happened?"

"We split up after Gabe died. I couldn't look at him anymore. Gabe was all we had to keep us together. We were married sixteen years. I don't really want to talk about my ex too much, if you don't mind."

"You don't mind me asking, how old are you?" Mikey asks.

Donna laughs. "I like that you asked me that. You're young enough not to know."

"Not to know what?"

"You don't ask women that question."

"Sorry."

"It's okay. I'm thirty-nine. I look older." She says it not as a question because she knows it to be true. The last three years have beaten her down, and she feels like she's aged ten years. "Somebody at work thought I was in my late forties."

"You don't look old."

"It's okay. I don't take any offense. I'm okay with looking my age. I'm okay with looking older than my age. I don't want to look like a girl. I didn't want to look like a girl when I *was* a girl."

"I'm twenty," Mikey says, suddenly nervous. "I turn twenty-one tomorrow."

Donna lights up. "Well, happy birthday."

"Thanks. Doesn't mean much to me, really."

"You have a girlfriend?"

"She broke up with me a while ago."

"Gabe was in love with this girl he was afraid to talk to. Carissa, that was her name. He didn't even give himself the chance to get his heart broken." She pauses. "You sure you don't want some crumb cake? I wish I had more to offer. My mother would've said I should be ashamed. Have someone over and have nothing good to put on the table."

"I'm okay, thank you."

"My parents are dead, both of them."

"All of my grandparents are dead."

"We've got a lot of dead people between us, huh?"

Mikey shifts uncomfortably in his chair. He wraps his hand around the mug of coffee. "Death is weird," he says.

"It sure is," Donna says, and she laughs again.

Mikey laughs, too. He stands up, pushes away from the table. "I should probably go. Thank you for the coffee."

"It was nice talking to you. Really. I'm off tomorrow. I know it's your birthday, but come by, if you want. I'll just be here with my records."

Mikey's eyes drift back to her crates full of LPs in the living room. "You've got a lot of records."

"I enjoy listening to music. Do you?"

"I've got some tapes."

"If you come back, we can listen to music," she says, and she can't really believe that she's said it, but she has.

Mikey nods.

She walks him back through the living room to the front door. "Don't forget the books," she says.

"You're sure?" he asks.

"I want you to have them. Now that I know you a little, especially. I'm happy they'll go to a good home."

Mikey leans down and picks up the box.

Donna opens the door. "Thank you again for bringing back the note," she says.

Mikey stops as he crosses the threshold to outside. "If I come by tomorrow, can I just come by? Or should I call first?"

"Just come by," Donna says, smiling. "I'm not going anywhere."

When he's gone, she goes back to the table and sits down in the seat where Mikey had been sitting. It's warm. She touches the handle of his mug, considers the bit of coffee that he's left, and she feels something she hasn't felt in a long time.

It's desire. She knows that. But she can't really distinguish what kind of desire. Is he a potential stand-in for Gabe? Someone she hopes to mother?

Or is it the other thing?

He's practically a kid, but she likes the way he looked at her, and she likes the way they talked, and she's bowled over by the things they have in common.

What she feels now is that there's a line between them, something that goes from A to B, and that maybe that line has always existed somehow, even though she's almost forty and he's only twenty going on twenty-one, but that it only came alive in the moment of meeting.

She lets out a heavy sigh and drinks what little is left of his lukewarm coffee.

Nick's making the rounds. First Donnie and now Mikey Baldini. He wants the true story of what happened that night in the schoolyard. He's thinking that's his opening scene for the script: Donnie going after Mikey with the bat. Was he drunk? Was he sweet on Antonina Divino? Was he legitimately concerned for her, trying to play father since his own kid was dead and buried?

He remembers where Mikey lives because once he gave him a ride home from Bay Ridge. It's a pretty far hike. There were always a few boys from the neighborhood at Our Lady of the Narrows. Nick avoided them on the bus, but if he had the car—especially late, after a basketball game or a school play or some bullshit—he didn't mind giving them a lift. That bus ride could be torturously long, especially at night if you had to wait.

The time he'd given Mikey a ride nothing of note had happened. They must've conversed, but he doesn't remember about what. It was after a basketball game. Maybe they'd talked about the game. It was probably five or six years ago, before Mikey went up to New Paltz and got into whatever he got into, before the incident with Donnie Parascandolo, before his old man killed himself. He knew Mikey was back in the neighborhood because he'd heard it secondhand from Ava, who'd heard it from Rosemarie, who wouldn't stop talking about how worried she was for his future.

The Baldini house is sad and slumped, with green-speckled siding, loose roof shingles, and a rotting porch. There's still an Easter wreath up on the front door.

When he rings the bell, he's not sure what he's expecting. He's got it in his head that Mikey will answer and be amped to talk.

But it's Rosemarie who answers. "Ava's son?" she says. "What do you want?"

"Hi, Mrs. Baldini," Nick says. "I was hoping to talk to Mikey."

"Talk to Mikey about what?"

"Just a writing project I'm working on. Nothing to worry about."

"Are you loaded? You're like my son. He was loaded last I saw him, too."

"He's not home?"

She waves her hand, disgusted. "Who knows where he went? The lies. I can't anymore."

"I'll come back another time. I'm sorry."

"Twenty-one tomorrow. He was less trouble when he was a teenager."

Nick backs away. "Goodbye."

She swats the air and closes the door.

His next bright idea is to go see Antonina Divino. Antonina lives right around the corner from Donnie with her parents, Sonny and Josephine, so he backtracks. He should've just gone there first. She must be going into her senior year of high school. Nick's seen her around in her Bishop Kearney uniform. Model-pretty. Her hair's long, usually dyed pink or purple. Maybe it's not the smartest idea, a drunk guy going over to talk to a high school girl, but he's so excited he can't think about anything else. He'll talk to Sonny first. He'll be respectful as hell. Sonny will understand.

The Divino house is on Bay Thirty-Fourth, in the middle of the block. He can throw a rock and hit the back of Donnie's house. He stumbles through the front gate, leaving it open behind him, and nearly knocks over their metal garbage cans. Sonny's motorcycle is parked in the garden next to a Mary statue encased in glass. Flowers grow in the garden. The little purple

ones you can pinch with your fingers and make a puff of air with. A piece
of tape on the mailbox has their last name printed neatly in Sharpie. Nick
presses the bell three times. And then he bangs at the edge of the screen
door with his fist.

When Josephine Divino answers finally, Nick steps back so as not to
seem intimidating. She's wearing gym shorts and a Bart Simpson T-shirt.
She's only a few years older than him. Thirty-three or thirty-four. She had
Antonina when she was seventeen, a neighborhood scandal. Sonny was a
dropout who worked at a garage on McDonald Avenue and had a few girlfriends. Antonina was something like twelve when Josephine was Nick's age.
He can't imagine having a kid, let alone a near-teenager, under his command
about now. Josephine's almost as pretty as her daughter, with dark hair and
sharp features. She could pass for mid-twenties. He was three grades behind
her at St. Mary's. He remembers looking at her during assembly when he
was in the fifth grade and she was in the eighth. All the boys in the school
had a big crush on her because she was angelic and sweet and looked like a
woman. He remembers her plaid skirt, which she wore high on her waist so
it rode above her knees, and he remembers the pale blue leggings she wore
that the nuns weren't fond of.

She talks to him through the screen. "Nick Bifulco?"

"You remember my name," Nick says. "I'm impressed."

"What do you want?"

"I'm not selling anything, I swear." He focuses on trying to stand absolutely straight but then wavers and loses his balance and falls forward into
the door.

"Are you wasted?" Josephine says.

"I've had a few. I'm celebrating. Is Sonny here? Can I talk to Sonny?"

"Sonny's not here right now."

"His motorcycle's here."

"That thing doesn't work."

"Maybe I can talk to you?"

"About what?"

"Antonina." He pauses. "Is she here?"

Josephine eyes him askance. "Why do you want to talk to me about my daughter?"

"It's nothing bad. It's all good. Trust me. It's good news."

She pushes open the screen door and waves him inside. He smiles and nods and walks past her and then waits for her to lead him down a long hallway through a living room with a broken TV and a plastic cover on the couch and a deep green shag rug into a kitchen that smells strongly of chicken cutlets. He watches her as she walks. Barefoot. Behind her knees, the soft creases there. She's got killer legs.

"Don't be staring at my ass," Josephine says. "I get enough of that shit during the day."

"I was, I'll admit, admiring your legs," Nick says, chirping a little burp into his palm. "I'm sorry."

She turns around. "Legs I can deal with. Ass and boobs, you keep your eyes to yourself."

His eyes now are drawn to the shape of her under Bart Simpson.

"Nick?" she says.

"I'm sorry," he says.

"Sit down." She points to the kitchen table. A stack of scratch-offs is rubber-banded together next to a sugar bowl and a clutch of ripe bananas. "You want some coffee? I think you need some coffee."

Nick sits. "That'd be fantastic. Thanks."

Josephine goes over to the stove. She reaches up for a percolator in the cabinet over the range hood, and he watches her as she stretches, on the tips of her toes now, the muscles in her legs sinewy, collecting the pot with both hands as if she's stealing a baby bird from its nest. She gazes over her shoulder at him and notices him noticing her again. He looks down at the table, at the sugar bowl, at the scratch-offs.

"Tell me what you want to talk to Antonina about," Josephine says.

"Is she here?"

"She's in her room." Josephine runs water in the sink and fills the pot. She then spoons some Folgers into the basket, drops the basket into the water, and secures the lid. She gets it going over a high flame on the stove. She comes back to the table and sits across from Nick. "Coffee should only take a few minutes."

"Oh, that's great."

She puts her elbows on the table, clasps her hands together, and rests her chin on her knuckles. "I'm waiting," she says.

"For what?"

"For you to explain yourself. What do you want with Antonina? You know, my daughter doesn't need any shit right now. She's had a tough year. She's been down in the dumps."

"She has? I'm sorry. She's such a pretty kid. I'd guess she was happy."

"Pretty isn't everything." The percolator rattles over the gas. She gets up and turns it down. The coffee settles to a steady perk.

There's a sound of movement from behind the door at the back of the room.

"That's the stairs to the attic," Josephine says. "That's where Antonina stays now."

Feet clomping down the steps. The door thrown open. Antonina's standing there, framed by light from a bare fluorescent bulb hanging over her. She's wearing combat boots and a wool skirt and a purple crop tee. Her hair's cotton candy pink. Leather and silver-stud wristbands. Black lipstick. Eyes heavy with mascara.

Nick stands up. "Hi there, Antonina," he says. "You don't know me. I like the look."

Josephine shakes her head. "Don't encourage her, okay?"

"You're that teacher from OLN. What do you want?" Antonina says.

Josephine stares daggers at him, anxious to know what the hell his deal is. Nick turns down the corners of his mouth. "I am that teacher. I'm also a writer. I'm working on a movie script. It's my dream. Write a script, get it into Martin Scorsese's hands or something like that. I mean, I'm just in the beginning stages, but I need to talk to you."

Antonina struts over to the refrigerator and opens the door and takes out a Coke. She pops the tab and drinks some.

"I'm basing the main guy on Donnie Parascandolo."

"She doesn't want to talk about that piece of shit," Josephine says. She's still perched by the stove. She pours coffee in a Harrah's mug and hands it to Nick. "Black?" she says.

"Black's great," Nick says. "Thanks." He accepts the mug and blows down into the steam and sips the hot coffee.

"What can I possibly tell you?" Antonina says.

"Donnie picked my mother up on the Belt tonight. She'd broken down. He was being a Good Samaritan. You believe that? Took me a second to realize who he was. When I did, I thought, 'This is so interesting.' I remembered his reputation. I remembered the stories I heard around school about him hitting Mikey with the bat." Nick's talking animatedly to Antonina, but he's also addressing Josephine, the coffee mug balanced over his palm. He fears he's slurring his words. It doesn't matter. "I'm the guy to write about him, to dissect the psychology at work."

"Antonina shouldn't have been there that night," Josephine says. "She was fifteen. Mikey Baldini got all out of whack when he went upstate. Sonny would've kicked the shit out of him, given the chance. I don't think much of Donnie, but I don't have a problem with him hitting Mikey that night, that's for sure."

"He probably picked up your mom because he's trying to fuck her," Antonina says to Nick.

"Your mother does look nice," Josephine says. And then to Antonina: "Watch your mouth, okay?"

"I think he might have some interest in Ava. I was just over at Donnie's. Don's."

"You were over there?" Antonina says.

"I was over there. Around there. Whatever."

"You think he's gonna let you write a movie about him? That's pretty stupid. And dangerous. He's not a good guy. I've heard other things."

"Like what?"

"Like him breaking arms for Big Time Tommy Ficalora."

"Keep your nose out of it," Josephine says.

"Where'd you hear that?" Nick asks.

"Just around," Antonina says.

"I think you should leave," Josephine says. "Sonny's gonna be home soon. He won't like that you're here. He's got brass knuckles. He likes to use them."

Nick plucks up one of the scratch-offs and tries to write his number on the back with a golf pencil. The pencil won't write on the card. He finds something else to write on, a yellow Post-it notepad.

"You're pretty wasted," Antonina says.

"I'm not being untoward here," Nick says. "You think of anything I could use, just call me and let me know. You talk to Mikey lately?"

"I haven't seen Mikey since that night."

"You need to go," Josephine says to Nick.

Nick puts down the mug on the table, some coffee sloshing out and puddling around the sugar bowl. He places his hand on his chest, taking a poetic stance: "Donnie's the neighborhood in a nutshell. I'm the guy to write about him, about this place. We're talking real-deal stuff. This is history, and we can record it."

He staggers down the hallway and out the front door, leaving it open behind him, almost ripping through the screen door with his elbow and then letting that door clatter shut. He stands out front and considers Mary in glass and Sonny's motorcycle.

When he turns, Antonina's standing behind the screen, her face crisscrossed with shadows, her hair like a neon light in a bar window. She looks like maybe she wants to say more. She bites her lip and closes the door.

Antonina is on the fire escape outside her attic window, smoking, with her Walkman in her lap. She's listening to a mix her best friend, Lizzie, made her. It's got Siouxsie and the Banshees, the Cure, This Mortal Coil, Cowboy Junkies, Patti Smith, Television, Joy Division, Wire, Gang of Four, the Fall, and Echo and the Bunnymen. It's the best mix anyone's ever made her. She's finishing up "Tarantula" by This Mortal Coil on Side A now. It transitions into Cowboy Junkies doing "Sweet Jane." Lizzie is so good at transitions. Antonina can just picture her, perched over her tape deck, ready to pounce. Lizzie loves making mixtapes, staying up all night with a pot of coffee, her tapes and records spread out on the bed. Antonina's tried. She doesn't have the patience. She always fucks something up, cuts off a song too soon or has too jarring a transition. It's an art she hasn't mastered.

She can't believe that teacher came over asking about the night in the schoolyard with Mikey. He probably watches a lot of Woody Allen movies and thinks he's got a shot with her. Fucking freak. He must be thirty. Not that she wouldn't date an older guy, but it's sure as shit not going to be a loser teacher from Our Lady of the Narrows.

A script? The dumb piece of shit probably watched *Mean Streets* one time and thought, *I could write something like that*. Antonina loves *Mean Streets*. It's her favorite movie, hands down. De Niro in that movie. Jesus. She loves when he comes into the bar in his boxers, when he's introducing the Jewish girls from Café Bizarre to Harvey Keitel.

She looks over at Donnie Parascandolo's house. It's dark. She remembers when his wife still lived there. Donna. She works at Bishop Kearney, where Antonina goes to school. Antonina doesn't see her much, but every once in a while, she'll turn a corner in the hallway and Donna will be there and they'll ignore each other. Donna obviously doesn't like to think about living in that house. It brings back Gabe. That was tragic, him killing himself. Gabe was a year older than Antonina. They'd been at St. Mary's at the same time together. She didn't know him—a grade was a big difference in grammar school—but she used to see him in the gym at recess and wonder how he was the son of someone like Donnie Parascandolo. He seemed so tender, so grown-up, the kind of kid who acted more like an adult than most of the adults around. She didn't know that from talking to him or anything. It was just the way he carried himself. Always with a book. Mature. Holding doors open for nuns when the other boys in his class were spitting on girls to get their attention or arm-wrestling for five-buck pots or taking bets on who could get Sara Desiderio to blow them in the bathroom.

And Mikey Baldini. She hadn't thought about him in a little while. That night was weird. He'd been back for the summer from his first year at college when they started hanging out. They met at a party over at Gina D'Aniello's on Seventy-Eighth Street. Antonina had snuck down the fire escape one of the first times ever that night. Mikey was so different. He was from the neighborhood, but he had changed. Those gauges in his earlobes, that tattoo, his hoodie. He didn't smell like the city. He smelled like the country. He had stories about seeing hardcore bands at dive bars in Kingston and Pough-keepsie. He had stories about crust punks he knew who rode the rails and lived in tents in the woods with their dogs. He said he'd shot heroin but didn't like needles. Within a couple of hours of meeting, they were making out. She saw him five or six times after that. Lizzie had just lost her virginity to a guy who was in college, and Antonina figured it was her turn. The schoolyard seemed perfect. She'd pictured it happening on the cold cracked concrete. Maybe she was fucked in the head, but that seemed romantic to her. Out in the open on a summer night, all the sounds of the city around. But it didn't go down like that. Donnie happened. After he'd hit Mikey, she didn't know what to do. She thought she'd have to call an ambulance. But Mikey just yelled at her to get away and he ran out of the schoolyard, holding his face. He never spoke to her again, thinking she was off-limits. She sees him around now that he's back for good and they ignore each other, too. She wound up losing her virginity in the back of an '84 Toyota Tercel on Shore Parkway by Nellie Bly to a senior from Bishop Ford named Rico Ruiz. It was fast and awkward and mostly sad, but Rico wasn't too much of a jerk.

She drops her cigarette into the yard and goes back into her room. Her bed is a mess. Her floor's covered in crumpled clothes. She's got movie posters on her wall: *Pink Flamingos* and *Carrie*. They were getting rid of them at Wolfman's, the neighborhood video store where she likes to rent movies, and she took them off the owner's hands. She's got a small TV in the corner, a VCR right on top of it. She loves movies. She's gotten lost in them for as long as she can remember, watching anything on TV she could, renting tapes from Wolfman's and taking them out from the library and going into the city to track down arthouse and foreign and cult movies at Kim's Underground.

She's thinking about watching a movie now. She taped a few off of HBO over the weekend: *Light of Day*, *Frantic*, and *Christine*. She's thinking *Light of Day*. She likes Joan Jett.

Her phone rings. She's got her own line. She takes off her headphones, stopping Lizzie's mix, and answers, wrapping the cord around her wrist as she presses the receiver to her ear. She's guessing it'll be Lizzie, but it's Ralph Sottile.

Ralph had been a weird side effect of the night in the schoolyard with Mikey and Donnie two years ago. He's one of Donnie's cop pals. She'd seen him around before then. But he clearly hadn't been okay with what Donnie did, and that was the first sign he was different. The second was he showed up outside Bishop Kearney after school one day about a week later and gave her an envelope. In the envelope was a hundred bucks. He said it was for any trouble they'd caused her. He said to call if she ever needed anything, writing his number on the envelope. She called him a few days later, and he picked her up two blocks from her house and they drove to the Crosstown Diner out in the Bronx so they were far from the neighborhood. Ralph isn't a good-looking guy. He's heavy, he wears tired suits, and he's losing his hair. But he's not bad overall.

They don't fuck, her and Ralph. He's never tried anything like that. He just likes talking to her about school and about what she wants to do in life. He likes giving her money. She doesn't ask where it comes from. She's saving the money. She figures when she graduates next spring, she can take off with less trouble. She wants to get the hell out of Brooklyn. Maybe she'll just wind up in the city or maybe she'll go upstate or maybe she'll go farther. Maybe she'll keep going until something tells her to stop. She's not sure about college. She knows only that she won't be trapped into going where her parents want her to go, Hofstra or Fordham or St. John's. If she goes to college, it'll be on her own terms. Maybe a state school like the one Mikey went to, and she can just pay her own way by waitressing.

The weird thing is, using Ralph or not, he knows her better than anyone, other than Lizzie. She guesses she's a stand-in for the daughter he'll never have. Or maybe he just gets off on playing daddy.

"Can you meet me?" he asks now.

"Sure," she says. "Pick me up?"

"I'll be there in fifteen. Usual spot."

She hangs up the phone and then locks her door from the inside. Her parents won't come knocking. They don't bother her much these days. She crawls through her open window onto the fire escape and shimmies down the narrow ladder. She has sneaking out down to a science.

The next step is hopping the fence into Jane Rafferty's overgrown yard.

Jane's a shut-in, seventy-something, and her yard is dark. Antonina stays close to Jane's house and comes out on Bay Thirty-Fourth Street. From there, she books it up to Bath Avenue and then takes a quick right onto Bay Thirty-Second. Ralph always picks her up in front of a white three-family house with six Virgin Mary statues in the front garden among the tomatoes and peppers and zucchini.

Antonina gets there first, but Ralph pulls up in his red '88 Cadillac Brougham with its cross-hatch grille soon after. She knows about cars from her old man. She likes Ralph's car.

She gets in the passenger seat, pulling the door shut behind her. He's wearing a black bowling shirt and blue dress pants. He gives her an envelope. Same routine every time. Sometimes it's a hundred bucks, sometimes it's more. "A little something," he says.

"Thank you so much," she says, tucking the envelope in the tight little pocket of her wool skirt.

Ralph pulls away from the curb.

The Crosstown Diner has become their go-to spot. Depending on traffic, it can take thirty minutes to drive there or it can take two hours. Ralph's usual route is the Belt to the Cross Island and then across the Whitestone Bridge. The Bronx is the same city but a different world. Antonina had never been there before Ralph, not even to a Yankees game.

There's light traffic now on the Belt.

"Look at this scumbag piece-of-shit fuck," Ralph says, pointing over the wheel at a Ford Mustang that's cut them off. The driver seems to be pretty short. "Can barely see over the wheel. He should sit on a couple of phone books, fucking citrullo that he is."

Ralph curses a lot when he's driving. Antonina finds it endearing.

"I'm sorry, sweetie." He reaches over and pats her knee, as innocently as a man in his mid-forties can touch the knee of a seventeen-year-old girl. "I like the new hair—I tell you that?"

"Thanks," Antonina says.

"Your old man give you shit?"

"A little."

She thinks about Nick Bifulco and decides not to tell Ralph about his visit just yet, if ever. What good would it do? There's only one way Ralph would interpret Nick coming around. She's legal in New York at seventeen, and Nick's no doubt a scrubby little pussy-hound. And it might not be an inaccurate appraisal of the situation, after all.

The traffic gets heavier by JFK but then it clears up. In no time at all, they're getting off the Whitestone Bridge and Ralph is navigating his way through the streets, before turning onto Bruckner Boulevard. They park in the Crosstown Diner lot. Ralph does a couple of laps around his car to make sure it's secure and then they're approaching the chrome front of the diner, its red neon lights bright against the dark sky.

Inside, they're seated at their favorite booth, the blinds open so they can watch the cars out on the street. The waiter, in his black vest, his black hair slicked back, recognizes them and gives them menus. Ralph says they don't need menus. He's got their orders down. Chicken Française and an Amstel Light for him and a Belgian waffle and a vanilla milkshake for her. The waiter hustles off to the kitchen to fill the order.

"So, tell me something good," Ralph says to Antonina.

"I don't know," Antonina says. "There's not much to tell."

"How's Lizzie?"

"Lizzie's Lizzie."

"She make you another mixtape? I knew how to make a tape, I'd make you one. Sinatra, Dion and the Belmonts, Frankie Valli and the Four Seasons, Bobby Darin, that's the stuff right there." He pauses. "I never asked, what do you think of Madonna? I seen her in that *Dick Tracy* and *A League of Their Own*. Very good. I don't know from her music really. 'Like a Prayer,' I heard that on the radio a few times."

"I used to like her a lot. 'Papa Don't Preach,' that was my favorite song when I was like ten."

"Madonna Louise Ciccone. Italian girl. You already knew that, I'm sure."

Antonina nods.

"You like movies," Ralph says. "I bet you like her in that *Desperately Seeking Susan*."

"I do like that movie."

"Reason I ask, I could get you tickets to this Madonna show at Madison Square Garden in October, you'd be interested? You could take Lizzie."

"The Girlie Show? That's a big deal."

"So, I'll get you the tickets. They'll be the best. I got a guy."

"Thanks, Mr. Sottile."

"What'd I tell you? Call me Ralph. I like when you say my name."

The waiter brings their food. Antonina attacks her milkshake first and then picks at her waffle. Ralph tucks a napkin into the collar of his shirt, lifts his fork and knife, smiles, and digs in. His first bite, he looks happy as can be. While he's still chewing, he says, "Here we are. Our home away from home."

Antonina thinks about taking Lizzie to the city for a Madonna show. Maybe Lizzie's boyfriend, Chip, will get them fucked up beforehand. "I'm happy, too," Antonina says, and she realizes she's only partly lying.

Rosemarie is on her knees in the bathroom, cleaning the toilet, when the doorbell rings again. Mikey hadn't made too much of a mess, but she wants to make sure she scrubs the bowl good while she's thinking of it. She takes off her yellow rubber gloves, draping them on the side of the tub, and leverages herself on the sink as she stands.

"Hold on!" she calls out. "I'll be there in a minute."

She hopes it's not that Nick Bifulco again. Some nerve, showing up like that, drunk. She wonders if he's a homosexual.

But when she opens up, she sees it's Big Time Tommy and one of his sidekicks. Big Time Tommy is a large man. He's got a neck like a tree trunk. His skin is dark from tanning beds, and his hair is greasy. He's got bushy eyebrows. He wears a patriotic windbreaker and loose-fitting black slacks and black loafers.

The sidekick is little. Rosemarie doesn't remember him. He wears a leather Yankees jacket, a gold cross hanging on his chest over a blue muscle shirt. He's young, maybe in his mid-twenties, and he's got a fat lip.

The streetlight out front is on, reflected in the hood of Big Time Tommy's double-parked DeVille.

"Rosemarie," Big Time Tommy says, as a way of greeting. "You remember Dice?"

"What's the what?" Dice says, nodding.

"I didn't know you were coming today," Rosemarie says, holding the door open and stepping onto the porch. She never invites Big Time Tommy inside. It's a small act of defiance and resistance. Who she's really mad at is Giuseppe, for bringing this into her life and letting it outlive him. She guesses he thought his death would clear her name, but no such luck.

"I was on the block," Big Time Tommy says. "You know Slimeball Sally on the corner? He needed a talking to."

"I don't have anything ready for you," Rosemarie says.

Big Time Tommy turns and looks out at the street. Dice watches him. "Haven't I been good to you?" Big Time Tommy asks. "Ain't it nice I come personal, don't send one of my goons? You don't want to know my goons. Dice here, he's nothing. An accoutrement. And didn't I quit with the vig? Didn't I say just the principal would square you and yours? Maybe that was a mistake. Maybe I'm too generous. I see a grieving widow, my heart opens up. But this has been two years, Rosemarie. Two years, and you've barely made a dent."

"I've got bills, Tommy," Rosemarie explains. "The funeral put me in a hole. I've got the mortgage. Oil. Forget it. I work seventy hours a week at Sea Crest. I can't keep up. I need some compassion, that's it."

"And what about your bum son? He's still out of work? This kid could earn. This kid could earn for *me*."

"No."

"It's a way out. Mikey works off your husband's debt, and you get this weight off your shoulders."

"It's very generous," Dice says.

"Very generous indeed," Big Time Tommy says. "He's not a kid anymore. He's a man. Let him do a man's work."

As if on cue, Mikey turns the corner onto the block. She sees him before they do, and panic rises in her. She doesn't want Big Time Tommy to make this offer to Mikey. With Mikey's state of mind, who knows what he'll say.

Sure, that sounds great! And then, boom, her son's gone, a crook, shaking people down and breaking legs (not that he could break legs).

When the front gate opens with a whine and Mikey comes into the yard, carrying a box of books, Big Time Tommy smiles as he sees him and says, "Oh, look who it is! Speak of the devil, and he shows himself. Freak Show Mikey."

"Don't call him that, please," Rosemarie says.

Mikey's attitude toward Big Time Tommy has always been a mix of fear and disgust and reverence. Rosemarie sees all of those things on his face now, as he stops at the bottom of the stoop and looks up at them. "You're not supposed to be here," Mikey says.

"You keep a record of my comings and goings?" Big Time Tommy asks.

"No, it's just—"

"Just my balls."

"Yeah, just his balls," Dice says through a grin.

"I can give you something in a few days," Rosemarie says. "Tomorrow's Mikey's birthday. My brother, Alberto, comes tomorrow, I'll ask him for help. Come back in a few days, okay?"

"Alberto?" Big Time Tommy says, laughing, giving his attention back to Rosemarie. "What's he got for you, some sweaty twenties he forgot to shove up his favorite stripper's cooch?"

"I'll have something," she says. "Just go."

Mikey walks up the stoop onto the porch, edging around Big Time Tommy and Dice, standing next to Rosemarie by the door.

Big Time Tommy takes a couple of steps toward Mikey, throws his arm over his shoulder, and says, "How are you, Mikey? Tomorrow's your big day, huh? Twenty-one. I remember when I turned twenty-one. My uncle took me to a house of ill repute in the city. Gentle Vic Ruggiero was there. He paid my way. Class act, that Vic. That was a night to remember."

"I'm okay," Mikey says, stiff, uncomfortable with Big Time Tommy's meaty arm holding him.

"You a big fucking reader over here?" Big Time Tommy thumbs the box of books, takes notice of the books stacked on top. "*Salem's Lot*—fuck's that about?"

"Vampires."

"Leave him alone," Rosemarie says.

"Your mother's nervous," Big Time Tommy says, "because I was just talking about the possibility of you coming to work for me. A way of erasing your father's debt, I said. Plus, a good experience. Teach you how to be tough, how to survive on the mean streets."

"Me work for you?" Mikey asks.

"What do you think?" Big Time Tommy asks.

"No," Rosemarie says. "Absolutely not. We'll get you your money."

"Let Mr. Mikey here answer for himself."

"I don't know," Mikey says.

"'I don't know,'" Big Time Tommy says, mimicking him. "The coward's refrain. You *should* know. It's an easy yes. It'll grow you some balls."

Mikey doesn't say anything. Rosemarie tugs at the sleeve of his shirt.

Big Time Tommy continues: "I used to tell your old man something. 'Giuseppe,' I'd say, 'you can't live with your tail between your legs.' For a math teacher, for such a smart guy, he never played it safe, and I respected him for that." He lets go of Mikey, dramatically, and then pinches his cheeks with both hands. Mikey tries to escape but can't and takes the pinches like a kid who's just been accosted by a drunk uncle at his Holy Communion.

"This isn't right," Rosemarie says.

"Happy birthday," Big Time Tommy says. "Eat. Drink. Do whatever the fuck it is you do."

"Thanks," Mikey says.

Big Time Tommy turns, and Dice follows. They walk down the stairs together. Over his shoulder, Big Time Tommy says, "You change your mind, you know where to find me. Nine times out of ten, I'm at Twentieth Century on Bath. You know it? Vacant old disco dive."

Rosemarie puts her hand on Mikey's shoulder, and he shrinks at her touch. They go back inside. She's upset by the encounter, but Mikey doesn't seem particularly fazed. He places the box of books on the table.

"Where's that from?" Rosemarie asks.

"Someone was getting rid of them," Mikey says.

"They're what, water damaged?"

"They're fine."

"Don't be a junk collector."

"They're books. They're in good shape."

"We don't need more stuff." She realizes—as she gives him trouble about the books—that she's doing it because she's avoiding what she wants to say about Big Time Tommy. "You wouldn't get involved with Tommy, right?"

"Maybe I should," Mikey says, and she can't tell if he's just kidding. "Maybe it's work I'm cut out for."

"Don't even joke."

"I could help us. I could get us out of this hole Dad got us into."

Rosemarie sits down at the table with a huff, her elbows on her knees. She takes a couple of labored breaths. "Don't do this to me, okay? Just, please, don't. I went through enough with your father. You'll kill me."

"Ma, I'm kidding," Mikey says. "I wouldn't work for that animal. I just wish he wasn't around to bother us anymore. I wish someone would push him in front of a train."

"You shouldn't wish for things like that. God's got His reasons for guys like Tommy."

"He does, huh?"

"He must."

Mikey goes over to the sink and runs the tap, filling a glass with water.

"How's your stomach?" Rosemarie asks.

"It's fine," he says, pausing to take a drink. "I'm sorry I made a mess before."

She waves him off. "It's nothing at all. I'm glad you're feeling better. Where have you been? I was worried."

"I was just out walking."

"That old teacher of yours came around looking for you."

"Old teacher who?"

"Ava's son."

"What? Ava, your boss?"

"Yeah, Nick Bifulco."

"He was looking for me? Why?"

"I don't know. Very strange. Are you going out again tonight?"

"I'm just gonna sit down on the couch and read. You think Uncle Alberto has some money you can borrow to pay off Tommy?"

She shrugs. "We'll see tomorrow."

"He's bringing a new girlfriend?"

"Who knows with him."

Mikey grabs a book from the box and trudges into the living room and turns on the lamp. It's a lamp that's been in her family for fifty years. The shade is tattered and torn. A kind of pastoral scene is painted on the side of the body. Big, open field, children and dogs running through grass, a sunset in the distance. Rosemarie's never seen a field like that. She's never really seen a sunset like that either. The way the light hits the neighborhood, the way it glows over the rooftops, that she knows. But nothing like the lamp.

Mikey crashes onto the couch next to the lamp.

Rosemarie stands in the doorway and looks at him.

"What are you doing the rest of the night?" Mikey asks, eyeing her over the top of his open book. "Watching me read?"

"No, smart guy," she says, drawing back into the kitchen. "I'm gonna take a shower and paint my nails. Maybe listen to the news."

"Exciting," Mikey says.

"Very," she says, sitting in her chair at the table, trying not to think about Big Time Tommy, trying instead to focus on the meal she's making tomorrow. She wonders if she should call Alberto to tell him about Big Time Tommy's visit, to ask for money so she doesn't blindside him over dinner. She thinks she will.

The inside of Donna's apartment had been warm and sad. Mikey liked seeing her records. He likes that she likes music. He pictures her now, sitting in front of her turntable and speakers, dreamily getting lost in whatever she's listening to. He should've asked who her favorites are. She's probably never heard of the bands he likes. He saw a couple of album covers, but he didn't recognize anything.

He's thinking that most guys his age wouldn't find her beautiful. But he does. That feels like some sort of accomplishment. He loves how she said she didn't want to look like a girl, that she liked looking her age. She has this confidence of knowing who she is. She wears her defeat on her face, and it makes her stunning. He likes that she's divorced. He likes her dark hair with some gray mixed in and her pale skin. He likes that she wasn't wearing a lot of makeup. He likes that she has wrinkles, little notches next to her eyes and mouth. And she has a figure that no twenty-year-old could have.

He's still on the couch, feeling lonely. It must be eleven or so. He's read about a hundred pages of *Salem's Lot*. Rosemarie sat out in the kitchen for a while and painted her nails while listening to WINS. She's in bed now, and he wonders if she's sleeping. She never sleeps well. She tosses and turns and worries. With the unexpected visit from Big Time Tommy, it's probably even worse. Mikey could be in his bed, but he prefers the couch because it feels less permanent. When he's on the couch he feels that one day soon he could be sleeping somewhere better, maybe in a motel bed with a woman he loves.

He often dreams of living in motels. He wishes money wasn't required for everything. He thinks if the world was the way it should be, people could just travel around and do what they want and feel content. For him, that would mean having a car and just driving all over the country and seeing new places and eating in roadside diners and staying in the sorts of motels where complicated characters live in movies.

His head is spinning. A crazy fucking day. Asking Ludmilla out at the bank, going to Spanky's and getting a little bit drunk, finding Gabe's note at the library, meeting Donna, coming home to Big Time Tommy. And his mother said that Mr. Bifulco from Our Lady of the Narrows came around asking for him. He'd honestly forgotten that Mr. Bifulco lived in the neighborhood. One of the main things he remembers about him is that he talked about Hunter S. Thompson a bunch the year Mikey was in his journalism class. That wasn't nothing. It set him apart from the other dipshits on the faculty, the no-necks and the hard-core religious types, the fuckwads and the pushovers. But what could he possibly want?

What Mikey's thinking now is he was busting his mother's chops about actually working for Tommy, but maybe it's not the worst idea in the world. What other prospects does he have? He's tried the liquor store on Bay Parkway. The library is never hiring. He can't really do shit. Rosemarie said go into the city and find a temp agency. She's told him, he likes to read so much, maybe he can get a job in publishing. Start at the ground floor, in the mail room, and move on up until he runs the joint.

He puts the book down on the carpet, open to the page he's on. The spine is crinkled. He thinks of Gabe reading it. He thinks of what it must be like to go through with hanging yourself. He doesn't get why anyone would settle on that. Pills, he can understand. Take a bottle of something from the medicine cabinet and wash it down with whiskey. Maybe the fear there is in choking on puke. That would be a rotten way to go.

When he closes his eyes, he imagines Gabe—though he doesn't really know what Gabe looked like—hanging from a sturdy pipe.

He wakes up a few hours later to the sound of his mother clicking off the lamp. She always gets up at four thirty and takes a shower and makes tea and plays solitaire at the kitchen table with the radio on. It's as if she thinks she won't wake him.

That's what she's doing now. He just lies there in the dark, staring at the cracks in the ceiling. Eventually, he gets up and goes into his room and changes his clothes.

His room is an unmade bed with boxes stacked high in the corner and posters on the wall. He never unpacked those boxes after moving back from New Paltz. He's gotten rid of pretty much everything from high school and before, all the dumb baseball shit and wrestling toys and *Star Wars* guys. He's got a crate of clothes, T-shirts and sweatshirts and jeans. He thinks maybe he *will* go get that corduroy jacket of his old man's that his mother mentioned. He wants to see Donna again, and he wants to look nice for her.

The posters on the wall are the same ones he put up in high school. Elle Macpherson's *Sports Illustrated* swimsuit cover. John Carpenter's *They Live*, with Rowdy Roddy Piper's eye up close, one of those skeleton alien motherfuckers reflected in the sunglasses pushed low on his nose. The Jesus and Mary Chain's *Darklands*. The edges of the posters are all curled, and all three are off-center. His mom's tried to straighten them a few times, but she made them worse.

The room has a low ceiling, which makes it feel small. An old radiator that he's always found beautiful squats in front of the window. The view from the window is of the neighbor's backyard, overgrown with weeds, weights lined up on a patch of concrete. Mikey sometimes watches this neighbor, whose name he doesn't know, come out in the early mornings and pump weights among the weeds. It's too early for him yet.

Mikey sits on his bed and looks around. A room like this, one he's spent so much of his life in, holds stories, secrets, things not even his mom could know. Where he hid his first stash of weed. How he and his first girlfriend, Gia, had skipped out of school early and beat Rosemarie home and made out on his bed for an hour until Gia left out the window, using the ancient rusted fire ladder on the side of the house to get down from the roof. Where he hid cigarettes and airplane bottles of scotch. Bringing Sarah Williams from Fort Hamilton High over while Rosemarie was at work and eating her out on the edge of the bed while he kneeled on the floor. He remembers a crinkled gas station receipt that fell out of her pocket as she pushed her pants down.

One time, not long after Donnie Parascandolo clocked him with the bat and his old man had offed himself, Mikey sat here and actually did think about killing himself, too. It was only for a minute. And he didn't think about the how. Pipe or pills or knife or bridge—none of it crossed his mind. What he really thought about was what it would be like to be dead, if he would see things after he was dead, feel contentment or regret. He remembers wondering about his father, if being dead just meant being nothing forever, or if maybe it meant being a ghost on the streets.

He should take a shower, but he doesn't. He just changes his clothes, putting on clean underwear and jeans that his mother washed in the basement and dried on the line in the yard. He finds a yellow button-up shirt. The last and only time he wore it was his high school graduation.

When he goes back down to the kitchen, all the lights are on. His mother is working on the chicken parm, making the batter, getting the oil going.

"Happy birthday," she says, coming over, her hands coated in eggs and bread crumbs, pecking him on the cheek. "You look so nice."

"Thanks," he says. "I'm gonna get Dad's jacket. The one you mentioned."

"You're dressing up for your birthday?"

He shrugs. He doesn't tell her that it's not for his birthday, that it's because he's going to go back to Donna's to ring her doorbell. He thinks he should bring her something. That's what a man would do. Flowers. But maybe flowers are too much too soon. What else could he bring that would be a kind gesture? A record? Maybe he could find one in the basement. His father had some jazz records under his worktable, and his mother had stored away Uncle Alberto's records. He wasn't sure what there even was. He remembered going through them as a kid, sometimes cutting up the covers to make collages in marble notebooks.

"Are you going somewhere else?" his mother asks, suddenly suspicious.

"No," he says.

"Is there a girl?"

"There's no girl."

"When'd you meet her? Just yesterday? You're different today. That shirt."

"Oh, stop."

"Is she Italian?"

"Stop. Please."

He opens the door to the basement and turns on the light. He goes down the rickety steps, which could fall apart at any second, holding on to the railing. The oil tank looms like some great lost machine. His father's worktable is full of tools. The washing machine is running—his mother must've put an early load in. At the far end of the room, there's a closet. He finds his father's brown corduroy jacket and slips it on. It fits better than he thought it would. It smells like his father. Cheap aftershave and cheap beer. He digs around in the pockets and finds a couple of loose breath mints, toothpicks wrapped in cellophane, and a scrap of paper with bets he was making or had made.

At the bottom of that same closet are the records. Uncle Alberto's are in a cardboard wine box, while the ones that had belonged to his father are in a sturdy blue carrying case. He'd thought his father's records were under the worktable in the back of the basement, where his father would repair radios and Mikey would come down just to smell the soldering iron, but his mother must've moved them here. He opens the case first and is surprised by the good condition of the records. He recognizes some of the names. His old man was always talking about Monk and Miles and Coltrane.

The other box is full of Uncle Alberto's childhood records, stuff Mikey's more familiar with. Uncle Alberto is about Donna's age. He doesn't really like music anymore as far as Mikey knows, but he grew up loving the Beatles and the Rolling Stones and Cat Stevens. The records in this box are in worse shape.

He's not sure what to pick. Maybe it's stupid to show up with a record. Probably Donna already has everything that she wants. He hates the idea of pretending to know a record and just saying, "Here. I think you might like this."

A Neil Young record seems like a safe bet. He takes one called *Comes a Time* and carries it up to the kitchen. He notices now that his mother has stacked Gabe's books in the corner on the floor.

"What are you doing with that record?" his mother asks, her hands glistening with oil, blowing a hair out of her face.

"I'm going to listen to it," he says.

"You don't have a record player."

"I'm gonna find one at the Salvation Army."

"I had two. One was your father's, one was Uncle Alberto's. I put them out in the trash. But I kept the records. I don't know why. Why do we do anything we do?" She pauses. "The jacket looks good."

"It's not as big as I thought."

"My handsome son. There *is* a girl. You can tell me. What's her name? You like her? Is it Marilu on the corner? I've been trying to get you to ask her out. She's a sweetheart. She's got a good job at Main Pharmacy."

"There's no girl," he says. But he's thinking, *There's a woman.*

He leaves the house with the record under his arm. He's not even sure what time it is now, but it's light and he's been up for a while. Where he lives with his mother, on Bay Forty-Seventh between Bath and Harway, is about fifteen blocks from Donna's apartment, maybe farther. He wonders if there's any harm in walking past, just walking past. He imagines a scene from some shitty romantic comedy: He bumps into her just as she's coming out her front gate and she invites him in.

She did say to come by. She probably didn't mean in the morning. She's off. He bets she's sleeping in. He thinks of her in bed. He wonders if she's thinking of him. Probably not. She's got real problems to think about. Work, bills, the apartment. Or maybe she's just drinking coffee and listening to her records.

Speaking of which. He heads to Eighty-Sixth Street and stops for coffee at the first deli he sees, the Corner Joint. He's still got money left over from the teller. He also gets a buttered roll. The guy working the counter is in his fifties, wearing a Mets caps and reading the *Daily News.* "You have a good one now," the guy says to Mikey, pushing across the buttered roll wrapped in cellophane.

Mikey thanks him and goes outside. He sits on the curb, the record in his lap, and eats his roll while letting the coffee cool.

He remembers what his birthday used to mean to him as a kid. The feeling of being special. His mother hanging streamers from the wall, a "Happy Birthday" banner over the TV in the living room, taping balloons to the ceiling fan. Opening presents. His mother making chocolate cake. His father trying some stupid magic trick.

He throws out the cellophane his roll was wrapped in and walks toward Donna's place, sipping coffee.

When he gets there, he stands across the street and stares at the barred window of her ground-floor apartment, shades pulled, light glinting off the dirty glass. Another miracle would be her opening the shade, not surprised at all to see him.

Having spent time inside, he now considers the outside of the house. It's a two-family job. Yellow siding that's in rough shape. A roof that's missing shingles. Sagging gutters. A front yard overgrown with weeds and neighborhood debris, a hose half-covered in dirt and not attached to the water valve snaking along the perimeter by the rusted iron fence. The black mailbox hangs from a single nail, the names *Bonsignore* and *Rotante* written in bleeding Sharpie on a piece of laminated paper taped to the front. It's a big house, but like so many big houses in the neighborhood, it's neglected and feels small, and Donna's apartment is the smallest part of it.

He wishes he was the kind of guy who could volunteer to help fix something, anything. He doesn't know his way around a paintbrush or a hammer or any tool of improvement. As his father used to say, he's pretty goddamn useless. There's no point hiding it, pretending to be something he's not.

He gets nervous standing there, like it's wrong or perverted to be watching her window, so he does a lap around the block. He studies other yards, other mailboxes, considers garbage piled at the curb, passes an old woman pushing a shopping cart.

When he comes back, there's a slight change. Donna's front door is ajar.

He looks down at the sidewalk and thinks about going over to knock. Before his next thought, she's outside with a bucket of water, emptying it over the side of the stoop onto the driveway. She's wearing blue sweatpants, heavy-looking slipper-socks, and a purple sweater that hangs off her shoulder. Her hair is up. She looks over and sees him. His shitty romantic comedy is coming to life.

He waves, drops what's left of his coffee, so it splatters his boots. He picks up the Styrofoam cup and sets it on the hood of a parked car.

She waves back, smiling.

They meet in the street. He notices that she has a wrench in her pocket. "What are you doing here?" she asks.

"I don't know," he says. "I was just out walking. I got some coffee. I found this record in my basement. I thought you might like it."

"That's sweet." She holds up the bucket as a way of explanation. "I have a leak under my sink. I'm not very handy, but I'm giving it my best. Getting Suzette to call a plumber is like pulling teeth."

A car turns onto the block, beeping for them to get out of the street. They go back on the sidewalk, close to her fence.

"Happy birthday," Donna says.

"You remembered," Mikey says.

"Do you want to come in? I can make you another coffee."

"Definitely," he says.

She looks surprised but not put out. He follows her inside. She sets down the bucket inside the door. "As you can tell from what I'm wearing, I wasn't expecting company. I'm sorry."

"I can go. You said come by. I thought early might be okay."

"Oh, it's fine. I'm not doing anything. I'm just a mess."

"You look great," he says.

"That's nice of you. You *actually* look great. You're all dressed up. Are you doing something with your family?"

"Just my mom and uncle." He holds up the Neil Young record. "Have you heard this?"

"I love Neil Young."

"You already have it?"

"I have a ragged old copy. This is in better shape." She takes it from him and puts it on the turntable, blowing some dust from the record and then dropping the needle on the first track. She takes the wrench out of her pocket and leaves it on top of the right speaker. She props the record sleeve against the other speaker.

"I remembered there were all these records in my mom's basement," Mikey says. "Some were my dad's, some were my uncle's. They're just sitting there. I saw them, and they made me think of you."

"That's really sweet." She points to the couch. "Sit. I'll make coffee."

He sits on the couch and pulls a red pillow into his lap. It's a nervous thing he does. On the school bus, he'd always sit with his backpack in his lap. At Ginny's house, he'd do it and always worry that people would think he was trying to hide a hard-on.

He listens to the record, which he's never heard before. He's heard some Neil Young but not this particular one.

He watches Donna through the doorway as she fiddles with the knob on the stove, turning the gas up under the percolator. He's trying to get a sense of whether there's any interest on her part. Interest, that is, in the way he's interested in her. She's not checking herself in the mirror. She's not putting on makeup. She's not doing the things he's seen girls do when they're getting ready for a date. She's not self-conscious. But maybe that comes with age.

She returns with two mugs of steaming coffee and hands him one. "I'd already made some," she says. "Just had to heat it up."

"Thanks."

"I love the record. This sounds less scratchy than my copy. Thank *you*."

"You're welcome." He takes a sip of coffee, burning his upper lip and the roof of his mouth.

She must notice that he's winced. "Be careful. It's really hot."

He nods.

"Tell me more about your mom," Donna says, out of nowhere.

He wasn't expecting this. He doesn't want to talk about his mom. "There's nothing to tell, really."

"There must be something."

"I don't know. She's fine. She works at Sea Crest in Coney Island. She's a mom. She does mom things."

Donna laughs. "I'm a mom. I *was* a mom. What are 'mom things'?"

"I don't know." He pauses, trying to weigh his words carefully. "Cooking, cleaning, worrying, being on my back."

"I figured that's what you meant. That's not how all moms are. You know that, right?"

"I don't know."

"I bet your mom has all sorts of dreams."

"I guess," he says. And then without thinking, or even meaning to: "You're really pretty."

She laughs awkwardly, spilling a little coffee in her lap. "What?"

"I said you're really pretty."

"You're messing with me, right? I'm almost twice your age. *I* could be your mother."

"You would've had to have me pretty young."

Donna shakes her head. "No way," she says. "No way you're hitting on me."

"Things happen for a reason, like we were talking about yesterday," he says. "I found Gabe's books and then I called you and we met and we had all this stuff in common."

Donna stands up. The first side of the record ends, and the needle skips in the final groove, making a dusty noise. She goes over and pushes the tonearm back in its cradle. She sets down her coffee. She doesn't look at him.

"You should probably go," she says.

"I'm sorry," he says. He stands up, cradling the coffee against his stomach. "I didn't mean to make things weird. I really didn't. I'll go."

"Thank you for the record."

He puts down his coffee on an end table next to the couch on top of a pile of *Redbook* magazines and stands, his arms dangling awkwardly. "I'm sorry again," he says.

She turns to him. "It's okay," she says.

"Do you really want me to go?"

"I don't know. Maybe."

Ava wakes up with a start. A bad dream. Something about Anthony choking to death at the kitchen table while she sat across from him, unable to move. She can still feel it in her bones. He's dead already, and she's paranoid about him dying again. She looks at the clock on the bedside stand, illuminated by her dusty little Virgin Mary nightlight. It's four in the morning. The stillness of the house fills her with a new dread. She likes to be up no later than five so she can shower and have coffee in her robe and sit at the kitchen table with the radio on for a while before she leaves for work. But she knows she'll never get back to sleep now. She's wearing the thin summer nightgown she put on after changing out of her robe.

She still can't quite wrap her head around what Nick told her. Don's the ex-cop from the papers. And he apparently knocked Rosemarie's son in the head with a baseball bat over Antonina Divino. Rosemarie must not know about it, because Ava never heard that story from her.

Nick snuck out of the house for a while after they were done talking, and she's not sure where he went. Not Alice's. She puts on her slippers and goes out to the living room and sees that he's passed out on the couch, snoring, still in his work clothes, his hand shoved down his pants. She's got to talk to him about his drinking. Maybe she should ask Father Borzumato to talk to him. Not that Nick will listen. She hopes he gives up this idea of writing a script about Don. She can't see it leading to anything but trouble. Trouble for them or trouble for Don. She puts on coffee in the kitchen. When she's upset or sad or overwhelmed or when she feels like she's losing it and has no sense of what God's plan could possibly be, she sometimes picks up the phone and talks to the dial tone as if she's talking to Anthony. She does that now as she waits for the coffee to perk. "Anthony, I'm lonely and I'm tired and I'm sick of work. I miss you so much. I miss the way you touched me and talked to me. I miss your hair and your hands. I miss your dirty laundry. I miss the smell of your work clothes. I miss watching you eat and your smile. I miss being in church with you." She hangs up the phone and watches the coffee.

A rustling in the living room. The snoring becoming a cough. Nick's up. He comes out to the kitchen, clacking his dry tongue against the roof of his mouth. "Can I have some of that?"

"Sure," Ava says. "Where'd you disappear to last night?"

Nick rubs sleep from his eyes and yawns. "It's all coming together."

"You're still going on about this script?"

"I'm gonna talk to Paulie and Nina's son. Local Hero Phil. I know he'll help me out." Nick sits down at the table, yawns more dramatically, throwing his arms up over his head and smelling his armpits. "What are you doing up?"

Ava shrugs. She tends to the coffee, pours two cups, and brings them over to the table, sitting in the chair next to Nick. He thanks her.

"You're gonna shower and change before you go to school, right?" Ava says.

"I'm not going to school. I'm taking off. Call in for me, won't you? Tell Martha the secretary I'm sick."

"I won't do that."

"I need the car today. I'll drop you off."

"The car's in the shop."

"Damn, I forgot. I'll take the train with you to Coney."

"What are you doing in Coney Island?"

"Research."

"I'm sorry about our fight."

Nick sips some coffee and then stands back up. He walks over and reaches out and takes Ava's free hand. Her other hand's wrapped around the coffee cup.

"What on earth are you doing?" Ava says.

"Let's dance," Nick says.

"You're still bombed."

He tugs on her hand until she gets up. He pulls her into a tight embrace, puts his right hand on her back and his left hand in her right hand, and they rock back and forth slowly. He smells stale, his breath a blast of something rotten, the booze seeping through his pores. He puts his head on her shoulder, his eyes closed. "This is a celebration," he says.

"Okay, enough," Ava says.

"You remember when I was a kid and I'd stand on your feet and we'd dance?"

"Of course."

"Can I try that now?" He steps on her feet, stomping her toes, trying to keep the dance going.

"You're being stupid," she says, disengaging, kicking her feet out from under his, curling her stinging toes inside her slippers. She sits down and goes back to her coffee. "I wish I'd never broken down on the Belt, that's what I wish."

"Do you?" Nick says. "Don's sweet on you."

"Just shut up, Nick. Just please shut up. It's too early for this."

Donnie's pissed himself. Happens every now and again. He wakes up with the front of his jeans and the bed around him all wet. After popping that dumbass Dice at the Wrong Number, he did two more shots and drank a few more beers and watched as Dice and his buddies eyed him but never made a move, eventually disappearing into the night like the scared little shits they are. When Donnie got home, he played Super Nintendo for a while and then he just passed out in bed.

He doesn't usually remember his dreams, but now he remembers one he had about his parents. They were in a hospital. They were the only ones in the hospital. He was young in the dream, first or second grade, but his parents were old, both wobbly with dementia. His mother opened her mouth to talk to him and her teeth were all little buttons and then her eyes became bigger buttons. Not channel-changer buttons. Like buttons on a shirt. His father had the same button eyes and button teeth. All the walls around them became see-through, and he saw dripping pipes, mice, crawling things, shadows. No wonder he pissed himself.

He goes into the bathroom and takes off his pants and boxers and hangs them on the shower rod. Even the bottom of his shirt is wet. He takes that off too and avoids looking at himself in the mirror over the sink. He brushes his teeth with his finger. The foamy toothpaste comes away pink with blood.

He spits in the sink and then leans over and sucks up some water from the tap, rinsing forcefully until he feels some relief in his sore gums.

He heads out to the kitchen in only his socks and looks in the refrigerator. A bottle of orange juice with no cap on the top shelf. He downs it, spilling some on the floor, and tosses the bottle in the trash.

He searches for his cigarettes in the living room. Figuring they must be in the cushions of the couch, he feels around and comes out with a business card for a phone sex line and a crusty battery and a stale hunk of bagel. He pushes his hand down deeper, and sure enough, there's the case, lodged snugly against a flat part of the base. One cigarette left. How many did he give to Ava? His yellow Bic's on the table. He lights the cigarette and thinks about turning on the TV. Instead, he just sits, smoking, staring up at the ceiling.

Ava's floating there, smiling at him. He thinks about doing nice things for her. He knows she's got work today. He could brew some coffee and walk over to Flash Auto and check in about her car. He can just imagine Frankie nudging him and saying, "You fucking Ava Bifulco?"

And he'd say, "I'm trying, man."

Donnie doesn't have much money, but he's got some of what his parents left him. A little over five grand, last he checked his Williamsburgh Savings bank book. He didn't give a fuck about his pension. He didn't want anything from the force after they strung him up for the Dunbar thing. Whatever money he makes on his jobs with Pags and Sottile is cash, and he keeps it in the house. He's probably got about three grand under a floorboard in his bedroom. Donna doesn't ride him for alimony. He's thinking about his money now because he's thinking he should buy Ava something. Not a big something. Just a way of letting her know he's thankful he met her. Maybe a used car from Flash. They've got an '84 Oldsmobile Cutlass Ciera for two grand. It's gray and long, and he can just picture her behind the wheel. Maybe that's too much too soon.

What Donnie's not so thankful for is meeting Nick. That's the trade-off. The world gives you an Ava but it also gives you a Nick at the same time.

He doesn't know what the kid has up his sleeve. Coming around drunk like he did, that glint in his eye. What's the end game in that? It'd be a shame to have to beat the fuck out of him while trying to romance his old lady.

When his cigarette's done, he goes back into the kitchen to look for something to eat. Something plain. There's a half-open container of white rice in the fridge. He takes that out and sits down at the table and eats it with the plastic fork that he left in the rice. It's hard, gnarly with age, tastes like the refrigerator smells.

The kitchen's in the rear of the house. He pushes back the curtain and looks outside. He can see the backs of the houses on the Bay Thirty-Fourth Street side. Fire escapes, rotted siding, shingles dangling from roofs. Movement behind windows. One of the houses is the Divinos. Sometimes, sitting here, he looks out and sees Antonina Divino out on her fire escape, smoking. She's always changing now. With the different hair color, the boots, all the bullshit. Her window's kind of hard to see into from here but if he tilts his head in exactly the right way, he can see her getting ready for school in the mornings. When there is school, that is. It's summer. He wonders what she does with her days. He watches her window now and hopes she emerges. He thinks about her from that night with Mikey Baldini. In her bra. Her arms crossed over her chest. Such a little body.

When she pops out through that small attic window onto her fire escape with her own cigarette, he's only half-surprised. She's wearing a purple T-shirt and purple underwear, holding a Walkman and wearing headphones with orange foam ear cushions. Her hair's the pinkest pink he's ever seen. Like something from a costume party. There's a lot of color up there on that fire escape. She's all bunched up, sitting on her ass, leaning forward, her left arm wrapped around her legs, hugging them close to her, her right arm propped up on her knee as she brings the cigarette to her lips. He doesn't feel bad for scaring her that night with Mikey. What she learned, that was a good lesson. He bets she's been more cautious since. He holds out hope that, in a few years, she'll thank him for looking out for her.

The phone rings. Now he's expecting Suzy again, ready to chew him out, but it's Pags this time. "It's lined up," Pags says.

"Where and when?" Donnie says to Pags.

"We're meeting Tommy and Dice at Flash Auto," Pags says.

"Okay."

"We'll be there in an hour."

"I guess I'll get dressed," Donnie says, and he hangs up.

He goes upstairs to his room and hunts around in the top dresser drawer for clean boxers. He smells a pair. Good enough.

On the floor next to the dresser is a tattered brown throw rug. Under that rug is a loose floorboard. He kneels now, pushes away the rug, and removes the slightly warped length of wood. The cash is there in the hole, wrapped in plastic. He takes more than half of his stash, probably in the neighborhood of two grand, and sets it aside to bring with him. He's thinking it's a sign that they're meeting Big Time Tommy at Flash Auto. He's going to buy the Olds for Ava. To hell with *too much too soon*. He replaces the length of wood and smooths the rug back over it.

He puts on the boxers, finds some other jeans crumpled on the floor of his closet, and gets out a softball T-shirt from when he used to play. It says OLD GLORY in white script on the front of the red shirt. They were good, his team. This wasn't fatsos drinking beer and goofing off. This was fast-pitch, competitive as hell. A lot of the guys, they played college ball or even made it to the minors. He's got a few championship jackets in the cellar. Shortstop was his position. He could hit some homers when he needed to. His bat—the one he used on Mikey and still keeps behind the dresser in the empty room downstairs—was much desired by his teammates for its good juju.

Back in the hallway, the money in his pocket now, he stops outside the door to Gabe's room. He remembers standing here, hearing music from behind the door, whatever that heavy shit was Gabe liked, and knocking like a stranger. Next would be the clatter of Gabe pressing stop or pause on his boombox, followed by a mopey "Who's there?" Donnie would say, in a voice he could never duplicate again, "It's Dad. How you doing, bud?" Gabe's answer would always be one word: *good*, *fine*, or *okay*. This was Gabe pretty much the last few years of his life, ages eleven to fifteen. Before that, he was a kid and he had his joy, wasn't sad all the time. Donnie barely remembers that Gabe now.

Something tells him to go into Gabe's room. He hasn't been in a while, hasn't wanted to, but now the desire's there. Maybe Ava's unlocked something in him.

He opens the door. First thing he notices is it's cold in the room. A kind of bottled-up cold, like maybe he shut the radiator in here and forgot and this is like walking into winter. Or maybe it's cold because Gabe's ghost is around. Donnie believes in ghosts. He saw the ghost of his old man once in his childhood house, just shaving in the bathroom mirror, looking disappointed. Donnie doesn't feel Gabe now, and he always figured if he haunts anywhere regularly in the house it's the cellar, which is why he steers clear of down there.

The mattress is bare. Donna had stripped the sheets off the morning of the day Gabe did what he did, and it stayed that way. A desk in the corner has an alarm clock that's not plugged in, a few spiral notebooks from school, and a Golden Nugget coffee mug full of pennies, nickels, and dimes. Gabe's clothes hang in his open closet: Dockers, dress shirts, the suit he wore to Donna's father's funeral.

On the wall over the bed, a wall calendar is tacked crookedly. The tacks holding it in place are red and yellow. The calendar is open to April 1990, the month that Gabe killed himself. None of the days are marked in any way. There are no notes, no reminders.

The dresser is positioned strangely in the corner—that was Donna's doing. He slides open the rickety top drawer, and there's a mound of clean white socks inside. He closes the drawer.

What Donnie's struck by now is how ordinary the room is. There aren't any clues. It's just Gabe's room. It was Gabe's room for fifteen years, and now it's empty.

Donnie takes one last look around and then leaves, closing the door behind him. He goes downstairs and puts on his steel-toe construction boots. He's never done construction, but they're good for kicking in heads when he needs to.

"It's nice riding to work with you like this," Nick says to Ava, who's wearing a lot of her perfume this morning. "I'll walk you to Sea Crest."

"I hope you don't get fired from school," Ava says.

"I won't. It's summer. The kids who are there are all morons anyway. They sit there all day, picking their noses."

"You're terrible."

"It's true."

"I hope the car's okay, too."

"It'll be fine. Sal and Frankie will work their magic."

"Their magic? That's a laugh."

"You smell good."

"Shut up."

They're on the B train, sitting in the conductor's car. Nick's feeling good, barely hungover, maybe still drunk. The orange seats and the windows are covered in tags. It's only a couple of stops to Coney Island and then about a ten- or fifteen-minute walk to where Ava works. Nick will drop her off there, doting son that he is, and then he'll try to go see Captain Fred Dunbar, who lives in a walk-up on Mermaid Avenue with his girlfriend. That wasn't difficult information to obtain. Dunbar was right there in the White Pages.

He feels like the script's written and optioned already, championed by the great Phil Puzzo himself.

"I just hope you don't throw your life away," Ava says.

"You're being dramatic," Nick says.

"What about Alice?"

"What about her?"

"Have you talked to her since you had your big idea?"

"I'll talk to her later. After I do a few things. She'll be excited."

"You two should get married."

"We will. With all the Hollywood money."

Ava shakes her head. "You're being ridiculous."

They get off at the Stillwell Avenue station, the last stop, coming out on Surf Avenue. They go to a newsstand so Ava can get a pack of Viceroys. Nick hasn't been to Coney Island in a while, certainly not to visit Ava at work. Last time, he guesses, was two summers ago with Alice. An August day. They went swimming. Alice loves swimming. Nick doesn't. She looked amazing in her electric blue one-piece. The shitheads all had their eyes on her. Nick got jealous. He drank a lot of beer. He started a fight with some juiced-up guinea who could barely string a sentence together. He wound up with a black eye. He and Alice ate hot dogs at Nathan's afterward. She said she found it romantic that he was jealous.

He could use a hot dog from Nathan's right now. He wonders what time they open. Probably early. He bets nine. It's a little after eight. Ava's got to be at work by eight thirty. On the way back, after dropping Ava, after paying a visit to Dunbar, he'll grab a hot dog. He'll also call Alice. Thinking about her in that bathing suit eating a hot dog slathered in sauerkraut has his mind wandering to dirty places. He thinks of the phone sex they almost had. He'd like to tell her his big news, pour her some wine, ask her to put on that electric blue bathing suit, kiss her legs and her arms and her shoulders and her neck, kiss her through her bathing suit.

"I could use a hot dog," Ava says.

"I was thinking the same thing," Nick says. "Hot dogs for breakfast is the American dream. When I make it big, we'll have hot dogs for breakfast every day. Delivered to our door."

Ava laughs. She's loosening up a little.

They pass Nathan's and the freak show and go up on the boardwalk, cutting a right in front of Candy's Room, where Nick drank Schaefer beers with Alice that same summer day. It's a nice morning. Warm and not achingly hot. The beach is quiet. A few runners out on the sand. A few more on the boardwalk. Old men sitting on benches, taking the sun, talking. It's too early for the hustlers, for the punk-ass kids who'll try to grab wallets and hoot at any girl they see, for the carnival barkers, for the crude weirdos, for the boys with boomboxes, for the loud-talking girls with tattoos in skimpy bikinis.

Ava takes Nick's arm, and they walk the way parents and their adult children at weddings walk. Slowly, deliberately, as if something might be undone forever if they step wrong. Ava's wearing black slacks and a silk gold-braided blouse. She's got on those big dangly hoop earrings she likes to wear, lots of rouge on her cheeks, brick-red lipstick. Nick hasn't changed his clothes from yesterday. He brushed his teeth and sprayed some deodorant under his arms and on his pants. He looks out at the water now.

"I forget about this sometimes," Ava says.

"What do you mean?" Nick says.

"I mean Coney Island. The beach. The boardwalk. The Wonder Wheel. The Cyclone. Nathan's. The Parachute Jump. Everything. The way I dreamed about it as a girl even though it was so close. I go to the home five days a week. It's all right here, but I just pull into my space in the parking lot and I go into my office and I do my rounds and talk to who I need to talk to and I forget to look out the window at all of this. I take smoke breaks in the parking lot next to a dumpster. I should go out on the boardwalk."

"Start today," Nick says.

Ava lets go of Nick's arm and takes the new pack of Viceroys out of her purse as they pass the Parachute Jump. She peels away the cellophane, places a cigarette between her lips. She lights it from a book of matches she scored at the newsstand, puffs away Ava-style.

"I used to have such big dreams about Coney Island as a girl," she says. "So close and yet so far. Ten minutes by the subway. Bus is pretty quick, too. Five minutes by car. We hardly ever came as a family. Not to go to the beach, definitely not for the rides, not even for the Fourth of July most years."

"You and Daddy never took me growing up either."

"That's different. It was really starting to be a mess when you were a kid. It changed. It wasn't the same place it was when I was a girl. We came when we were newlyweds. We rode on the Wonder Wheel. Everything changes. Now I work here every day, and I just forget it's the place I dreamed so much about. That's sad, isn't it?"

"Pep up. I'll take you on the Cyclone any day you want to go."

Another smile from Ava. A guy on roller skates zooms by. He's wearing pink shorts and headphones and is heavily oiled up. They pass the Childs Building, the last of the beautiful old '20s structures still standing. Stucco, terra-cotta, nautical-themed medallions, marble columns. Graffiti all over the doors and walls. Nick homes in on thick green spray-painted letters that read SAVAGE-N-PEACHES.

Ava stops out front and drags deep on her cigarette. "You should've seen this place back then."

"I've read about it some," Nick says.

"There was a roof garden. I remember being up there and seeing a steamboat docked at the Steeplechase pier. So many people out on the beach. Once I saw this guy, missing both of his arms, and he was dancing right out front here. I'll never forget that guy, I don't know why."

"No arms will do it."

"What are you doing in Coney Island?" Ava says, finally asking the question he imagines has been on her mind all morning. "You take off, you've got this big script idea—why are you here? You said research. What research?"

Nick doesn't want to get into it with Ava again. He knows it's not the best idea to bring up Captain Dunbar.

But she intuits it. Ava's so goddamn sharp. "You're going to see the cop that Don punched, right?" she says. She drops her cigarette, and it falls into a slat between the boards under their feet. "I was looking at the *Daily News* you left out. I know how your mind works."

"Yep, I'm going there."

"You're just stirring up trouble. Phil Puzzo, what he does, he loves those mobsters he writes about. It's a very different thing. And he writes books. You don't even know what you're doing. What do you know from a movie script?"

"It's easy. It's all formatting. The dialogue's what's important."

"And you're just going to use Don as a model?"

"Exactly. He should be flattered, really. He's my Jake LaMotta, you know?"

"You're nuts."

They start walking again, not far from Sea Crest now. Ava clams up. Nick's not sure what else to say either. She turns to him, kisses him on the cheek, and then heads down the ramp from the boardwalk to West Twenty-Fourth. He watches until she turns into the parking lot and then keeps on walking.

Dunbar lives on Mermaid Avenue between West Thirty-Fifth and West Thirty-Sixth. It's strange to think that he's so close to Ava's work.

Nick stays on the boardwalk for a few more blocks and then heads down his own ramp, walking first up West Twenty-Eighth and then turning onto Surf. A man comes out of the corner store, pumping at a scratch-off with a nickel, cursing under his breath. Nick continues along Surf and then makes a right at West Thirty-Fifth. He's never been this far toward the western end of Coney Island. There's no reason not to be where everything is. This is all low-income housing, senior centers, bodegas, little two-family places with concrete front yards.

As he turns onto Mermaid, keeping his eyes open for Dunbar's address, he's thinking how stupid he is. In his excitement, he wasn't even thinking about Dunbar probably not being home. Oh well. He's come this far.

The place where Dunbar lives is a boxy house with gray siding. A silver Mercury Grand Marquis is parked in the front yard behind a chain link fence, eating up the whole space. There's some scattered debris from Fourth of July fireworks on the ground next to the car.

Nick opens the gate and climbs the steps to the upstairs apartment. He rings the bell.

From behind the door, a man's voice: "Who is it?"

"Sir, my name is Nick Bifulco. I just wanted to talk to you for a sec."

The door opens. Dunbar is standing there in his undershirt and basketball shorts, barefoot, a steaming cup of coffee in his hands. He's maybe in his late forties, hard-looking, fit, his eyes heavy and tired. "You know what time I got off work last night?" he asks.

"I'm sorry."

"You got some balls knocking on my door this early, whoever you are."

"I just wanted to ask you a few questions."

"What're you selling? Just get it out of the way. You a Mormon or whatever? You gonna hit me with that *let's talk scripture* shit?"

"I just wanted to ask you about Donnie Parascandolo."

"Jesus Christ. What is this?"

"I'm a screenwriter—"

Dunbar's raucous laugh cuts Nick off, his coffee sloshing up over the edges of his cup.

Nick withers a little.

"I'm sorry," Dunbar says. "Go ahead."

Nick, looking down at his shoes now, says, "Donnie's from my neighborhood. I'm writing a script where I'm kind of using him for the main guy."

A woman comes up behind Dunbar. She's probably a little younger. She's wearing an oversize Miami Dolphins jersey and nothing else that Nick can see. She's got dreadlocks.

"Who's this?" she asks. Her accent's Jamaican.

Dunbar, more awake now, laughs again. "He says he writes movies. He's writing a movie about Donnie Parascandolo."

"That's the guy who punched you?" she asks.

"Damn straight. He's a good subject, I guess."

"You want to know why I think he's a good subject?" Nick says.

"Not particularly," Dunbar says, dabbing at some coffee that's spilled on his shorts. "There was a pattern of behavior there," he continues. "It wasn't just him getting drunk and punching me. A lot led up to that. We gave him a shot to get help. He wanted no part of it. That's why he got the boot."

"I'm sure."

"What do you want to ask me?"

Nick draws a blank. What *does* he want to ask? He should've prepared something. He guesses he should ask for details, what Dunbar can remember about what happened, about anything that led up to it. "What do you remember?" he says.

"He had some grudge against me, I don't know why. He cold-cocked me at the bar. That's it. He'd been off the rails, like I said. Listen, I get it. I wouldn't ever say he was a stand-up guy based on what I knew of him, but when his kid killed himself, that was the end. We've all got ghosts. Typical self-destructive bullshit. But I get it. What I'm laughing at isn't him. I'm laughing at you. You come to my house, you say you write movies. Look at yourself. You want to know what Donnie *looked* like the night he clocked me? Not so different from how you look now."

Dunbar closes the door in Nick's face.

Nick stands there for a minute. He can hear the woman talking behind the door. When he finally leaves, he doesn't feel so much dissuaded as energized. Dunbar's a character too, a tough motherfucker.

Donna is taller than Mikey by a couple of inches. Standing this close to him, she's noticed for the first time that she's looking down on him.

"I'm not short," he says, as if reading her mind. "You're just tall."

She's about to speak but hesitates and then finds what she wants to say: "Mikey, this is nuts. You feel a bit of a connection with an older woman, you figure *what the hell*. Maybe you think I'm desperate. I'm not desperate."

"I don't think you're desperate."

"Maybe you think I'm cheap?"

Mikey swallows hard. "I think you're pretty and kind, that's it. You want me to go?"

"Let me flip this," she says, going over to the turntable and flipping the Neil Young record on the platter, dropping the needle gently onto "Human Highway." It was nice of Mikey to bring her this record, a gesture she appreciates.

"I'll go," he says.

"It's okay. You can stay longer."

He goes back to the couch. She sits on the floor cross-legged, her usual listening position, picking up the little Casio keyboard that was Gabe's and fiddling with the keys. Its batteries are dead. She doesn't look up at Mikey.

"I like this song," Mikey says.

"Me too," she says.

"Do you want to come to my house for my birthday dinner later? It's not really dinner. We'll probably eat at two. Like a Sunday."

She laughs a little. "What?"

"It's stupid. Forget I said it."

"It's not stupid. It's just, what would your mother think?"

"Who cares?"

"She'd think I was your date. She'd think I was some Pamela Smart type. I'm twice your age."

"There's something between us, I can feel it." He gets down on the floor and moves next to her. There's space between them—he doesn't make a move to touch her.

"You're impulsive, that's it."

"Tell me you don't feel anything."

"You're a stranger."

Mikey scooches closer. "It okay if I kiss you?" he asks.

She reaches out and touches his sagging earlobes, the slightly visible tattoo under his beard. Twenty-one. She knows how college is. He's so handsome. He's probably slept with a hundred girls.

In some way, she feels inadequate. She stayed home for college. She didn't live in dorms, didn't go to parties. She only slept with one guy before Donnie, and Donnie sure as shit didn't know about it. The guy's name was Gianluca Giove. She doesn't remember much about him. It wasn't a good experience. It happened in the back of Gianluca's parents' Pontiac Catalina station wagon, parked right there in their garage. Gianluca kissed like a bulldog. His hands were rough. His breath smelled of cheese. She was seventeen, and the Beatles were on the radio in the car. It was 1971. She felt terrible on her walk home. Sad, empty. She went to her room and cried for six hours straight. She feared pregnancy. She feared her parents finding out. She feared everyone calling her a worthless puttana. Gianluca moved on to Marie Antonaci. She met Donnie the next year. After that, it was Donnie and only Donnie.

Since they split—and for a while before they split—there's been nothing. She hasn't particularly thought of her body as being capable of pleasure, especially not since Gabe's death. She got her tubes tied when Gabe was eleven, thinking one kid was enough and divorce wasn't in the cards. She didn't want some drunken accident with Donnie. She also didn't know that she'd lose her one and only child.

Yesterday, with Mikey, was the first stirring of something. She wonders again how many girls there have been, how many girls have sat so close to him and fingered his strange earlobes like this. *Look at me, I'm jealous*, she thinks.

Mikey touches his earlobes now. "I kind of like them like this, all stretched out. My mother hates it. She thinks I ruined myself."

"What's it called?" Donna asks. "That kind of piercing?"

"Gauge piercing. I had these big-ass gauges in there. I had some friends who were crust punks—they got me into it."

"Crust punks?"

"They live in squats, most of them. Hop freight trains. Lots of homemade tats, like this one"—pointing to his chin—"and they dress crustie. All black, studded jackets, boots. They're usually in bands. They've got dogs, a lot of them. My friend Joanna had a dog named Whiskey. Their main thing is kind of saying *fuck you* to everything."

"They sound scary."

"Most of the ones I knew, they were okay. I wasn't one of them, though. I tried to be, I guess, but I was a fraud. They were devoted and disciplined in their way. I don't think most of them worried about anything. They didn't get depressed. They just did what they did, lived how they lived. They got sick of somewhere or chased out, they were on to the next place."

"So, they traveled around a lot?"

"Yep. They'd show up, usually when it wasn't freezing, and be around for a few months, and then—unless they had a particularly good squat, like they did this one time in Rosendale—they'd be gone. College towns and cities, that's what they like. College towns because there's always college kids they could take advantage of, hit up for money, whatever. You're eighteen, nineteen, you think that life is romantic, you get sucked up in it and become, really, a tourist."

"I went to Brooklyn College," Donna says. "I stayed home with my folks. I worked at a jewelry store in Kings Plaza on the weekends. I was a very boring college kid."

"No riding the rails?" Mikey says, smiling.

She laughs and then, out of some nurturing impulse, says, "Are you hungry? I can run to the bagel place and get egg-and-cheese sandwiches."

"I'm good," Mikey says. "But you never answered me."

"Answered you about what?"

"About this kiss."

"How many girlfriends you have?" Donna asks.

"I don't have a girlfriend."

He leans in, and they kiss. It's a strange feeling at first, her lips on his, his beard bristling against her skin. She tries to remember the last time she was kissed. Donnie, drunk, probably a few months before Gabe died. But that wasn't a kiss where she felt anything. It was mechanical, soulless. That's how kissing Donnie had been for years. She didn't feel kissed and didn't feel like she was kissing, not like it had been in the early days of their marriage, when a kiss from him could light her up. This is that kind of kiss.

She's making out with Mikey on the floor in the living room, "Four Strong Winds" playing in the background. She feels like a kid. Or maybe like the kid that she never was, never really had a chance to be. She should've made out with more boys on the floor while listening to records before getting married.

They kiss until the record ends. Donna wants to fill the silence with music. She pulls away and goes over to the turntable, taking the Neil Young record off the platter and putting it away. "I'm going to put something else on," she says.

"Okay," Mikey says.

"You like Bruce?" Donna asks, leaning over and thumbing through the vinyl in one of her crates. She holds up Springsteen's *Nebraska*.

"I've never really listened to him, to tell you the truth," Mikey says. "I mean, I've heard 'Born in the U.S.A.'"

"You've never listened to Bruce?"

"You don't like me anymore, huh?"

"I'm just excited I get to play him for you. This is my favorite song ever." She takes *Nebraska* out of its sleeve and puts it on the platter, dropping the needle into the second groove, placing it perfectly, "Atlantic City" coming on straightaway.

She stands there over the turntable, alternating between watching the record spin and watching Mikey's face for a reaction. She remembers the first time she heard "Atlantic City," driving in a car on the way to Atlantic City for the weekend with Donnie. It was the fall of 1982. Gabe was about seven. They had a babysitter lined up in Atlantic City, a daughter of a friend of Donnie's from the force. It seemed unbelievable that you could hear a song like "Atlantic City" while driving *to* Atlantic City. Donnie mostly liked it, but he was never a big Bruce guy. It was always weird to her that he loved Bon Jovi so much but was sour on Bruce.

She and Donnie stayed at the Golden Nugget and fought a lot while they gambled that weekend in Atlantic City. The babysitter wound up being a stoner who fell asleep while Gabe watched TV. The song didn't leave Donna's mind. As soon as she got back home, she went to Zig Zag Records and bought *Nebraska*. She loved the whole album, but "Atlantic City" was one she'd just keep setting the needle back on.

She's thinking now—not to get too deep about it—that a line like "Everything dies, baby, that's a fact, but maybe everything that dies someday comes back" is very different to a woman who's thirty-nine and has lost her only child. But being twenty-one and having lost his father gives Mikey his own perspective. She doesn't want to force that conversation. Maybe she doesn't even want to have it. This song used to mean one thing to her. After Gabe died, it meant another. It changes shape, it gets better and more resonant—that's what the best songs do.

"That's a great song," Mikey says when it's over.

"You liked it?"

"A lot. I'm a Bruce fan now."

"That's what I like to hear."

The record continues to play, the quiet devastation of "Mansion on the Hill." Donna sits back on the floor. She wants to kiss Mikey again. She does. He puts his hand on her arm. She's self-conscious about how she's dressed suddenly—in her sweats and slipper-socks and a light sweater she got off the sale rack at Century 21. She's wearing a bra, thank God. Her hair is pinned up. She hasn't taken a shower yet this morning. She thinks of her body's imperfections, all the ways she's aged, what it would be like to take her shirt off in front of Mikey. The girls he's been with, they still have their young bodies. She's got this body that's getting so old so fast.

Mikey's hand is under her sweater suddenly, touching her side. His fingers are warm against her skin. His touch doesn't feel invasive the way Donnie's did for so long. She opens her eyes while locked in a kiss. She studies his eyelashes, the place where his eyebrows come together caterpillar-like. She closes her eyes again and touches the sleeve of his corduroy jacket, which smells of mothballs. She likes the feel of the corduroy with her eyes closed. He's not overanxious, he's not moving too fast, and she appreciates that. He seems content with kissing.

Upstairs, they hear footsteps. Suzette Bonsignore is moving around, probably trudging to the bathroom. Her steps are heavy.

Mikey puts his hand farther up Donna's shirt now, touching her back. He moves away and kisses her chin, her jawline, her neck, her ear. He spends a while kissing her ear. His fingers play over the ridges of her spine. She takes a few deep breaths. Yesterday, she wouldn't have thought of something like this as possible. She's always been one of those people who thinks they couldn't do this or they couldn't do that, but how do you really know if something's possible or not until it actually happens? Here's Mikey now. This is happening. It's *real*. It wasn't expected. That's silly—what expectations has she even had this last however long?

Mikey backs off and looks at her. "Are you okay?" he asks.

She gives him a tender nod. "I'm perfect," she says.

Donnie walks over to Flash Auto early and scouts out the Olds Cutlass Ciera, parked at the far end of the yard, away from the garage. It's in good shape. He'll tell Sal and Frankie to give it to Ava when she picks up her Nova. She'll go home with two cars. Her shithead son can drive one. She'll feel like a champ, a gambler who's won big. She'll probably show up at Donnie's house and strip out of that suit of hers and screw his lights out like only an overworked widow can.

He goes inside to the office. Frankie's wife, Michelle, is at the desk. She's got a calculator in front of her, the phone receiver pressed to her ear, and is writing on a yellow legal pad, saying, "Uh-huh, right, yeah." She's working on a parts estimate. She holds up her hand to signal to Donnie that she'll be with him in a sec.

The office is cluttered. Repair manuals stacked on rusty filing cabinets. Stray batteries and mufflers in cardboard boxes. Quarts of oil and brake fluid and antifreeze. A couple of tires propped against a cracked mirror. The walls are covered in photos of the Italian soccer team that won the 1982 World Cup. There's a signed, framed photo of Phil Rizzuto next to a picture of Frank Sinatra playing Madison Square Garden in '74.

Michelle hangs up the phone. "Donnie, how's it going?" she says. "Tommy's not here yet."

"No, I know," Donnie says. "That '84 Cutlass Ciera in the yard, it still up for grabs?"

"Sure."

"It's a good car, right? Runs good?"

"Far as I know."

Frankie comes in through the door at the back of the office, wiping his hands on an oily rag, chewing on something. He's wearing blue work pants and a plain white T-shirt streaked with grease. He's got a crucifix on a heavy gold chain around his neck. His goatee is dusted with flakes of pastry crust. "Donnie, excuse me," he says. "I'm chowing down on some sfogliatelle a customer brought in. What's the good word? Tommy will be here in a bit."

"I was asking Michelle about that '84 Cutlass Ciera."

Frankie comes over, and they shake. "The Tempo break down on you?"

"It's not for me."

Frankie nods a little, his interest obviously piqued. "It's a good car. I did the work myself."

Donnie looks past Frankie, through the glass window in the door, into the garage, checking to see what cars are up on the lifts. "I want it. You're working on a car now, a Nova?"

"I am. Ava Bifulco's."

"Good. Yeah. This Olds is gonna be a gift for Ava."

"You know Ava?"

"I do now. When she picks up her Nova, tell her the Olds is hers, too. Two grand will square it?" Donnie takes the money out of his pocket and thumbs off a stack of hundreds. He hands it to Frankie.

"We've got a deal," Frankie says, smiling. "No tax."

"I don't need a receipt. Just give Ava the title and the keys and whatever else."

There's surprise in Frankie's voice as he says, "Piacere mio, amico. You and Ava an item?"

Donnie just smiles. "We're friendly," he says, imagining Ava coming in to check on the Nova and being shocked by the gift of a new used car.

Michelle's been eavesdropping the whole time, her ear tuned into gossip of any kind. Her eyes are wide, her mouth open. She's recorded all of this so she can repeat the information to anyone who will find it shocking. *Donnie Parascandolo and Ava Bifulco, who would've seen that coming?* He wonders if word will spread to Donna through whichever channels that dope moves. Probably someone Donna works with at Kearney. He doubts Donna knows anything of Ava—she wasn't that kind of person, in everybody's business, digging up dirt—but she'd probably still be surprised to hear he'd set his sights on a widow in her early fifties. A lot of guys in his position, they would've gone the other way, found some skank in her twenties, but Donnie's going the high-class route.

"I like that Ava," Michelle says now, as if reading his mind. "Very professional. An admirable woman."

Donnie likes that. He smiles again. "Admirable's right," he says.

Pags and Sottile show up a few minutes later. Frankie opens the other office for them, the one that Big Time Tommy uses. Sal comes in to say hey. He's shorter than Frankie by a full foot, has curly hair and big Popeye arms. He's not much of a talker. He's in and out.

Much of the time, Big Time Tommy hangs out at a former disco club he owns on Bath Avenue. This office is one of the many other places that he's got around the neighborhood, these different little meeting spaces he keeps. There's a desk and some chairs, a picture of Marisa Tomei in *My Cousin Vinny* cut out of a newspaper and taped to the wall. Other than that, the room's pretty bare. Donnie, Pags, and Sottile just stand there, leaning against the cold concrete wall. Sometimes Big Time Tommy's fifteen minutes late. Sometimes he's an hour late.

"My cousin called me this morning," Pags says, deciding to make small talk while they wait. It's a thing that drives Donnie crazy about him. Let the silence just sit for a few minutes. They've known each other a long-ass time. Can't they just appreciate not talking?

"Your cousin who?" Sottile asks.

"My cousin Andrea."

"Andrea who moved to Staten Island?"

"Right."

"How's she like it?"

"She doesn't like the dumps, I'll tell you that. And she's over the bridge four, five times a week. 'Why'd I even move?' she says. She still comes back to go to Alba. She says there's nowhere as good over there."

"Staten Island," Sottile says, and he shakes his head.

"Anyhow, she goes like this to me, she goes, 'You remember when we were kids and we used to hide in Nana's basement closet with all the olive oil and the wine?' 'Sure,' I says. 'You remember kissing me?' she says. 'What the fuck?' I say. This broad's married with three kids, and she's my cousin, and—not for nothing—she's not my type. 'I think you got me confused,' I says. 'You're right,' she says. That's how my morning starts. I'm fucked-up about it. What's it mean?"

Donnie says, "What do you mean, 'What's it mean?' You either made time with your cousin in your nana's basement or you didn't."

"I didn't," Pags says.

"Andrea's nice," Sottile says.

"So, you didn't," Donnie says. "End of story."

"But why would she say it?" Pags is honestly confounded.

"Maybe she dreamed it. Maybe you're somebody's fantasy, after all." Donnie laughs, makes a smooching noise. He wishes he had cigarettes. He forgot his case at home, forgot he needs a new pack.

Big Time Tommy comes strutting in a few minutes later with Dice on his heels. "It's the cavalry, waiting patiently for orders," Big Time Tommy says, plopping down behind the desk. Dice stands beside Big Time Tommy, arms crossed, his upper lip puffy where Donnie punched him. He's giving Donnie a look that's meant to be intimidating but is about as far from it as a man can get.

Donnie winks at Dice.

"Heard you two had a little spat," Big Time Tommy says.

"I told the guy don't touch my shoulder," Donnie says.

Big Time Tommy nods. "Dice is not a good listener, I'll agree on that front."

Dice just stands there and sits on his feelings. Big Time Tommy must've put him right in his place when he told him what happened.

"You got what for us today?" Donnie asks.

"I've got a guy off the rails is what I got," Big Time Tommy says. "Duke O'Malley."

"I remember him."

"He's in the hole for ten large and I know he's holding out, but there's the bigger issue of his mental health. He's going around saying, 'Fuck Big Time Tommy. I'm not paying that tubby bitch.' Antonio over at the Wrong Number says he came in with a sign the other day, like a homemade sign you make in grade school. Oak tag, glue, glitter. He's got written on it, 'Big Time Tommy Ain't Shit!' And a drawing of me where I look like Santa Claus. 'Tubby bitch,' you believe it? This mick must be off his meds. Number one, he's no Sissy Spacek. Number two, he works for Mr. Natale as a bookkeeper, which looks bad for me."

Mr. Natale is the other neighborhood big shot, Big Time Tommy's former mentor and biggest current foe.

Donnie says, "So, we shake him down for the ten, fuck him up if he can't pay? Easy enough."

"On the surface, it's nothing. But the word I got is he's hiding out in his house, ready for battle. I'm telling you, he's whacked out completely. You know Vlad? Vlad went over there yesterday, he says Duke thinks he's in a fucking Western now. Vlad rings the bell, Duke comes out geared up like John Wayne. He fucking draws on Vlad, shoots at his feet, says, 'Dance, you commie stooge.'"

"No shit."

"He lives with his sister, Duke does. She's sick in the head, too."

"So, we go over hot?" Pags says.

"In the least. Be ready for a showdown, is what I'm saying."

Donnie laughs. "Some Sergio Leone shit."

"This guy's laughing," Big Time Tommy says, motioning to Donnie. "You ain't gonna be laughing, believe me. Duke was in the Korean War. We're not talking about another Dice here. Take it serious, okay?"

He has Dice write down the address and then stands, paying his respects to Marisa Tomei on the wall by touching her picture longingly.

Antonina's plan is simple. She's going to leave a note for Mikey in his mailbox, let him know that Nick Bifulco will be coming around so that he's not blindsided. There's a lot she wants to say to Mikey, but she decides not to write a gushing letter. He probably doesn't even think about her except for the fact that hanging out with her got him cracked in the head with a bat.

She's in her bed, not really ready to get going with the day after sneaking back in late. Following the diner, she and Ralph had just driven around the Bronx, stopping somewhere called Orchard Beach and sitting in the parking lot in the dark, listening to Ralph's tapes. She always expected him to make a move on her, but he never did. This time, he talked to her about some of his favorite songs, the stuff he'd mentioned at the diner, what he'd put on a mixtape if he made one for her. She found it hard to imagine him making a mixtape.

After Orchard Beach, they drove home through Manhattan, taking the Bruckner to the FDR. Traffic blocked up the FDR. Ralph cursed a lot. Antonina liked looking out at the lights of the city. They crossed the Brooklyn Bridge, and she felt like a kid, coming home from some family trip she'd never really gone on.

Ralph knew the history of the bridge. He'd seen a show on PBS. He talked about the guy who designed it—she forgets his name now. How it opened a hundred and ten years ago. How they used to store wine in vaults on the Manhattan side—they called it the Blue Grotto because there was a shrine to the Virgin Mary or something. How they built the towers. He went into great detail on this, about how they sunk some stuff and how mind-blowing it was what they were accomplishing way back then. How the workers got the bends. How they used to have trains and streetcars running across. He said they couldn't build a bridge like it these days if they tried because everything's shit and no one cares that much.

She rolls over now and reaches around on the floor next to the bed, looking for a spiral notebook. She finds one, its yellow tattered cover etched with doodles, a pencil nudged into the wire spirals.

She opens the book to a blank page. It was supposed to be her book for some math class with Sister Renee, but she never took a single note. Instead, sometimes, she uses it as a diary. But her thing is she'll write on a page—about whatever, a normal day, or going with Lizzie to the city, or seeing some movie she really likes, or even about her first time with Rico Ruiz or one of her weird little Bronx trips with Ralph—and she'll say everything she wants to say, every feeling she has, whether it's complicated or not. Her thing is to be totally honest with herself. Or, at least, to try to understand what honesty even is. She'll write everything down and then she'll rip the page from the book, bring it out on the fire escape, light a smoke, and use what's left of the flame to set the paper ablaze. Sometimes it takes another match. She likes to watch the burning paper flutter down to the yard, crinkle into nothing amid the weeds on a broken patch of concrete. That shit's poetic to her.

What to say to Mikey is the thing she needs to figure out now. Maybe she should just let it go, let him deal with it on his own. What purpose could leaving a note for him serve other than suggesting that she has some desire to reconnect?

Well, does she? It's been two years. She's a senior now. He's home from college, a dropout. Maybe they should reconnect. They'd be smarter this time, wouldn't start stripping down in public. She knows places they can go.

So, she does still have a crush on him.

Sure.

After all, he's the only guy from the neighborhood she's ever known who has renounced being from the neighborhood. He looks different, acts different, talks different, even if the neighborhood is somehow buried deep in him.

She writes:

Dear Mikey,

That loser teacher Nick Bifulco from OLN came around saying he wants to make a movie about DP. He wants to talk to me and you about the night in the schoolyard. I don't know how the hell he even knows about it. He was drunk when he came over my house. I just figured I'd warn you. If you ever want to hang out, give me a call. I have my own line.

And then she signs her name with hearts over the *I*s and scribbles her number under that. She rereads the note ten times. Has she said too much or too little? Is she coming off as desperate? Or does it seem more like she's not even interested?

She's about to rip it up and try again, but then she decides that it's okay, it's fine. There's no way Mikey could think she was being too aggressive or that this was anything other than her looking out for him. Maybe the hearts are too much. She turns them into big inky dots instead.

She gets up and finds an envelope on her dresser and folds the letter, stuffing it inside and writing MIKEY in big letters across the front.

She takes off the boxers and Sonic Youth T-shirt she'd worn to bed. She borrowed the shirt from Lizzie and never gave it back. She's never even really listened to Sonic Youth. She puts on clean underwear she finds stuffed in the top drawer of the dresser and a bra hanging from her doorknob. Then one of her favorite loose-fitting flannels and her overalls. Finally, back into her combat boots she goes.

Her eyes are heavy, and her mouth tastes stale. She discovers a piece of gum in her jar of loose coins and pops it in her mouth. She stuffs the envelope in the front pocket of her overalls.

Unlocking the door, she goes quietly down the stairs from the attic, knowing her father will be at work and hoping her mother isn't around. She gives her mother credit for not bothering her, for not knocking when she shouldn't knock, for giving her plenty of room to fuck up. She's not a baby, after all.

In the kitchen, there's a note on the table from her mother: *Be back. Finish the coffee.*

She pours herself a cup from the percolator. It's lukewarm. She looks in the liquor cabinet under the sink and finds a bottle of sambuca stashed behind all the gin and Kahlúa and scotch. She splashes some into her coffee and leans against the stove, drinking it down in a few gulps.

On the way out of the house, Antonina notices that Jane Rafferty is sitting at her front window, watching her open and close the front gate. Antonina looks up and kind of gives her a half-wave. Jane's face is empty, full of longing. Antonina wonders if she's thinking about when she was a girl, how it feels to leave your house, your yard, to walk freely in the world. This thought makes Antonina sad. How do people get stuck inside like that? How do people decide to retreat from the world? She doesn't know Jane's story. She's never asked. Her mother and father say Jane's whacked in the head. She's never left the house that Antonina can remember. A cousin of hers brings groceries once a week. Antonina's mother says it goes back further than that—she's known of Jane since she was in high school, and even then, Jane didn't leave the house.

What if there was some heartbreak? Antonina's sure there had to have been. Most people don't just stop living out of fear. They stop living because something happens to make them stop living, right? Must be. Antonina wonders if anything like that will ever happen to her. Jane was a girl once. She didn't have pink hair and overalls and combat boots, but she was a girl, and she was probably a normal girl who left her yard and walked to school and work and to meet friends. Antonina's thinking she should knock on Jane's door one day, ask her if she needs anything. Why hasn't she ever thought to do that? A nice person would think to do that. Is she not nice? Not believing in the shit she's been taught at church and school doesn't mean she doesn't have to be nice.

She smiles at Jane, but Jane doesn't smile back. She just has that same gone-in-the-eyes expression, watching the outside world like it's boring TV.

Antonina heads toward Bath Avenue.

Mikey's house isn't that close. It's far enough away in the wrong direction that she never passes it on the way to school or the subway or wherever. The only time she's passed in the last couple of years is when Ralph happened to drive up his block one night after getting off the Belt on their way back from the Bronx.

She was only ever there once. They didn't do anything. His mother and father were both home. He had to get something in his room. He showed her around, quickly. She remembered seeing his boxers crumpled on the floor, a stash of condoms in an open tin box on his dresser, his *They Live* poster. The room had smelled of boy funk. She'd touched the spines of a few of his books and cassettes.

Mikey's mother, Rosemarie, had not been happy to meet her—Antonina remembered that much. "How old is this girl?" Rosemarie had said, looking her up and down.

"Sixteen," Mikey said, and Antonina didn't correct him.

Rosemarie shook her head. "You're in college," she said to Mikey. "Act like it."

His father, Giuseppe, she only saw through a doorway. He was in the living room, fumbling around with their VCR, and didn't seem to care who Mikey was with. It's so crazy to her that he killed himself the night they were in the schoolyard. That's another reason she's steered clear of Mikey. She would've hated to have to see him through that.

When she gets to Mikey's block, she takes a deep breath and tries to think of what she'll say if she happens to bump into him. Her plan is to just leave the letter in the mailbox, but who knows? Say he's sitting out front on the stoop. Say he sees her from a window. What then?

The mailbox is next to the front door. It's made of black plastic and opens like a toaster oven. She runs up to it and deposits the letter in the box on top of a Genovese circular and a menu for a Chinese restaurant on Cropsey.

She's headed back down the stairs when the front door opens and she hears Rosemarie Baldini's voice. "Antonina Divino?" she says, as if she's not a hundred percent sure. And maybe she's not, with the hair. It's been a while.

Antonina turns around. "Hi, Mrs. Baldini."

"Your hair is pink."

"It is."

"What're you doing here? Mikey's not home."

Antonina hesitates. She decides to tell the truth. Rosemarie could very easily open the mailbox, find the letter, and read what it says. "I was dropping a note for him."

"You two keep in touch?"

"We don't," Antonina says.

"A note about what, then?"

"Just . . . it's nothing. I wanted to give him some news. You can read it if you want to."

"I don't read my son's mail."

"I'm sorry I bothered you." Antonina begins to walk back to the gate.

"Have you seen Mikey?" Rosemarie says, her voice turning desperate. "He went out early this morning and he hasn't come back. It's his birthday. His uncle's coming over. I think there's a girl. You two haven't started up again?"

"No, I'm sorry," Antonina says, leaving the yard and not looking back, figuring that Rosemarie will stay outside for a few minutes to keep an eye out for Mikey. She feels bad for Rosemarie, she does. Her husband killing himself. Her son a different breed. It's like Jane. You can't figure those things. Life just throws them at you.

Antonina wonders if Rosemarie will read the letter she wrote. If she does, she wonders what she'll make of it.

At the corner, she turns left and is about to start for home when she sees Nick Bifulco hustling across the avenue to her. "What're you doing here?" Nick asks, slowing to a stop in front of her. "Commiserating with Mikey, huh? I'm back to try him again, too."

Antonina shakes her head and keeps walking. "He's not around."

Nick follows close behind. "Will you get a drink with me?" he asks.

She stops. "A drink?" she says.

"Sure," he says. "We can go to Spanky's Lounge. It's right over here. They'll serve you. I want to ask you a few things."

And then, regretting her answer almost as soon as the words are out of her mouth, she says, "Okay."

As she follows Nick toward Cropsey Avenue, headed for that shithole Spanky's, she thinks, *What's the point of being young if you don't do the stupid things you obviously shouldn't do?*

Rosemarie has the day off for Mikey's birthday, but it doesn't feel like a day off. She's been cooking and cleaning and worrying. She's not sure what time her brother, Alberto, will be over, and who knows what type of hot tamale he'll bring with him? Last time the girl was some kind of dancer. And she can't begin to guess where Mikey went this early, all dressed up. Must be a girl.

The visit from that Antonina Divino has her all mixed up too, coupled with the visit from Nick Bifulco the night before. Something's going on, and she can't piece it together.

She's still standing at the front door, having watched Antonina walk away up the block. That pink hair. What a disgrace. And the way she dresses. Those big black boots and stupid overalls. Makes sense now, she guesses, what her son was drawn to. She's another one who doesn't seem to give a damn about fitting in.

Must be a girl with Mikey, but not Antonina. If it was her, that's where he'd be in his father's nice jacket, walking around with her, out for breakfast at the Roulette Diner.

Rosemarie opens the mailbox and finds the envelope that Antonina left. She goes inside and sits down at the kitchen table and turns it over in her hands.

She taps her foot against the linoleum.

She studies the way that Antonina has written Mikey's name, looking for a clue.

What could be inside?

She knows opening it is wrong, a breach of privacy, but sometimes a mother has to do what a mother has to do. Sometimes, she reasons, privacy isn't a right for a kid who needs help. Twenty-one today. Not a kid anymore. A man. But maybe if she'd breached Giuseppe's privacy a bit more, she could've helped him see a way out other than suicide. Her concern leads her, fingers trembling, to rip open the envelope and read the note from Antonina.

She'll admit, her first reaction is relief that Antonina is warning Mikey about Ava's son, Nick. It seems that the main purpose of the note is to let Mikey know that Nick is a creep.

Beyond that, it doesn't make much sense. That "night in the schoolyard" Antonina's talking about—Rosemarie has no idea what this means. Mikey was seeing Antonina around the time Giuseppe died. In fact, he came home the very night Giuseppe went missing with a shiner, saying he'd been jumped in the schoolyard up the block by some guy from the Marlboro Projects. She remembers saying they should call the cops, but he played it tough, shaking her off, saying it was nothing, just a bruise, and the guy didn't even get his money. Could that be the "night in the schoolyard" Antonina's talking about? And who is "DP"? There's so much she doesn't know, so much she's been shut out from knowing. If something had gone on that night, any impulse or inclination to find out what it was had been swiftly buried by Giuseppe's disappearance.

Anyhow, Rosemarie has always known that Mikey has a life, maybe even *lives*, that she knows nothing about—especially up in New Paltz—and she wouldn't be able to tell his life story to a stranger, not past the age of fifteen or so anyway. After that, it becomes totally blurry to her, so much information withheld, so many gaps and dark patches. There were times when she felt like people who didn't know him at all knew more about him than she ever could.

She gets up and searches the junk drawer next to the fridge for an envelope. She finds one, its edges a bit crimped. She folds the note neatly, stuffing it inside the new envelope. She duplicates Antonina's penmanship as best she can, writing MIKEY in big letters across the front. She tosses the original envelope in the trash and leaves the new one, containing Antonina's note, propped against the glass bowl full of pennies and paper clips and used scratch-offs in the center of the table.

She goes over to the stove. She's got the chicken parm and garlic bread in the oven, cooking at three-fifty. The gravy is bubbling on the back burner, blue flames glowing under the edges of the pot. The water for the ravioli is humming at a low boil on the front burner. When they're about ready to eat, she'll turn up the gas and put the ravioli from Pastosa in gently. But she's not sure when that will be.

She goes into her bedroom and changes into nice clothes. A black blouse with gold sequins and black slacks. This is an outfit that she would wear to church. She wants to look nice for her son's birthday. She looks around at the bare walls of her bedroom, at the string dangling from the light in the middle of the ceiling, at the smudgy mirror over her sewing table. The top of her dresser is also empty. A few months after Giuseppe died, she put away their wedding picture. She couldn't look at it anymore. She also put away the handkerchiefs he usually kept folded and lined up there.

The bare walls tell nothing of her life. Other people—she's been to houses like this—have their stories plastered on the walls. Weddings, communions, vacations, school pictures. She has all that stuff, but none of it is on the walls. Her photo albums are buried at the bottom of her bedroom closet. Pictures pasted to crumbling black pages. She can't bring herself to look at them. It's too sad, thinking about all she's lost, about the possible futures that existed at the time certain pictures were taken.

Mikey, for instance, standing in the driveway on his first day of kindergarten in his St. Mary's uniform, smiling like he'd just won something, Giuseppe next to him, a proud father. That must've been 1978. She doesn't even need to dig around in the closet to find the picture. It's right there in her mind. Mikey is so happy. He could be anything. He could stay happy. Giuseppe looks like a different person than what he'll become. He doesn't look like the kind of person who would ever leave this son of his. He doesn't look like the kind of person who would throw himself from a bridge in desperation.

What will become of these photo albums when she's gone? What will become of the house? *Stop, Rosemarie. You're only forty-six.*

The doorbell rings. She sighs. She's not even sure who to expect. She wonders if she'd even be surprised if she opened the door and the ghost of Giuseppe was there, soaking wet, blue in the face, begging for her to take him back.

She ambles out of the bedroom, through the kitchen, and back down the hallway to the front door. She opens it on Alberto, who's looking less than dapper in cargo shorts and a tank top, the hair on his shoulders and chest matted with sweat. He's holding a paper grocery sack in his beefy arms. Having been thrown off by Antonina Divino, Rosemarie remembers that she'd called him the night before to ask if he could lend her money to fend off Big Time Tommy.

"You're early," Rosemarie says. "And you're alone. I thought you'd bring a new girlfriend."

Alberto smiles. "I'm seeing a real class act. Madeline, her name is. She's a regular at the Knights of Columbus dances. You'd like this one."

"I'm sure."

"Listen, Ro, I've got some bad news."

"What is it?" she asks, the disappointment palpable in her voice.

"I can't stay. I've got a thing."

"A *thing*?"

"Mikey here? I got a present for him. And I got something for you. I forgot the pastries and cookies, though. I'm sorry about that, too."

"Mikey's not here right now." She pauses. "You have to stay. Please. I made so much food."

"I'm sorry, sis. I can't." He leans in and kisses her on the head.

The smell of her brother is enough to choke her. That awful cologne he's wearing covering up the BO only slightly. "Come in," she says.

Inside, he puts down the sack on the kitchen table. "Smells good in here," he says.

"You don't know what you're missing."

"Nothing's ready, right?"

"The chicken parm only needs twenty minutes."

"And Mikey's not even here?"

Rosemarie shrugs.

"I'm in a rush," Alberto says.

"I could make you a quick sandwich. Mortadella and provolone."

"Forget it." He reaches into the sack and comes out with a wooden device of some kind. It's square with a small wheel that grinds back and forth through a notched groove by turning a handle. He puts it on the table. "That's for Mikey's birthday."

Rosemarie picks it up and turns the handle. "What is it?" she asks.

"Bullshit grinder," Alberto says, grinning. "Got it off a guy on Mulberry Street. Reminded me of Mikey."

"Real nice you make fun of your nephew like that."

"What? I figured he could grind his bullshit while he's loafing on your couch. He'll get a kick out of it."

Rosemarie sets it back down.

Alberto takes a shoebox out of the sack next. "And I got something for you," he says, plucking the lid off. Inside is a messy stack of twenties and a gun.

"What is this?" she asks.

"Some money to hold off Big Time Tommy. It's only about five hundred bucks. That doesn't work, you need it in a pinch, there's the piece. It's a Colt Anaconda. Won it in a card game." He pauses. "I shouldn't say that. I shouldn't mention card games. I'm sorry."

Rosemarie's never seen a gun. "It's loaded?"

"It is. I'm not saying go crazy. I just want you to feel protected. Hide it in the closet so Mikey doesn't even know it's in the house."

"I don't know."

"Tommy starts pressing, he's gonna stop being respectful because you're a widow. Something unexpected goes down, I just want you to be prepared."

Rosemarie thinks about it. Sometimes her brother does use his head. It's not a bad idea to be prepared for the worst. She doesn't have anything else in the way of protection, not an alarm, not bars on the windows, nothing.

"I don't know how to shoot it," she says.

"Just point it and pull the trigger and hope for the best. With Big Time Tommy, at least you got an ample target."

She nods.

Alberto picks up the grocery sack, which still has a few things inside. He leans over and kisses Rosemarie on the head. "I'm sorry again, Ro," he says. "Just watch your back. And tell Mikey I said happy birthday." He rushes back down the hallway and out the front door and he's gone as fast as he came, leaving her with a gun in the silent house.

The AC in Ava's office isn't working. She's made her rounds. Now she's sitting at her desk with the window open, doodling on a pad, craving a cigarette. She picks up the phone and dials Flash Auto. She wants to check on the Nova. She hopes it's nothing too serious. Michelle puts Frankie on.

"The bad news is," Frankie says, "it's the catalytic converter."

"Are you kidding me?" Ava says, scratching the pencil against the pad until the point breaks, her jaw tight.

"I know, I know. These things happen. It's not a new car. The good news is your boyfriend bought you the Olds Cutlass Ciera in our lot."

Ava's taken aback. "My boyfriend?"

"Donnie Parascandolo. He came by and said it was yours, paid for and everything. Lot of people have big problems with Donnie, but he's okay in my book. A solid individual. Loyal."

Ava really could use a cigarette now. "He's not my boyfriend."

"Well, your admirer, then."

"I don't think I can accept a gift from him like that."

"That's between you two."

"When's my Nova gonna be ready?"

"Gotta order the part. Give me until tomorrow to get you an estimate, okay? The Olds you can pick up whenever."

"We'll see."

"Okay there, Ava."

Ava ends the call and sits back in her chair. She decides to take her smoke break. She lets Jada and Straleen know she's stepping out for a sec and then goes to her usual dumpster spot and is about to light up before thinking twice about it. She heads for the boardwalk and finds an unoccupied bench and lights her cigarette. She really enjoys that first drag after such a hectic morning. These girls under her, they're one worse than the next. None of them listen. Many of them are not polite, not to her and not to the residents. Others are just flakes. Rosemarie took off today for her grown son's birthday, which Ava can't wrap her head around.

She watches seagulls circling over the beach, hears their squawks. She watches the water, sees a ship out on the horizon that's a dot. A small plane towing a banner passes over the beach. An ad for a radio station.

A guy sits down next to her. He's wearing red shorts that are inappropriately short, mismatched sneakers, and a heavy jacket that's blue and puffy. "Sweetheart," he says. "Good morning."

"I'm trying to enjoy my smoke here," Ava says, thinking maybe she's better off by the dumpster after all.

"Can I bum one?" he says.

"Christ. Fine." Her pack is in her lap. She opens it and passes him a cigarette.

"Viceroys?" he says, smiling wide, showing gold teeth. "My old man smoked Viceroys."

"I don't want to be rude," Ava says, "but this is my break and I'm trying to enjoy the quiet."

"Sure thing. Got a light?"

She hands him her book of matches.

His first match gets snuffed out by the breeze. He doesn't have any luck the second time either, the match sizzling between his fingers. He gets it the third time with a sigh of relief, stands, and hands her back the matches. He bows dramatically and sings his thank-you.

Ava watches as he struts away, puffing over his shoulder.

She thinks about Don buying her this Olds. Going overboard with the Good Samaritan thing now. She doesn't even know him. It's weird, but it's also romantic. She's not sure that's what he was going for, but what else could it be? You get into your forties and fifties and you start to want to just cut through all the bullshit. His thinking probably being that flowers wouldn't get the job done.

Or maybe he's been beaten down and rejected so much by people in the last few years that he feels the need to do wild, over-the-top stuff to make an impression. *Thanks for dinner. Here's an Olds Cutlass Ciera.*

She should accept the car.

No, she shouldn't. What would Anthony say?

Don's off the force—where'd he get the money for the car?

And what would any of this lead to anyway? The way Don drinks. His background. She's gonna what? Go to bed with him?

Her thoughts stray to Nick. She thinks about him knocking on that police captain's door. To bother him like that. She doesn't like what she's seeing in Nick since this dumb script idea took root. She hopes he comes to his senses.

She stands up and walks out to the railing and looks down at the sand. Crinkled cellophane and a grease-stained paper plate blow past. She can't remember the last time her feet were in the sand. She keeps the cigarette pinched between her lips as she reaches down and takes off one shoe and then the other. She's sick of them. She needs better shoes. She sets them off to the side. She walks down the three steps from the boardwalk to the beach. Her bare feet feel good in the sand. She closes her eyes and takes a deep drag off her cigarette. More seagull squawks. The sound of waves rolling in at the shoreline. To hell with it. She grabs her shoes and walks all the way down to the water.

At Sea Crest, they'll be wondering where she went. She doesn't care. After this, she'll walk to Nathan's and get a hot dog and an orangeade and she'll sit at one of the tables and just people-watch. Let them come looking for her. She's so dependable. *Too* dependable. It's her turn to be a flake.

Her feet are in wet, dark sand now. She sees a horseshoe crab scurrying, feels the pinch of a broken shell against the bottoms of her toes. She has her shoes under her arm. She finishes her cigarette and tosses the butt behind her in the general direction of an orange garbage can, missing to the left. She takes a few more steps forward and lets the waves break around her feet. It's cold. Colder than she expected. The surf comes in faster and harder now and sloshes up at her ankles, wetting the cuffs of her slacks.

The sun glows on the ocean.

Ava thinks of her grandparents. All four of them came over from Italy. Her mother's parents from Naples. Her father's mother from Calabria. Her father's father from Sicily. Ava knows the names of the places, but she can't picture them. Italy is just a word. She remembers wishing, as a girl, that she'd been born there. She still wishes she spoke Italian. Her father spoke some with his parents, her mother more with hers. Neither of them taught her a word. She picked up a few expressions but that's it. She wonders what it means to be from a place but not to know the place at all. This makes her sad. All she's done is look at the ocean, and now she's heartbroken about Italy.

She steps back and immediately regrets having put her feet in the water. They're caked in dry sand. She trudges back to the boardwalk.

She sits on the first bench she comes to—a different one than before because she's entered via a ramp a little ways up the beach—and knocks the sand from her feet. She looks over at Sea Crest. The place where she's worked for too long. She's so tired of it. She can't imagine that humans were intended to just grind away their days at jobs that make them feel empty. She thinks about Italy again. She'll never get there.

Nathan's it is. She puts her shoes on and walks back the way she came with Nick, mostly staring out at the pier. Seems like there's a party going on, early as it is. A Puerto Rican flag. Some camping chairs. A boombox blasting salsa music. Men in speedos, dancing. Women who could be twenty-five or forty-five pointing and laughing.

Leaving the boardwalk, she passes the freak show. A man out front—top hat, neck tattoos—barks at her. She keeps walking. At Nathan's, there's no line. She orders an orangeade and a frank with sauerkraut and sweet onions. She waits and then takes her food over to one of the green tables under an umbrella. The orangeade is perfect. So is the hot dog.

She chews. She dabs at her mouth with a yellow napkin. She watches people at the other tables. Families in bathing suits. Drunks. A high school kid with a droopy backpack and a Walkman. A leathery, toothless woman in a wide-brim straw sun hat.

An Olds Cutlass Ciera, imagine that. She shakes her head.

Ava feels unburdened. She decides not to go back to work. She can stop at a payphone and call over there and tell them she's not feeling well. They won't think twice. They know she doesn't call in or leave unless something's really up. Straleen can just take over for the day.

After the hot dog, Ava walks to the Wonder Wheel. She wants to be up in the air, looking out over Coney Island, seeing everything. She's never up in the air.

People are milling around by the kiddie rides in Deno's. A small crowd having nothing to do with the rides. Something must've happened. A fight, maybe. She stands next to a woman wearing a green tracksuit, the zipper open on the jacket over a Lady Liberty bikini top. The woman's breasts threaten to flop out each time she moves her arms or takes a breath.

"What's going on?" Ava says.

The woman shrugs. "Something with the cops. Now everybody's talking. When it happened, nobody gave a shit."

Ava takes a quick glance at the woman's breasts. She wishes she felt free enough to walk around in the world like that.

The woman notices. "Ain't a free show," she says.

"I'm sorry," Ava says.

"They're massive. They're impressive. I know."

"I admire your guts."

"We can go under the boardwalk and you can suck on them for ten bucks."

Ava smiles. She can't tell if the woman's joking or not. She doesn't respond.

"You got a cigarette?" the woman says.

Ava takes out her Viceroys and hands the woman one.

The woman tucks it behind her ear. "Thanks, doll," she says. "I'm saving it for my first cold beer." She walks away from the scene, out onto the boardwalk, where she takes off her track jacket and starts doing a series of strange stretches while leaning against the railing. Her breasts are pendulous, bound to fall loose.

Ava walks down the tunnel to the Wonder Wheel and buys a ticket and waits in a short line for the next go-round. When the time comes, she climbs into a stationary car and the attendant closes the door behind her. The swinging cars make her nervous. She remembers them well even though she only went on once as a newlywed. Her and Anthony. The swinging cars slide on rails as the wheel makes its rotation. She was afraid she was going to throw up. She felt like they would just be ejected out onto the pavement below and they would splatter there like bugs. Anthony laughed at her. "This is the safest ride in the world," he'd said. They'd kissed after that. He'd put his hand inside her shirt. It was romantic.

The Wonder Wheel begins to move.

Ava thinks of Anthony kissing her in that swinging car. Thirty years ago. Nick was conceived around then. Maybe she should've gone in one of the swinging cars on the off chance it was the same car she'd been in with Anthony. Aside from a fresh coat of paint, she bets they're all still the same. Maybe the car holds the ghost of her good memory. Newlyweds. How young they were. How she loved Anthony. His callused hand inside her shirt. His lips on her neck, the scratchiness of his two-day beard. The smell of him. Coffee and aftershave. She wishes he was here with her now.

As her car rises, she looks out at the water and the beach first. The sun's reflection stretched out. Then she looks all around. The Parachute Jump. The Cyclone. Roofs of buildings with their uneven lines of slathered black tar. Seagulls and pigeons peppering the air. The streets getting more crowded. Faint thrum of that salsa music from the pier.

She thinks of the woman in the Lady Liberty bikini top. She was hard-looking, sure, but Ava bets she knows how to take real pleasure in things. And not just that bummed cigarette and the cold beer she was going to get. Letting someone kiss her and touch her and suck on her.

She remembers her shower the night before and lets her thoughts stray back to Don. If Nick hadn't interrupted her, she might have taken her own pleasure there with the water beating down on her head. She wonders if she should resume high above Coney Island like this. That's what Lady Liberty with all her great openness and freedom would do, no doubt. No one can see into her car. There's hardly anyone else on the ride right now. A couple in one of the swinging cars. A mother and her three daughters in another one. At the top of the turn, the wheel will pause and she'll have a swaying minute or two to get lost in her dream.

She traces her hand down under the waistband of her slacks. She undoes the top button to give herself more room. She pushes her hand into her blue-striped cotton underwear. She's looking out over Coney Island. She's hearing all the sounds, terrible and strange and wonderful, rides whirring, plunging screams from the Cyclone, more of the seagulls squawking, that distant salsa, kids crying and laughing and howling. She imagines Anthony touching her and then he's replaced by Don. She can't stop her mind from going there.

The car pauses high up. There's a breeze. Her breathing quickens. Her hand moves faster in her underwear. She watches the small movements in her forearm as she strokes. She forgets about the view. She thinks of all that she likes and has ever liked about her own body. She steadies herself with her other hand on the bench and squeezes her legs together tightly and then a kind of shiver goes up her spine and she tilts her head back and exhales.

She lights a cigarette for the descent.

She can't believe she's done what she's just done. She pulls her hand back and buttons her pants. Here, out in the open, on the Wonder Wheel, a ride for kids. She's never done anything like this. Not in public. Not really. Once, before Anthony, in a dressing room at Woolworths she saw herself in the mirror in her bra and underwear and was similarly moved. That was so many years ago. She was a girl. It was fast, too. An experiment. She just liked watching herself in the mirror. The way her neck tensed up. But the dressing room still seemed private. It didn't matter that no one could see her now.

And, she asks herself, what if someone could? What if someone had a clear view of her somehow? Binoculars, a telescope, her mind going wild. A woman in her fifties, alone on the Wonder Wheel, pleasuring herself. She wonders if she could be arrested for that. She feels like a vagrant now, the Catholic guilt hitting home like a brick. She adjusts her blouse and her slacks. At least she wasn't naked or exposed in any way. It was just a hand down the front of her pants. She ashes on the floor of the car. She thinks of God, licking the tip of His pencil, marking this one down on her record. That's how she thinks of God, as some sort of accountant with a big note-book full of sins.

She shouldn't feel shame, though. That's ridiculous. Think of Lady Liberty.

When the car comes back down to the bottom, she gets out and someone says something to her about not smoking, but she just rushes away, flushed, breathing hard for a different reason. She heads up the ramp, tossing her butt on the floor and stomping it out. She decides she'll head back for the train. Maybe she will go to Flash Auto and pick up the Olds. First, she needs to stop at a payphone and call over to work and tell them she's done for the day.

Spanky's Lounge is on Cropsey Avenue, not far from the Baldini house, edging back toward Coney Island. Nick guides Antonina there now, trailing his hand behind him like he's trying to coax a puppy to eat something good or shit somewhere appropriate. He's never had a puppy, but he always wanted one. Anthony hated dogs. Ava's no fan either. Alice had a dog, Sully. It died of cancer. It, he, whatever. Had these massive lumps all over that made him look misshapen. Could barely walk straight toward the end. Just slept in his dog bed while his lumps heaved. Nick's thrilled to be walking with Antonina, even if she's not giving him much yet. He's thinking about who will play her in his movie. Drew Barrymore would be good. She could do Italian. Alyssa Milano's the more obvious choice, but he wonders if she has the chops for it.

"When we get to Spanky's," Nick says to Antonina, "they'll have a phone booth. I'm gonna call Phil Puzzo. You heard of him? He's a neighborhood god. He's on his book jacket in a wife-beater with his arms crossed. His bio says, 'Philip Puzzo was raised on the mean streets of Gravesend and Bensonhurst.'"

"That's the guy who writes about mobsters and shit?" Antonina says.

"Right. That's him. He's gonna help me get my movie made. We'll worry about Mikey later."

"I think my mom blew him before she married my dad."

"Your mom blew Phil Puzzo?"

"She claims to have blown him. I don't know. She might've just made it up."

They wander into Spanky's Lounge, a dark little dive. Nick was here with Alice once, and they got pretty drunk and loud, daring each other to sing along to whatever was playing on the jukebox.

"My kind of joint," Nick says.

"This is so depressing," Antonina says.

The bartender is a scruffy little guy with bloodshot eyes.

"Are you Spanky?" Nick says, smiling.

"I'm Gibson," the bartender says. "What do you want?"

"Two cans of Schaefer."

He gets two cans of Schaefer out of the cooler and pushes them to Nick across the bar. No questions about Antonina's age, no request for ID. Gibson doesn't even look at the girl. Nick pays and leaves a buck tip.

He carries the beers and guides Antonina to a wobbly table back by a *Knight Rider* pinball machine. Michael and KITT loom brightly over them. Nick pulls out Antonina's chair for her, and she sits reluctantly, tucking her hair behind her ears. The jukebox, he notices, is unplugged.

"So," Nick says, "what were you doing at Mikey's?"

"I was warning him about you," Antonina says, without missing a beat.

"You still see each other regularly?"

"No." She takes a long slug off her beer.

"But you wanted to *warn* him about *me*? Wow. You know, I'm on to something here. Who's gonna play you in the movie, that's what I'm asking myself. Drew Barrymore? Maybe Winona Ryder. I'm gonna tell Phil Puzzo the whole deal. My bet is he gets right on the phone with someone"—Nick miming talking into a phone—"and says, 'You've gotta fucking hear this guy's story.' The people he knows, I wouldn't be surprised if I walked away with a movie deal."

"You're crazy."

Nick drinks some beer. "You know what? Maybe I am crazy. I think being crazy pays off. I think you've *gotta* be crazy." He pauses. "Tell me what it was like that night."

"It was Donnie being a tough guy, thinking he was protecting me," Antonina says, drinking more.

"What do you know about him working for Big Time Tommy? Where'd you hear that?"

"Around."

"You want another beer? I'll get you another." He goes to the bar and comes back with another can of Schaefer and two shots of tequila.

She downs her shot without waiting for him to make a toast and then finishes the first can of beer, quickly moving on to the second.

It's not that Nick's trying to get Antonina wasted. She's as old as one of his students. Or as young as one of his students. He just wants her to talk more, to work through and process what she's seen and what she knows about Donnie. He wants to know about the night in the schoolyard, sure, but she's Donnie's neighbor, so she must have other important insights into his character. Nick also thinks she's free-spirited and totally unpredictable, and he wouldn't mind seeing how that turns out. She's playing coy now, but she reminds him of a younger version of Melanie Griffith in *Something Wild*. He pictures himself traipsing after her in the city, her swinging from lampposts and pulling up her shirt to flash taxi drivers and taking him to some shithole Times Square motel where he could feel the electric crackle of her youth. Alice fades into a far corner of his mind. He thinks how Antonina would snap on him like a glove. Those lithe legs of hers. That face full of beautiful damage. He'd lick her pink hair, and it'd taste like sugar.

Nick smiles, digs around in his pocket, and comes out with a quarter. "I'm gonna go use the phone. I'm gonna call Phil's folks and see if they'll hook us up. If I get in touch with him and he says he'll meet, maybe you'd like to come along?" He stands, looks around for a phone booth. It's nudged back between the bathrooms, its glass door slashed with graffiti. "Just think about it."

"You have another quarter?" Antonina says. "I want to play pinball."

"Sure," Nick says. He takes out another quarter—he's got two more left—and plunks it down on the table in front of Antonina. She grabs it, gets up, and goes to the pinball machine, dropping the quarter in and hip-checking the machine to loosen a stuck ball or something. As he struts to the phone booth, chest out, carrying his beer with him, he keeps his head turned, staring at Antonina in the golden glow coming off the machine, all that litheness and tightness, that cotton candy pinkness.

He knows Paulie and Nina's number by heart the way you know the numbers of neighbors who you might need to tell to move a car because of alternate-side parking or because someone's blocking their driveway and you saw the guy go into the Laundromat across the street or because the mailman delivered something of theirs to your house. They're good folks, Paulie spending summers shirtless in the front yard, listening to Bob Grant and ballgames, hosing down his car, mowing his little lawn, trimming his little hedges, tending to his tomatoes. Nina's hard and boozy with a great Kathleen Turner voice. She plays bingo at the church a lot and goes to Atlantic City twice a week on a big gray bus that leaves from near Seth Low Playground. She smokes two packs of Pall Malls a day. She calls the kids on the block *turds*. She says their parents spoil the hell out of them. Paulie and Nina love their son. They love being the parents of a big-shot writer. They love that he drops names of friends like De Niro and Danza. Nick punches in the number.

Nina picks up after one ring. "Who's this?" she says.

"Nina, it's Nick Bifulco."

"Well, what the *fulco* do you want?" she says, laughing at her own inane joke. As if he hasn't heard it all from the kids at school. *Mr. Bifucko*. "Mr. Bi, are you bi?" High school kids can do almost anything with any name, but his is especially well-suited to cheap jokes.

"I was wondering, hoping really, that you could put me in touch with Phil. I'd like to talk shop with him. Writer to writer."

"You write? I didn't know that."

"I do. I mean, I'm just getting started on this movie script. It's about the neighborhood. I was hoping I could just ask him a few questions, get his feedback."

Silence on the other end. Then the rasping sounds of a lighter. Nina inhaling. "You want what, his number?"

"That'd be great."

"He's got a lot on his plate. He's working on a new book."

"I understand. I just need a few minutes of his time."

"How's Ava?"

"She's good."

"At church, I see her in the back. She leaves right after Communion. I don't get to chat with her. I told Father Borzumato, she must have places to be. Busy woman, I says. You don't go to church, Nick?"

"I go in Bay Ridge with my girlfriend," Nick says, which he did do once or twice with Alice and her folks.

"You still with that hot-to-trot number?"

"Alice, yeah," Nick says, rubbing between his eyes, unsure of how to reel the conversation back in.

But then Nina circles back around. "Phil's number," she says after another prolonged exhale. "I've got it right here on the fridge. I don't remember anything anymore. Not even my son's number. You got a pen?"

He looks around. He doesn't have a pen. He puts down the phone and rushes over to the bar and asks Gibson the bartender if he can borrow one. Gibson tosses him a cheap promo pen that reads DR. DICK VOLLUCCI, CHIROPRACTOR. Nick snatches up a cocktail napkin and heads back to the phone booth and tells Nina he's ready. She gives him the number. He writes it down, runs it by her to make sure it's correct, and thanks her. She groans and tells him to say hi to Ava and ask her to stop by for coffee one day.

He hangs up the receiver and then picks it up again, pushes in another quarter, and dials Phil's number. He looks over at Antonina, bent over the machine, still playing that same quarter. A pinball wiz. As the phone rings, he readies a short speech.

But there's no answer.

He lets the phone ring twelve times before giving up because twelve's a number he likes. He's superstitious about it.

He goes over to Antonina, tucking Phil's number away in his pocket, and leans on the machine next to her.

"How'd it go?" she asks.

"Looks promising," Nick says. "I got his number from his mother. She's excited for me to talk to Phil. I couldn't get through to Phil yet, though. I'll try him back later."

"You're such a fucking loser," Antonina says, finishing her game by letting the plunger snap back and then returning to the table to drink her beer.

"Hey, that's not nice." Nick bristles at being called that. Whatever else Antonina is, and he can think of a few things she might be, she is clearly not a loser. She's like one of the girls he sees with boys across the street from Our Lady of the Narrows after three, running, kissing, swatting away hands. She's serious. Cool. That hair. Those overalls and boots. She's probably already, at seventeen, slept with twice as many people as he has in his life. She's probably done hard drugs. She probably tastes like sucking a mint in a downpour. He goes back to the table and sits across from her. "You don't even know me. How can you say that?"

"I don't need to know you."

"Are you drunk? Maybe I shouldn't have bought you that shot."

"Get me another one, and I'll tell you everything I can think of." Antonina practically shotguns the rest of her second beer. "Another beer, too."

"Yeah?" Nick scurries to the bar and buys two more shots and another beer. He's still got half of his first beer left.

He sets the shots on the table, and Antonina picks the first one up and pounds it, slamming the glass back down. He's about to go for the other shot, but she gets to that one first, too. She washes it down with some beer.

"Okay," she says. "Now I'm feeling loose."

"About Donnie and Big Time Tommy?"

"Are you trying to fuck me, Teacher Man?" Antonina says, looking and sounding pretty drunk. "Don't you have a girlfriend?"

Nick's thinking about his job and his reputation suddenly. He imagines Sonny Divino coming through the door with his own bat, finding out that Nick's getting his seventeen-year-old daughter loaded early as hell on a summer day. "I'm not. I didn't try anything."

Antonina stares over at the pinball machine. She's quiet for a few moments. "You can kiss me."

"What are you talking about?" Nick says.

"That's what you want. So, kiss me." She turns to him. Her mouth is a bright oval.

"Antonina." He scooches his chair closer. The truth is he would like nothing more than to kiss her. He's thinking, seriously, *Seventeen's plenty old, right?* He's thinking, *It's just a kiss.* He's not thinking how she might just be fucking with him. Girls at this age, they're mercurial. One minute, it's *You're trying to fuck me, loser.* The next, it's *Kiss me.* That doesn't change really. He leans in slowly. His breath smells bad. He can taste it. He bets she puts something on her lips that tastes sweet. He bets his whole mouth will soon taste like raspberry or vanilla. When his face is only inches from hers, he closes his eyes.

Antonina pulls away, laughs at him, swats at his chest. "See what a pathetic fuck you are?"

Nick's face goes hot. He feels stupid and irrelevant the way only a high school girl can make you feel. He remembers the feeling well from his high school days. Helen Passantino from Fontbonne. She made him crazy and then tore him apart. He's dumb, falling for Antonina's little act.

He doesn't say anything at first. And then, after thinking about it, he says, "Just tell me about that night in the schoolyard or Donnie working for Big Time Tommy. Anything. Please."

She stands up and flips Nick off. "Thanks for the drinks, asshole," she says. "Good luck with your movie." Then she walks out of Spanky's, and there's nothing he can do to stop her.

They keep pieces in the trunk of Sottile's car for just such occasions, squirreled away under a pile of rags and rope. Sottile's car is an '88 Cadillac Brougham, parked at a hydrant in front of Flash Auto. People know not to mess with it. They use Sottile's car more often than not these days because Donnie's lost his cop privileges. And Pags, well, his '82 Chrysler Imperial broke down last year and he's too lazy to have it fixed.

They get in the car, Donnie riding shotgun, Pags in the back.

"What do you think?" Pags says to Donnie.

"This Duke's what, in his sixties?" Donnie says. "How much trouble could he be?"

"I knew a guy, sixty-seven, his name was Johnny Christmas Lights," Sottile says. "He got that name because he was the master of doing his house up for Christmas. Dyker Heights, you know? Those big displays. Johnny owned a pork store in Long Island City. He was fit. Did martial arts, I don't know the kind exactly. Aikido or whatever. These two mooks tried to rob him when he was closing one day. Sawed-off shotguns, ski masks, the works. What's Johnny Christmas Lights do?"

"What?" Pags says.

Sottile demonstrates while driving. "Front-of-the-head strike to one, *bam*. Chest thrust to the other, *bang*. These little shits are on the floor, writhing around, can't breathe. Johnny Christmas Lights grabs the shotguns, sweeps these guys out the door like sawdust. Sixty-seven he was at that point in time."

"Fuck are you saying?" Donnie asks.

"I'm saying, don't underestimate this Duke. I don't want to get clipped by some loose-cannon golden-ager because I took him for granted."

Donnie shakes his head. "There's no such person as Johnny Christmas Lights," he says.

"You don't believe me he's real?" Sottile asks. "He's dead now, but he was one hundred percent a real guy. Ask around."

They drive over to where Duke lives on West Ninth Street between Highlawn and Avenue S, parking at another hydrant. Duke's house has weather-beaten blue siding, flaky shingles on the roof, sagging blue gutters, a front porch with rotting beams, and a fenced-in yard scattered with plastic shopping bags. Donnie takes it in. The plastic bags look like they're growing there, white stringy weeds among the dust and dirt.

They go to the trunk, pop it, and get the pieces, Donnie and Pags looking around before tucking them into their waistbands, Sottile dropping his to the blacktop before recovering it by awkwardly stooping with a groan.

"Let's fucking do this," Sottile says, and then he erupts into a coughing fit.

"You gonna have a heart attack on the way in?" Donnie says.

"I'm good," Sottile says.

They walk in the front gate, trying to be as quiet as possible, Donnie leading the way. His hand is at his side, ready to draw. They climb five steps to the porch, and Donnie scopes out the windows. Blinds drawn, no obvious action inside that he can tell.

Pags instinctively thumbs the bell.

"Fuck you doing?" Donnie says.

"Ringing the bell," Pags says. "We gonna just stand here like a bunch of citrulli?"

From inside, a woman calls out: "Who is it?"

"Census Bureau!" Pags says, with joy in his voice.

Donnie shakes his head. "Who's gonna open the door for that?" he says in a whisper.

There are two doors. A screen door—the screen battered around the edges, several holes covered with clear tape—and the inside door, made of heavy wood, a curtained window in the center of it. Donnie reaches out and tries the screen door, but it's locked.

An old woman peeks out from behind the curtain. Donnie can't make out much about her yet, but she's got a grizzled face and a shock of white hair screwed on her head. She gives them the once-over. He wonders if she saw him reach out and try the handle on the screen door.

"Census Bureau, huh?" the woman says.

"You Miss O'Malley?" Donnie asks.

"I'm a person living in this house, and you're ringing my goddamn bell."

"We'd like to have a word with you and your brother."

"That so?"

Donnie's hand goes to his waistband. He's secure knowing the piece is there. With Big Time Tommy's warning, he's not sure what to expect. A bullet could come whizzing through the glass any second and catch him in the throat. He moves off to the side a little, figures he'll let Pags or Sottile take the hit if that's the way it goes down.

But the heavy wooden door is flung open from the inside, and the woman is standing there behind the screen. She's in a rainbow muumuu and fuzzy slippers. Her skin is tough. She has a pack of cigarettes tucked in the sleeve of the muumuu. She's smiling a wild smile. "Come on in," she sings. "The water's nice. The sharks don't bite."

Donnie's spooked by her singing. The words sound like a theme song for a TV show he's never seen, but he's pretty sure she's just making them up.

She unlocks the screen door and continues her song: "Come on in. Take a seat. We've got apples. We've got meat."

"What the fuck?" Pags says.

Donnie grabs the handle and opens the screen door slowly.

They follow her inside, down a cluttered hallway, into an even more cluttered and somehow lopsided kitchen. The linoleum on the floor is red, cracked in places, edged with tumbleweeds of dust. The table is covered in folded-open napkins, used in place, it seems, of a proper tablecloth. A cuckoo clock hangs from a peg on the wall; it's not wound up, a spring having erupted from the bottom, dangling there. The ceiling is corkboard. The windows over the sink are closed. There isn't an AC in sight. It's hot in the little kitchen.

"Have a seat," the woman says. "I'm Vera, by the by. Lived in this dump my whole goddamn life."

Donnie, Pags, and Sottile sit on wobbly wooden chairs around the table.

"Where's your brother?" Donnie asks. "Duke's his name, right?"

She points to the back of the house. "He's in the shitter. Usually takes about an hour in there. I says to him, I says, 'Don't your legs fall asleep, okay?' He just shrugs. A man will sit on a can until he's blue in the face, that's the only thing I've learned in this stupid life. You want some Entenmann's?"

"We're good," Donnie says.

She trudges over to the refrigerator, opens the door, and narrates what she sees: "Duck sauce, old yogurt, month-old cold cuts, canned carrots, an Egg McMuffin. Shit. I don't even have the crumb cake I offered. Duke must've eaten it. That's why he's in there, shitting up a storm. He's got an uneasy tum-tum."

"Can you go get your brother?" Pags asks.

"I'm not getting within ten feet of that bathroom door," Vera says.

"We've got some business with him."

"Census Bureau, you said."

"Sure. Right. Counting heads."

A voice comes booming from the back of the house: "Who the hell you talking to out there?"

Vera yells back: "Census Bureau!"

"Census Bureau, my balls!" A toilet is flushed, and a door whines open loudly. Heavy footsteps follow.

Donnie looks at Pags and Sottile, letting them know they should be ready for anything.

Duke comes through a dark doorway at the back of the kitchen. He's squat and heavy. A brutal stink coasts on the air behind him. He's wearing clothes like he's in a Western. Ten-gallon hat. Shitkicker boots with spurs. A shirt with snap buttons. Jeans and a shiny belt buckle with his name embossed on it. Gunbelt around his hips, an antique-looking six-shooter strapped in a holster there, bullets tucked in little loops on the side of the belt. He's even got that John Wayne strut. But when he talks, it's the thick, ugly voice of the neighborhood.

"Fuck you little snatches want?" he says.

"Holy shit, a real Brooklyn cowboy," Pags says.

"You're with Ficalora, and you got the balls to come in my house?" He turns to his sister. "Vera, you've gotta use your bean. These shitbirds ain't Census Bureau. They're Ficalora's goons."

Vera shrugs apologetically. "It's all the same to me."

"You owe, you owe," Donnie says to Duke. "You work for Mr. Natale, right? You know how it goes."

"I say who I owe," Duke says.

"Let's talk reasonable, okay? Al più potente ceda il più prudente. You know what that means? 'Better bow than break.' Just give us the ten large, and we'll be on our way."

Duke's hand hovers over his piece. "Get out of my house, you fucking guinea."

Donnie leaps up and pushes back from the table. In an instant, he's jumping at Duke, toppling him to the ground, knocking off his stupid-ass hat. He takes out his own piece and clocks Duke in the side of the head with the grip. Duke is flat on his back, a pained look on his face. He's not even trying for his piece. He's an old man who's playing dress-up, that's it. Donnie can't believe Big Time Tommy took the threat seriously. Vlad must have a real streak of limp-wrist in him too, like Sottile.

"Where'd you find this fucking getup?" Donnie says. "Some mail-order catalog?"

Duke, stunned, doesn't respond.

"That's where he got it all, yep," Vera says. She's standing away from the action.

"You go around disrespecting Big Time Tommy Ficalora?" Donnie says to Duke. "Where you get the balls for that? You're gonna pay up or I'm gonna drop you off in Brownsville dressed like this. You'll fucking wish I shot you. Where's the dough?"

Duke groans.

Donnie hits him again with the grip of the gun. A cut opens over the old cowboy's bushy right eyebrow. "Where's the dough?" Donnie asks again, his voice restrained.

"It's under the sink," Vera says. "Don't hurt him anymore."

Donnie leans over and strips Duke's gun from the holster on his belt. It looks like the kind of dipshit piece that would've probably exploded in his hand. He tosses it to Pags and then scrambles over to the sink, flinging open the cabinet beneath the dirty chrome basin. Two boxes of Depends are stuffed under there among bottles of dish soap and rusty pipes and blooming bunches of plastic Pathmark bags.

"In the boxes," Vera says.

"You shouldn't have let them in," Duke says to his sister. "I told you not to answer the door. I told you let me answer the door."

"Sometimes I get sick of not answering the door," Vera says.

Donnie pulls the diaper boxes out from under the sink and opens the flaps. There's more than ten large in there. A lot more.

They're splayed out naked on the brown-and-gold rug on Donna's living room floor, Donna curled against him, listening to a record by someone named Garland Jeffreys who Mikey's never heard of. The record is called *Ghost Writer*. Donna says it's one of her favorites. The song that's playing now is "New York Skyline."

"You like it?" Donna asks.

"It's really good," Mikey says.

Donna sings along with it under her breath for a moment, something like, "Hindsight, foresight, sometimes we've got no love at all. New love, true love, sometimes we've got no sight at all." It fits the moment, and that's why she's singing it. She's got a nice voice, he can tell, even though her singing is only a whisper. The song sounds like feelings he's had that he can't name, just riding the subway or walking around the city. He likes when songs hit him that way.

He sure wasn't expecting this to happen with Donna, for it to go this far this fast. Maybe that jacket of his old man's is a good luck charm.

When Donna had first taken off her clothes, she kept talking about how she was ashamed of her old body, how it had been a long time since anyone else had seen her naked, and how it felt wrong. He said she looked beautiful, which is sometimes a thing you just say to a girl, but he meant it. Her body has a wisdom to it. He's never seen anything else of the sort. He thinks of the word *natural*, like her body's been through the things it's been through, giving birth and grieving for Gabe especially, and that's the purpose of a body, after all. To live. To wear down from living. If anyone should be ashamed, he'd told her, it should be him, with his nothing body, his hairy shoulders and back. She'd laughed and touched the swirls of dark hair on his shoulders. Her discomfort faded quickly.

He's also realizing that his body has never had that sense of purpose, that he'd been trying to give it purpose when he had his chin tattooed and those gauges put in his ears. Never, that is, until now. Until his body was with her body.

It was, Mikey's thinking, the best it's ever been. New in some unexpected way. While they were sitting up against the couch, Donna on top of him, one of her hands on his shoulder and the other on the arm of the couch, he'd seen something in her face he'd never seen before. Her eyes closed, biting her lower lip, the expression of pleasure was absolutely and totally real. That look was the kind of thing that could make you love someone forever, and it had set his mind wandering. There could be more of this, a life with Donna and her records. He feels like he's known her for a long time already.

"I can't remember the last time I was so happy," Donna says now, and then she claps her hand against her forehead.

He watches the way her body resonates from the vibration of the touch.

"I shouldn't say that," she continues.

"Why?" Mikey asks.

"It's too much pressure. On you. On me."

"I'm really happy, too. Just so you know."

He can't see her face, but he feels her smile. "Life still has some surprises up its sleeve, I guess," she says.

It strikes Mikey as such an innocent, beautiful thing to say. He's thinking, *People aren't impulsive enough. They don't open themselves up to times like this enough.* That's one thing New Paltz taught him. *Be open. Go where you're guided.* "You'll come with me, right?" he says.

"Where?" Donna says.

"My birthday dinner."

"I don't know."

"Please."

"I'd need to take a quick shower and get dressed. I can't meet your mother looking like this." She pauses. "Do you think she'll be able to tell? Maybe it's a bad idea."

Mikey doesn't really give too much of a fuck what his mother thinks. In fact, he knows she will not be happy about it, and he doesn't mind the thought of seeing her sweat, wondering what the hell he's doing with a woman twice his age. He knows where his mother's mind will go: Donna's taking advantage of him, using him. He doesn't want to put Donna in a bad spot, but he likes—and has always liked—the idea of challenging his mother into new ways of being. The reckless son's refrain: *Deal with it.*

The first side of the record ends. Donna gets up, one arm hugging her chest. He watches as she tenderly places the tonearm back in its cradle, flips the record, drops the needle carefully. Standing there over the turntable, she's a painting. It's a moment Mikey will hold on to.

Donna disappears into her bedroom first, closing the door behind her, and then the bathroom within the bedroom. He hears her turn on the shower, the clanging pipes, the full thrust of the water. He pictures her in the shower. He wonders what she's thinking. He wonders if she's worried he didn't use a condom. Do women worry about that at thirty-nine? Maybe she's on the pill from before or maybe she had her tubes tied. It wasn't smart, but it's nothing to stress about right now. He's always been lucky before. He imagines having a child with her. When their child is twenty-one, he'd be forty-two and she'd be sixty.

He goes into the kitchen and grabs some paper towels, wiping himself off. He finds his clothes and gets dressed, even putting his father's jacket back on. He sits and listens to Garland Jeffreys sing about being wild in the streets. The shower runs for a while.

When Donna comes back out, her hair wet, she's wearing a floral dress. It's tan and cream with brown patterns and brown buttons down the front. It's got two slits on the bottom. The back is cinched with ties. She's wearing brown flats on her feet that match the dress. "I'm sorry I took so long," she says. "I had to shave my legs."

"It's okay," he says. "I like your dress."

"I got it a few years ago, before Gabe died. I've never even worn it. It's just been sitting in my closet."

"Maybe you bought it for today without even knowing it."

She smiles, going over to the record player, shutting it, and putting the Garland Jeffreys album back in its sleeve. "Maybe. I like thinking things like that. I like thinking I was doing something for a day I didn't even know— couldn't possibly have known—was coming."

The walk back to Mikey's house is slow. They walk the way people walk when they've been intimate but they're still getting to know each other. Each step is measured. Mikey's considering things he's never looked at before. Iron gates with red, rusty points. Drooping mailboxes. Skinny sidewalk trees. Old cars under tarps. Cats in windows. Ads for manicure joints and car service joints. Toppled tin garbage cans. Signs for new Chinese places. Tags thrown up on bus stops and telephone poles. Donna seems to be doing the same thing, running her hand against whatever they pass. Chain link fences. The bristly branches of front yard bushes. The red brick of an apartment building.

They count Virgin Mary statues. On one block alone, there are twenty in varying states of weather-beaten decay. A couple are behind glass, protected from the elements.

On his block finally, Mikey points to his house, the house where he grew up, the house he left a few years ago and is back living in now.

Donna stops in her tracks. "This is a bad idea," she says.

"It's fine," Mikey says, but he knows she's right. He's instigating his mother. Maybe he's looking to give her a reason to challenge him.

"I don't know your mother from school or anything, do I?"

"She went to Lafayette."

A look of concern passes across Donna's face. "So did I. How old is she?"

"Forty-six. Rosemarie Baldini."

"What's her maiden name?"

"Russo."

"I don't know her, I don't think. Maybe I'll recognize her. Maybe she'll recognize me."

"Come on," Mikey says, taking her by the hand. Her hand is soft, like she's just rubbed it with lotion. The red polish on her nails is chipped. There's a blue vein that pulses from her middle knuckle to the edge of her wrist. "Don't be scared."

Walking up the steps to the porch, Mikey can sense that his mother's in the hallway, waiting for him to appear at the front door. He lets go of Donna's hand. As he goes to ring the bell, the door opens, and his mother's standing there, harried. She comes out onto the porch, letting the door close behind her. She's wearing a black blouse with gold sequins and the slacks she usually wears to church, dressed for his birthday dinner.

"Where have you been?" his mother asks, her eyes not even seeming to acknowledge Donna's presence yet.

"I'm not that late," Mikey says. "Uncle Alberto's not here?"

"He couldn't stay." Now his mother's eyes move to Donna. She takes in the floral print dress, the brown flats, the dark hair streaked with gray. "Who the hell are you?"

Donna puts out her hand. "I'm Donna Rotante."

"I know you?" His mother doesn't stick her hand out to shake.

"No, I don't think so. I'm a friend of Mikey's."

"'A friend of Mikey's'?"

"Ma, Donna's my guest," Mikey says.

His mother is agitated, her neck bulging. "This is her, the girl you got all dressed up for this morning? She's no girl. She must be close to my age. What's this about?"

"Let's just go inside. It's my birthday. She's my guest." He takes Donna's hand again. He can feel that she's shaking.

His mother's eyes zoom in on the hand-holding. "This is a joke, right?" she says. "Uncle Alberto put you up to this? She's one of *his* girlfriends. You're having fun with me."

"This was a terrible idea," Donna says.

The way she says it, something registers in his mother's face. She knows now it's not fake, that Donna's with him. "Did you sleep with my son?" his mother asks. "How fucking old are you?"

Mikey can't think of a time he's heard his mother curse like that, except maybe once or twice in the heat of battle with his old man. "Ma," he says. "Don't be like that."

"'Don't be like that,' he says. My son's got it all figured out, let me tell you." She pauses, gives Donna the once-over again, keeps her eyes on her as she addresses Mikey: "Where'd you find this washed-up puttana, some street corner?"

Mikey was expecting trouble from his mother, discomfort and disappointment mostly, but not such cruelty. "Ma, what the fuck?" he says.

"Watch your mouth," she snaps back.

Mikey looks at Donna. He can tell she's about to cry. "I'm sorry," he says. "I didn't think she'd be like this."

"It's okay," Donna says. "I told you it wasn't a good idea. I'm gonna go."

His mother does something he could never in a million years have anticipated her doing. She spits on the ground in front of Donna and says, "Good riddance." Not fake-spits. Really does it. An act of total and utter disgust.

Donna shakes her hand loose of Mikey's and runs down the steps and out of the front yard. Mikey doesn't chase her. He knows she's going home. He knows he'll follow her there eventually. He's so angry he's almost calm.

"I can't believe you," he says to his mother.

"*You* can't believe me? You show up late, with a woman twice your age? I don't know where you come from, I really don't, you think you can act like that. How long's this been going on? Look at her. She's desperate. She's taking advantage of you. Use your head for once. You're twenty-one now."

"I'm so sick of you," Mikey says. He storms past her into the house.

"Come eat," she says.

He ignores her and heads straight for his room. He gets an old hiking backpack he bought in New Paltz out of his closet and fills it with underwear, socks, jeans, and T-shirts. He stuffs Gabe's paperbacks—which his mother had placed neatly on his bed—in there on top of the clothes.

He looks around and considers what else he needs, *really* needs. He's leaving. Not for a few nights. For good. That was the last straw. He doesn't need much else, he decides. Maybe just his toothbrush, toothpaste, and deodorant, which he finds stashed in his dresser drawer and zips away in the front pocket of his pack. He's going to go to Donna's, try to make amends, and then take it from there.

His mother comes into the room. "Where you think you're going now?" she asks.

"I'm leaving, and I'm not coming back this time," he says.

"Don't say that." His mother sits on his bed, thumbing the threadbare comforter. "Please don't say that."

"You need to have your own life." He slings the backpack over his shoulder and leaves the room, the house, and his mother without looking back. He can hear her behind him some of the way until, out of the yard, her cries fade, and she's the past. The sidewalk that he's on is the present. Donna's the future.

He walks with his head down, floating on his anger, feeling real purpose. He's going to go to Big Time Tommy. He's going to work off his father's debt for Big Time Tommy so he doesn't have the burden over him of leaving his mother with it. He doesn't want to see her again, but he also doesn't want her to wind up shot at her kitchen table. His plan is he's going to work until he makes more dough and then he's going to leave. Go someplace different. California, Canada, Mexico, who knows? He's going to, hopefully, stay with Donna until then. He's going to, hopefully, talk her into coming with him.

When he gets back to Donna's, he knocks gently, and she answers the door, mascara stitching her cheeks. She's been crying hard. "You're back?" she says.

"I'm sorry," he says. "It was my fault for putting you in that position. It made me realize that I can't stay there anymore. I can't stay here, in this fucking neighborhood, much longer either. You want to run away with me?"

She laughs the way a woman laughs after she's been crying. "Run away?"

"I don't know where yet. I need to square this debt my mother and I inherited—I won't get into that now. I need to make some money, and I know a way. But then I want to leave forever. I figure it'll take a few weeks, maybe longer. Maybe by fall, I can hit the road. Can I stay with you for a while? And, if you still like being with me, maybe you'll want to come along when I leave?"

Donna smiles, wipes her cheeks with the heels of her hands. "Come in," she says, her voice crumbly. "It was only a few minutes, but I missed you. I really did."

Ava pulls out of Flash Auto behind the wheel of the Olds Cutlass Ciera. It's clean on the inside. A piece of Palm Sunday palm is wrapped around the mount on the rearview mirror, and a St. Christopher medal is clipped to the visor on the passenger side. There's what looks like a cigarette burn in the fabric right under her thigh. It's the only thing wrong she can see.

She felt moved and surprised when Frankie just dangled the keys in front of her, no strings attached. He said that "Donnie P." was an okay guy in his book. He said it was a good thing too, because the part for her Nova was gonna take a couple of days longer than expected and he was glad that she wouldn't be stuck without a vehicle.

Ava grips the wheel tightly, turns carefully out of the lot onto Bath Avenue. She feels like she won something in a casino. Like she yanked a lever and coins poured out at her feet. She feels that low electric hum that comes with winning.

Where Don lives, it's not too far from here. She knows it's right across from P.S. 101, which is only a couple of blocks away.

She makes a U-turn at the corner and pulls back into the driveway at Flash, facing an open garage dock where a red Caddy is up on a lift. She leaves the engine on and runs back in to ask Frankie for Don's address.

"You don't know his address?" Frankie says, thumbing some grease from his hands onto the midsection of his blue jumpsuit.

"I told you," Ava says, "he's not my boyfriend."

"He must really like you." Frankie smiles, showing a smear of grease on his teeth. "Understandable."

"He's just trying to do a nice thing, I guess."

"Sure. You're gonna go say thanks, huh? Maybe show up in your birthday suit?"

Ava ignores the comment. She asks again for the address.

Frankie writes it down with a stubby golf pencil on the back of one of their business cards. "He's not far," Frankie says.

Ava nods and thanks him and goes back to her new car. She puts the business card in the ashtray.

Her thought is she'll go to Angelo's on Twenty-Fifth Avenue and get a box of pastries and cookies as a small way of saying thanks, and then come back to Don's and just ring the bell. He likes to drink. Maybe she should get him a bottle of something, too. Or maybe that's encouraging the wrong kind of behavior.

The car drives like a dream. It's not nearly as rickety as the Nova. It's been well-maintained. She wonders if it belonged to an old lady who hardly drove it and kept it in her driveway under a tarp and got the oil changed more than she needed to. Ava looks down at the mileage and confirms it. Barely fifty thousand miles.

She finds a spot at a meter on the corner of Twenty-Fifth Avenue off Eighty-Sixth Street. A B train headed back to Coney Island thunders by on the El, drowning the neighborhood in noise. She looks across the street at some kids playing basketball. They're sweating and running and yelling, but the yells are lost in the rumble. When the train finally passes, she hears the foul language the kids are using.

She ducks into Angelo's, and the girl behind the counter greets her. She picks out a nice assortment. Sfogliatelle, cannoli, sfinge, S cookies, a few rainbows and pignolis. The girl sprinkles some sugar on top, weighs the box, and ties it with baker's twine.

The sight of the baker's twine launches Ava into a new reverie. Anthony coming home with a box of sesame biscuits and savoiardi, her two favorites. She didn't have the girl put any in Don's box because she doesn't want to be tempted to eat any if he invites her in to join him for coffee or something. She loves that baker's twine. She used to love to watch Anthony cut it with his little yellow paring knife and then unravel it carefully. She liked to tie the twine around the tip of her finger until it became plump and red and she'd start wondering about the names for the lines on her hands and what they all meant. She'd loosen the string right when she felt like her circulation was about to be cut off, and Anthony would shake his head and say she could be a real whackjob sometimes. To her, that twine is one of the most beautiful things in the world.

She goes back out and gets in the car, placing the box from Angelo's on the passenger seat. She watches the boys playing basketball. One of the boys dunks and hangs from the rim. She pulls away from the curb and makes a left under the El. She picks up the business card and scans Don's address, memorizing it: 116 Bay Thirty-Fifth. She says it over and over in her head. She imagines herself knocking on the door with the box, Don surprised and thankful, telling her to come on in. Birthday suit. Frankie had some nerve.

Antonina is on her fire escape, feeling pretty drunk after the shots at Spanky's. She'd enjoyed fucking with Nick Bifulco—what a loser. She's not sure what to do now. Weird encounters with Mikey's mother and Nick are enough to derail her whole day. Her mom's still not home. She hopes Lizzie will call soon, though it's pretty early for Lizzie. Maybe they can go into the city. It'd be nice to go now, half-drunk, and head straight to the Keyhole Cocktail Lounge or Seven Bar, other places where she'll be gladly served, and just keep drinking. Or she hopes Mikey calls. She'd invite him over to talk about Nick. She wonders if he'd actually come. Probably not. Her bet is he doesn't even call. Maybe his mother won't even give him the note.

The phone in her room rings, and it surprises her. She goes to it, hoping for Mikey or Lizzie, unsure who else might be calling her. No way Nick got her number from somewhere.

She picks up after six rings. "Hello," she says, trying to sound mysterious, picturing her own lips close to the receiver like in a movie.

"It's me," Ralph says in a low, deep voice.

He's never called so early in the day. "What's up?"

"I just saw you out on your fire escape."

"You what?"

He talks in a whisper, his hand over the mouthpiece: "I'm at Donnie's. We lucked into something good. I've got a gift for you. For your future."

"I don't understand."

"Just meet me at our usual spot in an hour. I can't talk. I've gotta square things here—there's some drama right now—but I'll be there, and I'll give you what I've got for you. Okay?"

"Okay."

She hangs up and goes back out to the fire escape, bringing her Walkman with her this time, gazing down at Donnie's house. She can see into the kitchen slightly. She's seen Donnie sitting at the table there before, and she knows he's seen her. But she doesn't see Ralph now. She just sees a shaft of light hitting the linoleum.

She wonders what it could be that Ralph wants to give her. She wonders what makes her act the way she acts around Ralph as opposed to the way she acted with Nick. She guesses it's just that she could see through Nick and that Ralph's a mystery to her. Nick's just a loser who's stuck between youth and middle age. She saw the way he looked at her almost immediately. But Ralph's making a surrogate daughter of her. There's something sweet about that.

Headphones on now, she presses play. Lizzie's mix. Gang of Four's "Damaged Goods" picks up in the middle. She knows Patti Smith's "Because the Night" is next. She likes knowing the tape inside out, its familiar transitions, the track list in her blood.

Donnie's thinking that wannabe-cowboy Duke, in his position as book-keeper for Mr. Natale, had been skimming off the collections that came to him. Not too dissimilar from what Donnie was doing, ultimately. But Duke had been doing it on a larger scale, and Donnie has no idea how the hell he's gotten away with it. There's close to a hundred large in his diaper boxes.

Donnie, Pags, and Sottile are back at his house, going over what's turned into a major score. Donnie stopped for cigarettes on the way, and he's refilled his case. He's smoking now. He'd really been jonesing for one.

The money is laid out on the living room floor. But there's turmoil. His idea for the split is that the first ten goes to Big Time Tommy to cover the debt, and the rest they do fifty-forty. That's fifty percent for him, twenty each for Pags and Sottile. Which means he'd get fifty large and they'd get twenty each. Pags isn't happy about it, of course. They're scrapping in the living room, while Sottile's disappeared into the kitchen to probably call for a pedicure appointment or some shit. He won't cry over the twenty.

"Why do you deserve more?" Pags says.

"It was my discovery," Donnie says.

"Your discovery, my balls. This is bullshit."

"So, do something about it."

Pags, who was a Police Athletic League boxer before he turned donut-belly, lashes out with a quick jab and hits Donnie square in the center of his face, knocking the cigarette to the floor, his nose taking the brunt of it.

It hurts like hell. Donnie's gushing blood all over his shirt. "What the fuck?" he says, as he scrambles for a rag or an old shirt to jam under his nostrils. He settles for a lace doily on an end table next to the couch—something Donna dressed the house up with.

"I'm sorry," Pags says. "I meant to pull the punch."

"Could be you broke my fucking nose, shitmook."

"Jeez. I'm sorry, man. I am. You're really bleeding there."

Donnie scrambles for more doilies, a rag, anything. "Help me out. Find something I could use."

Pags scores a *Daily News* sitting on top of a pile of junk in the corner. He hands it to Donnie.

Donnie shrugs and uses the newspaper as best he can.

"You always put yourself first," Pags says to him, sitting on the couch, acting mopey and crushed. "You got no fucking loyalty. You were that way with Donna, too. The people who do for you, you don't look out for."

"You're saying what?" Donnie says, the back sports page knotted under his nose, catching drops of blood. "Why's my ex-wife's name in your mouth? I got no loyalty? I wasn't loyal, I would've cut you out of my life years ago. I need this moral-high-ground shit like I need a hole in my noggin."

Pags shakes his head.

The doorbell rings, the ding echoing through the house. "Now who the fuck is that?" Donnie says. He goes over to the window and draws back the curtain.

It's Ava, standing there with a white bakery box. She's wearing a gold blouse and neat black slacks and big earrings. She's got makeup on. She's primping a little, checking her hair with her free hand to make sure it's not poofy. He thinks of how he looks in his jeans and blood-splattered Old Glory shirt, his nose mashed.

Scanning the street, he sees the Olds Cutlass Ciera parked in a spot a couple of houses down. She's come to say thanks. She's brought cookies.

He should just let it go. Let her keep ringing and think he's gone even though his car is still there. Maybe she'll figure he went up to Eighty-Sixth Street for groceries or coffee. Maybe she'll leave him a note. Few hours, things'll settle down and he'll go to her.

Donnie lets the curtain whisper closed.

Ava rings the bell again.

Donnie walks out into the hallway and stands by the door, putting his hand up to it. He swears he can smell Ava. A good dose of the kind of perfume a woman like her should be wearing. Flowery. Powdery. He wants to smell it across a fancy dinner table where there's wine and brick-oven bread and veal marsala on clean white plates. He wants to smell it as he kisses behind her ears.

"Don, you in there?" Ava says. And then a long pause. She's so close he can hear her breathing. "Don? I just want to say thank you so much."

Something in her voice gets to him, and he opens the door with the chain on.

"Don?" she says again, peering in through the opening. "What happened to you?"

"Nothing," he says, taking the newspaper away from his nose and tossing it on the floor. The bleeding's stopped. "Now's not a good time. I'm sorry."

"I just wanted to say thank you." She holds up the box. "I got you some cookies and pastries. It's not much. What you did, getting this car for me, it was so thoughtful. And unnecessary." She motions to where the car's parked. "It's right there. It drives beautifully."

"It's not a junker," Donnie says. "I'm glad you like it. Use it in good health."

Ava smiles. "Were you in a fight?"

"Nothing too serious. Just some fisticuffs with a pal over a disagreement. He's still here, cooling down."

"Do you need anything? I can go to the store for you."

"It's the middle of the day. What happened to work?"

"I said to hell with work for once." Ava's smile growing wider. Mischievous. "I sweat blood for them over there. I deserve a break."

Donnie takes the chain off the door and then opens it just wide enough that he can slip out. He pulls it shut behind him. He doesn't want her to meet Pags or Sottile or to see the dough in the living room. He's standing close to her on the stoop.

She gasps. "Are you okay?" she says.

He throws his hands up. "Fine. Just took a good shot to the nose."

"You've got blood all over you."

"I'm fine. Here, let me take that off your hands." He snatches the box from her. He plucks at the string with his teeth.

"You shouldn't use your teeth," Ava says.

He chews through the string, unravels it, and then puts his face over the box, breathing deep. "These smell great. Been a long time since I had any of this. My parents loved savoiardi."

"They're my favorite, too."

"You didn't get any?"

"They were out."

He paws out a pignoli cookie and shoves it into his mouth whole. "Oh, goddamn," he says. "That's so good."

"You're just gonna eat them out here on the stoop? How about some coffee?"

"I'm sorry. I can't have you in there right now. It's my buddy. He's a mess. The place is a mess."

"I understand." Ava takes a step down.

"You smell good," Donnie says, letting the top of the box fall shut, the cookie worked to a paste in his mouth. "Better than the cookies."

Ava laughs a little. She takes another step down. "You could just come back to my house," she says. "I'll make coffee. If you want, I can clean up your face. I have hydrogen peroxide. I could even wash your clothes, try to get the blood out so it doesn't stain. I don't have a dryer, but I'll hang your jeans and shirt on the line, and you can wear something of Anthony's. I have bags full of his old stuff in the basement. I bet you're about the same size."

"You'd do that for me?"

"Sure. Of course."

"I've gotta say," Donnie says, "that's about the nicest offer I ever got. I could stand being cared for a bit." He looks back at the door, thinks about Pags and Sottile and all the dough. He thinks about Nick, who might just show his worthless mug at home while Ava's patting him down with cotton balls soaked in peroxide.

"That's a yes?"

He opens the box and grabs a sfinge, taking a monster bite, his shirt now dusted with powdered sugar and flakey pastry debris on top of the blood. "Let me just run inside for a sec. Wait here."

He goes back in and stuffs fifty grand in one of the boxes. "What are you doing?" Pags says. "Who's out there?"

"A friend of mine. I'm going with her."

"You're something else."

Sottile comes in from the kitchen and sees Donnie with the box and says to Pags, "Where's he going?"

Pags goes to the window, looks out at the stoop. "He's got some broad out there."

"And what're we supposed to do?" Sottile says, looking distracted. "I got things I gotta take care of."

"You take the ten and drop it in the office at Flash for Tommy," Donnie says to Sottile. And then to both of them: "Keep the twenty each for yourselves. Beyond that, I don't give a shit what you do or don't do."

"This fuck's something else," Pags says.

Donnie carries the box up to his bedroom, locking the door behind him. He pushes aside the throw rug, removes the loose length of floorboard, and buries the fifty grand there in the plastic-lined hole. It barely fits. Pags stays behind, he'll never sniff it out. Not that he'd have the balls anyway.

He thinks about changing clothes, but he likes the idea of going with Ava all bloodied up. He thinks about her pulling his softball shirt off over his head.

At the bottom of the stairs, Pags is waiting for him. "What the hell's going on?"

"I like her," Donnie says. "I'm going on a date."

"And the money?"

Donnie reaches out and gives Pags a gentle slap on the cheek. "Don't let the dough come between us, boyo. You got twenty large for doing nothing, zilch, jack shit. You already busted my nose as retribution. Hang out. Drink my booze. Celebrate."

"You're an evil bastard," Pags says, defeated.

Donnie goes outside, and Ava's still there, waiting for him. "I was getting worried," she says.

"Let's go," he says, a big smile on his bloody face.

This woman is poison, Rosemarie thinks.

She's sitting at the kitchen table, which she's set for two. The chicken parm is getting cold on the stove. She made the ravioli despite telling herself she should wait, and it's turned to mush. She's bitterly angry. She can taste the bitterness on her tongue.

A boy like Mikey, he's sensitive, impressionable. This woman, this *Donna*, she caught him at a time when he's especially fragile, pliable, and she's bending him to her will.

Mikey's always liked girls, but this is different. This middle-aged woman wore her agenda proudly on her face: Corrupt and destroy.

They were out there, women like that. Rosemarie had seen them her whole life. She'd had to beat them off Giuseppe with a broom in the first years of their marriage. Temptresses. Puttane.

Forget the ones just after a buck. She could at least understand their motives in going after well-off guys.

It's the others who truly rattle her. The ones—like the bar tramps who pursued Giuseppe—who revel in breaking up marriages, in causing chaos. The ones—like Donna—who want to steal the sons of good women, to make something else entirely of them, to feed off their youth.

Vampire bitch, that's what this Donna is.

Rosemarie says a prayer and crosses herself.

Donna Rotante. She knew a Rotante back when she was a kid. Skip Rotante. They called him Skids. He ate glue and got in fights in the school-yard. She wonders if Donna is related.

She keeps her phone book in the hallway closet. She goes there now, retrieves it, and lugs it back, folding it open at the empty end of the table and searching the *R*s.

What was Mikey thinking? He must have known how he would devas-tate her. And leaving like that. He must've come home with this old tramp wanting an excuse to walk out. She should be as mad at him, but she knows he's under a spell.

How do you break a spell like that?

She finds a *Rotante, D* on Eighty-Fourth Street a few columns into the *R*s. She takes note of the address. She's going to confront this woman and bring Mikey home.

How she'll do it exactly is the question. She considers, first, a lie that isn't that far-fetched: Big Time Tommy is on her heels, and she needs Mikey's help desperately. Or, even better, she brings the note from Antonina Divino and exaggerates the conditions of their encounter. Maybe she can lure Mikey away from this washed-up puttana with a young pink-haired beauty.

She's being crazy.

He packed a bag, so what?

Mikey seeing Donna and bringing her to dinner was simply an impulse thing. Rosemarie overreacted. She was rude. As a mother, she should've learned by now that it's better to let things like this run their course natu-rally. Mikey likes the exoticism of an older woman, that's it. How long could it possibly last? A week, a month? Then the luster fades. He sees Donna as not that different from her, his mother, and he's skeeved out. And all of this for nothing. Maybe she should feel bad for Donna. Maybe this is what sad women do to try to find meaning in their lives. They don't find it in church, so they try to recapture some kind of youthful recklessness.

No, no, no.

Now she's being too nice. This Donna is a snake, no doubt.

She thinks of the gun her brother brought her just a little while ago for protection. Things happen for a reason—she believes that. Of all days, he chooses this one to express his concern over Big Time Tommy by arming her? Say she goes to this Donna with the gun. Say she shows it to her. Nothing too over the top. Put a good scare into her.

But what if Mikey's there? She's going to point it at him?

Maybe he deserves that kind of lesson. Maybe he deserves to have some common sense scared into him. She's his mother. She's looking out for his best interest. She's trying to steer him away from trouble, trying to teach him how to survive in this world. She has to threaten him to bring him home, where's the sin? A little hard love is what he needs.

She's hidden the gun in a hatbox in Giuseppe's closet on a shelf stocked with old cameras and electric razors wrapped in twisty cords and bottles of scotch he got for gifts and never opened. She takes the box down and brings it to the table and sits there with it in front of her. Eventually, she pushes aside the lid and looks at the gun.

She's being crazy. She's being her own kind of dumb.

Still. Sometimes a woman has to do things she never could've anticipated. She has to protect what's hers. She has to fight.

She touches the handle of the gun, traces her finger over the trigger and then the muzzle. She'll do what she has to do.

Ava shows Don inside. She turns the light on in the kitchen and slips off her shoes by the door. She leaves her purse there, too. She places the box from Angelo's on the table, the top lifting open a bit so that the paper and the sugared folds of pastries are visible.

"Where's your son?" Don asks, trailing behind her, looking around at all the quiet things.

"God knows," Ava says. "He took off from school. I'm sorry he had so much to drink last night."

"He came to see me afterward, you know that?"

Ava, on her way into the bathroom, pauses. "He what?"

"He came by my house."

"I didn't know. I'm sorry he bothered you. He gets these big ideas in his head."

"He was encouraging me to see you again."

"He was?"

Ava goes into the bathroom and gathers together an armload of first aid supplies. Hydrogen peroxide, cotton balls, Q-tips. She comes back out and Don's sitting at the table, leaning back in his chair. She puts down the supplies next to the box of pastries and cookies.

"What now?" Don says.

"I'll put on coffee," Ava says. "And then why don't you go in the bathroom and take off your clothes? I'll throw them in the wash and get you something to change into."

Don nods. "You're like an angel from heaven."

"You're the angel. Swooping down and saving me on the Belt. Getting that Olds. At first, I wasn't sure, I didn't think it was right to accept, but it was very nice of you."

"It's nothing."

At the stove, Ava gets the coffee started. She fills the percolator with water, scoops some Folgers into the basket, turns the gas on. She likes the way the flame lights up the condensation on the bottom of the percolator.

When she turns around, Don's standing, pulling his bloody softball shirt off over his head. Ava gets a plastic Waldbaum's bag and collects the shirt without touching it. She looks at him without his shirt on. Hair on his chest. Muscly arms. A little paunch. His jeans don't have nearly as much blood on them, but there's some. He has to take his boots off to slip out of his jeans. Ava looks away.

"Thanks for washing these," Don says, grunting as he struggles to step out of his jeans. He bunches them up and stuffs them in the bag with the shirt.

"Who was it you got in a fight with?" Ava says.

"My friend Pags," Don says. "Tony Pagnanelli."

She steals a quick glance of him in his boxers. He sits back down, his arms up on the table. His elbows are dry, rough. She thinks about putting cream on them for him.

"I'm going to go put the wash on," she says. "Watch the coffee. If it starts to perk, lower it so it doesn't go over."

"Sure," he says.

"Sorry. I don't mean to be bossy."

"I can handle the coffee." He smiles.

"When I get back, I'll clean up your face."

"Thanks, Nurse Ava."

She goes down the hall and opens the basement door. She flicks on the light. The stairs are rickety. She holds the railing as she descends, clutching the bag.

At the washing machine, she takes out the clothes and dumps them in. She crumples up the bag and sets it in a white basket off to the side. She starts running the water. She puts in a cup of detergent. She wonders if she should've put stain stuff on all the blood. She digs into the cold water and pulls out the shirt first and then the jeans, and she dangles them over the edge of the machine so they're dripping on the floor. She pauses the cycle. She takes down the orange bottle of stain spray and soaks them both and then stands there and waits, letting it go to work. Then she throws them back in and lets the cycle resume, the sound of whooshing water filling the basement. She closes the lid.

In the far corner of the basement, she finds the big black leaf bags full of Anthony's old clothes. On her knees now, she works at the knot on the first bag. She gets it open and reaches in, pulling out a pair of flannel pajama pants. She holds them to her nose. Smell of mothballs. She remembers Anthony walking around wearing only these pants and his slippers. That was the last time a man who wasn't Nick walked around without a shirt on in this house.

She digs farther into the bag and finds a matching shirt. Anthony never wore it that she remembers. It's no good for Don. Next is a faded pair of Levi's, also hung with the stink of mothballs. They'll work. She folds them neatly and puts them aside. She reaches back in and hits a run of T-shirts. Mostly shirts Anthony acquired at various bar benefits or charity drives at the Knights of Columbus. Some from the casinos. She finds one that looks like it'll fit Don well and isn't too worn out. It says ATLANTIC CITY in red script. Under that, there's a slot machine lined with fat 7s, a roulette wheel, a pair of dice showing snake eyes, and an ace-high royal straight flush of hearts. She folds it and puts it on top of the jeans.

It's been a while since she went through Anthony's things like this.

She searches in the bag a bit more, thumbing the well-worn fabric of an old work shirt and touching the gold buttons on a blazer he wore to weddings and funerals. She finds balled-up socks and frayed plaid boxers and white briefs with holes around the band.

She thinks again of rubbing cream on Don's elbows.

She closes the bag, tying it off as snugly as she can, and she stands. She picks up the clothes for Don and heads back upstairs to the kitchen, shutting the light behind her.

She finds him hovering over the stove, watching the coffee.

"Looked like it was about to go over," he says, "so I lowered it."

"Thanks," she says. "It makes a big mess when it boils over." He's practically naked at her stove. She thinks about Nick walking in right now. Her eyes find the floor for a second and then his feet, his legs.

"You got some clothes for me there?" Don says.

"I do," she says. "Let's get you cleaned up first, though. Sit."

He sits down.

She goes to work, dabbing around his nose with cotton balls soaked in peroxide. She uses dry cotton balls to soak up the blood. "You poor thing," she says.

"It's nothing," he says. "Bastard just tagged me right on the nose."

She's almost straddling him. She's looking down at his chest. Peroxide mixed with blood has made a pink froth and run down onto his stomach.

"You got any music?" he says. "It's so quiet."

"Not really. I can put the radio on. Nick has some tapes somewhere."

"You don't like music?"

"Oh, I don't know. I don't really listen to much. I like what Anthony liked. Dion. Frankie Valli. Sometimes it's nice to hear the Beatles. What do you like?"

"Bon Jovi. You know them?"

"Not really."

"I saw them in '87 at MSG on the *Slippery When Wet* tour. They were great. That tape and *New Jersey*, I like those a lot. I had them around for a while. Probably still in my car. I don't listen to music much anymore. I used to."

"*Slippery When Wet*?"

"Right. 'Livin' on a Prayer.' 'You Give Love a Bad Name.' You don't know those?"

She shrugs. She throws out some of the used cotton balls. She goes over and turns the radio on. WCBS. Oldies. They're playing "Seasons in the Sun." Reception is crackly. She remembers when it was big in the mid-'70s.

"I don't know this song," Don says.

"It was a hit," Ava says.

The coffee is perking at a steady low hum on the stove. She shuts the gas.

"I feel better," Don says. "Thank you."

"Do you want to put on your new clothes? We can have some coffee with cookies and pastries."

"I'd rather you take your clothes off."

Ava spurts out a laugh. "What?"

"Take your clothes off. Start with your blouse."

"Excuse me. You've misunderstood my intentions."

"Come on. Here I am." He sits up and pulls down his boxers and kicks out of them and he's naked on her chair in her kitchen with the smell of coffee in the air and Anthony's old clothes piled nearby.

"You're hurt. You must've gotten a good knock on the head."

"I'm serious."

"This is why you bought me the car?"

"No. Don't say that. I like you. You like me. Look at me. I'm a lover, not a fighter."

She gives him the once-over. His lower half is obscured by the table. His nostrils are edged with caked blood. She feels like she might bust out laughing. It's irrational. She's embarrassed, not scared. "Get dressed."

"Take off your blouse and pour me some coffee," he says. "Please. I want to see you walk over to me in your bra with a cup balanced on a saucer. That's my dream right now."

"You're nuts."

"I say what's on my mind."

"And what if Nick were to walk in?"

"He's not walking in."

Don's right, whether he knows why or not. Nick's off chasing some fantasy. Ava thinks back to the Wonder Wheel and the risk she took there and how she felt afterward. Would it be so wrong to give herself over to Don, to let loose a little, to have fun? She and Anthony had fun together. They played their little games. He even bought her a vibrator one time. He got it at some adults-only shop in the city. After seeing a movie one night at the Benson Twins, he gave it to her wrapped in a nice box like it was a diamond bracelet. She opened it and felt shocked. She remembers putting her hand over her mouth. She remembers him saying how he wanted to watch her use it. She felt silly, that bullety thing buzzing between her legs, but he seemed to like watching her with it. She was sprawled on their bed. He sat in the corner on her mother's old sewing bench. This happened more than a few times. Nick was in high school and out most weekend nights. She started to really enjoy it. Anthony started to think she was enjoying it too much, more than she enjoyed him or even him watching, and he tossed it unceremoniously in the dumpster of the Mobil station on the corner of their block. She's thinking of that now, and she's thinking, *Games are okay. Games are what humans do. Let yourself have fun.* What the hell. She starts to unbutton her blouse.

"There you go," Don says.

She feels her face flush. She slips out of her blouse. She stands there in her bra and slacks. The radio shifts to a loud, whoopy-voiced announcer. He's saying things about the song that just played or the song that's about to play. She pours Don a cup of coffee in one of her nice china cups and clanks it down on the matching saucer. She carries it over to him slowly, methodically, and his eyes take her in so fully that she feels alive in some new way.

Twentieth Century was a disco club back in the neighborhood's *Saturday Night Fever* days. Now, from the outside, it's just a vacant brick building on Bath Avenue nestled between a barbershop and a three-family house, the ghost of a flashy sign looming over its doorway. Big Time Tommy owns the place and, by all accounts, just kind of stretches out in there, using it as a base of operations. Mikey's never been inside, but he's heard things. That there's a stained-glass dance floor. That a who's who of celebrities and wannabes used to hang out and get high at the joint in its prime. That once a woman hanged herself from a disco ball and that she haunts Big Time Tommy's crew.

When Mikey rings the buzzer, he's not sure what to expect. He's got a speech prepared, about settling his father's debt first and foremost, about keeping his mother out of harm's way. He won't advertise the fact that he's trying to make enough dough to take off and start a new life somewhere else. He's just glad that Donna was so open to him, so willing to ignore what had happened with his mother and settle into something new.

Dice opens the door and smiles when he sees Mikey, his upper lip even more purple and swollen than it was the day before. He calls over his shoulder, "The kid's here!"

Big Time Tommy's voice bounces back from the darkness of the club: "Freak Show Mikey? Bring him in."

Mikey follows Dice inside.

The club is wide-open and dank, almost feels like a warehouse. Pretty high ceilings. No glass dance floor remains that Mikey can see, but some of the far walls are mirrored, if layered with dust. Narrow standing tables are set up around carpeted beams that run from floor to ceiling, donuts of polished wood where people were once meant to set drinks. A drooping disco ball is suspended from a heavy-duty cord over the center of the room. It looks like a lone planet left from some sort of sad solar system display. It doesn't reflect any light because there's no light for it to reflect, but many of the facets no longer have a mirror surface, and the disco ball—which must have once seemed magnificent to dancers below—is patched with dark, empty spots.

Big Time Tommy is sitting at a desk with a half-eaten hero on white butcher's paper in front of him. Mikey can see that it's broccoli rabe and sausage.

No one else is around, as far as he can tell.

"This is kismet," Big Time Tommy says, munching on a heel of bread, a stringy piece of broccoli rabe hanging over his lip onto his chin. "You know from kismet? Meant to fucking be, Freak Show."

Mikey wastes no time: "I want to work for you. I want to clear my father's debt."

"That's very good news." Big Time Tommy pauses, plucks a piece of sausage from between the pieces of bread, and jaws it noisily. "But there's now much, much more to talk about."

"What do you mean?"

"Get our friend a chair," Big Time Tommy says to Dice.

Dice grabs a folding chair that's leaning against the wall next to the front door and brings it over to Mikey, popping it open and setting it close to Big Time Tommy's desk. Mikey sits.

"I've got a crisis," Big Time Tommy says. "And you, well, you've got demons you didn't even know you had. I'm here to lay it out. We can help each other."

"I just want to clear my father's debt. Maybe make some extra money."

Big Time Tommy holds up his hand. "I understand. But your old man, kid, he was the victim of independent antics. I said one thing, but another thing happened. I've covered for said antics in the interest of my own name, but those responsible no longer deserve the reprieve I've granted them."

Mikey feels lost. "I don't get it."

"The ex-cop that fucked you up, Donnie Parascandolo, he and his pals, Pags and Sottile, they're on my payroll. My issue now is I've discovered they've been skimming off their collections, culminating in the misguided decision to take a haul they weren't anticipating from piece-of-shit Duke O'Malley, who turned out to be a more accomplished skim artist, and to keep it for themselves. I got the report straight from Mr. Natale, who Duke's been ripping off. Short of it is, Donnie and his guys fucked me."

"Again, I'm lost here."

"Two years ago, that night you got clocked with the bat, your old man died."

Mikey leans forward.

Big Time Tommy continues: "It was Donnie who did it. Pags and Sottile were there, but it was Donnie who dumped your old man off the bridge. It was *not* on my say-so. I had them going after him the next day. I had them kneecapping him, breaking an arm, something, anything to get him to pay up. Way it goes. I did not okay them clipping him. That was Donnie acting independently. I don't know why. I don't know if the beef with you set him off. I was not, in no way, interested in making a widow of your mother and leaving you without a father. I liked your old man. That's why I've been trying to go easy on you and Rosemarie."

"Donnie Parascandolo killed my father?" Mikey says, unable to wrap his head around it. If someone had asked him to draw a line from Donnie to Giuseppe, he wouldn't have been able to, because there was no connection to make. You can live in the neighborhood your whole life and not know thousands and thousands of people. Mikey had never figured the incident with Donnie for anything more than coincidence.

"Listen, I'm no psychiatrist. Donnie's kid killing himself really fucked him up. I've got sympathy for the guy—to a point. But now he's gonna pay. And I'm giving you the opportunity to get the revenge you deserve."

Mikey's head is spinning so hard, he almost missed it. *Donnie's kid killing himself really fucked him up.* Can't be. Can't fucking be.

"Donnie's kid killed himself?" Mikey asks. "What was his name?"

"Don't get soft out of the gate," Big Time Tommy says.

"I'm not. I just need to know."

"Gabe."

Mikey repeats the name: "Gabe Parascandolo."

They were hitched, Donnie and Donna. Sixteen years, she said? Jesus Christ. That on top of the fact that his father didn't off himself and was actually murdered unjustly by this ex-husband of the woman he's just fallen for. He's in the heart of a fucking soap opera. He's swimming in the blood of a fucking soap opera.

"You knew the kid, maybe?" Big Time Tommy asks.

"I didn't," Mikey says.

Big Time Tommy finishes his pitch as he finishes his hero, talking with his mouth full: "What I want you to do is to simply get your revenge on Donnie. Kill him, and your old man's debt is erased. You and your mother are in the clear."

"I'll do it with my fucking bare hands," Mikey says, anger filling him from the ground up. He pictures Donnie pushing his old man off the bridge. He pictures Donnie in bed with Donna. "I'll choke that motherfucker until he's blue."

"I like the passion," Big Time Tommy says, "but I think you should take a weapon." He turns to Dice: "Get the trunk for Freak Show here."

Dice disappears into what must've been the coatroom of the club and comes out pulling a steamer trunk behind him. He opens the trunk at Mikey's feet. It's full of guns, knives, swords, brass knuckles, nunchucks, other things Mikey doesn't have names for.

Before Mikey chooses, Dice gives him a pair of black batting gloves to put on. "Get the bastard good for me," Dice says.

Mikey doesn't know from guns. He's never even held one. His luck, he aims a piece at Donnie, the fucking thing backfires in his hand.

Instead, he takes out a machete. It's got a black handle, about six inches long, and a blade that's about three times that and sheathed in black leather. He wonders what he'll look like walking through the streets with a machete. A psycho on the loose. It doesn't matter.

What matters now is getting Donnie. After that, there's still the dream of escaping, of a life with Donna, and it's actually possible now, even if he'd have to run from his crime straightaway. Who the hell cares? Life on the run could be great—his mother absolved, Donna at his side. He's not mad at Donna for Donnie. He's sorry for her, that a piece of shit like that guy had been her husband, that he'd been poor Gabe's father.

He takes the sheath off the machete and looks at the silver blade, which zings a flash of light up at the disco ball.

"Good choice," Big Time Tommy says. "Go with God."

Donna's a mess, just sitting at her kitchen table with her head in her hands. She's been a mess before, over Gabe certainly and over Donnie plenty, but this is a different kind of mess. Her life was one thing yesterday, and it's a different thing today, all because she met a boy by chance.

And that's what he is. A boy. She went to his house to meet his mother as if they were going to prom together. This is the kind of thing people do when they're Mikey's age—sleep together within twenty-four hours of meeting, fall in love—not when they're almost forty. She must be losing her mind. Holding it together after Gabe died had been a carefully orchestrated balancing act of grief and routine. It's gushing out now, the desire for change, the desire to live.

Mikey's backpack is on the floor over near her records. She doesn't believe he was being manipulative, but she does think a big part of him wanted that reaction from his mother, wanted her to act in a way that would make him leave the house on principle. Another form of behavior that makes perfect sense at twenty-one.

That woman was awful. The way she stared at Donna. The way she spit on the ground at her feet. Donna would like to cut her some slack for being a widow, but she can't. She looked and acted demonic. That's really what Donna's still sick over. It'd be one thing if Rosemarie had taken Mikey aside and said, "What's going on? She's too old for you." But going all Linda Blair was uncalled for. Donna was putting a lot on the line by being there, putting her trust in the moment, and to have it thrown back in her face like that was crushing.

She doesn't hold it against Mikey. And she won't ever. She's not sure what to expect of this relationship with him, but she sees something good in his eyes. She wonders if he'll tire of her in a week or month. She wonders if she'll tire of him, a kid who throws his backpack on the floor like that.

But that's the difference between someone who has lost it all and isn't willing to take risks and someone who lives by the seat of her pants, who lives for adventure and experiencing new things. She's tried the one way. Maybe she should try the other.

Mikey's talking about leaving, about getting out of the neighborhood. It's a good idea. She has a car. When he's ready, they can just go. Why not? What's to lose? With Gabe and her parents gone, what holds her here any-more? Certainly not her job.

She pictures herself on a highway with Mikey in her piece-of-shit Mer-cury Lynx that's ten years old, the sun hitting the blacktop in front of them, mountains in the distance. There's a whole country she hasn't seen. She can live in a Springsteen song with him. Hit the road running, never let up, fuel it all with love.

Could that kind of life be maintained? *Who cares? Give it a shot.*

The debt Mikey mentioned—that must have been from his father with the gambling, what he owed Big Time Tommy. She wonders how deep they're in. It seems wrong that Mikey and his mother should inherit that debt, especially if that's why Giuseppe killed himself, to free them of it. Mikey said he knew a way to make money to get out from under the debt. She guesses that's what he's out there doing. She hopes he isn't doing some-thing too stupid. He is impulsive, after all. She wonders if he's so impulsive that he'd have the notion to break into a house or try to rob a bank. Maybe he's just trying to make an arrangement with Big Time Tommy.

She takes a napkin from the holder on the table and pats at the corners of her eyes, the white paper coming away black from the little bit of mascara she'd put on. She looks down at the dress. She doesn't regret it. She feels nice in it, pretty even. Rosemarie calling her a whore like that. Imagine her, a whore? Mikey's only the third guy she's ever even slept with, which is crazy to think about. When he gets back, she's going to kiss him before he has a chance to say anything.

She takes a deep breath and goes over to her turntable. *Ghost Writer* is still on the platter. She starts it over on the second side. "Lift Me Up" comes on. Standing there in her dress, waiting for Mikey to return, this song about being lifted higher by love feels more romantic than ever. That's what's happening to her. She's being lifted above the neighborhood. This is where the tears and grief live, down here in these houses, on these cluttered sidewalks and avenues. Slowly, slowly, slowly, she's going higher and higher with Mikey, until they float away. It's nice to think like a kid.

An anxious rapping at the door. Could it be Mikey, back already? What did he do? She's imagining mistakes he could make, trouble he could drag with him wherever they go.

She lifts the tonearm from the record, the needle scratching because of the hastened motion, and then the apartment goes silent except for the knocking. "Who is it?" Donna says.

No answer.

She looks around for something to wield. The wrench she'd been using earlier on the sink is still there on top of the speaker. She picks it up and holds it across her chest. "Who's there?" she says again, suddenly spooked.

Her mind goes a million places. She's now tangled up in whatever Mikey's father got him tangled up in.

Why wouldn't whoever's knocking answer her?

She reels her wild imagination back in. Maybe it's an elderly person who can't hear well. Every once in a while, someone like that—from St. Mary's usually—will come around looking for Suzette.

She approaches the door with the wrench held at her side.

She unlatches the lock on the deadbolt first and then puts her hand on the knob, turning it cautiously and pulling open the door.

She's shocked to see Mikey's mother. She's wearing the same black sequined blouse and black slacks, dressed like she's going to a wake, not hosting her son's birthday dinner, lunch, whatever. She's got a gold knockoff purse slung over her shoulder, the kind you buy on Eighty-Sixth Street for cheap at one of those dive storefronts. It's still got a price tag hanging from the strap.

"What are you doing here?" Donna asks.

"Can I come in?" Rosemarie says.

"Absolutely not."

"Is Mikey here?"

"He's not here, no."

"Can we talk like women?"

"I'm not talking to you."

"Where is Mikey?"

"I don't know."

Rosemarie looks past her into the apartment, notices Mikey's backpack on the floor. "I know Suzette Bonsignore," Rosemarie says. "Your landlord, I take it. Maybe I should go talk to her."

Donna ignores the empty threat, pressing the hand holding the wrench against the doorframe as if she's about to say, "Goodbye, get lost."

"What's with the wrench?" Rosemarie says, stepping forward, her little feet over the threshold. "You gonna whack me one?"

"I didn't know who was knocking. You wouldn't answer. I figured I better be prepared."

"I didn't think you'd open up if I said who it was."

"You're right."

"I'm sorry for how I acted."

"Are you really?"

"Give me five minutes, please. I'm just concerned for my son."

With that, Donna makes the decision to let this woman into her apartment, against her better judgment.

Rosemarie sits on the couch and takes in the room, her eyes lingering on the crates full of records.

Donna sets the wrench back on top of the speaker. "Well?" she says.

"He's got a life ahead of him, my son, and he doesn't know what it is yet," Rosemarie says. "How long you been seeing him? He doesn't tell me anything."

"We just met."

"And you're coming home with him to dinner? You're not some dumb girl. What're you, thirty-five, forty? Imagine yourself in my shoes. I look around, I can tell you don't have kids. That's a different life, not having kids."

Donna is on the verge of tears again. Mikey is only a few years older than Gabe would've been. How would she react if he was alive and came strutting through the door with a woman twice his age? Impossible to say since he's gone forever. If Gabe was alive, she'd be a different woman. She thinks about saying, *I had a son*, but she doesn't. She doesn't owe Mikey's mother anything. She doesn't want to let her in that far.

Rosemarie continues: "I don't know you, I don't know your story, but let's just agree you need to part ways with my son before things get any more involved. I need to be a mother. I need to rein him in, regain control. Mothers do what I'm doing. We don't do what you're doing."

Donna remains silent. She faces the turntable, wipes dust from the surface of the record with an orange cloth she keeps nearby. She needs to bite her tongue. She shouldn't have allowed this woman in. "You're right," she says, her back still to Rosemarie. "You don't know the first thing about me."

"My son needs to get his head right. I'm not gonna let him go down the same path as his father."

Donna turns around, and Rosemarie has a gun pointed at her. Her first reaction is to laugh. This can't be real. Women like Rosemarie don't show up at your apartment with a fucking gun. She's just an overprotective, controlling mother, that's all. And they only met a short time ago. How could she possibly be pinning Mikey's downfall on Donna? Maybe it's just a power move. A nasty woman showing her claws. Probably the gun's not even loaded.

"You've gotta be fucking kidding me," Donna says.

"I'm not kidding."

"You met me for five minutes. Less than that."

"My brother came to me with this," Rosemarie says, her eyes tilting toward the gun, "to protect myself from Big Time Tommy. But things like that don't just happen. He must've known I'd need it for this reason. He has a sixth sense, I always said that."

"You're crazy."

"Mothers sometimes have to be."

"I'm going to go over to the phone and call the police. You go ahead and try to shoot me, okay?"

Donna takes a couple of steps toward the kitchen.

Rosemarie stands, the purse that was in her lap falling to the floor, an envelope with Mikey's name on it in big letters falling out, and she aims harder, both shaky hands on the gun now, one around the handle and the other cupping it, the pointer on her right hand wobbling over the trigger.

"I don't believe this," Donna says. "This must be a nightmare. I fell asleep. I'm dreaming this."

For a second, she convinces herself that's true and then wonders if she's even met Mikey, if he found Gabe's note and brought it back to her. How big a world can someone dream? If that's not real, maybe Gabe's not dead, maybe there was no Gabe, maybe she never even married Donnie. Maybe she's still a girl. Maybe it's 1970, and she just dreamed a whole possible future for herself. Could be. If you dream a future, it doesn't necessarily mean dreaming the whole of it. It simply means that you're set down at a point in time, say 1993, and your past exists behind you.

Forget it. Rosemarie is absolutely real. She's there, right there, and her shaking is getting more intense.

"Believe me, I don't want to shoot you," she says. "I just want you to promise that you won't see my son again. I'll take his bag, and I'll leave. He comes back, you don't answer. He calls, you don't answer. He'll forget about you. He'll move on to the next girl."

"Fine," Donna says.

"I don't believe you. You're a snake. You'll say one thing, and you'll do another. I can see it in your eyes. Mikey will come back and you'll laugh about how crazy I am. You'll take him away from me."

"I think you need help."

Rosemarie moves forward again, the gun coming even closer. Donna reads it as a lunge and ducks away, snagging the wrench from on top of the speaker. She swears Rosemarie's about to pull the trigger. The motion is there, she's ready, and what if this gun *is* actually loaded? What if Rosemarie is that kind of crazy? If she's crazy enough to shoot Donna, maybe she's crazy enough to get away with it.

That's what's running through her head when she lashes out with the wrench and slams Rosemarie in the side of the head with it.

A gash opens from Rosemarie's eyebrow to her hairline. Blood erupts from the wound. She looks stunned and then broken, like a clock that's stopped ticking, and the gun falls from her hand to the floor. She follows the gun, slumping over it, deflated at Donna's feet, the sequins on her blouse glinting in the thin shafts of light filtering into the room around the edges of the pulled shade.

"Oh, Jesus Christ," Donna says.

She looks at the wrench, its jaws streaked red. She sets it back on the speaker, wishing she'd never picked it up to begin with. She leans over the body. There's a world of blood, pooling outward on the rug. The floors aren't level, but she's never noticed just how exactly off-kilter the room is until the blood starts to run toward the couch on the big area rug. She thinks, stupidly, of the shop on Eighty-Sixth Street where she bought this flat weave rug when she first moved in and how much she paid for it, bargaining the seller down a hundred bucks.

She touches Rosemarie's shoulder and tries to turn her so she can see her face. She says her name. She thinks of Mikey. She thinks of what she'll need to do now—call 911, get an ambulance here, the police. Mikey said he might be gone the rest of the day. She has no way to contact him. She says the woman's name aloud, this stranger who showed up at her house with a gun, threatening her. She wasn't wrong to protect herself.

Rosemarie said *she* was protecting herself, but from what? Donna was *actually* protecting herself. From a woman with a fucking gun.

Time is passing. There's still no response.

She closes her eyes. *Make this go away. Please. Make this be a dream.*

She's not talking to God. Who is she talking to?

She's shaking now. Worse even than Rosemarie was. She presses her hand against Rosemarie's shoulder again and allows the shaking to pass through her fingers into the sequins on the blouse, hoping it will electrify her into waking up. What then? An apology for clocking her with a wrench? Beats the alternative.

"Rosemarie, come on," Donna says. "Please don't be hurt."

The blood spreading thickly across the floor tells a different story. Rosemarie's fucking hurt all right. Maybe worse than hurt.

Donna replays the moment in her mind. Rosemarie was about to pull the trigger, right? That's why she took a quick swing with the wrench. It happened that way. Her hand was forced.

She looks at the phone on the wall in the kitchen. She considers the silence of the apartment. A creak upstairs must be Suzette adjusting herself on the recliner in front of the TV. Did Suzette hear the thump? Does sound like that travel up? Might the walls have rattled when Rosemarie fell?

The gun is just sitting there on the rug, almost touched by blood. If what Rosemarie said is true, Donna curses the woman's awful brother for bringing it to her. The gun entered the picture, and Rosemarie lost all sense. She thought of it as a way to regain control.

Donna knows someone—*knew* someone—who was good in bad spots. For all his other faults, Donnie could always act, whatever the severity of the situation was. Be it a simple mess of broken glass, or a car accident, or deeper and darker things she didn't know much about, Donnie could always be counted on to respond. Tony Pagnanelli and Ralph Sottile called, needing something, needing help, and he'd be there in a flash. And they reciprocated, his pals. It was the same with her.

Once, years and years ago at Kings Plaza, she was being followed by someone to her car, and she stopped at a payphone, called Donnie, and he answered, thank Christ, and was standing right in front of her with his bat, Tony and Ralph at his side, ten minutes later. She'd marveled at how fast they'd gotten there.

Even the practical stuff with Gabe he'd had to handle: the church, the wake, the cemetery. She couldn't do any of it. It was Donnie who paid the bills, Donnie who signed the forms, Donnie who shook the hands that needed shaking. Part of it was his job. Part of it was just who he was.

It's a stupid idea to call him, but the situation doesn't make sense. He'll walk her through what to do, give her the guidance she so desperately needs.

She wonders if she does manage to call him now, if he'll respond in the same way he would've when they were married, if he'll still feel that deep loyalty to her.

She doesn't want to do it, but she's not sure what else to do.

She goes to the phone, shaking harder and harder with each step. She dials Donnie's number, her former number, from memory. She thinks of the cellar. She thinks of Gabe. She fears hearing Donnie's voice.

But it's not Donnie who picks up.

It's Tony Pagnanelli. Pags.

"Donna?" he says, his voice full of shock.

She breaks down crying.

"What is it?" he says.

The words get caught in her throat. "Is Donnie there?" she manages to say.

"He's out. Tell me what's wrong. I'll help you."

"I don't know what to do."

"Go ahead and tell me what it is, sweetheart."

She tells him, all of it, because what else can she do? He tells her he'll be right over, not to move, not to call anyone, not to open the door for anyone but him. She says okay and hangs up the receiver and sits at the kitchen table with her back to Rosemarie.

Ava takes off her wedding ring and puts it on the counter in a blue plastic bowl. She washes her hands with Dawn dish soap. She stays facing the sink, looking down at the drain. When she turns back to him, she's crying. Just a bit, but there are tears on her cheeks and a tremble in her chin. What they've done, she feels bad about it.

"That wasn't nice?" Donnie says.

"It was," she says. "I'm sorry."

"You seemed to like it."

"It wasn't you." She tosses him a dish towel from a rack next to her.

He wipes himself off and then walks over to her, still naked, throwing the towel in the sink and leaning against the counter. He reaches out and puts his hands on her chest. Her bra is black, plain, pills of lint on the straps. "I'd like to see these," he says.

"Don," she says.

He lowers the straps off her arms. She doesn't stop him. He likes the way she's half-bursting out of her bra. She's got good cans for a woman in her fifties.

She slips the straps back on and puts everything in place. "I've just gotta use the bathroom," she says. "I'll be right back. The clothes, they're right there. Get dressed in case Nick comes home."

He nods and reaches for the jeans.

Ava disappears into her bedroom, shutting the door.

He puts on the jeans without his boxers, which are still balled on the floor. He puts the shirt on next. Ridiculous Atlantic City thing. A little tight on him. Must've been a pretty skinny fuck, this Anthony.

He leans over the sink and drinks water from the tap. He takes a squirt of dish soap and washes his hands first and then rubs some into his chin and rinses it off under the stream.

The phone rings again.

"Just let it go," Ava calls out.

But he bets it's her son, so he goes over and picks up. "Yeah?" he says.

"Who the fuck is this?" Nick says on the other end. Donnie hardly even knows him, but he sure as shit recognizes that voice, though the drunken warble of it has faded.

"Who the fuck is *this*?" Donnie parrots back to him.

"Where's Ava? I called her at work, and they said she went home. Is she okay?"

Donnie covers the phone with his hand, talks close to the mouthpiece. "Ava's terrific, bud. Best she's been in a while. I ate her pussy until she howled."

"Jesus Christ. Leave there now."

"Nah. You got a stepdaddy now, bitch." Donnie laughs and hangs up.

He goes back to the table and snags a rainbow cookie from the box and shoves it in his mouth whole. It's soft, fresh, fucking delicious.

He sits in the chair where all the action went down. He pulls closer to the table and looks up at the fluorescent light overhead. It makes green dots in his eyes. He remembers, as a kid, thinking that staring at a light like this would give him some kind of X-ray vision. He wanted to see through walls, through clothes. He wanted to see the whiskey tucked into the sock band of his least favorite nun at school. He wanted to see skin. He wanted to see heat. That and the ability to stop time, those were the big desires of his childhood.

Ava comes out in a terry cloth robe. She doesn't sit. She goes over to the sink and puts her ring back on. "Did you answer the phone?" she says.

"I did," he says.

"Who was it?"

"No one. They hung up. Probably thought they had the wrong number."

"If it's important, they'll call back. Probably work. They're helpless without me." She studies him in her dead husband's jeans and shirt. "The clothes look good on you."

"A little tight, but not bad."

"I can get you something else."

"It's fine."

The phone rings again. Donnie's sure it's Nick, and he's not sure what exactly will happen, what Nick will say and how Ava will react.

"Hello?" Ava says into the phone.

But it's clearly not Nick. She's listening. He's listening to her listening.

"I know, Alice," Ava says, rolling her eyes to tell Donnie she's got to deal with this. "Some harebrained scheme. He hasn't been in touch?" And then, after a beat: "I'll tell him to call you as soon as he gets home. Yeah, I don't know what's gotten into him." She hangs up.

"Who was that?" Donnie says.

"Nick's girlfriend. I think I mentioned her yesterday. Alice."

"Sure."

"She's looking for him. He's . . . forget it." She points to the coffee she poured him, the cup she carried over on a saucer with her blouse off. "Your coffee's cold. Let me heat it up and pour you a fresh cup."

"Okay. If it's not a hassle." He's honestly—despite the fact that it wasn't Nick on the phone after all—surprised that Ava's not giving him the boot.

But Ava seems pretty content. He thinks the tears must just be about the ring. He wonders if she considers what she did cheating. Some women would. Women are strange.

"You don't need to wear it," he says.

"Excuse me?" she says.

"The ring. You don't need to wear it anymore."

"I've been told."

"You didn't cheat on him. You *can't* cheat on him. We were just having fun. Don't feel guilty about it."

"I don't work that fast. I shouldn't. It's not right." She fidgets with the ring on her finger. "Poor Anthony, he's probably rolling over in his grave." She goes to the stove and turns the gas back on under the coffee. She empties his old coffee in the sink and rinses the cup.

"I, for one, had a great time," Donnie says, smiling. "Can I tell you something?"

"What?" Ava says, not looking at him.

"You just do something to me. You're the first woman I can think of in a long time that's true of. It stopped with my ex-wife pretty early on. You're classy, you're smart. The way you smoke. Your voice. You know who you remind me of? Susan Sarandon. The actress. You know? She's half-Italian. Her mother's name was Criscione. You see that *White Palace*? She's hot in that. Mid-forties and she's got them all beat."

"I'm older than Susan Sarandon," Ava says, obviously flattered.

"What's a few years? You look good."

"I look worn down."

"Let's go to your bedroom. I'll show you how good you look. I can be ready to go again, you want."

Something of a smirk from her. He wonders what she's got on under that robe, if she left on her bra and underwear or if she's naked underneath. He's surprised she put on the robe at all. He was thinking she'd come back out fully dressed, shaking off the encounter and deciding to head back to work for the afternoon.

When the coffee's boiling again, she shuts the gas and pours them both cups. She brings them over, no saucer for him this time, and sets them on the table, fanning out napkins like cards. She sits across from him and picks at the shell of a cannoli.

"I wasn't going to have anything," she says.

"But you worked up an appetite." He paws up another rainbow cookie and devours it. He sips his steaming coffee. "Eat the whole thing. You deserve it. I want to see you licking up the filling."

"Don! You're bad. Everything is dirty with you."

"Not everything."

But she does pick up the cannoli, balancing it on her palm, nibbling at the shell mouselike, finally tonguing up some filling, her lips dusted with powdered sugar.

"See, that's sexy right there," Don says.

"This is so good," she says, and she doesn't stop. Her bites get bigger. Soon, it's gone, just a scatter of crumbs remaining in her palm, her mouth full of the pastry, chewing in a way where her whole face seems to be moving, her eyes closed. When she finishes, she washes it down with some hot coffee.

"Look at you," he says.

"I'm such a pig. I can already feel that in my ass."

"Have another one. I like to see a woman eat."

"Are you sick in the head?"

"Maybe."

"I'll just try one of the S cookies. Dunk it in my coffee."

"There you go."

She dunks the cookie in her coffee and then brings it to her mouth, holding it over her outstretched palm. It's spongy from the coffee and in danger of falling apart. She takes a big bite, half the cookie, and the rest wilts in her palm. She laughs. She eats the remaining coffee-soaked half from her palm like she's on a desert island and it's the first food she's seen in months. She laughs as she chews. "I'm disgusting," she says, her mouth full of cookie gristle.

"I love it," Donnie says. "Go for broke."

"I'll explode!"

"Today's the day of living dangerously."

She takes a pignoli cookie out of the box this time.

"That's the stuff," Donnie says. "Melt in your mouth."

"Anthony liked these," Ava says, and she seems to catch herself too late. "I don't need to tell you everything Anthony liked. Sorry."

"It's okay. It's the texture. Nothing better." Donnie shakes his head. "Eat up. Put it on your tongue like a communion wafer."

"That's blasphemy!"

"Is it? I bet Christ's real body tastes just like that."

"Don't say things like that." Ava draws back, slumps her shoulders, seems genuinely hurt.

"It's a joke. I'm sorry, hon."

"Don't call me *hon*."

"You with the don'ts. It's starting to feel like we're at the end instead of the beginning."

"Two don'ts. That's all. Two." Ava finds her Viceroys and lights one. "Let me tell you about my history with *hon*."

"It's a term of endearment."

"Not the way a lot of men use it. All fucking day. Excuse me. I don't like to curse. All day. *Hon* this and *hon* that. 'Who are you calling *hon*?' That's what I want to say. You're the maintenance man. You're the whatever."

"Leave the maintenance man alone. He's got it tough. His mother just croaked. His wife's banging a gangster named Z-Bone."

Ava takes a long draw off her smoke, looks at him with quizzical eyes. "What are you even talking about?"

"I'm imagining a life for the maintenance man. His name's Luis."

"His name's not Luis, the guy I'm talking about. It's Ted. Ted Nowak. He's a Polack."

"Okay, okay." Donnie puts his hands up in surrender. "I'll leave the maintenance man alone."

"Then, forget it, there's the other guys. The guys that think they're somebody. The doctors. They're the worst."

"No more with the *hon*. I get it."

"Can I ask you something?" Ava says, leaning forward on her elbow, her cigarette perched between her fingers, the wedding ring seeming to glow.

"Oh, boy," Donnie says. "Maybe I need another cookie." He takes an S cookie and turns it to mush in his coffee and eats it just like she did, over his palm, catching spongy dark crumbs. "Okay. Shoot."

"What happened, how do you feel about it?"

He looks around, at the walls, at the light overhead, searching for her meaning. What he *did*?

"Well, Ava," he says. "I like it. It's a good place to be, down there between your gams. Warm. A great little rut to dig around in. Makes me feel like a squirrel."

"Not *that*."

"Then what do you mean?"

"Your son."

Donnie leans back. *That*. How's she know? People just know things, he guesses. A neighborhood like this, word gets around. More likely, she didn't know or at least didn't put two and two together and then her son remembered, told her everything he could think of, the whole public file.

Ava blows smoke away from him. "Did you go to church about it?" she says.

"Why?" he says.

"Maybe you should. Father Borzumato at St. Mary's, he's a good guy. I talked to him a lot after Anthony died."

"Me and priests don't get along great. You want me to tell you all about Father Pepe and Monsignor Vallone and how they beat the shit out of me when I was an altar boy?"

"I remember Father Pepe and Monsignor Vallone. They were kind."

"Yeah, if kind's getting loaded and knocking the shit out of some of us. And Vallone, his tastes ran more deviant with some of the effeminate boys."

"You're saying what?"

"Why you think they moved Vallone so hush-hush?"

"No. Not that."

"You put your trust in these fucks. They got their end games. Some of them, it's about trying to throw a bang on one of their nun pals. The others, they're into the boys. They never tried to fuck me. I want to make that clear."

Ava stubs out her cigarette in the Cento can, picks a tobacco fleck from her lip. "How come I never knew you growing up?"

"You're a little older, I guess is why."

"I was probably in seventh grade when you were just starting out. Did you have Sister Bernadette for kindergarten?"

"She was the worst. She looked like a rat."

"I liked Sister Bernadette. I saw her not that long ago at church."

"She must be two hundred."

"She remembered me. She said I was one of her favorites."

Donnie takes a cigarette. Ava lights it for him. "There any of that scotch left?" he says.

"Let's just talk," Ava says. "Did you have a favorite year?"

"Second grade wasn't the worst."

"Who'd you have?"

"Miss Schwartz."

"I must've missed her."

"Jewish lady teaching in a Catholic school, you believe that? Only lasted a couple of years. She lived on the same block as the school. Just a nice lady. Had the blackest hair. She wasn't like the nuns. I saw her one day sitting on the front stoop outside what must've been her apartment building, just listening to music and polishing a pair of shoes. She gave me the biggest smile and wave. That's one of my favorite memories from being a kid. I felt like I was somebody."

"That's so sad," Ava says.

"What's sad?"

"A kid should have a lot of great memories. Not just a stranger waving at him."

"She wasn't a stranger." His turn to draw deep on his smoke. He crinkles his forehead, looks past her at the radio, which he wishes was still on. All this goddamn talk. "I've got good memories with my folks and my aunts and my uncles. Big Sunday dinners. My old man taking me on the train to the Bronx to see the Yanks."

A hard minute of silence. Just the sounds of them smoking. A clock ticking in another room, barely audible, a tiny heartbeat for the house. He hadn't noticed it before now.

"Being a cop must've been hard," Ava finally says.

"It was what it was. I got in young."

"Talk to Father Borzumato. Just talk to him. You're not signing up for anything."

"I don't think so, Ava."

Antonina is waiting at the pick-up spot on Bay Thirty-Second. When Ralph arrives on foot, she's taken aback. He's carrying a gym bag, sweating hard in his tight-fitting polo shirt and wrinkled chinos, out of breath. He looks all around, watching to see if anyone's watching him, and says, "Pags took my car. An emergency."

Antonina nods. It feels strange to be in the neighborhood with him outside of his car. In the Bronx, she feels comfortable. In the car on the Belt, she feels comfortable. Here, she feels exposed. She's sobered up after the early drinks, and her nerves are frayed, which doesn't help.

"I'm sorry," Ralph says.

"It's okay."

"I just want to give this to you right now, anyway." He hands her the bag. "Maybe we can meet later when I get the car back and go to the Bronx?"

"What is it?" she says, inspecting the outside of the small bag. It's one of those small tubelike bags, black with white handles, and it's got rings of dust etched into the fabric.

Ralph whispers, "I came into some bread today. I don't need it all. I want you to have some. For your future. Maybe it'll help, with college and everything."

Antonina doesn't need to unzip the bag to believe him. "How much?" she asks.

"Ten thou," he says.

Panic sets in. She's standing on Bay Thirty-Second with a dirty cop, ten thousand bucks in a gym bag she's holding that he gave her. Who knows where he got it? Lots of things to say race through her mind. *I can't take it. Why me? Where's this money from? Did someone die over this?*

Instead, what she says is simply, "Thank you."

"There's more, and I don't need all of it," Ralph says. "I fly solo. You're a special girl. I want you to have every opportunity."

Money makes the future look different. She's thinking—in a flash—college isn't a bad idea. She's got this money. She doesn't have to depend on her parents. She can go to a state school and learn to make movies or something. She can get out of this neighborhood, out of this city with its broken sidewalks and groaning buses and muggers and people getting killed on the train for sneakers, go see some trees and lakes and mountains and shit like that. Mikey had told her how nice it was in New Paltz, how sometimes he'd just walk off into the woods with a sleeping bag and a bottle of wine in the spring and sleep on the ground.

Ralph reaches out and touches her hair, taking a couple of strands between his fingers. "I ever tell you I like the pink?" he says.

She's thinking of changing it. She got a color called Psychedelic Sunset last time she was at Manic Panic in the city with Lizzie.

"I'm gonna go," Ralph says. "I'll call you later. Two nights in a row, we'll go to the Bronx. This one'll be a celebration. We'll toast to your future."

She honestly doesn't know what to say. She nods and smiles.

Ralph leaves, walking back toward Benson Avenue.

She races home—her mother's still not there—and goes into her room, locking the door behind her. She unzips the bag and empties the money on the bed. Ten thousand dollars doesn't look like as much money as she thought it would. Ten banded stacks of ten hundred-dollar bills. She touches the edges of the money. She tries to think of where she should hide it. In her closet? Under the bed? Maybe she can get her own safe deposit box at the bank. Or maybe that's dumb. It's dirty money, and the bank is equipped somehow to sniff it out. She imagines herself buying a car at Flash Auto with cash, paying for her college tuition with cash, buying more dyes at Manic Panic and more movies at Kim's Underground.

She hides most of the money on the top shelf of her closet in a half-empty box of tampons, keeping out three hundred so she can have some fun, and then she stuffs the gym bag under her bed. She doesn't like seeing the gym bag because she doesn't know who it belonged to. She'll have to remember to toss it in the trash.

She goes to the phone and calls Lizzie, who picks up after four rings. "You want to go to the city?" Antonina asks.

"Your parents won't be pissed?"

"No one's around. I've got some money. We could go to the movies, go get drunk, and then go hear music." She's thinking it'd be cruel if she's not here when Ralph calls, but she can't worry about that.

"Hell yes," Lizzie says. "I'll meet you at Bay Parkway."

Antonina locks the door from the inside and goes out on the fire escape, thinking that when her mom comes home and finds her door locked, she'll just think she's not feeling well and let it be. She smokes a cigarette. In a few minutes, she'll descend the ladder into the yard and run to meet Lizzie at the train.

Nick looks at the payphone in Spanky's Lounge and shakes his head. That can't have been real, Donnie at his house with Ava. It must've been some sort of auditory hallucination. He's heard of that. It's a real thing. He called, Ava wasn't home, the phone just kept ringing, and then he imagined the conversation with Donnie. But, of course, he knows it is real.

Before that, he'd gotten through to Phil Puzzo. They'd made plans to meet at Nick's house in an hour or two—Phil owed his parents a visit anyway, and he could use a home-cooked meal. He said he'd stop by for ten, fifteen minutes, until his mother had the food ready. Nick had given him a quick pitch, and Phil said he was familiar with the Donnie P story, but he wasn't sure it'd be enough for a script or a book or anything. Donnie's a nobody, he said, and no one will give a good red shit about neighborhood melodrama. Nick would have to dig deeper. Still, maybe he—Phil Puzzo, neighborhood god—could give Nick some pointers on how to fill it out.

It was disconcerting, ultimately, but Nick doesn't want to pass up the chance to meet Phil, who's been gone from his parents' house for twenty-plus years and doesn't come back all that often. Nick's got clay, he knows that much, and maybe Phil can help him shape it into something good.

The next call Nick makes, with his last quarter, is to Alice, who should be getting home from summer school soon.

It rings and rings. Nothing. He gets his quarter back. He'll try again in a bit. Give her time to get through the door.

His mind goes back to what Donnie said. Nick highly doubts that this goon was going down on his mother. That's just Donnie fucking with him, trying to get in his head.

But now Nick's got a picture in his mind that he can't shake, his mother on her four-poster bed with her legs spread, Donnie lurching on his knees in front of her, his head buried in her crotch. Nick doesn't want to think about it, but he finds that he can't stop. He keeps seeing Ava's face, her neck, her hands, her clothes bunched on the floor the way clothes only get bunched when they're taken off in a fever. He thinks of Ava's thighs, her butt against the bed. He knows the way Alice looks when he's down there, the way she bites her lip and grips the sheets, the way she sometimes palms her breasts, the way her eyes seem closed and open at the same time. He imagines those things to be true of Ava now. He never thought of his mother biting her lip or gripping her sheets. He's thought of her breasts but only in the way that a man thinks of his mother's breasts—they might as well be wooden spoons in the kitchen—but they never jumped into his mind at a time when they shouldn't have.

Donnie saying *pussy* like that. Nick had never even thought of that word in relation to his own mother. Not really. He'd thought of it in relation to the mothers of other boys, sure. He had started out dreaming of them, after all. Mrs. Torregrossa and Mrs. Loverde and Mrs. Telesco. Even Mrs. Angilletta with that fierce armpit stink of hers. He'd dream of what was between their legs and what wasn't even before he knew anything with any sort of certainty. Tits you knew right out the gate. They were like the sun and the moon. Institutions. A boy couldn't help but dream of them, to wonder about them. But down below was a mystery. A lot of early schoolyard talks, between arm wrestling bouts, revolved around speculating on women's private parts. Could it be that there was something with teeth or claws? Some boys, guided by older brothers, whispered of bushes. This was, he's thinking, third grade. Other boys had sisters, so they had general information, but general information in those days transformed into wild gossipy news from the edge of hysteria. One kid, Edmund, concluded that women had starfish stuck there and that only husbands could peel away those starfish. Another kid, Lucas, who later became a rabid panty-sniffer, told tales of needing to chip away ice with a hammer to get to a pool of maple syrup deep inside.

But there was that one time with Ava. He was in fifth grade by then. He came in from playing basketball with his friends. He was sweaty. He wanted a peanut butter and banana sandwich. He opened the back door, ball under his arm, and heard moans. He stopped himself from going in. He took a step back and kept the door open a couple of inches. His father was off from work that day or home early. Either way, he was locked in an embrace with Ava at the kitchen sink. Ava was slouched over his shoulder. His hand was wedged down her pants, and he was pumping it up and down. They hadn't noticed the door, hadn't heard him turning the handle or his footfall on the threshold. Now, he was watching them in this strange ritual. "You're so wet," his father said. Ava laughed and moaned and said, "You make me wet." Nick remembers puzzling over why she might be wet. This was the '70s, and he was still a kid. He didn't have porn the way kids have porn now, where you can just walk into a video store and look through the big boxes behind the saloon doors in that little private room and bring them up to the counter like a loaf of bread. He didn't even remember seeing any dirty magazines at newsstands in the neighborhood. His friend Cal had passed along a sleazy novel called *Topless Waitress* with a great cover. Nick had leafed through but never read it, then he hid it at the bottom of his closet, the cover seeming like the only good part, the words too small and crammed on the crumbling pages. And now his father was saying how wet his mother was and his mother was saying he made her that way between moans and Nick can think back to how strange that sounded then. He remembers thinking they must be talking about the sink or the shower or something to do with washing up. Finally, Nick's old man stopped for a second, Ava's pants not allowing enough movement, and he pulled them down around her thighs. Her underwear, too. He licked his hand and put it back between her legs. She was almost sitting up on the counter. Nick remembers catching just a glimpse of Ava's privates and then letting the door whisper shut and retreating back out into the yard, throwing his ball down, almost hyperventilating.

His learning picked up after that. More books were passed to him. Eventually magazines. He actually read instead of just looking at covers and pictures. He and his buddies went to Times Square to see movies when they could. They'd all jerk off during the movies, not saying anything about it to one another afterward. Nick's first sex had been with a hooker in a sad hotel over a liquor store near the Port Authority. Her name was Provenance, no shit.

He has a story. Everyone has a story. Ava must have one too, a long one that—like so many others—begins with a mix of curiosity and shame, wonder and fear. Her first under-blanket explorations. Rubbing against something. Long showers. Priests and nuns and mothers unveiling their don'ts and won'ts. Was there a boy before his father? Were there back seats? Had there been men since his father died? Desperate sessions in closets at Sea Crest? Now there was Donnie and, whether or not it was real, Nick was seeing it as real.

Nick is surprised that he's never given more thought to Ava's desires. He's seen her as a mother, as a widow, as someone who works herself to the bone. But beyond cigarettes, he's never given a thought to what pleasure is for her or what it might be. If Donnie wasn't Donnie, maybe he could find it in his heart to be happy for her. He feels guilt about going over to Donnie's, encouraging him in the name of getting close for the script. Maybe Ava does need a boyfriend. But not this guy.

He goes back to the bar and orders another can of Schaefer. He looks at the pinball machine and half-expects to see Antonina slumped there. She's not, of course, but he feels like he sees some sort of heat outline of her.

He heads to the payphone and dials Alice again. This time she picks up, breathy. "Nick?" she says. "Where on earth are you?"

"Can you come get me at Spanky's Lounge?" he says.

"I just talked to Ava."

"You did? Is she okay?"

"Yeah, why? What the hell are you doing at that dive?"

"It's a long story. I'm thinking. I don't feel like walking all the way home."

"Sechiano wasn't happy."

"I don't care about Sechiano. Things have changed."

"What do you mean, 'things have changed'?"

"I'll tell you all about it. Just come get me."

"Are you in trouble?"

"Please. Just grab your keys, go get the car, and come get me. You remember Spanky's, right?"

"Just tell me what's going on."

"Ava, please. Just come get me." He catches himself. "I mean Alice. Sorry. My head's a million places. I'll explain everything, I promise."

A dramatic pause. She seems to be holding the phone away from her ear, thinking it through. "Fine," she says, her voice brimming with derision. She was worried, but now she's upset. Number one: He's putting her out. She doesn't like to get in her car. She doesn't even really like to drive. He pictures her in that spot on the Belt where Verrazano Bridge traffic empties down from a ramp, and when she's in the middle lane, as she always seems to be, she has a panic attack about whether she should yield or keep plunging on. Number two: He's made that slip before, calling her Ava instead of Alice, and it freaks her out. Once, after dinner at her place, they were cleaning up and he came up behind her, his hands soapy with dishwater, and he hugged her to him and said, "That was delicious, Ava." She turned around and looked at him like a cockroach had just crawled out of his mouth. It was an honest mistake, he'd said, their names both starting with A. The next time it happened, they were at a hotel in Atlantic

City for a weekend of gambling and to see a show. They were showering together. She was giving him head under the heavy thrust of water. He wasn't thinking about Ava at all. He wasn't worried about her for any reason or anything. Relaxed as hell, he'd said, "Oh, Ava." It'd just wandered from his mouth, and he gasped, shocked beyond words.

It was, obviously, a far worse offense, and Alice ceased what she was doing and stormed out of the shower. "Do you want to fuck your mother, weirdo?" she'd said. "No, of course not," he'd said. He begged and pleaded and said it was just his brain messing with him, wanting to wreck the moment. He remembered how upset it had made her last time, and it must've been his subconscious doing the very thing he knew not to do in that moment. In psychological terms, it was self-sabotage. He was prone to it. She seemed to buy this and things settled down, and he never did it again until now.

Funny, he was just thinking how sexless Ava has always been to him, and now he's remembering these times, making the mistake again.

"I'm sorry, Al," Nick says over the phone to a hanging silence.

She lets out a desperate breath. "I'll be there in fifteen minutes," she says, and hangs up.

He brings his beer over to the same table he'd sat at with Antonina and drinks it down fast and then orders another one and gets a buck changed to quarters for the pinball machine. He tries his luck, beer up on the glass, lights flashing. He's nowhere near as good as Antonina.

When Ava convinces Don to take a walk, that some fresh air will be good for him, she doesn't tell him she's got a destination in mind. She changes into a pair of jeans and her own T-shirt, one she bought at a ninety-nine-cent store on Eighty-Sixth Street a few summers before, right when the Gulf War started. The shirt's got a drawing of Saddam Hussein on it with a green missile going through his ears like a knife-through-the-head prop, and it says THIS SCUD'S FOR YOU in big, blocky green letters. Don compliments her on it. Nick always makes fun of her when she wears it.

Tired of her work shoes, she puts on sneakers. She takes Don's arm as they head out of the house. She can tell he's getting shaky for a drink.

They walk up West Seventh and make a left at Bay Parkway. They pass the Marboro Theatre, continuing on Bay Parkway and circling through Seth Low Playground like high schoolers playing coy. That's the way she sees it, anyway. She's not sure what Don sees. She knows he's got deep, deep darkness inside. She let herself get carried away with him. She tells herself it's understandable. She's sympathetic to her own sudden desperate desires. God will forgive her for acting irrationally. She's been a decent person her whole life. A little indecency isn't going to sink her.

Ava looks around the park. Old-timers playing chess. Kids on the jungle gym and playing basketball and being pushed on swings. A woman in a big pink hat is sitting on a bench under a tree with pink flowers, feeding pigeons stale bread. Ava thinks back to taking Nick here when he was little. She'd sit on a bench, smoking, and watch him play. He'd get picked on. She'd try not to intervene. Maybe she should've intervened.

"We could go to a bar," Don says. "Good one I know right on Kings Highway. Not a bad hike from here."

"I don't think so," Ava says.

"What then? Just take in the sights?"

"Sure, what's wrong with that? All the sweets I ate. I need to walk it off."

"Nothing's wrong with it, I guess."

They leave the park and take Stillwell Avenue. Ava's idea is to make a right on Twenty-Third Avenue and bring them past St. Mary's school, where they both went, years apart, to reminisce about that a bit more, and then to turn onto Eighty-Fifth Street and stand in front of the church. She's there every Saturday night and on every holy day. It's been like that her whole life. The original church burned down when she was in her twenties. For a couple of years, while they rebuilt, Mass was held in the auditorium. Anthony always went to church with her. He had his own rosary beads. He was an usher for about a decade. She knows Don doesn't go to church anymore. She just wants him to see the place. Someone who's been away from it for so long just gets close, things tend to come back. That's the way she feels, anyway. You see the stained-glass windows, you smell the smells, you see the cross, how can something not get stirred up? She won't pressure Don into talking to Father Borzumato about his son. Maybe she'll just try to talk him into going inside and lighting a candle or kneeling quietly and saying a little prayer. Now she's got that song in her head. *I say a little prayer for you.*

"Can I ask you something?" Don says.

"Oh boy, what is it?" Ava says. "I'm nervous. Go ahead."

"You said yesterday you've never been out of the city except for Jersey."

"Right."

"Would you want to go out of the city with me?"

"Go where?"

"On a trip. I just came into some dough. I don't know. Maybe Italy. You were saying you wanted to go back to the old country."

Ava stops walking and looks at him. "Italy?"

"Right."

"You serious? We barely know each other."

"I like you. I mean, *obviously*. You get older, a day's like a year. You know how it is. I don't need more information. I like you. I want to get out of here. I want you to come."

"Oh, I don't know." She pauses, looks up at the telephone wires, a pigeon perched on a streetlamp. "Can I ask *you* something? You said you have an off-again on-again girlfriend, didn't you? Who is she?" Ava's surprised at herself for not thinking of the woman Don mentioned yesterday before now. She doesn't think he said her name.

"She's nothing. Forget her."

"You said you were off-again?"

"Way off. Never to return. She's nothing. She was always nothing."

They make the right onto Twenty-Third Avenue. She's steering him without him being aware of it. She's thinking he must really like her to invite her to Italy. And buy her a car. She's struck by the insanity of it all. Things like this must happen to people, opportunities for adventure must arise, but it's never been there for her. The neighborhood has been it. She's thinking people must cross paths for a reason. She's thinking it was maybe destiny her car broke down and Don picked her up on the Belt. She believes that could be true. God's got a plan. Don needs her, and she needs him. Don and Ava. Got a ring to it. She sees them sitting at a table in a fancy restaurant, a white tablecloth between them, Don cleaned up, Ava dressed to the nines. They could be good together. They could have adventures. She could get his head straight. She loses her train of thought and can only think how he could do what he did to her back there in the kitchen every day, make her feel good. Nick's a grown-up. Let him fend for himself for a while. Let him propose to Alice. With her and Don together, maybe he'll let go of this stupid script idea. She's got some vacation time saved up at work. A couple of weeks in Italy would be a dream come true.

"You're not messing with me, are you?" Ava says. "Please don't mess with me."

"I'm serious," Don says.

She's trying not to think too much about what Anthony would have to say about Don. Oh, he'd hate him. Such bravado. Anthony wasn't a big talker and he definitely wasn't a big bullshitter. No one was more straightforward than him. She could imagine him calling Don a chooch. She wonders if they ever crossed paths. Walking under the El. Getting pizza. She's sure she herself must've crossed paths with Don before, even if only in passing at one of the markets on Eighty-Sixth Street or maybe both of them on line at Meats Supreme or buying scratch-offs at Augie's.

"Where we are right now," Don says. "You remember what happened here?"

They're on Twenty-Third Avenue between Eighty-Second and Eighty-Third Street, standing in front of a chain link fence plastered with *Beware of Dog* signs.

"What?" she says.

"Big mob hit. The Brancaccios whacked Vin Volpe. This was '83."

"Sure, I remember that. He was sitting in his car, right?"

"Waiting on his goomar. She lived in Apartment 2C. Right there." Don points at a red door on the ground floor of a three-family house. "Stacey Lombardozzi. She was eighteen. Her claim to fame was she fucked Travolta. Supposedly." He pauses. "Banged. I'm sorry. Excuse my language."

Ava swats at his arm. "You think you're funny. I remember the *Daily News* the day after that. That picture of him in his car. I was working. Otherwise, I probably would've walked over and been part of the crowd that gathered."

"I saved that paper for a while. 'A Bloody End for Vin Volpe.'"

"Were you on duty?"

"I didn't work in the neighborhood. My precinct was in East New York. Fucking war zone over there."

"Right. I knew that."

As they pass in front of St. Mary's school now—it runs from corner to corner between Eighty-Fourth Street and Eighty-Fifth Street—Ava stops and looks up at the red brick, the high, dark, stained-glass windows of the convent. Not that high, in reality. As a kid, she thought the school was the tallest building in the world. It was, after all, at three floors, one of the tallest in the twenty blocks or so she lived within. And she thought the sisters lived so high up and watched over everything. She remembers waiting out here, on these weathered gray steps, in her plaid checkered jumper and cross tie and kneesocks, for the doors to be thrown open by Sister Maura. Her world was so small. Her world is still so small.

"You remember this?" Ava says to Don. "Sitting out here, waiting for school to start?"

"I was late a lot," Don says. "Sister Maura, she'd come out and knock me in the ass with a yardstick when I buzzed after the door was locked."

Ava's struck by how different people can have such different memories of a place. To her, these steps speak of carefreeness, of youth, of her body growing and changing over the years she stood and waited here, of good times with her friends, games of hopscotch and skully, sweet gossip whispered in ears, notes passed back and forth, dreaming of after-school egg creams.

"We'd meet out here for fights on Wednesday afternoons," Don says. "That was fun."

"Fights?"

"We'd pit whoever against whoever, you know. Make it like a boxing match. One of us would be ref. One would hold up round cards and act sexy. Someone would usually get their ass kicked pretty fast. I was one of the better ones. I knocked Onofrio Scotto out with one punch. Everyone scattered."

"The sisters never came out to break it up?"

"Once or twice. They were probably up in the convent by then, hitting the whiskey. I saw Sister Eleanor watching once, eating popcorn. You remember her? I got a kick out of the mean ones."

"She picked up my friend Marisa by the ear. Off the ground a foot, maybe more. Marisa's ear hurt for a week. I thought Sister Eleanor was gonna rip it off."

"That Sister Eleanor had some real chops."

"Let's pass by the church."

"That's what this is? A ploy to get me into church? Come on. Now who's messing with who?"

"I just want you to see it."

"I've seen the fucking church my whole life. It's ugly. You think Jesus is just gonna appear to me and say, 'Come back to me. Tell me how you really feel about your dead son.'?" Don makes a mocking gesture, like he's blessing something that's not there.

"I do think that, yeah."

"Just my luck. I find the woman of my dreams and she's a religious nut." He allows himself, though, to be led by the arm around the corner and up Eighty-Fifth Street to the church.

They stand on the steps. Don leans against the railing.

The church is bell-shaped, its glass doors like mirrors on a summer day like this. Stained-glass windows wrap around the sides. Ava loves those windows. So much of her life has been spent pondering them, kneeling before them to light candles, stuffing singles into poor boxes on the concrete walls between them. She remembers Sister Lena taking her aside one day, as she gazed up at the windows after a round of confession, to ask if she knew who Frau Ava was, if she was named after her. Ava said no, not that she knew of. She wasn't named for anybody. Her mother liked the name Ava because of Ava Gardner, but she wasn't named for Ava Gardner, who broke Sinatra's heart. Sister Lena told her that Frau Ava was a poet and an anchorite a long time ago. That's all Ava remembers. She never looked into who Frau Ava was or even what an anchorite did. She remembers the word *anchorite* so vividly, feeling important because Sister Lena assumed she knew what it meant.

Now she looks up at the gold cross on top of the steeple. The sunlight hitting it. She loves it, too. The way you can see it over the El and through telephone wires. She's unsure how someone can look at that cross and not see or feel Jesus. She's been unwavering in her faith, even with Anthony dying. Even with Nick's agnostic ways. While she was in the hospital with Anthony, holding his hand, dabbing at his head with a wet washcloth, while he squirmed and complained of pain, she'd talk to Jesus, and she swears she even saw Him sitting there across from her once, looking the way she'd always expected Him to look. Radiant. Like His eyes were telling her there'd be peace on the other side of the suffering.

Don doesn't seem particularly impressed by the cross or the windows. He doesn't seem called back to some good memory of the church. Ashes thumbed on his forehead. Feeling restored after confession.

"Nothing?" Ava says.

Don gives a frozen look, stares straight at the front doors of the church. "I see him! He's right there on the front steps. He's looking at me." He busts up laughing.

"That's not nice," Ava says. "It's really not."

"Where's Father Borzumato? That's his name, right? You want me to talk to him?" Don claps his hands together. "I'll talk to him. I'll tell him a few things. You think he'll mind if I call him Borz? Maybe Father B is better? Like we're old pals."

"Stop."

Don turns to Ava. "Listen, Ava. Forget this. I just had a thought. There's what's real, and there's what's not real. I want to get out of here for a while. I want to get out of my house. Out of the neighborhood. Italy. Like I said. Come with me. I've got this dough. We'll travel like royalty. Go to JFK or

LaGuardia and get on a plane and just take off. No looking back. Leave this
all behind for however long we want."

"I don't know," Ava says, her eyes darting back to the church. "Let me
think about it for a while."

"Now. Let's go now."

"You just bought me the car. I've hardly had the chance to use it."

"Leave it at your house. It'll be there when we get back. Pack a bag, if you
want. Or don't pack a bag—we can get all new clothes in Italy. Let's have an
adventure. People, they live their whole lives, they don't have an adventure."

"You're crazy," Ava says, but she's thinking about how he's reading her
mind. This desire for adventure. This desire to have a new life and experience
new things while she still can. Italy. She doesn't say anything, but she wants
so badly to nod.

Pags understands the magnitude of the situation as soon as he gets there. He tells Donna to go take a shower, he'll take care of everything. She's not sure what he means, at first, but she listens.

In the shower, it hits her. Pags will make it like this never happened. And that's what she wants. That's why she called Donnie in the first place. Donnie wasn't available to take care of it, so Pags is stepping in. He was always sweet on her. He seems happy to help.

Sometimes, you can make it seem like a bad thing that happened never actually happened. Donna knows that's true. Not all the time. Not with Gabe, obviously.

The water gets cold quickly. She remembers she just took a shower before leaving for Mikey's house, before setting these events in motion. Suzette will complain that she's using too much hot water. But using all the hot water seems like a luxury now. She doesn't want to be what she is. She can't believe that striking Rosemarie with the wrench was enough to kill her.

Her hands are still shaking. She can't totally settle into her new reality of believing that nothing actually happened.

She gets out of the shower and puts on different clothes, a red T-shirt and red gym shorts, bunching up the nice dress she'd worn for the first time and putting it in a plastic shopping bag.

Pags knocks on the bedroom door.

She opens it, her hair wet, feeling naked even though she's wearing these other clothes.

"You okay, kid?" he says.

She shrugs. "I'm not sure."

"I don't need to know what happened. It was an accident. You can't let it wreck your life."

She looks past him into the living room and sees the rug rolled up. The body must be in the rug. The rug must have soaked up all the blood from the body. The body no longer exists.

Pags continues: "I'm gonna go out and pull Sottile's car into the driveway. I'll take the rug right out the back door, put it in the trunk, and that's that. Don't worry, okay? Shit happens. We've got a guy in Brownsville who makes things disappear. He's got this vacant building, and he's got a tub and lye. You don't need to know the details. All you need to know is you're in the clear."

She nods. How can she live with herself after this? How can she face Mikey, or anyone?

Pags holds up the wrench and the gun. "I got *this* and *this*. They're going for a swim in the Gowanus Canal. You got anything else needs getting rid of?"

She hands him the dress in the plastic bag.

"Don't thank me, okay? You're always family, no matter what. This is what family does for each other. You take solace in the fact that nothing happened here today. You dreamed it all."

She nods again.

He leaves the apartment with the gun and the wrench. She hears the car a couple of minutes later, rattling down the long driveway to the back of the house. Her Lynx is parked out on the street because Suzette prefers to keep the driveway clear. Suzette might look out her window and try to figure out what's going on, but all she'll see is a man putting a rug in a trunk.

Pags comes in, propping the back door open with a cinder block he finds in the yard. She can hear the car idling just outside the door, at the back end of the driveway. He's wearing gloves now.

He stoops over the body. "When I'm gone, I'm gone," he says. "No mention of this. I won't tell Donnie or nobody, not ever. You can trust me."

"I don't know what happened."

"Hey, it's no biggie. You're not a bad person. You just keep it together."

He hoists the rug over his shoulder. She's afraid that blood will spill from either end, leaving a trail all the way through the kitchen and out the door to the car. But there's nothing else she can see. Maybe he's done something to prevent that.

He has trouble angling the body through the doorway and winds up smacking it a few times, first against the wall and then against the doorframe and then against the propped door itself.

Once outside, he pushes the rug into the trunk of Sottile's Caddy. There's plastic down in the trunk, she can see that. He has to sort of bend and smoosh the rug to make it fit, but he eventually crams it in there and closes the lid. She's watching all of this from the doorway, as if keeping an eye on a moving man.

He turns to her and dusts off his hands. "Easy peasy," he says.

She feels empty inside. He seems to understand what she's going through, so he just gets in the car and drives away, going slow the length of the driveway and then speeding up once he turns onto the block.

And just like that, he's gone. Rosemarie's gone.

Donna pushes the cinder block aside and closes the back door. She opens the cabinets under the sink and finds cleaning stuff, paper towels and some homemade solution she cooked up. The bucket's still under there collecting water from the dripping pipe, but she's put it in at a bad angle and some of the paper towel rolls are wet.

She looks around on the floor in front of the turntable and finds a smeared drop of blood not far from Mikey's backpack. She wipes it up. She doesn't find any more blood.

What she does see—and she can't believe she missed it before Pags left—is the new-looking gold purse that Rosemarie came in with, toppled right there on the floor next to the couch. The price tag says five dollars. The material is synthetic, almost rubbery. Donna can't help but think that Rosemarie bought it just for the purpose of carrying the gun.

But there's also the letter, or whatever it is, with Mikey's name on it. Other than that, the purse is empty. She rips open the envelope, expecting a letter from Rosemarie to her son, begging him to wise up. She's shocked to see it's from Antonina Divino, whose family lived behind her and Donnie. Donna never knew her other than to say hi when she still lived over there. Antonina goes to Bishop Kearney. She must've just finished her junior year. She's always got a different color hair, and the nuns give her hell for it. Donna can't make sense of how the girl even knows Mikey. Antonina was a couple of years behind Gabe in school.

She reads the note and can't make much sense of it. But being lost in trying to figure out the puzzle of what Antonina's saying gives Donna some momentary purpose, takes her head away from Rosemarie and the damage that's been done.

She rips up the note and stuffs it in the purse. She puts on flip-flops and walks outside with the purse clutched to her chest. The day is so bright. She's struck by how early it still is. She walks to the corner of her block and takes a right.

McDonald's is on Eighty-Sixth Street and Twenty-Fourth Avenue. Some kids are out front, skateboards at their feet, headphones on, eating burgers and letting the yellow wrappers fall to the sidewalk. She ducks into the back lot, where the dumpster is. She throws the purse into the dumpster, expecting it to make some noise, but it lands quietly on a knotted stack of plastic garbage bags.

Donna goes back to her apartment and puts Carly Simon's *No Secrets* on the turntable. She finds the blazer she was wearing the day before. That's where Gabe's suicide note is. She sits on the couch and reads the note over and over and listens to the record, fearing that she'll lose her breath and won't be able to catch it, fearing that reality won't allow her to lie to herself. She inhales and exhales deeply. She thinks about tearing up Gabe's note too, but she can't bring herself to do it. She stuffs it in the pocket of her shorts. Her mind plays a line on repeat: *I won't tell Mikey anything because there's nothing to tell. I won't tell Mikey anything because there's nothing to tell. I won't tell Mikey anything because there's nothing to tell.*

Mikey is in the P.S. 101 schoolyard. He hasn't been there since the night with Antonina. He's looking through the chain link fence at Donnie's house across the street. A car is parked in the driveway. Otherwise, the house doesn't tell him anything. He needs to get closer.

He walks through the opening in the fence and crosses the street, ducking behind a telephone pole for cover, the machete at his side. He's breathing heavily.

He expects to look up and see Donnie staring down at him from behind the curtain. Instead of backing off, he approaches the front gate of Donnie's house. He opens the latch as gently as he can, lifting it with the tips of his fingers so it doesn't make any noise. He then slides the gate open, hoping it doesn't creak or whine, which it doesn't, and he's careful not to slam it against the aluminum garbage can near the fence. Once in, he pushes the gate closed but doesn't snap the latch shut in case he needs to make a quick getaway.

He squeezes past the car, a Tempo, and goes down the alley on the side of the house, where he feels momentarily out of view. He passes the electric meter and a fire ladder hanging just overhead. A padlocked door that, he's guessing, leads to the cellar where Gabe killed himself. A lot of these old houses have them. This one's painted green, the paint peeling, the lock rusty.

Only two windows on this side of the house. The one on the second floor looks like a bathroom window. Frosted, small. Below that's a bigger window, and he's not sure what room's behind it, but it seems dark. The house has green asbestos siding. Mikey brushes against it, and some flakes off on his jacket. He looks up at the gutters, clumped with debris.

He goes around to the back of the house and crouches under another window. The ground in the yard is cracked concrete. A crumbling brick barbecue squats next to a cast-iron tub full of dirty water. He can see through the curtain slightly. Looks like the kitchen. A little table off to the left. He doesn't catch any movement, no shadows passing. He gets below it, sitting now, his back against the asbestos siding.

When he looks up, he sees the back side of the Divino house.

Antonina is out on the fire escape, smoking. She's wearing overalls, and her hair's pink. She doesn't see him. She flicks her cigarette butt away and descends the ladder into her yard, which is full of cinder blocks, sawhorses, blue tarps, and empty planters, and then disappears along the side of the house.

Pigeons scatter from their perch on the top post of the battered chain link fence that closes off Donnie's yard from the overgrown garden of the house behind him. Mikey can smell rotting figs from the fig trees in that yard, mushed grapes, tomato plants. He can see the golden bursts of squash blossoms through the diamond pattern of the fence.

Mikey stands and looks through the window into Donnie's kitchen. He doesn't see anything. He puts both hands on the window and pushes up, hoping it's unlocked. It is. He opens the window all the way and sets the machete inside. He's being as quiet as he can be.

He hoists himself onto the sill, climbing in through the open window.

He's standing in Donnie's kitchen now. That table's just to the side of the window. Formica top. An empty takeout container turned over on it. Dirty dishes are piled in the sink. One of the overhead cabinets is ajar, showing a rack of dusty spices that look older than him. He opens the refrigerator and gets hit with the smell of old ketchup.

The house is dead quiet. No voices, no anything.

Mikey picks up the machete and wanders down the hallway. In the living room, he sees empty Depends boxes on the floor. Leading away from the boxes toward the front door of the house is a small trail of blood that's browned the wood.

The feeling of being in the house isn't a good one. Walking here, he'd tried to inhabit a character—a man with a machete, out for revenge—but now he's seeing that he's just himself, and he's nervous as hell.

He goes upstairs and finds the bathroom. The toilet seat is up. Black pubic hairs cling to the rim of the bowl. He places the machete on the blue tiled floor, which is strewn with pieces of toilet paper and toothpaste caps and rusty razors. He kneels in front of the scummy toilet, fearing that he's going to puke. He looks down at the bowl and thinks, *These are the pubic hairs of the man who killed my father.*

He doesn't puke. He just stays that way for a while.

He gets up and goes back out into the upstairs hallway. There are three other doors. He tries one. It's a closet full of stiff towels and ragged comforters.

The next door opens on a cold room. He goes inside and shuts the door behind him.

It's Gabe's room, he can tell almost immediately. Bare mattress, desk, a beat-up old dresser, a closet full of high school kid clothes, a calendar on the wall.

He touches the clothes in the closet, the jackets and sweatshirts and pants.

He puts the machete on the bed and looks through the desk. In the top drawer, he finds a black-and-white picture of Donna from when she was a teenager. He imagines Gabe loved the idea of his mother in high school. Mikey never had a picture of Rosemarie like that. In fact, he's never seen a picture of her in high school or even from before her wedding day.

He looks closely at the picture. Donna must be fourteen or fifteen in it, which means it's from almost twenty-five years ago. The late '60s probably. She's wearing a knitted sweater dress. Her hair is pulled up in a bun. She's laughing. Mikey can't help but wonder who took the picture. She looks truly happy. He bets that's why Gabe loved the picture so much and kept it in his top drawer. It's the kind of picture that transmits joy. He traces his finger over Donna's young face. He feels close to her, close to Gabe.

He puts the picture in the pocket of his father's corduroy coat. He realizes how hot he's been in the coat on the walk over, how uncomfortable. It feels good to be in the cold room. He can feel the sweat drying on his forehead. He goes and sits on the bare mattress and stares at the back of Gabe's door. He unsheathes the machete and rests it across his thighs, at the ready. He'll wait right here for Donnie.

Alice stares daggers at Nick as he climbs into the passenger seat of her shitty Hyundai Sonata. She looks good. She's got that post-school glow. She's wearing a polka-dot-print sleeveless summer knit dress. Her hair is pulled up in a ponytail.

"What are you thinking?" she says. "You're gonna get fired. Sechiano's gonna hand you your ass. That's what you want?"

Nick moves around, uncomfortable in his seat, buckles his belt. "Just give me a sec here, Alice, okay?"

"Have you been drinking? And you haven't changed your clothes? Your breath fucking reeks. You look like a homeless guy."

"What else you got for me on your laundry list of complaints?"

"Now you talk in clichés? You hate clichés."

"Can't you be excited for me?"

"Excited for what?"

He starts rambling about his script idea, about Donnie Parascandolo picking up Ava when her car broke down, about Mikey and Antonina, about getting in touch with Phil Puzzo. He tells her about calling Ava and Donnie picking up. He leaves out the part about being with Antonina at Spanky's Lounge. He's not sure he's making sense. They're just sitting there, windows open, parked on Cropsey Avenue, people out on the sidewalk.

"Jesus," she says. "I'm worried about you."

Nick is looking at her and she looks good, but he can't help but let his mind wander back to Antonina, hunched over that *Knight Rider* pinball machine, jutting her hip against it to shake loose a ball.

"Hello? Nick? Are you there?" Alice pokes him in the shoulder. "I'm worried about you, I said."

"We're going to the house, okay? Phil's going to meet me there. He's taking the train from his place."

"You said Ava's there with this Donnie?"

"Crazy," Nick says, nodding. "We'll see. I'll take Phil to my room to talk to him. I need a few minutes in private, that's it."

Alice pushes the car into gear and thrusts away from the curb. It's a short ride back to the house, and Nick is antsy the whole way. He's anxious to talk to Phil. He knows Phil will be able to give him guidance and direction. Nick's always wanted to be taken under the wing of someone like Phil Puzzo. Ava's fine. Donnie was just messing with him. Maybe it's a good thing if Donnie's there. Maybe it's good if Phil meets him.

When they pull up outside, Nick notices a strange car in the driveway. An Olds Cutlass Ciera. He wonders who it belongs to. Alice asks if that's Donnie's car. He says he doesn't think it is, unless he has another one.

"Is Ava dating this guy?" Alice asks.

"When I talked to him on the phone, he said he'd just got done . . ." Nick trails off, pauses, thinks of what phrase might be least upsetting. "He said he'd just got done giving her oral sex."

"What the hell happened in the last day? Ava? *Ava?* I mean, she looks good, I guess, but she seems so icy. I thought she'd just moon over your dad forever."

Nick shrugs. "I don't know. I thought that, too."

They go inside. The kitchen light is on. Empty coffee cups are on the table. A half-filled box of pastries and cookies from Angelo's, as if Ava's been entertaining. The Cento can full of cigarette butts.

Alice sits at the table, exploring the cookies. Nick takes a lap around the house.

In Ava's room, he notices her robe's just tossed on the bed. Unlike her. He goes back to what Donnie said to him on the phone: *I ate her pussy until she howled.* The bed doesn't look like anything or anyone has been on it. It's still made. There's no mess. Just the robe. Nick shudders at the thought of Donnie eating out Ava. Maybe it really happened. Maybe on the floor or in the kitchen.

He goes to his room, and everything's in order. He gets his copy of Phil Puzzo's book off the shelf over his bed. *The True Story of the Diamond Den Murders.* That great cover with the chalk outline on the mirrored floor of the Diamond Den, that skanky old Bay Ridge club. He looks at the picture of Phil on the book. Toothpick in his mouth. Squinty, tough eyes. Nick puts the book under his arm. He's thinking he might as well get it signed by the great man himself.

On his way back through the kitchen, Nick takes a pignoli cookie and eats it while he's standing there. Alice is eating a rainbow. When he eats a rainbow, he does it in one big bite. Alice is taking these tiny bites, and it's unnerving him.

"So, what now?" she asks.

"We wait for Phil."

"You think Ava's out on a date with this Donnie?"

Nick shrugs. When he's done with his pignoli cookie, he takes another one. He looks down and there are crumbs all over his shirt and jacket. He swats at himself until the crumbs disappear. And then he goes into the bathroom and brushes his teeth with his finger. He should change his clothes, but he doesn't. He sprays on some deodorant. He doesn't like the spray kind, but he uses it now because he's thinking it'll freshen up his clothes a bit. He looks at his face in the mirror. His eyes are bloodshot. His hair's a mess. He runs a hand through it.

When he comes back out to the kitchen, he's met by Alice's restlessness.

"What do you think Phil Puzzo's gonna do for you?" she asks. "He's your neighbor's son, how come you never met him before? All you have is an idea. Probably everybody he knows comes to him with ideas. I knew a guy in college, Nathan, who was a great writer. He put out a book right after we graduated. His whole life after that was people coming up to him and saying they had the best idea for a book."

Nick looks at her. "Who's Nathan?"

"Oh, come on. Now you're jealous?"

"How come you've never mentioned him in all this time? He's a writer, I'm a writer. You dated him?"

"We did for a little while, yes." Alice avoids Nick's gaze. "Don't take this the wrong way, okay? You say you're a writer, but I've never seen you write anything."

"I'm always taking notes in my head. I've been waiting for my story to tell. This is it. And it's a live wire." He holds up Phil's book. "I just need a nudge. I need some connections. Phil's a big shot."

Alice shakes her head. "You've got so much right in front of you. You've got me. You've got a good job. And all you can think about is some stupid, farfetched dream."

"You don't think I've got it in me, writing this script, getting this movie made?"

She shakes her head. "I don't. I'm sorry."

He clenches his jaw but then settles into a smile. "You'll see. I'll surprise you yet."

The doorbell rings.

"Phil's here," Nick says, making a break for the door. "That was fast."

He opens the door on someone who looks almost like the man from the book jacket. The author photo's pretty old now, he guesses. He'd seen Phil outside his parents' house once or twice, back when Nick was a kid and Phil was around more frequently, but he's never seen him up close. Phil's probably in his late forties. *The True Story of the Diamond Den Murders* came out when Nick was in college. Since then, Phil's shaved his head bald and gotten a little puffier. His skin is Florida tan, and he seems to be wearing lip gloss. His clothes are flashy: a floral-print cotton shirt, linen trousers, leather monk strap shoes. He looks like he's just disembarked a cruise for assholes.

Phil bypasses a proper greeting. "Listen, kid," he says, his voice almost as Kathleen Turnerish as his mother's. "I don't have long."

Nick holds up his book. "I'm a big fan."

Phil's heard it all before. "That's nice."

"Come on in."

Phil follows Nick into the kitchen. His eyes light up when he sees Alice. "And who's this?"

"My girlfriend," Nick says.

Alice stands and extends her hand. "Hi, I'm Alice."

Phil takes her hand, almost brutal in his tenderness, and kisses the back of it with his greasy lips. "Pleasure's all mine. I'm Phil Puzzo."

"Take a seat," Nick says. "You want a cookie?"

Phil's still taking in Alice. "This is *your* girlfriend? No offense, but you've been called up from the minors before your time. She's major league, bud."

Nick laughs it off. "My script idea, it's a good one, right? Donnie might be here with my mother any minute. You can tell me what you think of him in person. He'll be a great subject—"

Phil cuts him off: "Let me stop you right there. I was talking to Bobby the other day—Bobby De Niro, who's a good pal—and we were talking about some project he's working on he wants to get out of. The guy doing it, he's an absolute hack. Thinks he knows Brooklyn, thinks he knows the mob. Bobby's kicking himself for signing on. I says to Bobby, I says, 'Someone should've discouraged that guy along the way.' Bobby laughs. 'You're right,' he says to me."

"I don't get it," Nick says.

"I'm here to discourage you. This Donnie's not only a bad subject. He's *no* subject. You don't know shit from a hole in the ground. I've got stories.

The guys I've met. The guys I've studied. Gaspipe Casso, Stacks Brancaccio. Listen, kid, I'm giving you free advice. I wanted a home-cooked meal from my mother, that's why I'm here."

Nick's hurt. He can feel it in his chest. Everyone thinks this idea of his is a joke. It's the worst hearing it from Phil because it means he doesn't look at him and see a fellow artist. He sees a wannabe hack.

Phil continues: "Anyhow, I'm really glad I came because I've had the great pleasure of meeting Alice."

Nick looks at Alice. He can't imagine that she'd be flattered by this kind of attention. She's probably not genuinely, but she does seem to be putting on some enjoyment of it to get back at Nick for his shortsightedness.

"You want to come over to Mama and Papa Puzzo's for a nice home-cooked meal, Alice?" Phil asks. "My mother's got the gravy going. My old man made the manicotti from scratch."

Alice turns to Nick and then stands up and approaches Phil. Nick figures she's going to slap the shit out of the guy. "You know what?" she says. "Sure, I'll come with you."

"What?" Nick says.

"Maybe you'll learn something," Alice says.

"Don't."

Phil puts his arm around the small of Alice's back and guides her down the hallway and out the front door. Alice doesn't look back.

Nick sits at the table with his head in his hands. Too fucking much, that's what this all is. He feels like crying. A real artist would sit here and get out his typewriter and channel the pain into his script. This neighborhood, this place, put down on the page all the ways it's tried to wreck him, get across the way he carries it in his blood like a disease. But he doesn't move. He's not even sure where his typewriter is. Anyhow, he doesn't know where to start, how to start, especially now with Alice having abandoned him. Even if it's just to prove a point, it stings. She's gonna be over there with Paulie and Nina and Phil, stuffing her face full of manicotti, Phil ogling her.

He eats a couple of more cookies and throws his copy of *The True Story of the Diamond Den Murders* in the direction of the trash, missing wide. Fifteen, twenty minutes he sits there like that, defeated, a bum who lost what he didn't even have.

When Ava comes in, wearing—to his surprise—her stupid scud missile T-shirt, jeans, and sneakers, she goes on the offensive before he can say anything. "I'm just having a little fun, that's all," she says. "I don't have to explain myself. If I want to go away, I can go away."

"Slow down," Nick says.

"I'm going away with Don. I'm packing a bag right now, and we're going to Italy for a couple of weeks."

"What?"

"You heard me."

Nick shakes his head. Unreal. "Where's Don, Donnie, whatever?"

"He's right outside, waiting for me. I was going to leave you a note. I'm glad you're here, so I can say goodbye."

"You're just gonna go to the airport and buy tickets to Italy? You're not gonna plan ahead? Reserve hotels? Rent a car? I'm no world traveler, but I don't think you can go just like that."

"It's an adventure. People have adventures, right? I deserve adventure in my life. Too long, I've lived cooped up."

Now Nick can only laugh. Between Alice taking off with Phil Puzzo five minutes after meeting him and Ava's proclamation that she's free and deserves some adventure in her life, what else can he do?

"Why are you laughing?" Ava says.

"Why not?"

Ava disappears back into her bedroom, ostensibly to pack a bag. Nick gets up and goes to the front door, opening it, and looking out at Donnie, who's leaning against the front fence like the freest man in the fucking world. Nick recognizes his father's clothes on Donnie. The Atlantic City shirt was a staple. His father would wear it around the house. Nick sees him now, kicked back in his recliner, watching the Yanks, fixing something on his worktable in the basement with a soldering iron, making a sandwich on semolina bread with provolone and capocollo. The shirt is a little tight on Donnie. Nick also notices that it seems like Donnie's taken a shot to the nose. He wonders what the story is there. Protecting Ava's honor, maybe?

Donnie looks up at Nick and smiles. "Hey there, fucko," Donnie says.

"Going on a trip?" Nick asks.

"Already took Ava to the moon. Figured we'd try Italy next."

"What do you want from her?"

"We're just having some fun, kid. Lighten up. What do you want from *me*? That's the real question. You've got an angle."

Nick looks at this man he's been thinking of as his possible subject since they met. Who was he to think like that? Alice and Ava were right. Number one was the question of where even to start. He'd read a couple of books on script formatting that he'd bought at a B. Dalton Booksellers in Staten Island, and an actor friend from school had given him a copy of Stallone's script for *Cobra*, but he didn't really have a sense of how he might build the thing. Say he did start with the schoolyard, Donnie hitting Mikey with the bat—where would he go from there? Number two, he wouldn't follow through. He'd get ten pages in and the whole project would lose its luster. He'd get distracted. He ignores Donnie's question. He *had* an angle, but there's no angle now. Just smoke from things backfiring so badly.

Nick looks up the block at the Puzzo house for any sign of Alice, but she must really be inside, must really be getting a kick out of putting the screws to him good.

"I bet you want to know where we're going in Italy," Don says.

"Do you even know?" Nick asks.

"We're playing it by ear. Maybe we'll find your mother's people. Or my people. Calabria. Sicily. Potenza. Bari. Lots of possibilities."

"How you gonna afford this? You're a rich guy?"

"I struck gold."

Ava comes out a few minutes later with a small suitcase, having changed into a white blouse, a blue skirt, and flats. "This is crazy. I'm not even thinking. I called work and told them to whistle Dixie for a couple of weeks." She turns to Nick and kisses him on the cheek. "Nick, did you see the new car?" She points to the Olds Cutlass Ciera in the driveway.

"New car?" Nick says.

"Don bought it for me from Frankie and Sal. So nice of him, wasn't it? The keys are in the dish on the table. Use it. The Nova won't be ready for a couple of days. When Frankie calls, you'll have to go pick it up. Leave the Olds in the driveway. I guess park the Nova on the street. What's somebody gonna do, steal it? Let them. Don't miss school again, huh? Last thing you need is to get canned. And—oh yeah—can you take the clothes out of the wash and put them on the line in the yard? Bring them in when they're dry, please." She takes a breath. "This is crazy. Italy! Can you believe it?"

"You're not thinking here, Ma."

"I think too much, sonny boy. I think too goddamn much." She pecks him on the cheek again and races down the front steps to join Donnie, who throws an arm around her and takes her suitcase.

"You ready, sweetheart?" Donnie says to Ava.

Nick can't take hearing his mother called sweetheart by this fucking guy. How'd she go from getting picked up on the Belt by a stranger to running away to Italy with him? *Sweetheart* is what his old man called her. *Sweetheart, we got any vermouth left? Sweetheart, the braciole is aces.*

"Take care of the old dump," Ava says to Nick now. "I'll write when I get there." And then she and Donnie walk away down the block.

Nick's alone in the house. This is maybe the most alone he's ever felt. He hopes Alice comes back after her lunch with Phil, just to say, "See how easy it is for me to walk away? Wake up, chump." If she doesn't, he's not sure what he'll do. Ava going to Italy on the fly with Donnie Parascandolo? How on earth did they ever get to this moment?

They walk to Donnie's house. Ava's flush with excitement. So is he, to tell the truth. It's the kind of excitement you don't feel much once you're beyond eighteen. The older you get, the more it starts to feel like you could never just drop everything and leave. They're making a vow together, Donnie and Ava, to feel free like kids.

"I have cousins," Ava says, as they turn onto his block. "I don't know how we'll find them, but we will."

"I have cousins over there, too," Donnie says. "They're all gonna be in for a surprise."

"Some of mine, I haven't seen since the wedding. They don't even know Anthony died."

"I can play Anthony, you want. I'm already wearing his clothes."

"Don't kid like that."

When they get to his house, Donnie—to his relief—opens up to silence. He's sure Sottile made the drop for Big Time Tommy at Flash Auto. Pags, he's another story. He's sorry he pissed him off, but the cut was fair. Anyhow, the money's gone, so he choked the deal down.

"Well," Ava says, taking in the place for the first time. "You definitely live like a bachelor."

Donnie shrugs. "I'll clean up my act for you, I swear."

Ava leans over and touches a flap on one of the diaper boxes. "You incontinent?" she asks, and laughs.

"I was just unpacking some junk," he says.

"Should we call about flights?"

"I say we just go. There's gotta be something taking off tonight."

She sits down and shakes her head. "I just thought of something. We're so stupid."

"What?"

"Passports. I don't have a passport. Do you have a passport?"

Don laughs. "What'd I ever need a passport for? Too many obstacles in this goddamn life. You want to go to Italy, you should just be able to go to Italy. The Italian blood I got, that should be my passport."

"I agree, but I don't think they'll let us on the plane."

"So, let's go to California. We take a red-eye to San Francisco. Go see the Giants play. They got their own Little Italy. North Beach, it's called. I heard about it on this show I watched."

"Why not?" Ava says. "I'd go about anywhere with you right now. I just want to get away for a couple of weeks."

"Right," Donnie says. "Who cares? We can throw a dart at the departures board when we get to the airport. I just want to hole up in a nice hotel with you and go out to eat and not think about New York."

Ava comes over and kisses him on the cheek. "We make a good pair, I think, me and you."

"Do me a favor. Go in the kitchen and call the car service. Tell them we need a lift to JFK. I got the number for a place on Twenty-First Avenue taped to the side of the phone. They'll be here in no time. I'm gonna go upstairs, get changed—no offense—and pack a suitcase."

He's thinking about the money under the floorboards. He's wondering if he should take it all. Maybe he should just take half, leave the rest if they're only going to be gone a couple of weeks. Why risk losing it? On the other hand, why not live it up? They could rent a fucking penthouse, get room service delivered, go out to high-end steakhouses.

Ava disappears into the kitchen to make the call.

Donnie grabs his cigarette case, which is sitting out in the living room. He goes upstairs to his room. He looks at his face in the mirror. Ava cleaned him up real nice. His nose looks a little fucked, and it's throbbing pretty good, but it's nothing he can't fight through. He finds a bottle of ibuprofen on top of his dresser and pops three in his mouth, washing them down with spit. He undresses, leaving Ava's dead husband's clothes balled on the floor.

He changes into fresh boxers, cargo shorts, and a Hawaiian-print shirt. As he buttons the shirt, he looks at himself in the mirror again. He's a man going on vacation. He's going to be comfortable on the plane. He's going to drink scotch and relax.

He packs a duffel bag. More boxers, some T-shirts and dress shirts, two pairs of jeans that are probably a size too small, mismatched socks. He tosses the cigarette case in there so he doesn't forget it. He pushes the throw rug aside and lifts up the floorboard and stuffs most of the money in the bag. What the hell? You only live once. They're going to live the goddamn high life, him and Ava. Maybe he'll talk her into Vegas after San Francisco, or maybe they'll go to New Orleans and eat like kings. He's not sure what he'll tell her about the money, but he'll come up with something good. The bag's coming on the plane with him, never leaving his sight. They find a fancy hotel first thing wherever they wind up, he'll put it right in the safe. He doesn't know much, but he knows fancy hotel rooms have safes.

He leaves a few grand in the hole so it's there if he needs it when he gets back. He guesses Big Time Tommy will catch up with him eventually, and he's going to have to figure a way out of that. Or maybe he'll just stay away longer. He puts the floorboard back and drops the rug in its place.

Anyhow, this wasn't Big Time Tommy's money, per se. The other dough he skimmed along the way—loose change, essentially—wasn't really either, and he's sure Tommy will just want him to pay off the insult through work. He won't dangle him from a roof or anything. He does, what the fuck? Donnie's not scared of Big Time Tommy and his numbnuts crew. Like that walking bag of dick scrapings, Dice.

Leaving the bag unzipped, he walks out of the room. He's thinking about what else he might need to do to shut the house down if he won't be back for a stretch. It's summer, so he doesn't have to worry about the heat. He should go around checking windows, maybe take out the trash, that's about it.

As he passes Gabe's room, he hears something.

Footsteps.

He pauses and sets down the bag on the floor, trying to be as quiet as possible. He can't have heard what he thought he heard. It was probably just Ava down in the kitchen, pacing as she talked to the car service guy. He's not used to the company, and it somehow sounded like she was up here.

But then he hears it again. Definite footsteps, coming from Gabe's room.

He presses his head against the door. He'd had that thought about the coldness being a sign of the presence of Gabe's ghost, and now he's convinced. This, of course, is the time he would choose to show himself, just as Donnie's ready to leave with Ava for the airport on this new adventure. What does Gabe want from him? He must be trying to tell him something with these footsteps.

"Gabe?" Donnie says. "That you? It's Daddy, Gabe."

He listens closer. No more footsteps, just silence now. *Look at yourself,* he thinks. *Standing here, talking to the ghost of your dead son. You're losing it. You lost it, motherfucker. What you heard was nothing. Go to Ava with your bag of money and ride off into the sunset.*

He's watched enough shows about hauntings to know that the best thing to do is ask a ghost what it wants. "Gabe, buddy, what do you want from me?"

More silence.

What could a dead boy want from his father? He and Gabe had their problems. Gabe was different from him, way different, way more Donna, and Donnie hadn't liked that. He hadn't done a lot of the things a father needs to do. He wasn't warm with the kid. He didn't make him feel loved. All that led to him calling it quits. If Donnie had been even just okay as a dad, maybe Gabe would've wanted to live.

It occurs to him he's doing what Ava wanted him to do. Facing down the loss of Gabe honestly for the first time. She wanted him to talk to a goddamn priest, but it took a ghost.

"Gabe, I'm sorry," he says, figuring an apology is the best place to start. "As an old man, I wasn't much, I know that."

A noise on the other side of the door. It sounds like a hand on the knob. Maybe that's all Gabe wanted, that *I'm sorry*, and now he'll open up and the room will be warm and that will let Donnie know that his son's at peace.

But when the door is flung open, it's Mikey Baldini standing there. He's wearing a corduroy coat Donnie recognizes as Giuseppe's and holding a long blade, batting gloves on his hands. Before Donnie can say anything, the blade comes at him. It's like the kid doesn't know how to handle it, so he just sort of lurches forward and thrusts it at Donnie. It goes straight into his gut, deep. He makes a noise, Donnie does, like the air's being let out of him.

Donnie's hands go around the blade, trying to yank it out with no luck, and he collapses onto his side, his head on the floor in Gabe's room, the rest of his body out in the hallway, the blade like something terrible that's sprouted from the center of him.

Ava calls up from downstairs: "Don, you okay?"

Donnie manages to look up at Mikey, who's stepping over him.

"That's for my old man," Mikey says.

The way he's curled on the floor now, the blade sticking out of his gut, Donnie watches as Mikey notices the duffel bag, money visible. As he picks up the bag, Mikey changes into Gabe. It's Gabe touching the money, reaching inside to see how much is there, looking shocked. It's Gabe walking calmly away, down the hallway, down the stairs. He's glad Gabe's got the money. No, it's Mikey Baldini. Donnie hears the front door open and close. Front doors sound a certain way.

Ava calls up to him again: "Don, what was that? The car service place has me on hold this whole time. I might try another one. You have the number for that place on Benson?"

Donnie's hands travel the length of the blade to the handle. He can feel the blood under him. The pain in his gut is like nothing he's ever known. It's like a meteor crashed there. He shouldn't pull the blade out, he knows, but he'll never be able to move with such a long blade stuck in him. He gets it out, he'll have to wrap himself with something. He's seen movies. Get down to the kitchen, wrap cellophane around his gut, while Ava—no doubt—panics and calls an ambulance. He can't speak.

He manages to get to his knees, right there in the doorway of his son's room. He can feel that the room is still cold. He sees his blood spreading out on the floor. He tries to pull the blade out, but he can't. The strength's just not there. He falls on his side again, but it feels like he's fallen into a deep pit, and everything goes black.

On the train into the city, Antonina tells Lizzie about the Madonna show that Ralph's getting them tickets to. They're sitting next to each other on the orange bucket seats. The car is otherwise empty.

Lizzie laughs. "That'll be weird," she says.

Lizzie's so pretty. Her mother's Chinese and her father's Italian. She's got this perfect black hair. She's putting on some heavy-duty makeup as they talk. Her mother wouldn't let her leave the house the way she looks now, with all that eyeliner and black lipstick. She's wearing a boy's flannel shirt, ripped jeans, and a pair of Doc Martens that she's covered in gold glitter.

They decide to skip the movie they'd talked about seeing at the Angelika and just go straight to the Keyhole Cocktail Lounge on St. Mark's, where the old Ukrainian bartender will serve them drinks to their heart's content, only charging them about half the time. They'll play songs on the jukebox and dance.

Lizzie dates a guy from the city named Chip. He's older and his band, Kill Chariot, plays at Coney Island High and Mercury Lounge all the time. Antonina's been to see them a few times. Lizzie says now, "Chip's friend's band is playing at Coney Island High later. Blessed Mother of Fuck is their name. I'm not sure if they're punk or metal, but they'll be loud. Chip says we can stay at his place overnight. You think you can get away with that? I told my mother I was staying with you."

"Of course," Antonina says.

Antonina watches out the scratched-up window as the train crosses the Manhattan Bridge. She looks at the light on the East River, the swarm of cars down on the FDR Drive. She imagines herself in the immediate future, putting back strong drinks at the Keyhole, wasted at Coney Island High in a jumble of leather and denim, getting lost in some music, any music.

If she and Lizzie go home with Chip, she wonders who else will be coming with them. They'll probably be up all night, partying. Last time she was at Chip's, she sat in awe as he shot up on a folding chair. That's all he has in his loft for furniture, folding chairs.

Antonina's going to spend every last cent of the money she brought with her. She hasn't even told Lizzie about it. Maybe she'll buy some drugs for them. Pills or weed. Or maybe they'll just shoot up with Chip. Lizzie did it once and said it was heaven.

She thinks again of the phone ringing in her room later, Ralph calling and her not being there to answer. She wonders how mad he'll be. She wonders if he'll go to the Bronx by himself and sulk. She wonders what lie she'll tell him eventually. The money he gave her deserves a good lie at least. She just wants to be a dumb kid with Lizzie right now, that's all.

"We're gonna get fucked up tonight," Lizzie says, dropping her voice dramatically on the last three words and sort of singing them. She finishes her makeup and turns, staring at herself in the glass as best she can. "I look okay?"

"You look great," Antonina says, smiling, seeing herself reflected in the glass over Lizzie's shoulder. Beyond that, over her own shoulder in the reflection, she sees the door between cars open and a hulking body squeeze through. She turns. It's Ralph. She knows this can't be a coincidence. Lizzie knows about Ralph, of course, but Antonina never anticipated that they'd meet.

Ralph smiles, holds up his hand, giving a little salute. He sits across from her and Lizzie. He's got dark pit stains under his arms, his forehead beaded with drops of sweat.

"You followed me?" Antonina asks.

"'Followed' is a strong word," he says.

Lizzie turns now and takes him in. She must know. She doesn't say anything, not yet.

"This is the famous Lizzie?" Ralph says.

"What the fuck, Ant?" Lizzie says, under her breath.

"Why'd you follow me?" Antonina asks Ralph again.

"I didn't," Ralph says. "Well, I did, but I didn't really. I wasn't setting out with those intentions. I saw you on Bay Parkway and I thought, 'Let me catch up to her.' That's it. You girls going into the city?"

"Dude, that's so creepy," Lizzie says.

"Antonina tell you about the Madonna tickets?" Ralph says to Lizzie. And then to Antonina: "'The Girlie Show,' you said it was called, right?"

"Please don't talk to Lizzie," Antonina says. "What do you want from me? It's not a good time."

"You girls are going where? Movie, concert, what?"

"How old are you?" Lizzie says to Ralph. "Are you trying to fuck her or what?"

"Lizzie, *stop*," Antonina says, feeling suddenly pissed at both of them, caught between them, these worlds colliding, unsure of what to do with Ralph or if Lizzie will now look at her and see a different girl. She imagines Lizzie's thinking, *You sneak out of your house to go to a diner in the Bronx with this sweaty piece of shit?*

"I don't know what I was thinking," Ralph says, taking a handkerchief out of his pocket and drying his forehead. "Maybe I can take you girls out for a nice meal? You got a favorite place? We can go there. How about Indian? That's something you can't get back in the neighborhood. Little India over there on East Sixth, you know it? A lot of good joints."

"You're a sad man, huh?" Lizzie says.

Ralph ignores her. "Can I talk to you alone for a sec?" he asks Antonina. "I earned that much, didn't I?"

Antonina nods. She puts her hand on Lizzie's knee. "Just give me a couple of minutes with him."

"We're getting off in two minutes at Broadway-Lafayette," Lizzie says.

"I know."

Lizzie gets up and moves about ten feet away, standing in front of a subway map like a straphanger, checking herself again in whatever reflection she can get on the glass over the multicolored lines veining the boroughs.

"What is this?" Antonina says to Ralph, realizing that he's crossed a line she long expected him to cross and then gave up on him ever crossing. This is not the way, or the time, that she expected it to happen. She's embarrassed in front of Lizzie. Put out. She can't help but think what it must look like, that *this* is the guy—worse-looking and older and more rundown than any father they know—that she'd been rendezvousing with. She can tell Lizzie's grossed out.

"I don't know *what*," Ralph says. "The money was nice, right? The money helps?"

Antonina's thinking, *Is this what the money bought you?* But what she says is, "I've gotta get off the train soon."

Ralph nods.

When the train pulls out of the Grand Street station, Antonina stands up. She starts to wander toward Lizzie, trailing a hand behind her, as if willing Ralph to sit and stay, to go to midtown or wherever else, to just let them be as they are. But he gets up too, and she knows he'll get off at Broadway-Lafayette with them and follow them up the steps. And then what? Will Lizzie ditch her? Will she be left alone with Ralph?

At Broadway-Lafayette, the doors ding open, and Antonina and Lizzie burst out onto the platform. Ralph lumbers out behind them.

"This is fucking creepy," Lizzie says, looking quickly over her shoulder at Ralph as they climb the stairs to the mezzanine.

"He's harmless," Antonina assures her.

"I know you think he's not trying to fuck you, but he's definitely trying to fuck you. I should stop and call Chip."

"What's Chip gonna do? Ralph's a cop. Besides, he's never acted like this before. Maybe something's wrong." Antonina looks back now, and Ralph's eyes are fixated on her as he huffs up the steps.

Antonina and Lizzie go through the turnstiles and up another flight of steps, coming out on the corner of Lafayette and East Houston.

"We can just lose him," Lizzie says. "He can't keep up with us."

Antonina's relieved that Lizzie hasn't given up on her. "Okay," she says. "Let's run."

They take off up Lafayette, headed for Bleecker. It feels good to be running. Antonina looks back at Ralph again and sees him standing by a halal cart, hunched over, out of breath, waving to her.

Finding Don in the upstairs hallway had been the biggest shock of her life. Her first thought was that it had to be a prank. A big sword like that. His Hawaiian-print shirt. So much blood. It looked like a horror movie. But then she realized it was really real.

Forget piecing it together, she told herself at once. *Forget how it could've happened, who could've done it. No time for that now.*

She'd only had the ability to scramble back downstairs and call 911, her finger shaking as she pulled the numbers on the rotary phone. After giving the operator the address and telling him that Don had been stabbed somehow, she went back to him and kneeled there and said a Hail Mary.

She looked all around, concerned that whoever had done it was still in the house.

But the house was quiet. The sound of the door opening and closing had been the sound of someone getting away with this.

The ambulance came from Victory Memorial. It took seven minutes. She knows because she was counting the seconds in her head, as she leaned there over Don, her hand on his shoulder, saying his name over and over, watching him struggle for breath.

The EMS workers called to her when they came in. They brought a gurney up. They brought the other things they bring. They started doing the things they do as quickly as they could. They had to take the blade out when they realized how hard it'd be to move him with it in. It was left behind on the floor. An attempt was made to stop the bleeding. One of the workers, a man, seemed scared. The other one, a woman, was all business, her jaw clenched. Cops showed as they brought Don out.

Ava's in the ambulance with Don now. She's sitting there while the EMS workers pump and pull and cut and do whatever else it is they need to do. She feels worthless. She's got blood on her hands, blood on her white blouse.

She closes her eyes and thinks about Don picking her up on the Belt. She can feel every fast turn the ambulance makes, every bump it hits. The sirens are drilling into her head. She thinks of her suitcase back there in Don's living room. She thinks of Nick having to hang Don's clothes on the line back at the house. She thinks of where she and Don might have gone if they'd actually made it to the airport. She can't believe they'd figured on Italy without thinking through the fact that they needed passports.

Whoever did this, it must've been revenge.

Ava thinks of how Don said he'd just come into some dough on their walk. That was when Italy had come up. So, he met her, he liked her, maybe he knocked someone off so he could have money to impress her with a car and a trip to Italy, to San Francisco, to wherever. Maybe this is her fault. She hadn't broken down in her piece-of-shit Nova on the Belt, Don would have kept on living his normal life, surviving in whatever way he'd known to survive before their lives came together.

She opens her eyes to the sound of Don flatlining. The EMS workers are in panic mode, getting out the defibrillator.

She's often around dying people at Sea Crest, old-timers at the end of the line, some of them dying alone, some dying surrounded by family. She was with Anthony when he died. That was difficult in a much different way. That was part of her going away forever. And she was lucky to be with both of her parents when they went, holding their hands, telling them how much she loved them and how happy she was to have been their daughter.

Don is a stranger but not a stranger. She finds it hard to reconcile the fact that there were only minutes, seconds really, between them being excited about traveling together and whatever happened to Don happening. Whoever did it must've been waiting there for him.

She's playing the scene back in her mind now. The room that he was partially in, that must've been his son's. She'll never have answers. She'll be asked questions, and she won't have answers. She'll go back to her life. It'll be like she never met Don.

"He's gone," the EMS woman says. "I'm sorry."

Ava gulps and nods, closes her eyes again. She rehearses a line she's sure she'll get to know by heart: "I didn't know him that well. We just met yesterday."

Mikey knocks on Donna's door. He's got Donnie's duffel bag in his hand. He paused on the way over to zip it shut but not before dumping Donnie's clothes in a corner garbage can and looking to see just how much money there was inside. Not only is his old man's debt with Big Time Tommy cleared, but Mikey has lucked into this starting-over money. He doesn't know how much exactly, but it's a lot. He can use it to split. He really hopes Donna will come with him. He's got to go now. He's got to talk fast. Trouble will likely be on his tail. There was a woman in the house with Donnie. Mikey's worried she got a look at him on the way out. Leaving the machete doesn't mean much, he hopes. He had on these batting gloves. He takes them off so Donna doesn't see them and stuffs them in the bag. He feels alive, electric, redeemed.

No answer. Where could she be? He looks up and sees a woman who must be Suzette Bonsignore staring down at him through dusty blinds. He doesn't know what time it is. It's still light, not even dusk. He knocks again.

Sitting there in Gabe's room, he hadn't been sure he'd be able to go through with it. But something possessed him, made it possible. Donnie came right to him. He thought of his father on that bridge.

If he and Donna leave now, maybe she'll never know what he did to Donnie. That would be easiest.

He doesn't have to go back to his mother. She'll be okay. It'll take her a while to adjust, but she'll realize he's an adult and he deserves his own life, even if it's not the one she'd choose for him. It's better for her not to know where he is, anyway. Say the police figure out it was him. They press her, she's got no answers. He hopes she feels gratitude that he cleared his old man's debt. He hopes that Big Time Tommy comes around and tells her the whole story, what Donnie did and how he got revenge for them. Maybe she'll understand him in a way she didn't before. Maybe she'll respect him. A few months, a year, when things have settled down and he's sure he's in the clear, he'll send her a card checking in.

Donna's crying when she finally opens the door.

"What is it?" Mikey says.

"Nothing," she says. "Are *you* okay?"

He looks over his shoulder. "I've gotta go. I can't tell you why, but I need to go now. Will you go with me?"

"Come in."

He unzips the bag and shows her that there's money inside.

"Where's that from?" she asks. She doesn't recognize the bag itself, thank Christ.

"It's mine now. It's ours. We can go anywhere."

She hesitates, looks back at her apartment, lingering on her turntable and records for a moment. "Okay," she says. "Let's just go. Let's start over."

Inside, Mikey gets his backpack. He notices that her rug is gone. Donna packs a bag full of clothes and toiletries. She wants to take the turntable and some of her favorite records. She selects a bunch that she wants to bring and then grabs her car keys from a hook on the wall. They make one trip out to her car, a Mercury Lynx parked on the street under a sycamore tree, and load the trunk with the turntable, the speakers, a crate of records, and Donnie's bag full of money.

Back inside, they grab their bags and she takes one last look around.

He kisses her. "You sure you don't want anything else?" he asks.

"Fuck it," she says.

They leave the apartment, closing the door behind them and not even bothering to lock it. She looks so cute in her gym shorts and T-shirt and flip-flops.

He gets in on the passenger side of the Lynx and throws his pack in the back seat. He takes her bag and puts it next to his.

She climbs in under the wheel and starts the car. The radio comes on. Some commercial. She puts a Van Morrison tape in. She looks at him and says, "North? South? West?"

He shrugs. "West, I guess. All the way west."

EPILOGUE

TWO WEEKS BEFORE CHRISTMAS | 1994

Ava's been in the hospital for a week after slipping on some ice up near Genovese and breaking her hip when she hit the concrete. Nick sits across from her in her room on the third floor of Victory Memorial, as he has every day after school since she wound up here. A cheap get-well card from Father Borzumato is propped on her nightstand.

The last seventeen months with Ava have been tough. She's become paranoid about getting sick, won't talk about anything other than not wanting to die. It all started with Donnie getting killed. It was either a random act of violence or maybe somebody paying him back for something. The police never figured it out. Either way, it shook Ava, made her older, made her want to live afraid.

Nick is in his school clothes. He's sitting on an uncomfortable green chair, the *Daily News* open in his lap, watching Ava try to eat the slop they serve her.

She's disgusted, rightfully so. She looks old and small in her gown. Her face is drawn in. The surgery on her hip had gone well, but it's a struggle for her to move even slightly.

"You've gotta try to eat," Nick says.

"You try to eat this shit," Ava says.

"You want me to get you something across the street? Minestrone?"

"Forget it."

Nick holds up the paper to the article he'd been reading. It's about Phil Puzzo. "Did you see this?"

"Did I see it?" Ava says. "Where am I gonna see it? This is me all day, laying here like a lump. What is it?"

Nick reads, fuming: "'Native son Philip Puzzo is back in the old neighborhood tonight with his new book, *The Bad Samaritan*. It's about ex-cop Donnie Parascandolo's descent from one of New York's Finest to low-level mob thug. Parascandolo was a man who lost his son to suicide and went badly off the rails, winding up gutted in what many assume was a gangland killing, though there's some speculation that his ex-wife was involved since she went missing the day of the murder. Along the way, Puzzo paints a portrait of a conflicted man still capable of kindness and sincerity. It's a slim, complicated piece of work, as is its subject, but Puzzo is up to the task, painting Parascandolo's fall against the backdrop of a Brooklyn at odds with itself. A powerful reading experience. Highly recommended. Puzzo will be signing books in the St. Mary's auditorium tonight at 6 p.m.' Jesus Christ, Ava. You talked to him for this?"

"I don't remember."

"You don't remember if you talked to Phil Puzzo about Donnie Parascandolo?"

"It was a favor to Nina. He came to Sea Crest one day after work. We sat out on the boardwalk."

"Was Alice with him?"

"No, she wasn't."

The day that Alice left with Phil Puzzo was the end of Nick's life in a way. She was enamored of Phil, and Phil—old and successful enough to be charmingly relentless in winning her over—said he loved her within a month, said he wanted to marry her within two. She said yes. She stopped teaching at Our Lady of the Narrows before the new year started. She moved into Phil's Boerum Hill brownstone. Nick had seen her only a handful of times since, mostly in those last months at school, and she wouldn't give him the time of day, which was crushing. His calls went unanswered. And, of course, he'd given up on his script idea before even starting it.

It didn't seem to bother Alice that Phil had stolen his idea. Nick wasn't sure about the book business, but Phil must've written *The Bad Samaritan* pretty quickly for it to be coming out already. Nick hasn't read the book yet, but he assumes that Phil's research was light, that he mostly made stuff up about Donnie. He'll get his copy tonight at St. Mary's. He'll do more than that.

The paper is from yesterday. He's known about the book for several weeks. He's had plenty of time to get amply upset about it. What he didn't know until the article was that Phil had the balls to come do an event in the neighborhood. That was unheard of. There weren't any bookstores. So, the bright idea—whoever's it was, probably some publicist—was to have Phil read and sign books in the auditorium of his grade school. Some of his childhood teachers, decrepit nuns, mostly the same ones who taught Nick and Ava, would be there to cheer him on. Nick figures that Alice will be there. Or maybe she'll have the smarts to stay away.

Nick's brain is churning. He's going to go, that's certain. He's going to stand in line and get Phil to sign his book, and he'll greet Alice warmly if she's there.

But he's going to bring the gun he bought earlier in the year. He'd gotten the gun for suicide purposes in a fit of February despair. It was sold to him out of the trunk of a car in an alley next to Spanky's Lounge by a neighborhood kid named Ray Boy Calabrese who sometimes worked for Mr. Natale. Ray Boy went to Our Lady of the Narrows, but Nick hadn't taught him, only knew him by reputation. Ray Boy didn't even blink when he sold Nick the gun, didn't recognize him from the halls. Not long after their meeting in the alley, Ray Boy got locked up for chasing poor Duncan D'Innocenzio—who Nick had taught in two classes—out into traffic on the Belt right near the spot where Ava had broken down in the Nova and Donnie had stopped to help.

Nick hadn't had the guts to eat a bullet like he hadn't had the guts to start his script.

But he's going to use the gun. *This* is why he got it. *This* is what it was intended for. After getting Phil Puzzo to scrawl a dedication in the front of the book, he's going to take out the gun and blow the thieving fucker's head clean off. Who's going to stop him, the nuns?

He looks at the clock. Four thirty. He's got just enough time to go home to pick up the gun and get changed. He wants to look sharp in case Alice is there.

"Where's your head?" Ava says.

"I'm thinking," Nick says.

She thumbs at something on her jawline. "Will you feel this? Do you feel a lump here? Do people get tumors in this spot?"

"You're in a hospital. Ask a doctor."

"These doctors. One worse than the next. I can't get straight answers."

"You're not dying. You don't have a tumor. You're going to live to ninety-five."

"God forbid I live that long."

"Well, what do you want? When do you want to die?"

"Give me until eighty-five. That sounds good."

"Okay, you've got until eighty-five." Nick stands, folding the newspaper under his arm, and walks over to the bed, kissing Ava on the cheek.

"That's it?" Ava says. "You're leaving already?"

"I've got plans tonight."

"A date?"

Nick nods.

"With who?" Ava asks.

"You don't know her. Woman from school."

"Italian?"

"Sure."

Ava looks satisfied. "Did you talk to anyone about when I'm getting out of here?"

"They'll move you to rehab tomorrow or the next day. Probably Sea Crest."

"I don't need rehab. And I'm not going there. Anywhere but there."

"I know you think you don't need it." Nick kisses her again, this time on the brow, and then he leaves the room.

He walks down the hallway and waits for the elevator. He thinks about the article. He's heard the speculation about Donnie's ex-wife, Donna, being involved in Donnie's death. He's also heard the speculation about Mikey Baldini and his mother, Rosemarie, being involved. It is peculiar that Donna, Mikey, and Rosemarie all went missing the day Donnie was killed, but none of it adds up to anything of value. Just two empty houses and an empty apartment, lots of stuff left behind. Nick figures that Big Time Tommy Ficalora has answers, but nobody's getting them from him, not even Phil Puzzo, who claims to be so tight with the mob.

Outside, he finds that the Nova has been ticketed because he parked too close to a hydrant. He should feel lucky it wasn't towed. That'd screw up his whole plan.

He drives home on the streets, foregoing the Belt, figuring there will be too much traffic this time of day. The ice from the week before is mostly gone, though it's still cold and damp, and the sidewalks are sloppy. People are walking around in hulking coats and heavy wool hats. Christmas lights are up on Eighty-Sixth Street, shining bright. He sees red and green reflected in the grimy blacktop.

He parks right in front of his house, lucky to get such a good spot, and goes straight to his room. He changes into the nicest thing he owns, a suit he bought at a JCPenney for his friend Nino's wedding. Nino teaches history. Nick went to the wedding with Alice. She'd picked out the suit.

He combs his hair and puts on cologne.

He gets the gun from the bottom drawer of his dresser. It's wrapped up in a blue handkerchief. He doesn't even know what kind of gun it is, but he knows it's loaded. He puts the gun in the pocket of his jacket.

He walks to St. Mary's, thinking the cold will do him good. It's not that long a walk, especially moving fast, and he shows up just as the church bells signal six o'clock.

A few people are standing outside the front doors of the school. He smiles at them and walks in.

Nick hasn't been in the auditorium since his last day of eighth grade. He remembers it seeming vast, cavernous. It's small. The wood on the floor is scuffed to a fleshy color. Folding chairs are lined up in rows, most of them occupied. An American flag is hung on the wall behind the stage. Next to the flag is a big wooden crucifix, suspended by some kind of wire.

Phil is sitting at a cheap card table on the stage, books stacked on either side of him. He's wearing a heavy leather jacket over a red sweater, black corduroy pants, and shiny black shoes. He's got a full head of hair now, which must be a wig.

Alice is in the front row. Nick can tell her back from anywhere.

He stands behind the last row of chairs and looks around. He recognizes some faces. The second row is occupied by nuns he remembers from school. Sister Maura, Sister Eleanor, and Sister Lena. Over by the door, old Sister Bernadette stands with her arms crossed, looking agitated, her white hair piled on her head in frosty curls. He doesn't remember anything about their order, but these aren't nuns who get all geared up in nun outfits. They're wearing regular boring old lady clothes.

There's nobody else he sees that he knows except for Sonny and Josephine Divino, who are sitting in rapt attention. Nick wonders whatever happened to Antonina. He guesses college. He imagines her now, hooking up with some cute boy in her warm little dorm room, and he wishes he was still in college.

Sister Thomasine, who Nick also remembers well, introduces Phil Puzzo. She says a few words about the book, insisting that it's "difficult but necessary," and then lists some of Phil's accomplishments.

Phil stands. He talks about putting aside the book on the Brancaccios he'd been working on to write *The Bad Samaritan*. "When a story feels urgent like this, one can't ignore it," he says. He reads the opening chapter of the book. It's fucking Donnie picking up Ava on the Belt. He's reading things Ava told him.

Nick's so mad he can't see straight. He doesn't want to wait to buy the book and then plug Phil. He wants to shoot the fuck right now, as he reads his bullshit. He wants him to fall back, a hole in his head, the wig blown off. He wants Alice to think it's romantic that he's shot this bastard over love and honor.

He takes out his gun and aims it at Phil onstage. He's shaky, but how hard can it be? Phil's not a tiny target. No one sees Nick because he's in the back. The only one who might have him in her sightline is Sister Bernadette, and she's ninety if she's a day.

Phil certainly doesn't look up and see him. He's staring down at the page, wrapped up in the glory of his own words.

Nick's about to fire when he notices, out of the corner of his eye, that Sister Bernadette's charging him.

"Gun!" Sister Bernadette shouts, and the crowd starts shuffling around nervously, everyone looking over their shoulders or lowering their heads into their laps.

Nick can't fucking believe it. He's still got his shot. "You thieving hack!" he calls out to Phil, just as he simultaneously pulls the trigger and Sister Bernadette makes contact with him, pushing him with her old, bony out-stretched arms and knocking him to the floor, the gun skittering away under the chairs in front of him.

The force with which Sister Bernadette pushed him was pretty impressive, he's got to give her that. He never would've guessed she'd be able to budge him, let alone take him down. He looks up to see if he's at least hit Phil, but he hasn't. Phil's ducking behind the card table like the coward that he is. What Nick's hit is the crucifix next to the flag, causing it to sway, a hunk of Christ's arm chipped away.

"You stay right where you are," Sister Bernadette says.

Nick looks at the door. He's clear. He could probably make a break for it. He's afraid to look back toward the stage. He's afraid to see Alice staring at him, whispering to whoever she's sitting next to about what a fucking loser he is.

"Yes, Sister Bernadette," he says. "I will."

Antonina follows her friend Janice down North Front Street, past the Bakery, and across North Chestnut. Janice is hopping around, excited. She's the first friend Antonina made here in New Paltz back in August during her orientation. Janice is from New Rochelle, but her family's originally from the Bronx. She's wearing her usual l.e.i. jeans, which Antonina had never even heard of before meeting her, and a tie-dyed hoodie. She's got a claret red wool coat she scored at the Salvation Army for five bucks on over that, and a wool hat her friend Luna knitted her is pulled low on her head. Her Walkman's always got this mix an old boyfriend made her with Joni Mitchell, the Allman Brothers, and Richie Havens. She's half-listening now, her headphones half-on. She's not the best friend that Antonina would've expected, but Janice is great, free and funny and up for anything.

Antonina's changed in her time here, too. Her hair is back to its natural color, brown, and she hasn't washed it in over a month, taking Janice's advice and rubbing it with some kind of hippie oil she gave her. She's thinking about dreadlocks. She hasn't shaved her legs in a month either. She has her combat boots and overalls on, still a go-to outfit. She's wearing thermals under the overalls and a man's bomber coat Janice didn't want anymore. She doesn't have a hat on. Her ears are cold.

She had her last final of the semester yesterday and aced it. It was a pretty good first semester, all told. She liked her classes, especially English 101 and Art History. She works three nights a week at a coffee shop called the Sleeping Turtle, where these hardcore bands sometimes play. Lizzie's in Boston and has come down to visit twice because Boston freaks her out. Antonina's going back down to Brooklyn in a few days. Her dad's coming to pick her up when the dorms close for winter break.

Antonina's made out with ten people since moving here, not that she's really keeping track. Seven guys and three girls. She's slept with two of them, one guy and one girl. The guy's name is Lane. He's from outside Syracuse and is in one of the bands that plays at the Sleeping Turtle. Jan's Long Crawl, they're called. She's slept with him a few times, actually. He's kind of dumb. He smokes a lot of weed. The girl, her name is Celeste and she's in her mid-twenties and works at Earth Goods on Main Street. They drank a bunch of wine one night and went back to Celeste's apartment in the attic of this rooming house on Church Street and had a really nice time.

She can't believe she wound up at Mikey's school. She wonders whatever happened to him. After Donnie was murdered, Mikey went missing. It's hard to imagine he didn't have something to do with Donnie dying, even if no one seems to care. She doesn't think Mikey could've killed someone, but she guesses there are a lot of people like that, who seem incapable of something until they're not. She wishes it was the future, and there was some way to get a glimpse of where he is and what he's doing. She'd heard a rumor from her mother that Donna Parascandolo or Rotante or whatever hired Mikey to kill her ex-husband and that they were having an affair and ran off together. That was some real Pamela Smart shit she just couldn't buy into. Antonina knew Donna from around Bishop Kearney, and she was no Pamela Smart. But she *is* gone, too.

She saw Ralph a lot her senior year of high school. He was pretty fucked up about Donnie getting offed. Whatever had happened, if he knew or not, he didn't go into it. He seemed like he was under a lot of stress, but all she knew for sure was that no one had killed him. He was happy about her going to college and thought a state school that wasn't too far from the city was a good call. He was happy she wanted to use the money for college. He still calls her, once a week. Her roommate, Sky Suarez, thinks it's weird this old dude who isn't her father always calls her. It *is* weird. Ralph wants to come up for a visit, but that'd be even weirder.

She's been pretty good with the money. She's mostly used it on tuition and books. She's got the income from the coffee shop, and she's starting work study next semester. If she plays it right and keeps working, she might not have to get financial aid at all.

She's been good about the money, that is, except for the drugs she occasionally buys. Like tonight. She got these shrooms she's carrying around in her pocket for her and Janice from Lane's friend Eric. They're walking down to Huguenot Street to eat them and trip in the dark with all these houses and graves from the 1600s and 1700s around them. Maybe they'll go on the Rail Trail and sit on the banks of the Wallkill.

It's dark out now. She likes that it's dark early. The dark feels different upstate. It wraps you up in a good way instead of just hovering over you.

When they get where they're going, standing under a streetlight in the center of quiet Huguenot Street, Janice lowers her headphones and says, "Okay, hit me."

Antonina fumbles around in her pocket and comes out with the baggie of shrooms. She empties the pieces into her palm. They look like bark. Janice divides them and takes half of what's there. They toss them in their mouths at the same time and chew frantically.

Antonina waits for something exciting to happen, for the dark to come to life, for bodies to rise from the ground or for the houses to take flight. This is her first time with shrooms. Janice has done them before. She tells her that they'll take hold soon, that this is going to be the best fucking night of her life. Antonina's ready.

But nothing happens. For a long time, an hour at least. They wander up the road past dark houses, and everything feels totally normal and boring. "You got ripped off," Janice says.

"Tell me about it," Antonina says. "I'm gonna kick Eric's ass."

"He should be afraid. I wouldn't fuck with you."

They walk back to campus, stopping on Main Street to pet a dog tied up outside the Main Street Bistro. Antonina's furious. She keeps expecting something to suddenly shift, for this to be part of it, this feeling that nothing will ever happen until something does. But it stays the same.

They head up Plattekill Avenue, past the fire department, cutting through Peace Park. When they get back to Antonina's dorm, Bouton Hall, Janice gives her a hug and says, "We'll have the best night of our lives next time."

Antonina goes inside, checking her mailbox in the main alcove and finding an early Christmas card from Grandma Divino. Her note is illegible. She's included a crinkled five-dollar bill and a couple of scratch-offs.

Antonina's room is on the third floor. On the way up, she sees a boy she knows from her Social Issues & College Life class and a girl she met at Take Back the Night.

The third-floor girls' end of the hallway has been decorated for the holidays by her RA, Rebecca. It looks like the hallway of a kindergarten. Wooden soldiers and menorahs cut out of construction paper. A couple of wreaths. A big board that says HAPPY HOLIDAYS in glue and glitter.

Sky is sitting in bed when Antonina gets back to her room, eating a bag of potato chips and watching *Edward Scissorhands* for the ninetieth time. "How'd it go?" Sky asks.

"A bust," Antonina says.

"Eric screwed you? I told you he was sketchy."

"I don't know. I guess so. Nothing happened."

"Your man called."

"Ralph?"

"Who else?"

"He say what he wants?"

"He said he'll call back. And he has, twice already."

Antonina sits at her desk and runs her fingers over the edges of a stack of CD jewel cases and cassettes that she has piled next to her textbooks. What could Ralph want so desperately? There hasn't been another incident like the time he followed her and Lizzie into the city, but she always worries that it's coming.

Sure enough, less than two minutes later, the phone rings. She picks up.

"Hey, sweetie," he says, and he sounds bad, different. "I've been trying to get you."

Antonina looks at the floor. She can feel Sky's eyes turn from Johnny Depp on the TV screen over to her, not wanting to miss this as it unfolds. "I was out," Antonina says to Ralph.

"Let me guess, with Janice?" Ralph says. "She's a good friend, right? I don't know about that Sky, though. She's not so nice to me."

"What is it? What do you want?"

"I'm at the diner. Can you meet me here?"

"In the Bronx? I can't."

"No. In New Paltz. Right across from the movie theater. I don't know the name of the joint."

"You're here?" Antonina keeps her eyes on the floor but hears Sky sit up and shuffle around.

"Can you meet me? I'm in a bad spot. We are. Me and Pags both. I just want to say goodbye."

"What are you talking about?"

"Please," he says.

"Okay, I'll be right there." She hangs up.

"What the fuck, dude?" Sky says. "He's in town? This is creepy. You're eighteen. He's what, forty-something?"

"I've gotta go," Antonina says, without hesitation. "Can I borrow your car?"

"The keys are by the TV."

Antonina stands and goes over to get the keys to the little shitbox Camry Sky inherited from her brother. She's thinking how Ralph's been good to her. She doesn't know why exactly he's chosen her to be the closest thing he'll ever have to a daughter, but she owes him this much at least. She's never heard him as desperate as he sounded on the phone.

"What's this guy got on you?" Sky asks. "I've known girls with pimps, this is how they act."

"It's hard to explain," Antonina says.

"You shouldn't lead him on."

"That's a fucked-up thing to say." She opens the door and walks out of the room.

The Camry is parked in the lot next to Bouton. Antonina finds it after searching up and down the rows of cars, getting in under the wheel. She keys the ignition, and the radio blasts on. That shit music Sky listens to. Like something from a club she'd never go to.

She backs out of the space and then leaves the lot. The Plaza Diner would've been a pretty long walk, but it should take her only about three minutes by car. Up South Manheim, right on Main. It's in a strip mall across from the movie theater where she goes at least once a week to see whatever's new.

When she pulls in, she notices Ralph's Caddy parked at the lonely end of the lot, no other cars around it, the engine idling. He doesn't seem to be inside, but the windows are fogged. She wonders why he would leave it running.

She parks away from it, close to the entrance, and gets out of the car. She comes to this diner sometimes when she's pulling an all-nighter. The coffee's okay, and she likes the feel of the place. Maybe what she first liked about it, in fact, is that it reminds her of the diner where she'd go with Ralph in the Bronx. It's not as flashy, but it's got the same vibe.

Inside isn't crowded. Five college boys sit at a table off the kitchen. A guy in paint-splattered overalls is at the counter with a gyro and a glass of soda.

She sees Ralph sitting in a booth by the window, facing the lot, so he can keep an eye on the Caddy. He looks bad. More ragged than she's ever seen him. He's sweating hard, the way he was the day he followed her to the city. He's wearing a gray suit that seems to be stained with grease and a yellow dress shirt. He's huddled over the table with a cup of coffee in front of him, his arms crossed over his chest as if he's hugging himself.

Antonina sits across from him. "Your car's running out there," she says.

"You're a sight for sore eyes," Ralph says.

"What's going on? Why are you here? What's wrong?"

The waitress, an older woman with stringy gray hair and red glasses held together with scotch tape, drops off a menu for Antonina, asking if she wants coffee.

Antonina nods, pushing the menu to the side of the table.

"Let me tell you something," Ralph says. "I want to be forthright with you. My intentions, maybe, have never been clear."

"You really don't look good."

"It's the end of the line for me, kid. Pags, too. He's out in the car. We started fucking up a long time ago and never stopped. It finally caught up with us the way it caught up with Donnie."

Antonina looks out the window at the Caddy. "Pags is in the car?"

"What's left of him. I don't know where we're going. Just running away. I needed to see you, to say goodbye. Ain't I helped you? Ain't I been an okay guy to you?"

She tries to see through his clenched arms. Is he shot? Is he sitting at this table with her, wounded, dying? What should she do?

The waitress brings Antonina's coffee and asks if she wants anything to eat without looking up from her pad. Antonina shakes her off, and the woman scurries away, pushing her glasses up her nose.

"I'm gonna go to the payphone and call nine-one-one," Antonina says to Ralph.

"Don't," he says, reaching across the table slowly and putting his hand over hers. There's blood on his cuff. She can also see with some definition now that blood is blotched on his yellow shirt over his belly. "Maybe I'm dead already," he continues. "Maybe this is heaven. A diner with you."

"Ralph," Antonina says, not sure what else to say, angling her legs as if she'll burst out of the booth and bolt for the phone, but not moving.

He bites down on some passing pain and then seems to come out of it. "I never asked nothing from you in return, right? I'm asking you now not to call no one. I just wanted to see your pretty face one more time." He pauses. "You know the song 'This Is All I Ask'? Written by Gordon Jenkins. A lot of people do it, but Sinatra's version on *September of My Years* is the best."

"I don't," Antonina says.

Ralph sings, half in a whisper, his voice breaking: "'Beautiful girls, walk a little slower when you walk by me. / Lingering sunsets, stay a little longer with the lonely sea. / Children everywhere, when you shoot at bad men, shoot at me.'" He cuts it off there, coughing into his palm, the coffee cups on the table quaking.

Antonina's never heard him sing. Not in the car on the way to the Bronx, not anywhere. She'll never forget it, the sound of singing that isn't singing at all. It's the sound of death. She thinks he must be delirious.

He recovers from his cough and starts talking again: "I never tried nothing funny with you, that wasn't my aim. I wanted you to know. I love you like a daughter. A woman lost a baby once and then she died too a few days later, that's a true story. That baby was mine. Little girl. Stillborn. Nicole Raffaella. The woman was my wife, Danila. We was married three months—this was forever ago. I always wanted a girl to spoil, you understand that? I wish I had more dough to give you on my way out the door."

"I'm sorry," Antonina says.

He waves her off. "The past is just the past," he says.

"Are you shot?"

"A little," he says, smiling, trying to make light of it.

"A little shot? How's someone get a little shot?"

He shrugs. "Ambushed by a couple of Ficalora's dumbest goons. Should've seen it coming. Made it this far since Donnie and thought we were in the clear. What're you gonna do? Pags is worse off."

"You're just gonna let him die in the car out there?"

"Time's up. We're nobodies. We got nobody. You're the only person I care about. I just wanted to wish you well."

Antonina can't believe this is happening. She's crying before she knows she's crying. She doesn't expect it, so she's surprised by the feeling of tears on her cheeks.

Ralph struggles out of the booth and stands. The blood is mostly obscured by his jacket, so she's not shocked he managed to make his way into the diner without creating a scene. He leans over and touches her hand again. "I ain't gonna try to give you a smooch or nothing, don't worry. I don't want you to remember me stinking like this."

"You're just gonna leave?"

"Goodbye, kid. Best of luck in everything." He squeezes her hand, and then he shuffles out the door of the diner.

Antonina watches through the window as he struggles down the steps, holding on to the railing like he's ancient and frail, and then heads for the Caddy and climbs in.

He backs the car up slowly and proceeds to drive out of the lot, making a left, going toward the Thruway.

Antonina sits there. She sips the coffee that she hadn't previously touched and uses a napkin to dab at her cheeks. She looks across at the spot that Ralph occupied only moments before, the Naugahyde dented and patched with red duct tape. She looks for traces of him, drops of blood, anything. She considers his coffee cup and lets out a breath. She's thinking, *Imagine if this is heaven.*

Mikey's not sure exactly when Seattle became their destination, but that's where they've been for about a month now. Before that, they spent time in Detroit and Chicago and then they went south to Memphis. After that was Oklahoma City and then Albuquerque and Phoenix. Finally, they made it to the West Coast and lingered in several cities in California—San Diego, Los Angeles, Salinas, and San Francisco—before making up their minds to keep going north. They took their time getting through Oregon and then decided Seattle was it. Well, Mikey decided. It was stupid, but he'd seen *Singles* back when he was still at New Paltz, and he thought Seattle looked cool. He told Donna about the music scene. She went along with it.

Gas and motels and food adds up, but the money's gone pretty far. They had to dump the Lynx and buy a new car in Phoenix—that was a killer, especially since they had to bypass traditional routes. What they wound up with was an '87 Pontiac Grand Prix. The other thing that hurt was having to put down security, first month's rent, and last month's rent on this apartment in Seattle. But it's a nice place, in a neighborhood called Ballard. There's a record store not too far away and a movie theater and a view of some bay or another within walking distance. They don't have much, just an air mattress on the floor, Donna's turntable and records, the books of Gabe's he brought with him, and a tiny fake Christmas tree strung with lights set up on the kitchen counter. He doesn't smoke, so he's set up the cigarette case he found in Donnie's duffel bag as a sort of decoration next to the tree. Donna had seen it early on and hadn't recognized it as Donnie's, so there was no problem there.

They have about fifteen thousand dollars left. Mikey's hidden it in the bottom of a bucket full of paint supplies, brushes and rollers, under a scrunched-up blue drop cloth, believing that no one would ever break in and think to look there. Traveling with the money for so many months, having it in the trunk of the car or in a bag they had to carry around with them, had been stressful as hell.

Mikey's walking to the post office now. He just shaved for the first time in weeks, his chin tattoo exposed. He doesn't get looks for it here like he did other places. It's midafternoon. He hasn't told Donna where he's going. She's back at the apartment, wearing stretchy pants and a new SuperSonics sweatshirt, putting together a bookcase they just bought.

He's thinking about his mother for the first time in a little while. He hasn't looked back since killing Donnie. He hasn't so much as checked a New York newspaper to see if his picture's on the front page. His life on the road with Donna has been a life of abandon. He never said anything about Donnie, not even that he knew who her ex-husband was, that he was the same guy who'd hit him in the face with a bat back in '91. Never mind not telling her what he learned from Big Time Tommy, that Donnie had killed his father by dumping him off a bridge, that he had not merely been following orders but had done it to be cruel. Hearing Donnie apologize to his son's ghost had led Mikey to believe that what Donnie had done to his father had been the result of his own suffering. If he had to know that kind of pain, others must, too. And Mikey had become his target that night. Not because Donnie wanted to fuck Antonina, as he'd first suspected. Just because Mikey was a kid with his whole life in front of him.

Mikey hopes his mother's okay. He realizes it must be hard for her, him leaving the way he did with no explanation. He doesn't have any sense of

what she knows or doesn't know. All he has is the clean conscience that came with getting revenge and clearing his father's debt. Of course, she might still have no idea it was Donnie that killed her husband or her son that killed Donnie in turn. The world lets you know what you need to know to survive. She'd call that the hand of God. He's not sure what he calls it.

What he's thinking now is it's about time he lets his mother in on the fact that he's still kicking, that she still has a son who loves her. Maybe it's a bad idea to send this postcard he's got in his pocket, but he has to. He owes it to her.

When he gets to the post office, he buys a stamp and puts it on the card. The front is a picture of the Space Needle. On the back, under the stamp, he's scrawled his mother's name and address. He thinks of their old house, of the life he had there, of the life she continues to have there. It must seem so empty to her. He can't imagine how sad she's been. He hopes it's gotten easier over time.

All he's written on the card is: *Dear Ma, I love & miss you. —M.* No return address. He drops the card in the mail slot and leaves the post office, feeling as if some weight has been lifted.

He can't talk to Donna about his mother. He's brought her up once or twice, and Donna's shut it down. Their meeting had been brief but intense. It'd obviously shaken Donna up.

On the walk back to the apartment, he takes out the turquoise snakeskin leather wallet he'd bought at a roadside stand in New Mexico. He keeps the picture of Donna as a teenager that he found in Gabe's room there. He often looks at it when he's out because he can't look at it when he's with Donna. She doesn't know he has it and, he hopes, will never know. That would mean lying about where he found it—in one of Gabe's books, he'd insist—or telling the truth. But he likes having the picture. It makes him happy to see a young version of her laughing like that, just as it must have made Gabe happy. He tucks it away as he turns onto their block.

Back at the apartment, Donna's got the bookcase put together. It's wide and deep. She's lined up Gabe's books on the top shelf. She said she wants to start reading more. He sees that Gabe's note is there next to the books, wrinkled and creased.

"What do you think?" she asks.

"It's a good thing you're so handy," Mikey says. "I can't do shit."

"I like you just the way you are."

Mikey pulls Donna close for a kiss. They've been lucky so far, in every way. He feels like the luck will hold.